4/04

Casting the First Stone

This Large Print Book carries the
Seal of Approval of N.A.V.H.

Casting the First Stone

Kimberla Lawson Roby

Thorndike Press • Waterville, Maine

Published in 2002 by arrangement with Kensington Books, an imprint of Kensington Publishing Corp.

Thorndike Press Large Print African-American Series.

The tree indicium is a trademark of Thorndike Press.

The text of this Large Print edition is unabridged.
Other aspects of the book may vary from the original edition.

Set in 16 pt. Plantin.

Printed in the United States on permanent paper.

Library of Congress Cataloging-in-Publication Data

Roby, Kimberla Lawson.
    Casting the first stone / Kimberla Lawson Roby.
        p. cm.
        ISBN 0-7862-4860-2 (lg. print : hc : alk. paper)
    1. Married women — Fiction.   2. Spouses of clergy —
Fiction.   3. African American women — Fiction.
4. African American clergy — Fiction.   5. Large type
books.   I. Title.
PS3568.O3189 C3 2002
    813′.54—dc21   2002032321

For my husband, Will,
the man who makes my heart sing every day
of the week.

And for my mom, Arletha Stapleton,
the woman who brings great joy into my life,
the same as her mother always did for her.

Acknowledgments

As always, I thank God for blessing me, over and over, time and time again.

With much appreciation to:

My wonderful husband, Will, for suggesting the storyline for this novel, and for making the last nine years of my life the best ever. You make my life so complete, and I love you with all my heart.

My mother, Arletha Stapleton, for inspiring me and for encouraging me to keep my faith in God, no matter what. I am amazed at how tremendous your own faith has been during your struggle with a brain tumor, and how you still manage to keep a smile on your face daily. And even more amazing, is how you always continue to encourage everyone else you come in contact with. Witnessing your illness has been the most painful experience I have ever had to endure, but I am so thankful that God has allowed me the opportunity to take care of you and be here for you whenever you

7

need me. I love you, Mom, in more ways than I could ever explain.

My brothers, Willie, Jr., and Michael Stapleton, for being so proud of their big sister. I love both of you so very much.

My best friend and sister, Peggy Hicks, for giving this novel its title and for proving that two women don't necessarily have to share the same blood in order to love each other like sisters — which is what we are; my girl, Lori Whitaker Thurman, for being such a caring and dependable friend for more than a decade, and for being so concerned about my mom; my girl, Kelli Tunson Bullard, for being such a great friend for the last twenty-eight years. I love all three of you.

My aunts and uncles, Clifton, Jr., and Vernell Tennin, Mary Lou and Charlie Beasley, Sr., Fannie Haley, Ben Tennin, Sr., Ada Tennin, and Bob Tennin for looking after your sister (my mother) the way you do. Whether it is calling her, visiting her, cooking for her, or taking her to doctor appointments, you are always there, and I thank God for each of you.

And words simply cannot express my love or gratitude for Sylvester and Rebecca Bell, Deacon Willie James Howard and Lori Thurman, for driving my mom all the way to Madison, WI, to the University Hospital for her radiation treatments on the days when I needed to complete the rewrites for this book. And to Steven and Peggy Hicks for driving her there for special MRI testing while I attended Book-Expo. And I don't want to forget the drivers in 1997 when my mom received her first round of radiation treatments during my tour for *Behind Closed Doors*: Howard Campbell, Eva Jones, Bernice Garmon, Barbara Lett, and Jeffie Jones.

The first readers of *Casting the First Stone* — Lori Thurman, Dorothy Wright (our weekly conversations are such a blessing), Tammy Roby (my sister-in-law and book club leader), Peggy Hicks, Keith and Shari Grace, and Karen Young. I know I pressed all of you with a tight deadline, and I am indebted to you for your excellent constructive criticism. It really does make a remarkable difference.

Much thanks to the Kensington family:

Karen Thomas, my wonderful, wonderful editor, who always has the best suggestions and ideas for my work. You are so supportive and such a blessing to me and my writing career; Laura Shatzkin, my publicity director, who makes my life so much easier when it's time to market and promote my work. What would I do without you? Then there's Laurie Parkin, my publisher, who I haven't known for very long, but who shows me great support no different than if she'd known me for the last ten years. I thank you for just being you; Jessica McClean, another godsend to my writing career. I appreciate everything you do to promote my novels to the bookselling industry. You are one of the most genuine and caring persons I know, and I am elated that our paths were able to cross; The entire Kensington sales force for working so diligently to make my books available to readers everywhere, and for that, I am forever grateful; Walter Zacharius, Kensington's founder and CEO, for having confidence in me when I was still a self-published author, and for maintaining that confidence since the very beginning.

And to my new agent, Elaine Koster — the best agent in the whole wide world. Your enthusiasm for my work and your genuine concern for me as a person allows me to sleep peacefully, and I am so thankful that I was able to make contact with you. More thankful than you could possibly ever know.

To Sally Anne McCartin and her wonderful assistant Jacqui Daniels, for organizing my tour in such a smooth and organized manner. I spent quite a long time away from home with *Here and Now*, and you guys really gave me the support I needed when I was out on the road.

To my author friends — E. Lynn Harris (my advisor and initial inspiration), Shandra Hill (my weekly and sometimes daily phone buddy), Eric Jerome Dickey (my other inspiration and comedian), Lolita Files (my first real AOL buddy), Patricia Haley Brown (my cousin who I grew up with), Victoria Christopher Murray (my California buddy — thanks for hanging out with me during my stay in L.A.), Colin Channer (my other comedian), and Yolanda Joe (my Chicago buddy). Much love to each of you.

To the bookstore owners who gave me the "big push" in the very beginning — Emma Rodgers at Black Images in Dallas, Frances Utsey at The Cultural Connection in Milwaukee, Sherry McGee at Apple Book Center in Detroit, Donna Lucas at X-pressions in Indianapolis, all the rest of the independents, and Barnes & Noble here in Rockford.

To the women's book club in Rockford — Norma Joseph, Tamara Lott, Carol

Craig, Estelle Black, and all of the rest of the members for the great dinners and discussions; to the African American Women's Book Club in Philadelphia — Iris Roundtree, Karen Holmes, Pamela Ray, Judianne Winston, and each of the rest of the members for sort of adopting me as your own; to Monique Ford and the members of Circle of Sistahs in Philadelphia for your support as well; to Salena D. Castle and each of the members of R.A.R.E. Book Club in Memphis for the wonderful dinner and discussion; to Cathy Brown in Sacramento, CA, for all your support. And to all of the book clubs throughout the country who attend my events and who take the time to read my work and then discuss it.

And finally to all of my readers everywhere, I thank all of you for your current and continued support.

Also, when you have a chance, I would love to hear from you, so please e-mail me at *Kim@Kimroby.com* or visit my Web site at *www.kimroby.com*.

Blessings always,
Kim Roby

Prologue

Eight years earlier

"I have something real important to tell you," Curtis said to Tanya, the woman he'd been dating for quite some time now. "Probably one of the most important things I will ever have to tell anyone."

"Okay," she said as calmly as she could, though in reality she was about to spill over with curiosity.

"Remember when I told you that I thought God had called me to preach?" he asked.

"Yes," she acknowledged.

"Well, no matter how hard I've tried to ignore it, I know now that I have to accept it."

Tanya reached out to hug him and they embraced for a few seconds.

"I'm really, really happy for you, because I know you've been struggling with this for some time now," she said.

13

"I always knew it was the right thing for me to do, but I guess I was sort of hesitant because I didn't want to do anything that would disappoint God. This is a serious commitment, and I didn't want to accept my calling until I was sure I could be faithful to the pulpit. I know it's not going to be easy, but, Tanya, I really do believe that I can make a difference in a lot of people's lives."

"Honey, I know you can. And you will, so long as you continue to follow God and you always remember to put Him first."

"My vision is so great, and what I want more than anything is to encourage people to live their lives in the right way and to teach them the word of God so that they truly understand it. So that they truly understand what they have to do in order to be rewarded with eternal life."

His words were powerful, and Tanya felt a sense of serenity just listening to him. She'd known for the last couple of years that Curtis was destined to be one of God's leaders. He'd always been a decent person, and not once could she ever remember him wanting to party with his friends or do any of the things that most college men seemed to enjoy doing. He was different, and that was the main reason why she'd been so attracted to him. He was so respectable and straitlaced, if you will. Which had been fine with her, because alcohol, drugs, and wild parties hadn't been her forte, either.

Curtis continued. "I'm telling you, sweetheart, the sky is the limit as to what I can accomplish with my ministry. Maybe I'll even become senior pastor at one of the prominent churches here in Atlanta. Or maybe I'll even build my own church. But more than anything, you know what I eventually would like to do?"

"What's that?"

"Become an evangelist, so that I can take my ministry all across the country. And who knows, maybe even to other parts of the world where people are a lot less fortunate than we are."

"You've really got it all planned out, don't you?" Tanya said, laughing.

Curtis laughed with her. "I guess I do."

"Well, there's nothing wrong with being ambitious, because that's what will make all the difference in the world for you as a minister. And I want you to know that I am so proud of you for making this decision."

"I'm glad to hear you say that, because I wasn't sure how you would react to being

15

with a minister," he said, grabbing both of Tanya's hands.

His face was serious, and Tanya wondered what was next on his agenda.

"You know that I love you, right?" he asked.

"Yes."

"And you love me, right?" he asked, staring straight into her eyes.

"You know I do. I always have."

Curtis sighed deeply, moved from the sofa and kneeled in front of her on one knee. Then he pulled out a small, felt-textured box.

Tanya covered her mouth in disbelief.

"Sweetheart, will you marry me?"

Tanya swallowed hard with tears flowing down her face, but quickly answered his question. "Yes, Curtis. I will."

He smiled at her, stood, and pulled her up from where she was sitting. They held each other closely and Tanya felt like melting to the floor when her future husband kissed her. She was so in love with him, and she could tell that his feelings for her were the same. And now he was going to be a minister, and better yet, maybe even a pastor of his own church someday. He was so happy. They were happy together. And Tanya couldn't imagine life being any better than it was for them right now. But best of all, she had a feeling that they were going to be happy with each other always. And that was the one thing she'd always dreamed of.

Chapter 1

Tanya crossed her legs for what seemed like the hundredth time and gazed at her husband in disgust. She'd been sitting as patiently as she possibly could, pretending to pay attention to what he was saying. But the more she listened to his pathetic observations, the more annoyed she became. And just looking at the eight-hundred-dollar suit, the overpriced dress shoes, and the expensive gold watch he was wearing was enough to make any human being puke. She couldn't believe he actually had the audacity to stand before his three-thousand-plus congregation, practically demanding that they give more money. Exactly how much more *money* did he think these people could afford anyway? The majority of them were already obeying God's word by paying ten percent of their weekly incomes to the church, and to suggest that they should be giving anything more than that was simply ridiculous. That is, unless there was a reason for it. An important reason such as one of the families being left homeless due to a fire or flood. Or one of the less fortunate members needing assistance with emergency medical bills or help with burying their deceased loved ones. As far as Tanya was concerned, situations like those were fine, but anything else just didn't seem justified to her. Every Sunday Curtis laid down the same wretched guilt trip, and she was sick of it: "You are robbing God if you don't pay your tithes, and He will bless you even more if you give an additional offering."

It was so hard to believe that this was the same man she'd married eight years ago. She'd thought for sure that Curtis Black was the man of her eternal dreams. He was intelligent, responsible, attractive, and, without a doubt, the most spiritually grounded man she'd ever made acquaintance with. They'd met during her junior year at Spelman, his senior year at Morehouse, and had fallen hopelessly in love with each other immediately. He pursued his bachelor's degree in business, and she worked hard on her degree in psychology. Then, shortly after they'd each completed their graduate studies in counseling, Curtis announced that God had called him to preach, and that he wanted her hand in marriage. And for the first six years, they'd been happier than any married couple could have thought possible. Everyone said they were a perfect match, and their friends and family members always raved over how attractive the two of them looked together. Curtis with his tall, broad-shouldered body and deep-mocha complexion, and Tanya with her black, bobbed hairstyle and medium-cocoa skintone. But what all their admirers didn't know was that not everything that looked good was, and that her and Curtis's model marriage had long since turned into something very ugly and dreadfully different.

If they all only knew about the horrible rumors that had started only weeks after Curtis was installed as pastor of Faith Missionary Baptist Church, which was located on the south side of Chicago, and how Tanya had purposely tried to ignore each and every one of them — hoping these rumors were nothing more than vicious lies. That is, until those lies began floating in a mile a minute, from every possible direction, and she'd had no choice except to believe that at least some of what she was hearing had to be true.

The thought of Curtis sleeping with another woman had always made her cringe, but now Tanya's pain was slowly turning to rage. She hated the ground that he walked on and everything he stood for. She wished him dead on almost every occasion, and she wasn't sure just how much more of this facade of a marriage she could actually take. She was sick of him and sick of pretending that they were this perfect couple who loved each other more than life itself. And even worse, she hated him for not spending any time with their six-year-old daughter, Alicia — the same daughter who still worshipped everything that had to do with her father. She didn't deserve to be neglected by him in that way, and just thinking about how he treated her pissed Tanya off.

Oh, but enough was enough. And as soon as they arrived back at their South suburban home in Covington Park, wife of a pastor or not, she was going to show him a side of her that he'd never ever seen before.

Tanya snapped out of her daydream and watched her husband step away from the podium. She couldn't believe he was still begging for more money.

"We as black people have little, because

21

we think little, and I want you all to know that it's up to you and I to take care of Faith Missionary Baptist Church," Curtis said, walking down the center aisle of the beautiful sanctuary, just past the second pew where Tanya was sitting. "If you want me to take you places that you've never gone before, then we are going to have to get rid of these stingy attitudes. I can feel them throughout the entire congregation, and it ain't nothin' but the devil who is trying to convince you to hold on to those purses and those wallets. Who gave you those purses and those wallets in the first place? And who gave you those good jobs that most of you go to every day? And who gave you a roof over your head, clothes on your back, and food on your table? I'll tell you who. God did."

Curtis paused for a moment and shut his eyes. Then he opened them. "God has laid an important message on my heart. He wants me to ask every adult who is here right now to give an extra twenty dollars this morning."

Tanya noticed some of the members looking around at each other. Some even whispered to the person sitting next to them. And it was obvious that most of them were sick and tired of dealing with this same old Jim Jones-Jim Bakker-Jimmy Swaggert-need-more-money sort of mentality. She couldn't help but wonder just how far Curtis was actually willing to go when it came to getting what he wanted from these innocent people. But the more she thought about it, the more she realized that her husband really didn't have any limitations when it came to anything.

And that was the one thing that frightened her the most.

Right after the Black family changed out of their Sunday-go-to-meeting attire, they each sat down at the kitchen table to eat the barbecued rib dinners they'd picked up on the way home from church. Usually they sat in the dining room for Sunday dinners, but sometimes when they ordered take-out, they ate in the kitchen instead.

"So, baby girl," Curtis said to his daughter, "did you enjoy the service today?"

"Yes. You preached really good, Daddy," she said, smiling.

Tanya smiled, but only to pacify Alicia.

"And *you* sounded real good yourself when you led that song today," he complimented her. Alicia was a member of the children's choir.

She beamed. "Thanks."

"What about you, baby?" He turned his attention to Tanya. "Did you enjoy the service?"

"It was fine," she said, trying to keep her composure, because she didn't know how much longer she was going to be able to control herself.

"The spirit was really moving through the church today, wasn't it?" he continued.

"Yeah, I guess it was," she answered.

"Mom?" Alicia said. "Can I go next door to Lisa's?"

"I guess, but if they're in the middle of eating dinner, then I want you to come right back home."

"I'll bet they already ate, because they get out of church way earlier than we do," Alicia offered.

Hmmph, Tanya thought. Everybody got out of church earlier than they did. She didn't know a lot of African American Catholics, but their next-door neighbors never missed Mass on any week she could think of. And they were always home before noon every Sunday.

"Okay, but make sure you wash your hands before you go," Tanya instructed.

Alicia did what her mother told her, and then left the house in a hurry.

However, as soon as Alicia had barely

darkened the front doorway, Tanya lit into Curtis like a madwoman.

"You know, Curtis, I don't know who you think you are, but you are not God's gift to this earth," she said, shoving the wooden chair that she was sitting on up to the table as hard as she could. She'd tried to calm herself down during the drive home and then again when they first started eating dinner, but now she felt like she was going to explode.

Curtis frowned. "What are you talking about?"

"You know exactly what the hell I'm talking about."

"No. I don't. And I'd appreciate it if you wouldn't use that kind of language in my house," Curtis said, spooning up a helping of peach cobbler.

Tanya glared at him and wanted to slap that dessert right down his throat. "What do you mean, *your* house?" she asked, folding her arms, staring at him. "This house is just as much mine as it is yours. And you'd better get this through your head, too: I'll say whatever I feel like saying. Whenever I feel like it. You might control those tramps you sleep around with, but you don't control anything that has to do with me."

"Lord have mercy," Curtis said, squinting at Tanya. "This ain't nothin' but the devil tryin' to come between us, because Lord knows I haven't been sleeping around with any women."

"Curtis, please. I mean, why is the devil always responsible for everything when it comes to you getting caught up in your mess? And, if that's the case, then let me ask you this. Is he responsible for you laying up with practically every woman at the church who will have your little jack-leg preachin' ass?" Tanya said and was shocked at her own words. She hadn't spoken so profanely since college, and even more so since she became a minister's wife, and she wasn't proud of it. But it was just that she'd had it up to here, there, and everywhere with Curtis's sleeping around. She didn't have one ounce of proof, but that was only because he was always so smooth, slick, and secretive with his wrongdoings. But she knew what he was up to, because he'd long stopped satisfying her in bed, and, to tell the truth, their love-making was nonexistent. And no man, especially one who was as high-natured and passionate in bed as Curtis, could go without sex week after week, and, lately, month after month. No. Pastor Curtis Jasper

Black was definitely getting his needs fulfilled somewhere else. She was sure of it.

Curtis looked at his wife as if she was crazy. "Why are you doing all that cursing?"

"Now, which do you think is worse, Curtis? Me using the word hell and a-s-s or you running around all over town committing adultery? See, that's the thing with you, you're always pointing out what everyone else is doing wrong when all along, you're doing something much worse. And to think you're the head of a prominent Baptist church. Please."

Curtis shook his head in confusion. "I don't know what's gotten into you, but I'm going to pray for you. Maybe we need to pray together, so the devil can loosen his hold on you."

"What's gotten into me is that I'm sick of hearing all these rumors about you and these women, and I'm sick of you coming into this house sometimes as late as midnight and one o'clock in the morning. Claiming that you've been doing the work of the Lord. Claiming that you were at some Baptist ministers' meeting. Claiming that so-and-so needed you at the hospital all evening to pray for their dying soul. Or that Mary, Sue, and Jane needed you to

27

pray for their gangbanging son. Yeah right," she said, throwing the last of the dinner dishes into the dishwasher.

Curtis sighed deeply and then stood up from the table. "Look, I've had enough of this. And I won't be spoken to this way in my own house. I'm the head of this house, and you *will* respect me whether you want to or not. A wife has a place, and she should stay in it. And I'm only going to tell you this one last time. I'm not sleeping around with any women. I love you and Alicia, and I would never betray my family, regardless of what you and any of the rest of those gossipy women at church think. They're just jealous, and the sooner you figure that out, the better off we'll be."

"Jealous of what, Curtis?"

"Jealous of the way you dress, the kind of house you live in, and that brand-new Lincoln Navigator that you drive around in every day. The ones who are talking are the ones who wish they were in your shoes."

She couldn't believe how shallow and superficial he was. And what did material things have to do with anything anyway? And since she didn't know, she decided to ask him. "What do material things have to do with you sleeping around, Curtis?"

"Look!" he yelled at the top of his lungs.

"I've already told you a hundred times. I'm *not* sleeping around with anybody."

"Well, then, why don't you make love to me anymore? Huh? Explain that."

"Look, I'm under a lot of pressure, and being pastor of a church as large as Faith Missionary involves a lot of hard work. You know how tired I am every evening when I get home. But I promise, things will eventually get better."

"Maybe when hell freezes over, but then, I don't plan on staying around long enough to see if things will get better or not," she said, wiping the kitchen table.

Curtis laughed sarcastically and shook his head. Then he grabbed his car keys. "I'm out of here. And I hope the devil has turned you loose by the time I get back, because I really don't want to hear any more of these paranoid accusations."

As he turned to walk out of the kitchen, Tanya threw the wet dishcloth and hit him in the back of his head.

"See, that's why I'm never here. And for the record, maybe I don't make love to you anymore, because you're always doing all that nagging, and it really turns me off."

"If you were being the faithful husband that you're supposed to be, then I wouldn't have anything to nag about. And on top of that, what about Alicia? You hardly spend any time with her, and I'm sick of you neglecting her the way you do," Tanya said, and wanted to cry her eyes out. Partly because of how Curtis was ignoring their daughter, but mostly because he'd actually admitted that she turned him off sexually.

"Alicia knows how much I love her, and she also knows how busy I am with church business. As a matter of fact, she seems to understand that more than you do. And you're my wife."

"She's only a child, Curtis. And she'll believe anything you tell her because you're her father. But I'm not six years old like her. And I know for a fact that there isn't that much church business going on anywhere."

"Whatever, Tanya," he said, and opened the door leading to the garage.

"Where are you going?" she yelled behind him. "To lay up with Adrienne Jackson?"

"To lay up with who?" he said, laughing in denial.

"You heard exactly what I said. To lay up with Adrienne Jackson," Tanya repeated, becoming more angry by the second. She'd heard that Deacon Jackson's wife was Curtis's prime-cut mistress, and although

Tanya didn't have proof of it, she couldn't dismiss what she'd been hearing.

"If you must know, I'm going out to visit some members on the sick list," he said without looking back at her.

"Liar!" Tanya shouted. But Curtis shut the door. And it wasn't long before she heard him driving down the street.

Tanya sat down at the kitchen table and clasped her hands together under her chin. A thousand thoughts circulated through her mind. A part of her wanted to believe that her marriage had a chance, but things were so awful between her and Curtis that she was starting to seriously doubt it. He didn't seem to care about her at all anymore, and it had gotten to the place where he found any and every excuse in the book to spend time away from her and Alicia. She was so tired, and even though she was angry, she was hurt, too. And she was ashamed of the way she had spoken to him. He'd deserved every bit of it, but that wasn't her usual way of handling things. Her parents hadn't raised her that way, but as of late, she hadn't been able to control the way she felt, much less the things she said. Not to mention the violent and conniving thoughts she'd been having. The kind of thoughts that were totally against any- and everything she believed in. She'd been sure that marrying a minister would guarantee her complete happiness, because it certainly had for her aunt Margaret in Memphis, but now she knew that not *every* minister was sincere, and that some were merely playing with God. She regretted ever going out on a first date with Curtis. As a matter of fact, the only positive thing she'd gotten out of this whole ordeal was her sweet little innocent Alicia. And as much as she wanted to divorce Curtis, she knew she had Alicia to consider. She didn't know how much longer she could sleep in the same bed with Curtis, but she knew she had an obligation to her daughter. Which meant she had no choice except to continue living a life of complete turmoil until Alicia turned eighteen. Which, unfortunately, wasn't going to be until twelve years from now.

Tanya grunted at her last thought, and then heard the phone ringing.

She glanced up at the Caller ID box and saw that it was Curtis calling from his cellular phone. She wasn't in the mood for any more arguing, and she definitely didn't want to hear any more of Curtis's lying. But she reached and picked up the cordless phone just the same.

"What?" she said in a nonchalant tone of voice.

"Tanya. Look. I'm really sorry for arguing with you, and I'm even more sorry for not spending any quality time with you and Alicia. But I'm telling you. From this day forward, things are going to be different," he said, and paused. Then he continued. "You sound like you're ready to divorce me, and that's not what I want."

Tanya listened, but she was leery. Especially since Faith Missionary's bylaws specifically stated that in order for a minister to keep his position as pastor of the church, he had to be married. So, she couldn't help but wonder if that was his real reason for calling — the real reason he was sounding like he was in beg mode. A mode that the Reverend Curtis Black never thought he needed to shift into for anyone.

She switched the phone from one ear to the other, but didn't say anything.

"I know you're upset," he continued. "But we can work this out. I'll be home in a couple of hours or so, and we can talk then. All right?"

"I don't know that talking is really going to change anything. Because it's not like you can take back what you've been doing."

"Tanya. I'm telling you. No matter what you've been hearing, I'm not messing around with any other woman. I admit that I have purposely tried to find things to do just so I wouldn't have to spend so much time at home, but that's only because you and I have been having so many arguments. But for the millionth time, I would never sleep with another woman. You and I took vows before God, and I have a commitment to Him, you, and our daughter."

"Mmm. Hmm," Tanya said, rolling her eyes toward the ceiling in disbelief.

"I'll talk to you when I get home, okay? And . . . Tanya?"

"What?" she answered irritably.

"I love you."

Tanya didn't say anything.

"Did you hear me?"

"I heard you," she said in a so-what tone of voice.

"You're not going to say it back, though. Right?"

"Curtis, I think you and I are much too old to be playing these little teenage phone games, and if you want to talk to me, I'll be here when you get home."

"Okay, okay. I'll see you later."

Tanya hung up the phone and walked outside to check on Alicia.

Chapter 2

"Lord have mercy," Curtis moaned as he and Adrienne Jackson stirred in opposite directions the same as they always did when they made love at their secret getaway, which was a huge, contemporary-style condominium located over in Barrington, a northwest suburb of Chicago. A condo that was far enough from the church and its members to prevent any accidental run-ins.

"Is it good to you, baby?" Adrienne asked, obviously hoping that she was giving him the pleasure of a lifetime.

"Oh, yes." Curtis spoke the words loudly, and then quickly motioned his body upward and downward, over and over again, but in a strong and rough manner. Adrienne moved her body at the same speed to keep in sync.

And then, finally, they both groaned with total enjoyment.

They lay there holding each other for a few minutes, trying to catch their breath.

Then Curtis spoke. "You are really something else. You know that?"

"Is that so?" Adrienne said, smiling at him.

"Yes. You are," he said, sighing deeply. "I mean, you understand me better than anyone I've ever met, and I feel so connected to you."

"More connected than to your own wife?"

"Yes. As much as I hate to admit it, I do feel more connected to you. There's this special bond between you and I that she and I just don't have. At one time it seemed like we did, but it just sort of faded away over the last couple of years. She just doesn't understand me anymore."

"Well, *I* understand you," Adrienne commented while moving her shoulder-length hair to the side and kissing him on his neck. "And you know how much I love you, don't you?"

"Yeah, I do."

Adrienne laid her head on his chest. "What do you think happened between you and Tanya?"

"For one thing, she stopped believing in me. And on top of that, she started criticizing the way I was running the church. She's not aggressive like I am, and she just couldn't see my vision. I had so many plans for Faith Missionary, and I really needed a strong, supportive woman by my side in order to set those plans into action. But now I realize that Tanya just wasn't the right one."

"Well, why don't you ask her for a divorce? I mean, why should you stay in a miserable relationship with someone you don't want to be with?"

"It's not that simple. First of all, you know the deacons would kick me completely out of the pulpit, and secondly, it wouldn't look very good in the eyes of the congregation, especially since they all have so much respect for Tanya. Although, if they'd heard the way she was talking to me this afternoon, they'd be shocked. They'd see that she isn't as wonderful as they think she is."

"What was she saying?" Adrienne asked curiously, then raised her head to look at him.

"Just a lot of unnecessary stuff."

"Like what?"

"I don't even want to go into it, but believe me, she wasn't talking the way any *real* Christian should have been talking right after leaving church."

"Were you guys arguing?"

"Yeah, and it was almost like the devil took complete control of her, because one minute we were eating dinner and the next minute she was screaming at me like she'd lost her mind. She kept going on and on about nothing, and then I finally left."

"Did she say anything about me?" Adrienne asked in a slightly nervous tone.

"She mentioned your name, but she's only going by what those nosy women at the church are saying."

"Well, to tell you the truth, I'm starting to get worried about all the talk that's been going on around the church, too, Curtis. The last thing I want is for Thomas to find out about us," she said, referring to her husband. "He truly loves me, and it would kill him. And I couldn't bear having that happen. I feel bad enough as it is about us committing this horrible sin."

"Nobody's going to find out about anything," Curtis said, ignoring the last part of her spiel. "The deacons and trustees will never believe any rumors over what I tell them. They trust me completely. And what you need to do is stop worrying about what people are saying and thinking."

"But it's wrong, Curtis. You know it just

as well as I do."

Curtis stroked Adrienne's hair. "No man falls short of sin, and we're no different than anybody else. That's why we have to continuously pray every day to ask God for forgiveness."

"But I don't think God is too happy when people purposely commit sins just because they know they can ask for forgiveness right afterward."

Curtis took a deep breath, but kept silent.

Adrienne sat up on the side of the king-size black wrought-iron bed and looked back at him. "Honey, how long are we going to have to keep doing this?"

"It won't be much longer than next year."

"Next year? When, next year?" she asked in frustration.

"Probably toward the end, and that's only if I can get my financial situation in order by then."

"It's only the end of April now, so are you telling me it's going to be another eighteen months before we can finally move away from here?"

"I know it seems like a long time, but it really isn't."

"Why can't you just tell Tanya that you

want a divorce? I'm really tired of all this sneaking around. And I would much rather ask Thomas for a divorce than to keep betraying him the way I am."

"Baby, you know it's not that simple. This is a complicated situation, and it has to be handled very carefully. If I divorce Tanya, then I'll be forced to leave the church with practically nothing, and I can guarantee you, Tanya is going to do everything she can to take me to the cleaners. Plus, if there's a scandal behind all of this, I'll never pastor at another Baptist church for as long as I live. At least not one worth talking about. I know you're ready for us to start our lives together, but we just can't do this without the right amount of money."

"Why can't we just forget the money? As long as we love each other, that's all that really matters."

"Look," Curtis said, elevating his voice to an angry volume, "I grew up with not a pot to piss in nor a window to throw it out of, and I'm not about to go back to living that way ever again. Do you have any idea what it's like to wake up in the middle of the night with your little nine-year-old stomach aching to no end, because your mother sent you to bed completely hun-

40

gry? Or what it's like to sit in the dark, because your father used all his money on his women and didn't have anything left to pay the utility bills? No, I'm sorry, but I've worked all my life to get to where I am, and I'm not about to mess it all up now. You're just going to have to be patient," he said, raising his body up from the pillow. Then he stood up and walked over to the window. "And, anyway," he said, glancing back at her, "if it wasn't for the *money*, you and I wouldn't be renting this condo all the way out here. And there's no way I would have been able to buy you that leather furniture in the front room that you just had to have. And we won't even discuss this bedroom set that you had me purchase from one of the most expensive furniture stores in this area," he said, pointing at the glossy-textured black armoire and matching dresser. "You said you wanted this to be your home away from home, and that's what I've tried to give you," he said, and then turned back toward the window.

Adrienne walked over to where he was standing, placed her arms around him, and rested the side of her face on his back. "Honey, I'm really sorry, okay? I didn't mean to upset you, but it's just that I really want us to be together for good."

Curtis pretended to ignore what she was saying, because he could tell he'd already regained control of her every emotion. It had been that way since the first time they'd slept together, and he'd known all along that she'd do what he wanted, whenever he wanted, at any cost. If he told her to run, all she wanted to know was how fast. If he told her to flip, all she wanted to know was how many times and in what manner. And that's the way he liked it. Tanya was too independent for her own good and didn't know how to stay in a woman's place, but Adrienne depended on him for everything. She didn't like doing anything without his approval, and that was the one thing he loved about her the most.

"Honey, please don't be mad at me," she continued with a shaky voice. "If waiting is what you want me to do, then I'll wait. But it's just that I love you so much," she said with tears streaming down her face.

Curtis turned his body and faced her. Then he pulled her long, lean body toward him and hugged her tightly. "I didn't mean to raise my voice, and I'm sorry. But if you can just hold on a little while longer, I promise you that everything is going to work out just the way we planned it," he said, lifting her chin away from his chest. He kissed her passionately, and it wasn't long before they stretched across the bed and prepared themselves for another sinful session of lovemaking. But this time, Curtis found himself much too preoccupied to indulge in their usual acts of foreplay. He tried hard to concentrate, but he kept failing at it. And he knew what the problem was.

He was scared to death that his whole world was about to come tumbling down around him. Because if everything *didn't* work out the way he and Adrienne had planned it, that was exactly what was going to happen. Or something worse, if he wasn't careful.

Chapter 3

As soon as Tanya heard the alarm ringing on the digital clock, she reached toward the nightstand and shut it off. She hadn't slept more than a wink, and the last thing in the world she wanted to do was get dressed for work.

And it was all because Curtis hadn't remembered where home was until sometime after eleven, and the fact that they'd started arguing as soon as he stepped through their bedroom doorway. She'd asked him the usual where-have-you-been type of questions, and he'd told a sack of lies the same as he always did. Finally, when she'd become angry enough to kill him, she'd not said another word. But she still hadn't been able to sleep. Here, she'd tossed and turned all night, while Curtis slept like a newborn baby. He acted as though there were no troubles between them at all. Either that, or he simply didn't care one way or the other. She didn't know what his problem was, but what she did know was that he was barely hanging by a small thread, and that it was only a matter of time before she jerked it completely away from him. Every dog had his day, and Curtis wasn't going to be any different.

She looked over at her shadetree-preaching husband and rolled her eyes at him when she saw that he was still sound asleep. Then she sat up, reached for the remote control and blasted the TV.

Curtis sat at attention and looked around the room with his eyes bulging, trying his hardest to figure out what was going on.

"What's the matter with you?" he yelled.

Tanya just stared at him, and didn't say anything.

"You must be losing your mind or something," he continued.

She stood to the floor, strutted over to the walk-in closet and pretended like she didn't hear him. And she took the remote control with her. She knew it was childish, but she didn't see why *he* should be allowed to sleep so peacefully when *she* had to get her behind ready for work. She

45

didn't know how she was going to make it through the day, but she knew she couldn't call in sick. Partly because she'd promised to cover for two of her vacationing colleagues, but mostly because she despised missing work. She loved her job, and with the exception of Alicia, nothing gave her a more satisfying feeling than helping people. Especially when it came to helping them deal with their social problems. Counseling meant everything to her, and it was the one thing in her life that didn't have anything to do with Curtis.

She scanned through her clothing trying to decide what she was going to wear, until she heard Curtis screaming out her name like some maniac.

"Tanya!"

She had a mind to keep ignoring him, but instead she leaned out of the closet and tossed the remote control over to where he was lying. Then, without missing a beat, she pulled out her teal-green crepe suit, walked back over to the four-poster, cherry wood bed and laid the outfit on her side of it.

"What's wrong with you?" Curtis asked, frowning at her.

"What's wrong with you?" she asked sarcastically, returning the same question.

"There's nothing wrong with me, and I don't see what you're so upset about," he said confidently.

Was he serious? And who did he think she was anyway? Bessie Buffoon? And did he actually think she'd somehow forgotten that he'd stayed out till almost midnight? No, what he was trying to do was make her *think* that she was just imagining things. That he wasn't doing anything out of the ordinary, and that in reality, he was actually being the perfect husband. But Tanya wasn't buying into his deceitful little scheme. Not in the least little bit.

"Look, Curtis, I think it would be best if you don't say anything else, because I've really had enough of these lies you keep telling me."

"You and I just can't seem to get along at all anymore, can we?" he said, crossing his arms in front of his chest.

"No. We can't. And while I would like nothing more than to divorce your cheating ass, I'm going to stick this out until my baby has graduated from high school and gone off to college. But I'm telling you right now, I'm not staying one day longer than that," she said, and could feel her blood practically boiling. Curtis brought out the worst in her, and she was getting to the point where she couldn't even stand to look at him without becoming severely pissed off.

"I thought we were going to talk about this?" he said, and Tanya could tell she'd gotten his attention. But then, she always did whenever she threatened to leave him.

"Talk? We were supposed to *talk* yesterday evening when you got home, remember?"

"And that's what I tried to do, but as soon as I walked in here, you started going off the deep end."

"What did you expect for me to do? I know good and well you weren't at any nursing home or any hospital till sometime after eleven o'clock. I don't care what you say."

"I told you," he said, breathing deeply, "I stopped at Brother Richards's house to see how he was doing, and then we got to watching the basketball game, and before I knew it, time had slipped right by me. You know how wrapped up I get during the playoffs."

"And I guess Brother Richards didn't have a phone for you to use, either?" she asked, pulling her periwinkle lace bra and matching panties from the top right dresser drawer. "Is that what you're telling me?"

"Look, Tanya, I'm sorry. I messed up, okay, and I admit it. But you and I have got to try and work things out."

"How can we work things out, when you're steadily spending all your time with somebody else?"

"Jesus Christ," he said in a fed-up tone of voice. "When are you ever going to stop making these crazy accusations?"

"When you start spending time with Alicia and me the way you used to. It was never like this in Atlanta, and I hate the day we ever moved here."

"How can you say that?" he asked, stacking two pillows behind his back. "We didn't have nearly as many members at the church down there, and now we have over three thousand. And if we hadn't come to Chicago, we wouldn't be living nearly as well as we do."

"You've known all along that I couldn't care less about all these material things. Because what good are they if a person is completely miserable in their marriage? I would give it all up right now if it meant one week of real happiness, or that I could go to sleep one night with peace of mind, knowing that you were being the faithful husband and the dedicated father you're supposed to be."

"I promise you, we *will* spend more time together. But you know I have to put some time into preparing my sermons each week, not to mention all the other things that every pastor in the country has to do if he is trying to run his church successfully. I can't be everywhere at the same time. You knew how much time I was going to have to put into this ministry when we made the decision to come here, but now you're acting like you can't deal with it."

Yeah, she *had* known that taking on a prominent church like Faith Missionary was a major responsibility and that Curtis would have to occupy a good portion of his time away from home, but lately, the amount of time he spent away from her and Alicia had become downright ridiculous. Her mother had told her that marrying a pastor was pretty much the same as marrying a doctor, and that the only noticeable difference was that doctors responded to their patients, and pastors to members of their congregation. Although Tanya had long since discovered that the latter was much worse, because there was no way of knowing when someone might need praying for or when someone might pass on to their glory. But even with all of that, things had been much better between them when Curtis resided over New Covenant down in Atlanta. They'd only had a few hundred members, but they were happy. And there hadn't been any rumors. That didn't mean Curtis wasn't doing anything, but at least she hadn't had to hear about any of his wrongdoings. And he seemed to have more time for her, too. They did everything together, and he treated her like an angel. She hadn't wanted to leave her parents, but she was willing to follow her husband wherever God wanted him to go. Which is exactly what Curtis had told her. That he'd prayed about it, and that God had instructed him to make their home in Chicago.

But now she wasn't so sure about their decision. As a matter of fact, she wasn't sure about anything anymore, because it was hard for her to believe that God would purposely lead anyone into a life of total corruption. The kind of life she wouldn't wish on anyone she could think of, and the kind that involved lowlife mistresses and way too much money.

"Look, I've got to get Alicia up for school, fix her something to eat, and then get dressed for work," Tanya said, pulling a

51

black satin robe from the closet and wrapping it around her body.

"Can't you go in late?" Curtis asked, sounding genuine. "I really think we need to continue our discussion. Things are getting out of hand, and something has to be done about it."

She didn't know whether to believe his so-called sincerity or not, but something told her that he was only trying to make things right with her, because he could tell she was serious about divorcing him. But she decided to humor his suggestion. "I can't miss work today, but we can talk this evening when I get home. That is, if you're going to be here."

"I'm going to the church around noon to take care of some business, but I should be home around five or so."

She didn't believe him, but since she didn't want to create any more waves between them, she decided to be cordial. "Fine," she said, walking out of the bedroom. Then she headed down the hallway and into Alicia's room.

"Wake up, sleepyhead," she said, opening her daughter's pink miniblinds.

"Mom," Alicia complained, and covered her head with a pink sheet and mauve comforter.

"Little girl, it's almost six-thirty, and you know you have to be out of here by a quarter to eight," Tanya said, pulling out Alicia's crisply starched blue jean jumpsuit that she'd just picked up from the cleaners a few days ago.

"I'm too tired to go to school, Mom," Alicia said with her head still buried under the covers.

Tanya didn't have the slightest idea why Alicia was so sleepy, because she'd tucked her in shortly after nine o'clock. But maybe she was ill. "What's the matter, sweetheart? Don't you feel well?" she asked, sitting down on her daughter's bed and pulling the comforter back. Then she felt her forehead to see if she had a temperature, but she didn't. "Do you feel sick?"

"No, Mom, I'm just tired," Alicia said, opening her eyes slightly.

"Why are you so tired?"

Alicia hunched her shoulders.

"Do you feel sick to your stomach?"

"No. But can I stay home with Daddy today?"

"Honey, Daddy has to go to the church, and if there's nothing wrong with you, then you have to go to school."

Alicia gazed into her mother's eyes but

remained silent.

"Now, I'm going downstairs to fix you some breakfast, and I want you to start getting dressed," Tanya said, walking toward the bedroom entrance.

"Mom?"

"What is it, honey?" Tanya said, turning to look back at her.

"Why were you and Daddy yelling at each other last night?"

Tanya felt as though she couldn't breathe, and she wished she could crawl under a rock. She hated when Alicia heard them arguing, and since their bedrooms were at opposite ends of the hallway, she'd thought for sure that Alicia wouldn't hear anything. But on the other hand, she and Curtis *had* gotten pretty loud with each other, and even worse, Tanya had used a few choice words. And now she had to explain herself.

"Sweetheart," Tanya said, sitting back down on Alicia's bed, "sometimes Mommy and Daddy don't always agree on everything, and that's why we were a little upset with each other last night."

"But you guys were yelling so loud," Alicia said innocently.

"I know. But everything's okay now," Tanya said, lying. She didn't like lying to her daughter, but she didn't have the heart to tell her what was really going on.

"Well, who is Adrienne, and why does Daddy keep saying that you don't know what you're talking about?"

Tanya swallowed hard with embarrassment. Alicia was so intelligent and much more advanced than the average six-year-old about to turn seven, but it was at times like this that Tanya wished she wasn't. Alicia understood far more about the situation than Tanya wanted her to, and she was making this whole conversation more difficult by the minute. "Look, honey," Tanya said, trying to explain this whole mess the best she could. "There's some things that mommies and daddies can talk about, but little girls can't, and this is one of them. Can you understand that?"

"Yes," Alicia said, clearly not satisfied with her mother's response. But it was obvious that she knew better than to debate with her about it.

"Now, you get up and get dressed, okay?" Tanya said, rubbing Alicia gently down the side of her face. Then she stood up.

"Mom, can I ask you one more thing?"

"Yes, what is it?"

"What does paranoid mean?"

Tanya couldn't believe what she was hearing, but she knew exactly where Alicia had discovered this new complex word of hers. And she had Curtis to thank for that. He'd insisted that she was paranoid at least three different times during the night, and Alicia had obviously overheard him. Which meant if she'd heard him say that, chances were she'd heard just about everything else they'd said as well. But if Tanya could help it, this was going to be the last time. Her own parents hadn't argued in front of her when she was growing up, at least not to the extent that she and Curtis did, and she wasn't going to burden Alicia with any more of their problems, either. "Paranoid is when someone is afraid that something is happening, when it really isn't."

"Oh," Alicia said as though she understood the definition completely.

Tanya wasn't sure if she did or not, but she was glad that this conversation was almost over. She could have easily ended it right when it started, but since she and Curtis had been careless enough to argue right in front of her, she felt she owed Alicia at least some sort of an explanation. Which was a lot different than the way her parents would have handled the situation. Not once had they ever allowed Tanya to question them about any "grown folks business." But Tanya had learned early in her counseling career that sometimes it was good to have these awkward discussions, because, in the end, they were usually beneficial for everyone involved.

"So, is that it?" Tanya asked, smiling at her daughter.

"Yep," Alicia answered, standing up.

"Give me a hug," Tanya said, extending her arms out to Alicia who was a little too thin but a lot taller than most children her age.

As they continued their embrace, Curtis stuck his head through the doorway. "Hey, pumpkin," he said to Alicia.

"Good morning, Daddy," Alicia said, pulling her arms away from her mother, practically running over to her father.

Curtis picked her up. "Daddy's baby girl is getting too big for him to be lifting," he said, laughing.

"Oh, Daddy. No, I'm not," she said, clasping her hands together behind his neck. "Daddy, can I stay home with you today?" she asked, and then cast her eyes at her mother.

"Alicia," Tanya said in a serious tone. "What did I already tell you?"

"Now, sweetheart, you know we don't do

that when one of us tells you something, right?" Curtis asked Alicia.

"I'm sorry," she said.

"You know better than that," Tanya added.

Alicia gazed at her mother shamefully.

Curtis slid her down his side until her feet were steady on the floor. "Isn't it time for you to start getting dressed, young lady?"

"Yes," she said. "But you and Mom can stay in here and talk while I go wash my face if you want to."

Curtis looked at his daughter and smiled. Then he turned his attention to Tanya with the same gesture of affection.

Tanya smiled back at him for the first time in weeks, and at that particular moment, she honestly wished they could get their marriage back on track. She knew it probably wasn't going to happen, but at least it would be nice for Alicia. And her, too, for that matter.

Chapter 4

"Girl, the last thing in the world I ever wanted to think about was filing for a divorce," Tanya said to Nicole, the closest friend she had in the Chicago area. They were on their way to an Empowerment of the Black Woman conference at the Hilton Towers Hotel down on Michigan Avenue, but right now they were having breakfast at a crowded local restaurant.

"I don't know, Tanya, I think maybe you're jumping the gun a little on that one. I mean, I know you and Curtis are having some problems, but do you really think things are so bad that you're ready for a divorce?" Nicole asked, and swallowed a couple of sips of coffee.

"I don't see what other alternative I have, if our situation doesn't get any better. We had a long conversation earlier this week, and although he seems like he's trying to pay more attention to Alicia and me, there's no way I can just simply dismiss all the rumors I've been hearing. Especially since I know for a fact that not everyone is lying on Curtis," Tanya said, raising her fork and taking a bite of her pancakes.

Nicole nodded her head slightly in partial agreement, and it was obvious to Tanya that she didn't want to comment one way or the other.

"Now, come on, Nicole. You know good and well you've been hearing the same stories as I have. If not more."

"Yeah, but people talk all the time, and you can't really rely on what other people are saying. Sometimes people start rumors just so they can break up someone else's relationship. Shoot, you know misery loves company, and I'd be willing to bet that the women who are talking don't even have husbands themselves."

"Oh, I'm well aware of that, but when you keep hearing the same names over and over again, and at the same time, you know your husband has more than his share of lost time, I think you have to have some common sense."

"Don't get me wrong. I understand exactly what you're saying, but all I'm saying is that divorce should be your last resort —

the last thing you even think about until you've done all you can to try and work things out with Curtis."

"But that's just it. I *have* been trying. Practically begging if you really want to know the truth. And still, things aren't getting any better."

"But you just said it seemed like Curtis was really trying to make things better this past week."

"I just don't know. I really don't know what to do," Tanya said, sitting back in her chair, folding her arms in frustration.

"Well, don't look at me, because the last thing I'll ever do is advise you to get a divorce. I offered my two cents to a good friend of mine two years ago, and it was the biggest mistake I ever made. She's miserable without her husband, and I'll never forgive myself for sticking my nose in their business. I mean, who was I to decide whether she should stay married to her husband or not?"

"But if she asked you for your honest opinion, then, as her friend, you had an obligation to tell her what she wanted to know."

"Not about something as serious as divorce. And I'll never do that for you, either. I mean, don't get me wrong, I care about you the same as if you were my own sister, but I just can't give you any advice when it comes to ending your marriage with Curtis," Nicole said, scanning the restaurant so she wouldn't have to look at Tanya directly.

Tanya didn't know if she should be upset with Nicole or not, but the more she thought about it, the more she realized that it really *wasn't* Nicole's place to tell her what she should do. Not about something as serious as this anyway.

"Okay, I guess maybe I'll let you off the hook this time, since you feel so uncomfortable about all of this," Tanya said, smiling at Nicole.

"Good," Nicole offered, smiling back in a relieved sort of fashion.

"So, how's Eric doing?" Tanya asked, changing the subject to Nicole's husband.

Nicole sighed. "Don't even ask. That's a whole 'nother story in itself."

"Why? What's going on?"

"Girl, I don't know. It just seems like the more successful my business becomes, the worse his attitude gets. I mean, he pretends like he's happy for me and all, but I can tell he practically resents what I'm doing."

"But he was the main person pushing

you to start your own business."

"Yeah, but when I was doing motivational speaking for the firm I used to work for, I wasn't earning nearly as much as I do now. And I definitely wasn't getting as much national exposure."

"Are you sure that's what's wrong with him? Because Eric seems so much more level-headed than that."

"Oh, I'm sure. Because just last week when I received a five-thousand-dollar check in the mail for a speaking engagement I did in Los Angeles, he copped an attitude then, too. I mean, it was one of the largest checks I've gotten since I went out on my own, so of course I was excited about it. But when I showed it to him, do you know what he had the nerve to say? *It's just money.* I mean, can you believe that?"

"You've got to be kidding?" Tanya said, scrunching her eyebrows.

"No, and that's not the first time he's made a remark like that. Because two months ago, when I told him that I'd been asked to speak at a women's business convention in New York and another conference at Harvard University which was scheduled for the same day, he seemed like he was upset about that as well. Especially

63

when I asked him which one he thought I should go to. At first, he didn't answer me, and when I asked him again, he practically yelled, *'It's not like it's that big of a deal, Nicole, so why don't you just pick one.'* And I can't tell you how hurt my feelings were after he said that."

"You know, why is it that some men seem to have such a huge problem when their wife gets just a little more attention or makes just a little more money than they do? I mean, it's so childish for a man to act that way. And I have to admit, I really believe that if I made more money than Curtis, he would probably react the same way, too. Curtis's life is built completely on money and material goods, and as far as I'm concerned, that means he has a major self-esteem problem. So, imagine how low his self-esteem would be if he wasn't bringing the highest salary into our household."

"Well, Eric isn't caught up in having a bunch of material stuff, but I do think that for whatever reason, my success is making him think less of himself. And it's really too bad, because even though he doesn't earn as much as I do, he earns more than enough from the construction company he works for."

"You know, I'll never forget when that one author was here last year signing copies of her book, and she said that the main reason she's come so far with her writing is because of the support and enthusiasm her husband has shown her. I can still remember the look on his face when she started reading from her book. He seemed so proud. And when one of the women asked him how he felt about his wife traveling all the time, he told her that most of the time he travels with her, but on the few occasions that he can't, he stays home and keeps a good watch on all the money *their* books are bringing into *their* bank account. It was so funny, but it was so wonderful to meet a man who clearly didn't care about who made the most money, and one who understood that all of their money belonged to both of them."

"Hmmph. I'll tell you one thing. I'd give anything to have Eric feel that way about what I've accomplished so far. I've worked so hard to get where I am, and he's making me feel so guilty about it. Almost like I should have continued working for someone else. But I have to say that although I made less money when I was with the firm, at least we were happy with each other back then."

"Well, all I know is that you need to sit him down for a serious discussion before things stretch too far out of hand. If he's feeling that insecure, what you've got to do is make him see that he's the most important thing in your life. And it probably wouldn't hurt for you to take him along on some of those business trips. You guys have a good marriage, and sometimes all it takes is a little communication to get things back to where they used to be."

Nicole laughed at what Tanya said.

"What's so funny about that?" Tanya asked in a baffled tone.

"You always give the best advice, but I guess that same advice isn't good enough to be applied to your own situation, though, huh?" Nicole commented with a smirk on her face.

Tanya shook her head and rolled her eyes toward the ceiling, smiling, because she knew Nicole was right. She knew she had an obligation toward making her marriage work. When she'd made the decision to marry Curtis, she'd promised to be with him until death. And although he was making it extremely hard for her to stick to that particular vow, she knew she had to put forth her best effort toward keeping their family together. It wasn't so much what she felt she had to do, but she knew that's what God expected from her.

Nicole and Tanya sat a while longer, left a tip on the table, paid the cashier, and walked outside to Nicole's utility vehicle. Then they drove downtown to the women's conference.

Once they'd found a vacant parking ramp, Nicole parked her silver-toned Dodge Durango on the top level, and then she and Tanya walked four blocks to the hotel. They couldn't believe the number of women who had already arrived. The turnout wasn't nearly as widespread as it was when they'd gone to the Today's Black Woman Expo a couple of months ago, but still there were hundreds of attendees perusing the various booths, and some were entering designated conference rooms to hear a variety of featured speakers.

"What do you want to do first?" Tanya asked Nicole.

"I don't know. Maybe we should check out one of the seminars," Nicole said, glancing through the brochure she'd been given when they'd first walked in. "There's three going on at ten o'clock, which is in fifteen minutes."

"Which ones are they?" Tanya asked,

looking over Nicole's shoulder at the schedule of events.

"One is Empowerment of the Black Woman in the New Millennium, the next one is How to be Black, Female, and Financially Free, and the third one is How to Have a Successful Black Relationship in the Twenty-first Century."

"Hmmph. That last one sounds like the one for both of us. As a matter of fact, what we need to do is find a couple of seats in the front row, as bad as our marriages seem to be doing," Tanya said, laughing.

Nicole laughed with her. "I don't believe you. Well, they're offering it again later this afternoon, so we can either check out all the exhibits now and go to the seminar later, or we can go to the seminar now and do the booths when that's over with."

"I think we should go to the seminar now, because the booths will be open all day," Tanya said, moving her sunglasses away from her eyes and then placing them on top of her head.

"Sounds good to me. I think the conference room is over here," Nicole said, pointing.

When they entered the room, which was already filling up, they took seats to the left of the aisle in the tenth row. They sat for a few minutes chatting, and then the opening speaker stepped up to the podium.

"First of all let me say how delighted I am to have been given the opportunity to speak with all of you today," said a beautiful, cappuccino-colored, thirty-something woman dressed in a classy-looking, royal-blue suit. "My name is Candace Livingston, author of *How to Have a Successful Black Relationship in the Twenty-first Century*, which is also the title of this seminar."

"That's the hairstyle I've been trying to describe to you," Tanya leaned over and whispered to Nicole, referring to the speaker's micro braids. She'd been wanting to get her hair braided for the longest time, but she'd been somewhat hesitant — hesitant because, as much as she hated to admit it, she'd thought braids were just a little too ethnic to be worn by a pastor's wife. But most of that crazy mentality had come from Curtis, the man who had a certain uppity image to keep up. Although, lately, she'd been getting closer and closer to the point where she didn't care what he thought. And to the point where if she wanted braids, braids were exactly what she was going to get.

Nicole nodded her head in acknowledgment. "Those are nice. I really like them. Maybe that's what I need to get done to my hair, because I'm getting sick of pulling it back into this ponytail all the time. And I just can't see sitting up in some beauty salon five to six hours every week, either."

"I agree," Tanya said.

"Relationships between men and women can be difficult, but at the same time, they can be the best thing to ever happen to human beings in general," the speaker commented, glancing across the audience. "My grandmother used to say, 'Marriage is what you make it,' and after years of making terrible decisions and mistakes with a number of relationships myself, I now know exactly what she meant by that particular phrase. Even if two people aren't married, the relationship still requires a huge amount of communication, understanding, and, most of all, a lot of give and take. Both parties have to be willing to contribute not fifty, but one hundred percent of what they expect to receive back from their partner."

The audience seemed mesmerized, and after Candace spoke for another twenty-five minutes or so, she took questions from those in attendance. There were many raised hands throughout the room, but she pointed to a middle-aged woman sitting in the second row.

"First of all, I'd like to commend you on your book, which I've read, and your ability to sort of tell things like they are. My question to you is: what would your advice be to a woman who is married to a man who doesn't want to do anything except watch football, basketball, baseball, and any other kind of *ball* most men can't seem to get enough of? Now, my husband was a wonderful father to our children when they were growing up, he's a wonderful provider, and he's even been what I consider to be a great husband for thirty years. But he never wants to take me anywhere. I mean, I want to go to dinner, to a movie, or . . . shoot, to a nice hotel to have buck-wild sex."

The audience roared with laughter, and the speaker herself couldn't help but burst out laughing at the woman. But when everyone finally settled down, she answered her.

"Well, first of all, you need to sit your husband down and tell him how you feel. Don't yell at him, but tell him why you feel the way you do. Explain to him that while you love spending time at home with him, you also want to spend time with him at other places, too. If he's willing, make a date with him, the same as the two of you probably did when you first started seeing each other. Since Saturday and Sunday are obviously popular days for TV sports, try to do something with him every Friday. And if you discuss it ahead of time, maybe he'll sacrifice one of those weekend days as well. And as far as going to a nice hotel, remind him of how important romance is to you, and that spending a night or week-end at a hotel is a lot more romantic than sleeping in your own bed. If you know what I mean," the speaker said, smiling at the woman who asked the question.

"Yeah, I know what you mean," the woman said. "I'm just hoping I can make my husband understand that even though I just turned fifty, I still need to get my sex on in a hotel room every now and then, the same as any other young woman."

Tanya and Nicole laughed again with everyone else. This woman was hilarious, and they couldn't believe she was speaking so boldly and telling all of her business in front of all these women she'd never even seen before. They looked at each other and shook their heads.

"She is really something else," Nicole said.

"Yes, she is. But you gotta give it to her, she knows what she wants, and she's definitely not afraid to do whatever it takes to get it," Tanya said, crossing her legs.

When the audience settled down again, Candace pointed at a young lady toward the back of the room who had her hand raised.

"Hi. I'm a college sophomore studying prelaw, and I'm wondering what your advice would be for a career-minded African American woman who dates a man who is not very ambitious or college-educated but seems to have a problem with women who are?"

"You have no idea how often I'm asked that particular question. And according to my colleagues, it's not just African American women who sometimes have this sort of problem. It's successful women in general who either make a ton of money or who have made a name for themselves at their jobs, in their communities, or even nationally, in the case of well-known celebrities. But even in your case, it can sometimes come about when young women date men who have never been to college and don't plan to. Or sometimes the problem can even arise with men who are very well educated. To put it plainly, these men have a serious self-esteem problem and a great deal of trouble with insecurity. And any man who makes you feel you should not be doing everything necessary to better yourself or one who makes you feel you should apologize for being successful is simply not the right companion for you. When you see the first wind of this sort of attitude, you need to end the relationship immediately. Now, on the other hand, if you're already married to someone like this, I highly suggest going to a marriage counselor. Most people don't think so, but low self-esteem, insecurity, and jealousy within a marriage can cause very severe marital problems. Eventually, the husband resents the wife for being successful, and the wife resents the husband for not supporting her or for not being happy about her accomplishments. And it's my opinion that unless mental and physical abuse are going on in a marriage, both parties have an obligation to do everything they can to make their marriage work. We all have choices, and if we make the choice to marry someone, then we have to be willing to work through the problems as well. Which is why I'm saying to you as a young student with your whole life ahead of you, get rid of negative people as soon as you discover them, and you'll end up a lot better off in the long run."

Nicole looked over at Tanya and then back up at the speaker. She couldn't believe this particular subject was actually being discussed. She felt as though the speaker was speaking directly to her. And now that she thought about it, she was starting to realize that Eric *had* made little comments when they'd first gotten married, after she'd told him that she wanted to go back to school part-time to obtain her master's degree. He'd even joked about her only wanting to go back to school so she could make more money than he did. She'd blown it off back then, but now she couldn't help but see how clear the signs of his insecurity had been from the very beginning. It sort of pissed her off, but one thing was for sure — no one was going to make her feel guilty about being successful. She was proud of how far she'd come with her career, and he was going to have to either accept it or find some very-glad-to-be-a-housewife sort of woman to marry. Because she wasn't the one. She never had been, and she was never going to be. No, it was like the speaker had just said, she should not have to apologize to anyone for being successful. Not even to her own husband.

A massive amount of thoughts paraded through Tanya's mind, but what she played over and over again was what the speaker had said about choices. That "if we make the choice to marry someone, then we have to be willing to work through the problems as well." She'd known that all along, and she believed in that theory with everything she had, but it was just that Curtis didn't seem to be putting any real effort into making their relationship work. Yes, he'd been doing better for all of one week, but she knew it wouldn't be long before he resorted to his same old infidelity. His same old lies. And his same old tricks. She knew she could make it without Curtis if she had to, but deep down what she really wanted was for the two of them to find the love they once had for each other. Which was why, starting tonight, she was going to put forth her strongest effort ever toward working things out with him.

Chapter 5

Tanya turned the front-door lock with her key, waved good-bye to Nicole, and stepped inside the front entryway of their solid brick, two-story home. They'd spent the entire day at the conference, and she couldn't remember when she'd ever felt more motivated, inspired, and so empowered. Not just as a black woman, but as a wife and mother as well. She had everything. A beautiful daughter, a wonderful career, and a successful husband. And even though Curtis hadn't been showing her the same love and affection he had when she'd first met him, she was sure that things were only going to get better as time went on. They just had to. She hadn't been this happy in a long time, and it was amazing how a relationship seminar could help make a world of difference in the way a person felt. Not just about herself, but about life in general.

She kicked off her flat, black shoes, dropped her black Coach duffle-style purse on the sofa, and gazed around the sunken family room. She could tell the cleaning service had been there, because everything looked immaculate. The family room was always the hardest room to keep clean, because that's where they each spent most of their time. And sometimes, when they didn't feel like eating at the dining-room table, they ate dinner in there as well, watched TV, and even entertained their closest friends when they visited. She picked up today's issue of the *Chicago Tribune*, and then headed up the winding wooden staircase to see what Alicia and Curtis were up to.

Tanya peeked her head through the partially closed doorway of her daughter's room and smiled. "So, what have you been doing all day, young lady?"

"Hi, Mom, look what Daddy bought me," Alicia said with her face lit up like a Christmas tree.

"What's this?" Tanya asked, reaching for the gorgeous, chiffon, lavender-colored dress.

"Daddy bought it for me when we went to the mall today."

"Well, wasn't that nice of him. It's beautiful, Alicia," Tanya said, glancing at the tag to make sure the size was a seven slim. Alicia could wear a size six with no problem, but sometimes she needed a seven to help out with the length. Which was what size this dress was.

"Can I wear it to church tomorrow?"

"Did you try it on at the store?"

"Uh-huh."

"Did you come out to show your dad?"

"Uh-huh, he had to zip it up for me, and he said it looked fine. He said I was going to have on the prettiest dress in the whole church tomorrow."

Tanya smiled. "Well, it sounds like to me you've already gotten permission to wear it."

Alicia smiled back at her.

"I'll tell you what. Why don't you try it on again, so I can make sure it fits you the way it should." Tanya hoped it did, because she knew Alicia was going to die if she said that it didn't and that they were going to have to take it back to the department store to exchange it. Partly because she'd set her mind on wearing it, but mostly because her father had bought it for her. She cherished everything he gave her, and this lavender dress was not going to be an exception.

"It fits really good, Mom. It really does," Alicia said, hesitating.

"It fits really *well*," Tanya corrected her daughter. "I'm sure it does fit, but I want you to try it on again, so I can see for myself."

Alicia removed her sleeveless jean shirt and matching pants reluctantly, and then slipped on the dress.

Tanya zipped it up. "Turn around, so I can see the back of it."

"See. I told you, Mom. It fits really good . . . I mean, well."

"Yeah, I guess it does," Tanya said, watching her daughter twirl around in the center of her bedroom. "I guess you can wear it tomorrow."

"Thanks, Mom," Alicia said.

"What's your dad doing now?"

"He's in the bedroom getting ready to go to a church concert."

A what? Tanya thought to herself. He hadn't mentioned a word about going to any concert when she'd left for the conference this morning. No wonder he'd been so receptive to spending the entire day with Alicia. Not to mention that expensive little dress he purchased for her, even though her birthday was still a couple of months away. She couldn't believe him.

She'd known all along that he wouldn't be able to keep up his little good husband, good father front. It was all too good to be true, and she couldn't believe she'd made the decision to put forth every possible effort to make their relationship work. She felt like storming into the bedroom, calling him everything but a child of God, and then throwing every piece of clothing he had to his name outside their master bedroom window. But then, maybe she was overreacting and what she needed to do was give him the benefit of the doubt.

"Well, after you get out of your dress, you can go downstairs to watch The Disney Channel, and I'll be down there after I see what your dad is up to."

"Okay. Can we get some pizza?"

"You still haven't eaten yet?" Tanya asked, since it was already after five o'clock.

"We ate at the mall, but now I'm hungry again."

"Okay, we'll order one in a little bit."

Tanya left her daughter's room, walked into her own, and shut the door.

"So, where are you getting ready to go?" Tanya said as calmly as she could, removing her black linen blazer. Then she sat down on the beige loveseat.

"To a youth concert at one of the churches over on the west side," Curtis said, pulling his necktie as tight as he could stand it. "How was the conference downtown?"

It was just like him to answer her so nonchalantly and then conveniently change the subject. She was so sick and tired of this. As a matter of fact, she was sick and tired of *being* sick and tired. But she was still going to remain calm. "The conference was fine. Why didn't you tell me this morning that you were planning to go to a concert this evening?" she asked, switching the conversation back to where she wanted it to be.

"I didn't decide to go until after you left."

"Did you forget my cell phone number?" she asked sarcastically.

"No, but I didn't think you'd want to go after spending all day at your conference. I figured you'd be too tired to come home, get dressed, and then leave right away."

Now, who exactly did he think he was kidding? Surely not her. And who was he to decide whether she would be too tired to go anywhere or not? She'd tried to keep her cool ever since Alicia had informed her that her father was getting dressed to leave, but she wasn't sure just how much more of this garbage she could swallow. She'd made a commitment to work hard on their relationship, but now she was starting to see that it really wasn't worth her while or her time. She couldn't understand why he always had to spend so much time away from home. Away from her and the daughter he claimed he loved so much. She wanted to scream at him, but instead she just glared at him as he sat on the bed pulling on his socks and slipping on his black dress shoes.

He looked over at her, and saw how furious she was becoming. "So, I guess you have an attitude about me going to church. Right?" he said innocently.

Tanya squinted. "Curtis, what do you expect me to do? Run in here with a smile on my face even though you're about to leave Alicia and me here all alone on a Saturday night like you always do? Is that what you expect me to do?"

"No, but I don't see why you have a problem with me going to a youth concert. Especially since our own youth choir is participating in it."

She'd seen the announcement in last Sunday's bulletin about Faith Missionary's youth choir singing at a concert, but in all honesty, she really hadn't thought too much more about it. As a matter of fact, it had totally slipped her mind. But that still didn't excuse the fact that Curtis hadn't asked her to go with him. He never asked her to go anywhere, because chances were he probably wasn't really going to any church concert in the first place. And even if he was, he was probably only going to be there for a hot second. No, what he was planning to do was lay up with one of his many women. She just knew it. But she decided to play as dumb as he thought she was just to see how he'd react to her next question. "Do you want me to go with you? I can shower, change, and be ready in less than twenty minutes."

Curtis stood up, and pulled on his grayish-black suit coat. At first he tried to ignore the question, but then he answered her. "The concert starts in thirty minutes, which means I have to leave now, or I'll be late. Plus, we don't have a babysitter for Alicia."

That part was true. They would never be able to get the babysitter over to their house on such short notice. Not on a Saturday night anyway. But still, it really irked her that Curtis was actually using the babysitter for an excuse. Because if he had truly wanted her to go, he would have asked her this morning, and then they either could have made babysitting arrangements or taken Alicia right along with them. Especially since she loved singing anyway. She was a member of the children's angelic choir, and nothing would have suited her more than to hear the older children singing in a concert. But of course Curtis didn't care about any of that. He didn't care about anything except how fast he could get dressed, and how quickly he could run out of the house, jump into his little Mercedes, and spend the rest of the evening doing what she didn't even want to begin trying to imagine.

"So, what time will you be back?" Tanya asked with her legs crossed and arms folded.

Curtis sighed in disgust. "Look, Tanya. I can't put some time limitation on God's work, because you never know when the spirit will get to moving. And if you must know, I have a counseling session that I have to do after that."

"A counseling session?" she screamed. "What kind of counseling goes on at ten-thirty or eleven o'clock at night? I know that concert won't be over until somewhere around ten! You must think I'm stupid or something." She hated doing this with Alicia in the house, and she'd promised herself that she wouldn't argue with Curtis in front of her anymore, but she'd had all she could take, and she wasn't about to let him leave without giving him a huge piece of her mind.

"Why are you doing all this yelling? Don't you have any respect for this family? Or more importantly, don't you have any respect for yourself?" Curtis said, frowning at her. Then he grabbed his wallet from the dresser and placed it in his pants pocket.

"You make me sick to my stomach," she said with her teeth gritted together. And she felt like killing him for the way he was treating her. The way he was trying to play her for a natural fool. The way he was dismissing everything their marriage was supposed to stand for. She knew it was wrong to hate anyone, but she was slowly but surely beginning to hate her own deceitful husband. "Curtis, how can you ask me that, when you're the one who stays out all night, every night? From where I'm sitting, you're the one who doesn't have any respect for this family. You have a lot of nerve blaming me for anything when you know all you're about to do tonight is go hop into bed with one of your sleazy tramps."

"Whatever, Tanya. I'll see you when I get back. Whenever that is," he said, and opened the bedroom door.

Tanya rushed over to the door and slammed it closed. "Oh, so you think you're going to just walk out of here like I'm no big deal, I guess. Right? Well, I'm sick of being left here all the time like some single parent."

Curtis glanced at the door, and then turned his head to look at Tanya who was now facing him. "I'll tell you what. You'd better not ever slam this door closed again when I'm trying to walk out of it," he said in a threatening tone. "Now, move out of my way before you make me late." He opened the door again, strutted out into the hallway and down the stairs.

Shortly thereafter, Tanya looked out the window and saw him backing out of the driveway.

She couldn't believe the way he'd just spoken to her. It wasn't so much the words he used as it was the way he spoke them. He sounded as though he was going to physically abuse her. He'd never done anything like that in the past, but for the first time ever, she could tell he just might be capable of it. At first, she became more angry, but the more she thought about her sad situation, the more sad she became. And she couldn't help but play Curtis's words over and over in her mind. And the look he'd had on his face made her feel even worse. If she didn't know any better, she'd swear he was on crack cocaine or something like it. He was so moody, selfish, and rude, and she didn't know what else she could do to make him transform back to the man she'd married in the first place.

She'd been so optimistic when she'd left the seminar, but now it seemed like she was fighting a losing battle. And she was doing it all by herself. She was so emotionally bankrupt that she didn't know who to turn to or what to do about any of this. She didn't want to bother Nicole, because it seemed like her friend had her own problems with Eric, and she didn't want to tell her parents, because they'd be worried sick about her and Alicia. But it was getting to the point where she didn't know how much longer she'd be able to keep her dreadful marriage a secret. She'd hoped that things would get better with time, but they hadn't. And now she didn't see how she could go another day without talking to her mother. She wouldn't let on about what was going on in Chicago, but it was just that she needed to hear her voice. She needed some sense of comfort, and her mother had always been able to give her that in the past.

Tanya left her bedroom, looked into Alicia's room, and saw that she had already gone downstairs. She hoped her daughter had gone down to the main floor before her conversation with Curtis had blown completely out of proportion.

When she arrived in the family room, Alicia never even turned to acknowledge her mother's presence. Tanya could tell that she was completely engrossed in one of her TV programs, which probably meant that she hadn't heard, let alone paid much attention to what she and Curtis were arguing about.

"Honey, I'm going to order the pizza, and you can keep watching your movie until it gets here. I'll be up in my bedroom, so when the delivery guy comes, I want you to come get me before opening the door."

"Okay, Mom," Alicia said, not even slightly taking her eyes away from the television screen.

"Alicia? Did you hear me?"

"Yes, Mom. I won't open the door until I come get you."

"Okay now, make sure you don't," Tanya said, and then headed back up to the second floor. When she arrived in her bedroom, she closed the door halfway, sat down on the side of the bed, and then dialed her parents' phone number.

"Hello," her mother answered, sounding as pleasant as always.

Tanya's plan to keep her marital problems hidden failed immediately, and instead of speaking, she burst into tears.

"Hello? Who's calling?" her mother asked with concern.

"Mom," Tanya said in a trembling tone of voice.

"Tanya, is that you, honey?"

Tanya took a deep breath, sniffled a couple of times, and wiped her face with her right hand. "Yes, Mom, it's me."

"Honey, what's wrong?" her mother asked, already sounding upset.

"Mom, I can't stand it here. My marriage is falling apart, and I'm so miserable I don't know what to do."

"What's going on with you and Curtis?" her mother asked, obviously surprised.

Tanya sighed heavily. "Mom, he's never here, and he doesn't spend any time with

Alicia or me at all anymore. And we argue almost every single day."

"When did all this start?"

"It's been going on for a while now, but I really thought that things would have gotten better by now."

"What is it that you guys are arguing so much about?"

"Everything. You name it, we argue about it. We don't agree on anything, and it's getting to the point where I don't see any other alternative except to leave him."

"Leave him?" her mother said in astonishment. "Things can't be that bad."

"Yes they are, Mom."

"Well, it's got to be more than just the arguments that have made you feel like you want to leave him."

Tanya knew her mother was going to want more specifics, and that was the one reason she had never brought this situation up in the past. She didn't want to burden her with any of this, but she knew her mother would worry even more if she was left with unanswered questions. "Well, for one thing, Mom, he is definitely seeing other women. Or at least one woman for sure."

"Not Curtis?"

"Yes, Mom. There have been rumors

going around about Curtis and one of the deacon's wives for a long time now, and I have a feeling that he's sleeping around with more than just her. I know it's probably hard for you to believe, but I know, with everything I have, that most of the rumors are true."

"Honey, I am so sorry, and you don't know how much it hurts me to know that you and Curtis are not doing well with your marriage."

"I know. But I don't know what else to do. I've tried to reason with him, but he's not listening. And whenever I ask him about where he's been all night, we end up screaming at each other like two enemies. And Mom, you know that's not good for Alicia. And I refuse to keep subjecting my baby to this type of environment. She doesn't deserve it, and it's not right for her to keep going through this."

"Mmm. Mmm. Mmm," her mother added, and Tanya could tell her mother couldn't believe what she was hearing. "I really hate to hear this, Tanya."

"I know, and that's why I didn't want to tell you about it," Tanya said, and then quickly continued. "And Mom, please don't tell Daddy about this. Not yet anyway, okay?" She hoped like everything that he wasn't in the same room as her mother, witnessing their conversation, because her father had never really cared that much for Curtis to begin with.

"I won't, but, Tanya, I want you to know that you can come to me with anything. I'm your mother, and that's what I'm here for. I don't care how bad something is, I want you to be able to talk to me about it. I love you and Alicia more than anything in this world, and I want to know when something is going wrong for either one of you."

"I just didn't want to burden you."

"Honey, you're my daughter, my only child, and it's my job to be here for you whether anyone else is or not. If you can't trust and lean on your own mother, who else can you really turn to? So, I'm telling you from this day forward, don't you ever feel like you can't come to me. All right?"

"All right, Mom," Tanya said, and then made another decision as soon as she answered. "Mom, I need to get away from here for a while, and I'm going to make some plane reservations for Alicia and me, so we can come visit you and Daddy next weekend."

"Well, you know your daddy and I would love nothing more than to see you and our grandbaby, but I really think that you should stay there and try to work things out with Curtis. Maybe you need to put everything on the table so that he understands it. Maybe all you need to do is show him that if things don't get any better, you're leaving him for good."

"I've threatened him with that so many times that now he doesn't believe one word of it. One time, he even laughed about it. Plus, I'm through talking to Curtis, because talking isn't getting us anywhere."

"Well, I guess you know best, and maybe a break from each other is what the two of you need."

"Maybe. But whether it is or not, I know that I have got to get away from him, the church, and Chicago."

"Well, your father just walked in, so I'll let you speak to him, and then I want to speak to Alicia when you two finish."

"Okay, Mom, and remember. Don't tell him about what's going on. I know I'll have to tell him when I get there, but I'd rather wait until then."

"Don't worry about it," her mother responded discreetly. "Now, here's your father."

Tanya waited for him to get on the phone, and prayed that she could keep a dry face until their conversation was over with.

Chapter 6

Tanya picked up her black strapless patent-leather sandals and placed them neatly inside of her pullman suitcase. With all of the chaos she'd encountered over the past week, she'd had no choice but to save the packing for this morning. She despised rushing around gathering clothes, shoes, and toiletries at the last minute, and she wished she'd been more organized than she had been earlier in the week. She'd been forced to work until eight in the evening on Monday and Tuesday, she'd spent Wednesday evening arguing with Curtis, which drained her completely, and then she spent all of yesterday afternoon and evening doing everything from going to the mall to picking up her and Alicia's clothing from the dry cleaner's. She was taking this trip to relax, but now her nerves were running wild, and she could already feel the early signs of a tension headache.

She placed a few more pieces of underwear and a few pairs of linen shorts in the suitcase, zipped it closed, and hoped she hadn't forgotten anything important. She'd been up since 3:00 A.M., but now it was already five o'clock. Their flight was at seven-thirty, and that meant they needed to be out of the house within the next half hour if they wanted to arrive at O'Hare Airport an hour before departure. She pulled her suitcase and garment bag off the bed and set them both near the bedroom doorway. And just as she turned to walk back toward the dresser to make a final check, Curtis walked into the room.

"Ready?" he asked in the happiest tone of voice she'd heard him use in weeks.

"Almost," she answered disappointedly. She knew the whole reason she was taking this four-day trip was to get away from her husband, but a part of her had hoped that he'd beg her to stay home with him instead of taking the trip down to Atlanta. But it hadn't happened. As a matter of fact, if anything, his attitude seemed to be better than ever, and they hadn't argued one time since the big blow-up on Wednesday night, which had erupted as soon as they'd finished dinner, and he'd informed her that he wouldn't be coming straight home from Wednesday-night prayer service, because he had some paperwork to go over at the church. And that he wanted to prepare the outline for his weekly sermon. Tanya knew he was lying, and hadn't waited more than a second to tell him exactly what she thought about him and his hypocritical sermons. But of course that hadn't stopped Curtis from leaving, and it certainly hadn't convinced him to come home until he was good and ready. Shortly after two in the morning.

"Your flight leaves at seven-thirty, right?" he asked, glancing down at his wife's luggage. "Are these ready to be taken downstairs?"

Well, wasn't he the considerate one? He'd never cared about helping her with her luggage in the past, and the more she thought about it, the more she couldn't help but remember that time she'd gone to a business conference in Dallas. The man had seemed completely put out when she'd asked him to carry her luggage downstairs and out to the car. Of course, they really hadn't been speaking to each other during that particular week, but he was still her husband, and it was his responsibility to help her with things like that. Not because the luggage was too heavy for her to handle, but simply because it was just the right thing for him to do. She wanted to ignore his question, but decided her current thoughts were far too petty to make a big deal out of. Or at least Curtis would think they were too petty anyway. "Yeah. You can take both of those down if you want. And Alicia's suitcase is ready, too."

"I just loaded hers into the trunk a few minutes ago."

Tanya didn't say anything, and she was sort of hurt over the fact that he was trying his best to get them out of the house and over to the airport as fast as he could. And even though she didn't want him to know how she was feeling, she spoke the obvious words before she could catch herself. "Curtis, how can you be so happy about us leaving?"

"I'm not happy about you leaving. But I really think you need a break from work, and it will be good for Alicia to see all four of her grandparents. She hasn't seen them since last Christmas, and I know they all can't wait to see her as well."

"Then why can't you go with us? Why can't we go visit our parents as a family?" She knew she'd planned this trip so she could get away from Curtis, but now she wished to a certain extent that he was going with them. Maybe what they really needed was to get away from Chicago together.

"Tanya, you know I have church commitments to tend to. And with you guys not coming back until Monday evening, I wouldn't be back in time to do my sermon on Sunday morning."

"What would the church do if you had a heart attack or dropped dead, Curtis? I'll tell you what, they'd have one of the associate ministers fill in for you."

"Having a heart attack and dying can't be helped, but I'm not about to drop my responsibilities on one of the other ministers so I can take a vacation. Things like this have to be planned. We'll do something together a few weeks from now, okay? I promise."

How many fake promises was this man going to make? He'd been making them week after week, month after month, and she wondered just how long he was going to go on the way he was.

She shook her head. "Fine. You do what you have to," she said, picking up her purse. Then she walked past him and out into the hallway.

"Mom, are we ready to go?" Alicia said,

stepping outside of her bedroom.

"Yes, sweetheart. We're ready to go. Do you have everything you're taking?"

"Yep. I've got my Walkman, my books, and all my other stuff in my book bag," Alicia said, smiling. She was so happy about going to see her grandparents, as Curtis had suggested, and Tanya was glad to see it.

Tanya looked in her daughter's room, making one final check, and then they all proceeded downstairs. When Curtis loaded his wife's luggage, he closed the trunk, and drove out of the subdivision.

Once they entered the expressway, Tanya felt relieved. There wasn't very much traffic, since it was still so early in the morning, and now she was feeling the same way she had when she'd phoned her mother last Saturday evening. Like she wanted to get away from Curtis. Like she wanted to leave him for good. She loathed the emotional roller coaster she was riding on. On some days she wanted to divorce Curtis, but there were others when she wished they could make up and live happily ever after. She just couldn't understand it. With all of the rumors of infidelity, all of the lost time, and all of the hypocrisy her husband was practicing, it was clear that she really should get rid of him without thinking twice about it. And she was sure that she would think lowly of other women who stayed with men like Curtis. All her life, she'd wondered why women stayed in abusive relationships, because Lord knows she'd seen enough of it at the center, and she never could understand how any woman in her right mind could stay married to a man who was sleeping around with every tramp that would have him. She'd even gone as far as saying that she would *never* put up with anything like that. Not from Curtis or any other man for that matter, but now she was doing exactly that. She wished she had never said the word never, and if she hadn't learned anything else over the last couple of years, she had learned one thing for sure: that a person didn't truly know how he or she would really handle a situation until they'd been forced to experience it themselves.

She felt stupid, and the last thing she wanted was to teach her daughter that she should stay in a marriage at any cost, even if it meant feeling miserable 365 days a year. It would be a long time before Alicia would have to deal with relationships, but Tanya knew a person's childhood always played a major part in their adult lives. People who were violent were more than likely abused as children, or they had watched someone else being abused on a regular basis. Women who were frigid when it came to making love with their husbands more often than not were sexually abused at some early stage in their lives. Those with low self-esteem were either called stupid, told that they would never amount to anything, or were completely neglected by their parents when they were growing up. Her thoughts were all based on psychological statistics, but just the same, she could see the logic in all of it. But then on the other hand, she hadn't watched her father abuse her mother, because he would never do anything like that. And as far as she'd known, he'd never messed around with other women, either. So, she couldn't help but wonder where her tolerance for Curtis's nonsense was stemming from. She didn't know whether it was learned behavior or something she'd been born with, but either way, she wanted it to end. She wanted it to end before it ruined both her and her daughter's life.

After they'd driven for another thirty minutes, Curtis drove onto the airport exit ramp, paid the toll, and continued driving toward the terminal. At least that's where Tanya thought he was taking them, until she saw him changing lanes and heading toward the main parking area.

"United is on terminal one," she offered.

"I know. But I don't want to just drop you off curbside and then take off."

She didn't know why not. He never wanted to spend any quality time with them on any other day of the week. And she couldn't help but wonder if he was going inside and up to the gate with them because he was being the considerate husband and father, or if it was simply because he wanted to be one hundred percent sure that she and Alicia really *were* going to be completely out of his hair for the entire weekend. But she really didn't have to wonder at all, because everything in her heart told her his reason was the latter.

"You really don't have to park, because once we check our luggage, we won't have more than forty-five minutes or so before they begin boarding the plane," she said, hoping that he'd change his mind, because she preferred that he drop them off and keep right on rolling. The same as he always had.

"Mom. Why don't you want Daddy to come in with us?" Alicia asked, obviously puzzled by her mother's comments.

"It's not that I don't want him to come in," she lied. "It's just that it would be quicker and more convenient for him to drop us off at the terminal. And we wouldn't have to carry the luggage through the parking lot, either."

Curtis looked over at Tanya, and then through the mirror at his daughter. "Daddy doesn't mind carrying the luggage, because that way he can spend as much time with his little girl as he can before she leaves."

Alicia smiled. "Thanks, Daddy. See, Mom, Daddy doesn't mind going inside the airport with us at all."

"No, I guess not," Tanya commented, trying to sound happy about it for her daughter's sake.

Once they'd parked the car, rented a luggage cart, and waited in the horrendously long line to check their luggage, they proceeded through the security area. Curtis had been asked to empty all of his pockets, but once he'd been cleared, they began walking toward the departing gate. As they continued walking, Alicia complained about being hungry, so they stopped at one of the restaurants for a bite to eat. When they'd finished they walked up to the gate, and took a seat. Alicia held a conversation with her father about any- and everything she could think of, while Tanya sat quietly reading a contemporary women's novel. She wasn't much of a reader when it came to fiction, but when she'd read the synopsis on the back of the book, she hadn't been able to resist purchasing it. It was almost as if the author had taken the storyline directly from her and Curtis's own sorry lifestyle. The two women in the story had everything: the career, the home in the suburbs, and they drove expensive vehicles, but, like her situation, their marriages were falling completely apart.

"What are you reading?" Curtis asked Tanya after Alicia told him she wanted to listen to her Walkman.

"A novel," Tanya answered curtly.

"What is it about?"

Why couldn't he just leave her alone? She'd wanted him to take the trip with them, and then when he'd lied and said he couldn't, she'd accepted that. Then when she wanted him to drop them off curbside and he didn't, she'd kept her mouth shut about that, too. But now that she was reading peacefully, she really didn't want to be bothered with his unnecessary questions. Questions that weren't going to make any difference to him one way or another.

"It's about two women who believe they have everything. You know, all the luxuries, but then they find out their marriages are in serious trouble."

Curtis grunted. "I can't believe you're even reading something like that. And I sure hope you're not being influenced by it."

"Being influenced by it how?"

"I don't know. For all I know, those women could be thinking about kicking their husbands out or leaving them for some other man," he said, laughing at his own pathetic joke.

"Well, after what I've read so far, I would definitely understand if they did come to that kind of decision. As a matter of fact, some men deserve to be left when they don't give their wives a certain amount of respect," Tanya said sternly.

"Hey, I was only joking with you. And it's not like those characters are real people. My goodness."

"The characters may not be real, but the chaos they're going through certainly is. And believe me, Curtis, I can surely relate to it."

Curtis shook his head, but didn't say

anything. Tanya could tell that he knew how hot she was, and that it was better for him to leave her alone. Normally, she would never embarrass herself by loud-talking him or anyone else in front of all these people, but she was so angry now that she just couldn't guarantee what she wouldn't do. She was hurt and frustrated, and there was no telling what she might say and how loud she might say it, if he kept pushing her.

Tanya and Curtis sat in silence until they heard the flight representative call Rows 20–25 for boarding. Tanya closed her book and grabbed her purse, and Curtis tapped Alicia, who was still listening to her Walkman, on the shoulder. When they reached the woman who was collecting the boarding passes, Curtis bent over and hugged Alicia, kissed her on the forehead, and told her that he loved her. Then he placed his forefinger under Tanya's chin, pulled her face close to his, and then kissed her on the lips. "I love you, Tanya. No matter what you think, I do."

"See you when we get back," Tanya said with no expression on her face.

" 'Bye, Daddy," Alicia said one last time. "Don't forget to pick us up when we get back, okay?"

"Don't worry, I'll be here, pumpkin. And don't you forget to kiss Grandma and Grandpa for me, okay?" he said, referring to his parents.

"I won't," Alicia said, waving at him.

Tanya and Alicia walked down the carpeted corridor leading into the plane. When they'd sat down and buckled their seat belts, Tanya gazed out of the window and wondered how long it was going to take for Curtis to call Adrienne and inform her that the coast was finally clear. That it was going to be crystal clear all weekend long.

Chapter 7

"Grandma! Grandpa!" Alicia yelled as soon as she spied her grandparents waiting inside the arrivals terminal. She was grinning from ear to ear, and instead of walking the rest of the way to where they were standing, she did a slow run, leaving her mother behind. When she finally reached them, she hugged her grandmother as tight as she could, and then her grandfather.

"How's my favorite granddaughter doing?" her grandfather asked, as though he had other grandchildren besides Alicia.

"I'm fine, Grandpa, how are you?"

"Well, I'm doing real good now that you're here."

Alicia smiled. "How are you, Grandma?"

"I'm good, and I'm so glad to see you," her grandmother said. "You're growing as fast as a weed," she continued, and then looked up at Tanya who was finally standing before them.

"Hi, Mom," Tanya said to her mother, and hugged her like she never had before.

"Hi, honey. It's so good to see you."

"How are you, Daddy?" Tanya asked. She hugged him affectionately, but she didn't want to hug him too tightly or too long, because the last thing she wanted to do was break down and cry right in front of him. Her father had always made her feel safe. He'd always given her the security and protection she needed when she was a child still living at home. And just seeing him made her wish that she could somehow turn back the time. She wished she could start her adult life all over again. Because if she could, she would certainly make some very different choices. She would never even consider marrying Curtis, and she would even think twice about ever getting married to anyone. This was not how marriage was supposed to be. It was supposed to be wonderful. It was supposed to be the best thing that could happen between two people who were of the opposite sex. She knew the divorce rate was as high as the sky, but she hadn't thought she would ever play a part in that set of statistics. She'd thought she and Curtis would be different. She'd thought that their love would withstand anything, and that it would see them through the good times as well as the bad. But so far she'd been completely wrong in her whole way of thinking.

"You doing okay?" her father asked when they'd released each other.

"I'm fine, Daddy. I'm doing just fine." Tanya hoped he hadn't sensed that something was wrong. She'd kept an everything-is-A-okay facial expression since she'd stepped off the plane, but maybe he'd seen right through it. He was asking a legitimate question no different than he always did, but for some reason, he sounded more concerned than usual. She knew her mother wouldn't have said anything to him, though, so maybe she was just paranoid. The same as anyone felt when they were in fact hiding something.

"Well, we'd better get down to the baggage claim area to get your luggage, so we can beat some of that lunch-hour traffic. It gets pretty ridiculous on Friday," he said as they all began walking.

"Robert, it's not even ten-thirty yet," Tanya's mother commented.

"Yeah, but, Elise, you know how these people are on Friday. Especially the ones who get paid today. They're liable to take an early lunch, and I don't want to get caught up in that bumper-to-bumper traffic on our way back over to Stone Mountain," he said, speaking of the suburb where they lived. "Plus, I know you guys are hungry, and all of the restaurants will be packed once twelve o'clock gets here."

"I guess you see that your father still worries about everything," Elise said to Tanya.

Tanya laughed, because her mother was right. He didn't like a lot of hustle and bustle when it came to anything. Just didn't have the patience, she guessed. The one thing she remembered, though, was that he always had time for his family. The thing she most admired about her father, the main thing she wanted from her own husband and wasn't getting. Curtis, Curtis, Curtis. And more Curtis. She'd flown to Atlanta to relax, and to get away from him, but she just didn't seem to be able to push him out of her mind. She still loved him, that's what the problem was. No matter how much he had hurt and neglected her, she still loved him. She'd been trying to tell herself that she didn't, but she did. She didn't want to love him, but that's just the way it was. But, she had to get him off her mind for now. She was there so that she and Alicia could spend some quality time with her parents, and that's what she was going to have to concentrate on. At least for now anyway.

Tanya felt a tremendous sense of peace and contentment as soon as she stepped across the threshold of her parents' home. She was so glad to be back there, and for the first time in months, she felt like a ton of weight had been lifted from her burdened shoulders. Her problems hadn't gotten any better, of course, but she was glad to be back in the midst of the people who had raised her, the people who had adopted her when she was only six weeks old. She never even liked saying the word adoption, because these were her *real* parents. She'd never met her biological parents, and most of the time, didn't care to. She had her curiosities the same as any other adopted child must have, but she didn't see a reason to look for someone who hadn't cared about anyone except themselves, someone who hadn't thought enough of her to raise her. Her mother had told her that her biological mother was a college student, and hadn't seen how she could continue her education and raise a newborn baby at the same time. And if she dropped out of college, she hadn't seen how she would be able to give her the good life she deserved. But Tanya had decided a long time ago that an excuse like that was a bunch of garbage. She wasn't buying into it, and she wasn't going to run around all over the country looking for her, either. Curtis had always thought she should try to find her biological mother, and even her biological father if she could, but she didn't see any real reason to do it. Although, she had to admit, that on some days she did feel like searching for her mother, just so she could look her straight in her face and ask her how — how on earth could she give away an innocent newborn baby? Her own flesh and blood. It was so completely insane as far as she was concerned, and while she strongly believed in adoption and not abortion, she didn't want to apply that sort of philosophy to her own situation. She knew her attitude was the result of a double standard, but she couldn't help the way she felt. And now that she was thinking about it, maybe that's why she was taking all of this crap from Curtis. Maybe being given away like she was a piece of clothing being donated to some charitable organization was the reason her self-esteem wasn't nearly where it needed to be. Maybe that's why she needed Curtis to love her. And why she needed him to spend time with her and Alicia as a family. She was a counselor, but she was starting to feel like she needed someone to listen to her own problems instead.

"Mom, can I call Jalen?" Alicia asked as soon as she'd gone through the house and taken a look in every room, checking to see if everything still looked the same. Jalen was Curtis's brother's little girl, and since they were the same age, Alicia always spent a lot of time with her whenever they visited Atlanta.

"Jalen is probably still in school, but we'll call her in a few hours to see if she wants to come over."

"Okay. But can I go outside in the backyard?"

"That's fine, but I want you to change into a pair of shorts first," Tanya said. It was the middle of May, but the temperatures were already in the upper eighties, something that was rare for Chicago, but pretty much the norm for Atlanta residents. She'd made Alicia wear a pair of jeans and a nylon jacket on the plane because of how cold the air-conditioning usually was, but now it was obvious that she didn't need any of those things. As a matter of fact, even shorts and a sleeveless shirt were still going to be too warm if she wanted to play outside. Atlanta's middle-to-late eighties were a lot different than Chicago's, because their eighties always felt more like nineties to Tanya.

"And if it gets to be too hot," Tanya continued, "you're going to have to come in until later on this evening."

"Yeah, sweetheart, we don't want you to have a sunstroke," Elise said to her granddaughter.

Robert walked back down the stairs and picked up the last of Tanya's luggage.

"Daddy, you don't have to carry all of that by yourself. I'll take it up later."

"Oh, this is nothin'. Besides, baby girl, I need the exercise."

"Well, I don't," Elise added. "What we need to do is find us a ranch-style home before we retire, because the older we get, the more we won't be able to walk up this huge flight of stairs every day of the week. Plus, what if we have surgery or get low sick? We wouldn't even be able to get up to our bedroom. This house was fine when we first built it, but now I'm starting to realize that we should have been thinking more about our old age. But you know how it is when you're in your thirties, you never even stop to think about it. But of course now that we're in our fifties, the subject crosses my mind on a regular basis."

"Mom, please. You guys aren't getting old. You probably are involved in more activities and take more vacations than anybody I know," Tanya said, dropping down on the sofa in the front room, a room that had been off limits when she was growing up.

Elise laughed and sat down in one of the mauve-colored, wing-back chairs. "Yes, we are, girl. Your mama and daddy are gettin' old."

"Maybe *you* are, but I'm not," Robert insisted as he walked back down the stairway. "A person is only as old as he acts, and you know I still have too much fire to be acting old. Right, Elise?"

"Robert!" Elise scolded him. "You see Tanya sitting here, and that baby is right upstairs."

"What? She can't hear anything all the way down here. And Tanya is grown."

Tanya burst out laughing at her father, because he was always saying things like this in front of her. It wasn't that he was trying to disrespect her, but it was just that he didn't see anything wrong with making these kind of jokes in front of his thirty-three-year-old daughter.

"Still," Elise said in embarrassment.

"I'm just lettin' my baby girl know I don't have one foot in the grave like some of these other middle-aged men runnin' around here."

Elise shook her head and finally laughed with her daughter. "Your father is a mess."

"Well, I guess we need to figure out what we're going to do for dinner this evening," Robert said. "You got something special that you want, baby girl?"

"Not really, Daddy, but it would be nice if you grilled some steaks and sweet corn."

"Sounds good to me," he said. "I guess I'll run out to the store and pick everything up then."

"Can I go with you, Grandpa?" Alicia asked, making her way back down to the main floor.

"Sure, baby. Grandpa would be glad to have you come along to the store with him. We'll stop and get us some ice cream on the way back, too."

"Yeah!" Alicia said happily.

"Now, you stay with your grandfather the whole time you're in the store, and don't run off to some other aisle without him," Tanya instructed.

"I won't, Mom," she said, pursing her lips together as if she didn't understand why her mother was telling her that.

"You two want anything special back from the market?" Robert asked his wife and daughter.

"You can bring some kind of cake back if you want, because I've really got a taste for something sweet," Tanya requested.

"I made a red velvet cake last night before I went to bed," Elise said, looking at Tanya.

"Ooh, Mom, you didn't. You know that's my favorite."

"I know. That's why I made it."

"Well, forget the cake, Daddy, unless you guys want one, because I'll probably eat the one Mom baked all by myself."

They all laughed.

"Well, let's go, sweetheart," Robert said to his granddaughter, and they both walked out of the house.

Tanya took a deep breath, leaned back on the sofa and stretched her legs as far as she could under the brass-and-glass coffee table. "Mom, you have no idea how good it is to be back home. I've been living in Chicago for two years now, but this is where home is always going to be for me."

"There's no place like home, I know, but I think you'd feel better about Chicago, if things were better between you and Curtis."

Tanya wasn't sure if she wanted to discuss this right now, but it was probably better to do it while her father was gone. She'd still have to tell him, but at least she wouldn't have to tell him all of the ungodly details. The kind that would make the hair he used to have stand up on end.

"Yeah, you're probably right, because even though I wasn't that happy about moving to Chicago, I didn't feel as bad about it when Curtis and I were getting along. I would have followed that man to Europe, if that's where he'd said we were going, and I would have been happy. But now, as much as I hate saying this, I wish I had never met him."

"I really hate to hear you saying that, and I don't understand at all what's gotten into my son-in-law. He seemed like he loved you more than life itself when you guys first got married, and never in a million years would I have thought he would start treating you and Alicia like this."

"Neither would I, Mom, but it's like I was telling you, he leaves home almost every single night, and I know he's messing

120

around with other women."

Elise shook her head in disappointment.

"Do you think maybe it would help if I spoke to him. I mean, I don't want him to think I'm sticking my nose in his business, but at the same time, I don't want to see you guys break up over something that can probably be worked out."

"I don't know, but I really doubt if he would listen to you. He's so defensive about everything I bring up, and he denies that he's doing anything wrong. He flat out lies, and he has an excuse for everything. And I would love nothing more than to leave him right now, and file for a divorce, but the truth of the matter is, I still love him, Mom," Tanya said with tears filling her eyes. "And no matter what he does, I can't seem to help it. I know it's stupid, but . . ." she said, barely getting her words out and covering her nose and mouth with both hands.

Elise stood up and then sat on the sofa next to her daughter. "Oh, honey, it'll be all right. Don't even worry about it," she said, pulling her daughter into her arms. Tanya laid her head on her mother's chest with her face still covered. And now she was crying uncontrollably.

Elise caressed her daughter's back, but

when she heard a key turning the front door lock, she looked up and saw Robert walking back through the doorway.

"What's wrong?" he said in an alarmed tone of voice.

Elise was speechless, and Tanya raised her head up, wiping her tears away.

"Oh, Daddy," Tanya cried, standing up and walking over to her father.

"What's the matter, baby girl?" he asked, embracing her. And she embraced him back like she was never going to see him again.

"Elise, what's going on?" he asked, hoping someone would give him an answer.

"It's Curtis . . ." Tanya said between deep breaths.

"What about Curtis? Is he sick?"

"No, Daddy, it's nothing like that."

"Then what is it?"

Tanya hesitated. "He's messing around with somebody else."

"He's what? What do you mean, messing around with somebody else?" he asked, gently pushing his daughter away from him by her arms, staring at her.

Tanya didn't say anything, and now that he was looking her straight in her eyes, she didn't have the courage or the nerve to tell him. She looked at her mother instead.

"Tanya thinks that Curtis is messing around with another woman, and he hardly spends any time at home with her and Alicia."

"You wait until I talk to that little jack-leg, wannabe preachin' . . ."

"Robert!" Elise yelled at him. "The girl is already upset, and you going off on Curtis is not going to make things any better."

"I don't care, I'm still going to call his no-good behind when I get back here. You know I never liked that little, shifty-eyed Negro in the first place."

Tanya's chest continued to elevate, and tears were still rolling down her face.

Robert noticed it, and grabbed her into his arms again. "I'm sorry that you're going through this, baby girl, but what you're going to have to do is file for a divorce. You don't have to take anything that that Negro is dishing out, and that's that."

"But she loves him, Robert. And it's not that easy to just walk out on somebody you love," Elise said, trying to reason with him.

Robert glanced through the living-room window at his granddaughter. "Let me get back out there before that baby comes in here and sees you all upset," he said. "But we're going to discuss this as soon as I get back. Now, are you going to be okay?"

Tanya shook her head yes, and Robert kissed her on the forehead. Then he left out of the door again.

Tanya sat back down on the sofa next to her mother and wiped her face again with both hands. "See, Mom, that's why I didn't want him to know about this. I knew he was going to be angry, and the last thing I want is for him to call Curtis. And what did Daddy come back in here for anyway?"

"Who knows. He probably forgot something, but after he saw how upset you were, he probably didn't think about it anymore."

"Mom, I'm sorry for breaking down like this. Sometimes I think I have everything under control, and at others, I feel like I'm falling completely apart."

"Honey, believe me, I understand how you feel, and you don't have anything at all to be sorry about.

"So, now. Why don't you go upstairs and wash your face, and I'll cut both of us a piece of that red velvet cake."

Tanya smiled and hugged her mother. "I love you so much, Mom, and I don't know what I would do without you."

"I love you, too. And no matter what happens, I want you to know that I'm always here for you. And don't you forget that," Elise said, hugging her daughter again.

Tanya headed for the stairway, and Elise strutted into the kitchen.

Chapter 8

As soon as Robert grilled four rib-eye steaks and a dozen corn on the cob, and Elise fixed her famous seven-layer salad, and a dish of baked beans, they each sat down and ate dinner. Now, though, Alicia and her cousin Jalen, who'd been dropped off by her parents a couple of hours ago, were playing in the backyard on a swing set, and Tanya, and her parents were sitting on the patio.

"Jalen sure has gotten tall. She's almost as tall as Alicia," Tanya commented.

"She sure has," Elise added.

"We don't usually get to see Curtis's family until you guys come down for a visit, so it's been almost six months since I've seen her."

"Now, who you should have married was Larry," Robert said, lighting his pipe and looking at Tanya. He was referring to Jalen's father and Curtis's older brother.

"Daddy, please," Tanya said, shaking her head in disagreement.

"Well, you should have. Because I'll bet if you had, you probably wouldn't be going through all this mess you're going through with Curtis. You know I always thought that Larry was the better brother anyhow."

"Robert, why don't you stop that?" Elise said, frowning at her husband. "Because criticizing Curtis isn't going to help anything."

"Well, shoot, I can't help it," he said, looking away from both of them. "As far as I'm concerned, that Negro needs to be beaten until he can't even holler anymore. And I'm the one who could do it for him."

Tanya couldn't believe how violently her father was thinking. Yes, he didn't like Curtis. And yes, he had *never* liked Curtis. But she couldn't believe he was taking this so seriously. He was acting like he wanted Curtis dead. Was he forgetting that this was his granddaughter's father? Was he forgetting his own Christian values? She'd never seen him so upset before, and it seemed like he'd become more and more angry as the evening went on. It was almost as if every time he thought about Curtis, his hostility rose to a whole other level. She'd known that he was going to be

127

upset, and that he would immediately suggest she divorce Curtis, but she hadn't expected him to go to such extreme measures with his opinions.

"Daddy, I know you don't like Curtis, but he's still my husband, and he's still Alicia's father. And it's not that easy to just up and leave someone you've been married to for eight years. Especially when you have a child with them."

"Well, which do you think is better, Tanya? Alicia seeing her father during weekend visits or listening to you and him argue like cats and dogs every day of the week. Because I know that's what you're doing."

Tanya didn't know what to say, because she knew her father was right. And although she would never admit it to him, she'd been having those same thoughts herself. But for some reason, she just couldn't force herself to actually leave Curtis. She didn't know what it was really. She kept telling herself that it was because she loved him, and because she didn't want to be the reason why Alicia had to live in a single-parent household, but maybe it was simply that she just didn't want to give up the tried and true. She and Curtis had a lot of history together, and she was scared to death of being alone. Nicole was her only true friend in Chicago, and if she divorced Curtis, she didn't see how she'd have any other choice except to move back to Atlanta where her family was. But that would mean that Alicia would only see her father on holidays and maybe during the summer. And that didn't really seem fair to her daughter, because regardless of how bad a husband Curtis was, Alicia still deserved to see him on a regular basis. Dr. Laura always insisted that on her radio program, and Tanya tended to agree with her. At least when it came to that particular subject anyway.

"Daddy, I have to work this out on my own," Tanya said, trying to reason with her father. "I know you're only upset because you care about Alicia and me, but Curtis and I have to work this out. And at this point, I don't know what I'm going to do yet. And that's part of the reason why I wanted to get away and come down here this weekend. I needed some time to think this through."

"Well, I don't know what it is you've got to think about," Robert said, obviously not paying attention to anything Tanya had just said to him. "I'm not saying it will be easy, but, baby girl, some things just aren't meant to be. It used to be that women stayed in marriages until death regardless of how their husbands treated them, but we're at the twenty-first century, and I just don't see how you can keep putting up with somebody who's trying to walk all over you."

Tanya sighed with irritation.

Elise noticed and decided to tone Robert down for the last time. "Look, Robert. This is none of our business, and if you don't have anything positive to say, then don't say anything at all. All this anger isn't helping anything."

"Elise, do you think I'm going to just sit by and watch some fake-ass, holy-rollin' minister treat my daughter like a dog? Well, I'm sorry. Maybe you can, but I can't. And if both of you want to know why I'm so upset, then I'll tell you why," he said, standing up and gesturing with his hands. "I'm sick and tired of these ministers running around here claiming that they've been called by God to preach and then they end up committing more sins than the average sinner who's running loose in the streets. They get up Sunday after Sunday judging everyone in the congregation when they know good and well they're doing much worse as soon as they step down out of the pulpit. Hell, some of them don't even wait for that, because you can see most of those fools gawking at the women in the church like they want to lie down with them right in the middle of the sanctuary. And you don't want me to even start talking about all the money they're fooling out of innocent people. Ridin' around in their fine cars and expensive suits and then looking like some drug dealer with all those gold rings lined up on every finger. It's a crying-out-loud shame how low-down some of these ministers are. And that Negro you're married to, Tanya, is no different."

Tanya looked at her father and then out in the yard at Alicia and Jalen who were still playing on the swing. She thanked God that her parents' backyard was huge, in a secluded partially wooded area, and was quite a distance away from the patio, because that was the only reason why the two girls hadn't heard her father going off like some maniac. Tanya loved her father, and she respected him with everything inside her, but she'd finally had enough of his criticizing. He'd made some very good points, but he was completely out of line. He was acting as if Curtis was betraying him instead of her, and she'd heard all she needed to hear. Her mother had tried to calm him once and failed at it, but Tanya was going to set him straight.

"Okay, Daddy. You've said what you have to say, and I've sat here and listened to it. But this is my marriage, and I have to deal with it the way I see fit. I love you, and I don't mean to disrespect you in any way, but what I need from you is emotional support. And that's it. I don't need to hear you criticizing Curtis, and I definitely don't want you talking the way you have been in front of Alicia. I mean, Daddy, what if she had been closer to the house and heard you?"

"Look," he said, pointing out toward the swing in frustration. "Those girls aren't paying us the slightest bit of attention, and even if they were, they can't hear anything all the way up here anyhow."

"Still. I don't want you talking about Curtis the way you have been when she's anywhere near you."

"Fine. You do what you have to do," Robert said, and walked into the house.

Tanya looked at her mother, who was furious.

"He really gets next to me when he starts rantin' and ravin' like that, and it really gets on my last nerve," Elise said, clearly irritated.

"I didn't mean to disrespect him, Mom, but Daddy was completely out of line."

"You did the right thing, because he had no business saying any of that stuff," Elise said, swatting at a mosquito with her right hand.

"I knew he was going to take it this way, and that's why I didn't want you to tell him until I got here."

"He'll cool down after he's had a chance to think about it, and you know he can't stand for you to be mad at him. Not his baby girl," Elise said, laughing.

Tanya laughed, but not as much as her mother, because she didn't know if her father really cared about her being mad at him or not. Especially since she'd never seen him so upset. Or at least not since when she was a little girl and their next-door neighbors kept allowing their German shepherd to do his business on their front lawn. Her father had been furious, and he'd yelled and screamed at them time and time again. And he had kept yelling and screaming until the day King came down with some respiratory infection and the neighbors had been forced to put him to sleep.

"I don't know, Mom. Daddy is so stubborn, and it doesn't help that he never liked Curtis."

"Honey, your daddy wouldn't have liked any man that you married. There's not one guy you could have brought home that he would have been crazy about, because he's never thought any man was good enough for you."

"I dated Bobby my last year in high school, and he really liked him a lot."

"That's only because he knew *you* didn't really like him all that much, and that nothing serious was ever going to result from you guys seeing each other. Trust me, honey, he's always wanted the best for you the same as I do. But it's just that he takes it to the extreme and has never learned how to let go of you."

"You think I should go apologize to him?"

"No, he'll be okay. But I will say this. He's not going to sit right with this until he knows you're happy again or that you've decided to leave Curtis for good."

"I know, Mom, and I'm going to get this taken care of as soon as I can. I'm hoping that Curtis will come around. I know it's doubtful, but that's what I'm praying for."

"Well, if it's meant for the two of you to be together, then you will be, and praying is the best thing you can do at this point."

Tanya turned her attention to Alicia and Jalen who were both holding imaginary mikes up to their lips singing as loud as they could, like they were musical superstars. Tanya and Elise laughed at them, and it wasn't long before the two girls realized that they had an audience. And it didn't take them more than a few seconds to skip their way back up toward the patio so they could put on a real show. Jalen acted sort of shy, but Alicia didn't have a shameful bone in her whole entire body when it came to performing. She did it all the time in Chicago. At home for her parents, for their guests, and at church in the little children's choir. She was a natural, and Tanya had a feeling that her daughter's musical talent was eventually going to take her places.

Alicia closed her eyes and sang Mary J. Blige's portion of "Lean on Me" by Kirk Franklin. And it seemed like she really felt what she was saying. It was so inspirational and so moving that Tanya looked at her with raised eyebrows. She couldn't believe how well Alicia knew the song, word for word. But then, V103 and WGCI had played it an awful lot when it first came out, and BET still showed the video pretty regularly. Tanya was so proud of her.

"Sing that song, baby," Elise said, praising her granddaughter.

"Just listen to my little Alicia," Tanya said, smiling, and thought, *No matter what happens with Curtis, I will always be here for my little girl, the same as Mom has been here for me.* Then she grabbed her mother's hand the way she used to when she was just a little girl herself — when she wasn't even quite Alicia's age.

Tanya had wondered when major fatigue would finally kick in, and now she was feeling it with full force. She hadn't slept more than a few hours the night before, and she couldn't wait to climb into bed. Alicia had wanted her cousin Jalen to spend the night, but since Jalen needed to attend ballet lessons early the next morning, her mother had thought it would be best if she stayed over tomorrow night instead. Tanya, Alicia, and Elise were planning to go shopping anyhow, and Tanya was sort of hoping to spend some time with just the three of them. Not that she didn't want Jalen coming along, but it was just that she wanted some time alone with both her mother and her daughter. And since her father always golfed on Saturday mornings, this was going to be the best time for them to do that.

Tanya walked into her old bedroom and gazed around. This was her old stomping ground, and although some of her best childhood memories were already sailing through her mind, she still felt a certain sense of confusion. She seemed to do fine when other people were around, but when she was alone, her marital problems always seemed to control her emotions. She'd thought Alicia was going to sleep in the room with her, which would have at least given her company, but Alicia had begged her grandparents to let her sleep with them, and of course they hadn't argued with her one bit. It was right up their alley, and since they only had a couple of days to spend with her, Tanya hadn't seen where she had any reason to be complaining about it.

She dropped down on the side of the bed, allowed her body to fall back, and then positioned her head on a pillow. She knew she needed to wrap her hair up, because if she didn't, come morning, she'd be looking like some wild woman. But she just couldn't seem to muster up the energy to take care of it. And worst of all, she hadn't even washed the foundation, blush, or the eye makeup from her face. This was an obvious no-no, since the slightest variation in her usual skincare regimen always caused her to break out, but at the same time, she just didn't feel like dragging her body all the way down the hall and into the bathroom.

She glanced over at the clock on the nightstand, saw that it was just after ten o'clock, and then closed her eyes. She wanted to phone Curtis, but she'd already spoken with him a couple of hours ago when he called to make sure they had made it safely. Which was actually a fine time to be calling since they'd made it to Atlanta earlier that morning. She usually called him whenever she traveled, but today she decided against it, because she figured it was probably better if he was the one left wondering for a change. Their conversation had been cordial, but that was pretty much the extent of it. He'd spent most of his time talking with Alicia, and there wasn't a whole lot Tanya wanted to say to him, anyway, in front of her father, who was still completely furious about the whole situation. But now that everyone was in bed, and her bedroom door was closed, she was thinking that maybe now would be a good time to call him. Maybe she could have a real discussion with him. It seemed silly to think that she had to fly hundreds of miles away from Chicago just to have a decent conversation with him on the phone, but at this point she was willing to try anything. But, then, what if he wasn't at home. There was always that chance, and even more so when she wasn't at home to confront or drill him about his whereabouts. She knew her feelings would be hurt if he wasn't there, and she was trying to raise herself to the point where she didn't care one way or the other. But there was no sense in lying to herself, because she really wasn't at that point at all. Last week, when she'd decided to take this trip she'd been sure that she wanted to divorce Curtis, and that, if nothing else, they needed time away from each other. But now that she was in Atlanta and he in Chicago, she still wanted to talk to him. She was sick of feeling this way, and what she wanted more than anything was to wake up one day with not a care in the world when it came to Curtis or her marriage. She was tired of the pain. Tired of begging. And tired of being made to look like a complete fool in front of every church member who knew what Curtis was up to.

She sighed deeply, but kept her eyes closed. Before long she dropped off to sleep without even realizing it.

"So, where's the deacon at now?" Curtis asked Adrienne sarcastically. She'd just phoned him about ten minutes ago for the second time that evening.

"He's upstairs sleeping. He's been asleep at least an hour or so, and if I had known that, we could have gone out to the condo like we planned."

"Well, you know I was ready and waiting, but you were the one who decided to stay home with him at the last minute."

"Honey, you know his blood pressure was sky high. And I just didn't feel comfortable leaving him. I know you don't understand, but it just wouldn't have been right."

"You're right. I don't understand. Here Tanya is gone for the entire weekend, and you've got me sitting here all alone on a Friday evening doing absolutely nothing," he said irritably. "And on top of that, you keep claiming that you're not even in love with the man anymore."

"Curtis, I'm not in love with him. But Thomas hasn't done anything wrong, and none of this is his fault. And what bothers

140

me the most is that he always treats me like I'm the best thing that ever happened to him."

"You're not in love with him because he bores you to death. You've been saying that from the very beginning."

Adrienne was speechless.

But Curtis continued saying what he had to say.

"Sometimes I think you have your priorities all mixed up. And if you and I are going to be together, you're going to have to do something about it. I have my needs, and I don't like you putting anybody else before me. And that includes the deacon."

"Honey, why are you acting like this?" Adrienne asked, sounding like a pleading ten-year-old girl. "Why are you so upset with me?"

"I just told you. You don't have your priorities in order," he said straightforwardly.

"Honey, you know how much I love you and how much I want to spend the rest of my life with you. And you know I would never put anyone before you unless it was necessary. I mean, what if something happened to him and I was gone?"

"Nothing is going to happen to him. You just said he's asleep."

"But who's to say what will happen in

the next couple of hours?"

"Like I said, nothing is going to happen to him. You've got yourself worried over nothing. But at the same time you keep telling me that you don't love him anymore, and that I'm the only person you want to be with."

"Look, Curtis. Both of us are married, and we have to see each other when we can because of it."

"What?" Curtis said angrily. "Don't you *ever* compare my situation to yours. I have a certain reputation to protect because of the church, so sometimes I'm going to have to spend time with my wife and daughter. You, on the other hand, can get away whenever you feel like it. It's not like you have any children or anything like that."

"Look, honey, I'm sorry, okay?" she declared. "I promise it won't happen again."

"You know," Curtis said curtly. "If you can't give me what I need and you can't be here for me when I need you to be, then we're going to have to end whatever this is we have going on."

"After all we've been through, how could you even suggest anything like that?" she said fearfully.

"Because maybe we're not right for each

other. Maybe you're not as dedicated to me as I thought you were," he said, leaning back on his bed.

"You know that's not true."

"I don't know, because that's what it seems like to me," he said, flipping through the channels with a smirky grin on his face. A grin that Adrienne couldn't see.

"Okay, honey, look. What can I do to make this up to you? I'll do anything you want, but please don't be angry with me."

"I don't know that there is anything you can do, because we'll never have another free weekend like this one for a long time."

"Driving out to the condo is too far, but I can meet you at that hotel we went to a few months ago if you want."

"I wouldn't want the deacon to pass out while you're gone or anything like that. Maybe you better stay there with him like you planned."

"No," she said in frustration. "He'll be fine for a couple of hours. He probably won't even realize that I'm gone."

"Are you sure, because just a minute ago, you said you didn't want to leave him."

"Honey, I'm trying to make things up with you, so just meet me in about forty-five minutes or so, okay?"

"See you then," Curtis said, and hung up the phone. He smiled at the fact that he'd gotten what he wanted. Just like he always did when it came to Adrienne.

But suddenly, his smile vanished when his eyes centered on the huge family wall portrait of him, Tanya, and Alicia. He didn't know why he did some of the things he did. He wanted to do the right thing, but at the same time, he didn't want to stop being with Adrienne. It was more like he couldn't stop being with her. He asked God to forgive him daily, and it was getting to the point where that was the only time he bothered to ask God for anything. He was starting to feel like Paul, the biblical character in the Book of Romans, who talked about his inner struggle with wanting to do the right thing, but not being able to do it. Curtis had read about Paul over and over again, but for some reason, he still wasn't able to change his way of thinking. And that bothered him. Sometimes it bothered him so deeply that he wondered why God had ever called him to preach in the first place.

Tanya opened her eyes and looked around the room mysteriously. It took her a few seconds to remember where she was, that she was at her parents' house in her old bedroom and not at her own home with Curtis. She gazed over at the clock and this time it was midnight. She sat up in the bed, and against her better judgment, she picked up the cordless phone and dialed her home phone number. She heard the first ring, and after the fourth, the voice mail system picked up, and she heard her own voice-recorded outgoing message. A nervous sensation whipped through her stomach, and she wished she'd followed her first mind and not made the phone call. When she heard a beep, she threw the phone on the hook. She wasn't about to leave that worthless husband of hers a message, and now she knew exactly what it was she had to do. She had to pray. Her prayer had always been to bring her and Curtis closer together. To make Curtis love her the way he used to. To bring Curtis home safely to her and Alicia. To make them a family again the way they used to be. But that wasn't the prayer that she needed to be praying anymore.

Tanya kneeled on the floor, leaned forward against the bed, and locked her fingers together under her chin. And she began to pray like she never had before.

She asked God to forgive her for the sins she'd committed in the past and even the ones she knew she might eventually commit in the future. Then she asked God to bless and watch over her daughter, her parents, her relatives, her friends, and Faith Missionary's congregation, which was sadly being misled. Then she asked God something that she hadn't asked Him for since the day she married Curtis. She asked Him to remove any feelings of love she had for her husband and to give her the strength to leave him for good.

Chapter 9

"Honey, are you awake?" Elise asked, knocking at Tanya's bedroom door.

"Yes," she answered, although she really wasn't completely awake until now. She'd heard the phone ring a couple of times, but all she'd done was turn over, trying to doze back off to sleep.

"Curtis is on the phone, and he wants to speak to you," her mother said, sounding wide-eyed and bushy-tailed.

Tanya didn't know whether to be happy or angry at the fact that he had the nerve to be calling her. She didn't want to talk to him, and she wasn't in the mood for getting into one of their usual arguments. But she knew there was no way getting around talking to him, so she decided that it was better to just get it over with.

"I have it," Tanya said when she picked up the receiver, and before long, she heard her mother hang up the other extension.

"Hello?" she said.

"Hey, sweetheart. How are you?"

She almost didn't know how to react to his question. She wanted to scream at him the way she always did whenever he pretended that everything was fine and that he was being the perfect husband. But she just wasn't in the mood for that today, and the more she thought about it, she definitely didn't want to raise her voice enough to where her father could receive wind of it.

"I'm fine, Curtis. How are you?" she asked in total sarcasm.

"I saw that your parents' number was on the Caller ID when I got up this morning. I had the phone turned off in the bedroom while I was meditating and studying the Bible, and then I guess I forgot to turn it back on before I went to bed."

Why was he still telling those same old lies? She was starting to wonder if he had some sort of psychological problem. Maybe he was a pathological liar. Maybe he really couldn't help it. Because surely no normal human being would continue putting up a facade with God and lying to his wife every single day of the week. It just didn't make any sense.

But who was Tanya kidding? Herself, she guessed, because she knew with everything she had that there wasn't one single solitary thing wrong with this low-down, trifling hypocrite except that he was simply lying to be lying. Lying because he had always gotten away with it.

Tanya was fuming, and oh, did she want to use a few choice words. But she decided to stay calm. "Curtis, why are you playing these games with me? You weren't at home when I called, so why don't you just say that? I'm fine with the fact that you weren't at home," she said, using the same untruthful tactics he had. "So, there's really no reason for you to keep lying. I know you think that by doing that, it makes everything all right between us, but it doesn't. So, I suggest you do whatever it is you want to do from now on, because I really don't care one way or the other."

Curtis paused as though he didn't understand what was going on. Then he spoke. "I know you don't believe me, Tanya, regardless of what you say, because you never believe anything I tell you."

"Whatever you say, Curtis," she said in a yeah-right sort of tone.

"I can't wait for you and my little girl to get home. It's not the same with the two of you gone, and I can't wait to see both of you. I know we've been going through some rough times, but it's like I told you a couple of weeks ago, things are going to get better."

Tanya didn't even bother commenting.

"Tanya, why are you always giving me the silent treatment when I'm trying to make things right with you? Why do you do that?" he asked, sounding frustrated.

"Hmmph. If you were really at home last night, and you haven't done anything wrong, then why are you trying to make things right?"

"Because I can tell you've got an attitude. You always have one. Every day of the week. Nothing I do is right, and you're always trying to get some sort of argument started between us."

She'd had just about enough of this trying-so-hard-to-be-cordial business. She'd tried to be as pleasant as she could, but this wasn't working for her. Not in the least little bit. Curtis was full of it, and needed so terribly to be told where to go. And she would have loved nothing more than to do it, but she wasn't about to give him the satisfaction of knowing how upset she was. Not today anyway.

"So, how's the weather in Chicago?" she

asked, playing his game right back with him.

Curtis laughed. "Since when do you care about the weather? Look, Tanya, stop pretending like you're not upset, because I know you are."

"Upset about what? If my memory serves me correctly, you didn't do anything. You were home last night meditating and reading the Bible. So, how could I possibly have a problem with that?" she said cynically.

"Just listen to you. Whether you admit it or not, I know you're upset."

Tanya repositioned the phone, but didn't speak.

"You and I have really got to talk when you get back here," he continued. "All these bad feelings between us have gone too far, and enough is enough."

"Hey, we're supposed to be going shopping this morning, so I'm going to have to let you go so I can jump in the shower and get dressed."

"Just like that, huh? Tanya, what is it that you want me to do? Tell me, and I'll do it. I've made a lot of mistakes over the last few months, and I apologize for any pain that I might have caused you, but now it's time for us to move on. So, whatever it

151

is that I can do to make things right with you, I'll do it."

She knew he was lying again, but she decided to humor him. And if for some far-fetched reason he wasn't lying, then that would be fine, too. "I want us to go to marriage counseling."

"Marriage counseling?" he said, clearly offended. "I counsel married couples all the time myself, so what good is that going to do for us?"

"It's not the same thing, Curtis. We need a third party to become involved before we can work this out."

"That's what God is for. He can work out anything, and that's who I'm counting on."

"I know God can work anything out, but he also gave us the sense to get help from knowledgeable professionals when we need it, too."

"I'm not going to any marriage counselor," he said matter-of-factly.

"Then you don't want our relationship to get any better, either."

"I do, but I just don't think that's the answer."

"You have a degree in counseling, Curtis, so how can you not see that that's the answer?"

"Mom," Alicia said, opening the bedroom door. "Can I speak to Daddy?"

Tanya smiled, and motioned for her to come in.

"Hey. Alicia wants to speak to you, so I guess I'll talk to you later or sometime tomorrow morning before church."

"So, that's it? That's all you have to say?"

"As a matter of fact it is. Now here's Alicia," Tanya said, and passed her daughter the phone.

"Hi, Daddy," Alicia said, filled with excitement. "Do you miss me?"

Tanya stared at Alicia and wondered just how her daughter was going to react if she was forced to live in a separate household from her father. The man she thought the world of.

Chapter 10

"I'll bet Daddy got here real early," Alicia said, stretching her neck, trying her best to see her father through the crowd of people. She and Tanya had just deplaned their returning aircraft and were walking down the corridor that led into the arriving terminal.

"I'm sure he can't wait to see you either, sweetheart," Tanya commented. She couldn't believe the weekend had gone by so quickly. They'd arrived at her parents' house on Friday morning, and now it was already after eight o'clock on Monday evening. But then, they had been fairly busy during most of their visit. They'd gone shopping as planned on Saturday, visited some of her and Curtis's relatives late that evening, and then gone to church and dinner on Sunday. And they'd even gone out and about this morning with her mother while she ran around and did a few necessary errands. Usually she was glad to get back home, but not this time. She wasn't in the mood for the same old routine or the same old arguments she knew she and Curtis would eventually get into. So, as much as she hated to admit it, she wasn't nearly as excited about seeing Curtis as Alicia was. She still had mixed feelings, and she'd tried to take this past weekend to think things over as much as she could, whenever she was alone, which was usually when she lay in bed at night. Curtis had called her early yesterday morning before leaving for church, but she hadn't had a whole lot to say to him. The conversation had been on the cool side from beginning to end, and hadn't lasted more than a few minutes. And on top of that, her father was still in a frenzy over the whole situation. He wasn't as angry as he had been on Friday evening, but Tanya could tell that he wanted wholeheartedly to fly to Chicago so he could wring Curtis's neck. He was so protective of her, and she wished she had never called her mother with the news and that she had never gone to visit them until after she'd made her decision about whether she was going to stay with her husband. And the sad part of it all was that she still didn't know what she was going to do. She was caught between a rock and a hard place, because no matter how she played everything out in her mind, she still had Alicia to consider.

"Mom, isn't that Deacon Roberson?" Alicia asked, looking up at Tanya.

"It sure is," Tanya said, already feeling a sense of rage building inside her.

"What is he doing here?" Alicia asked with no smile on her face.

"He's probably picking us up," Tanya responded.

They continued walking until they approached the forty-something, salt-and-pepper-haired deacon.

"Did you ladies have a good flight?" he asked, smiling.

"Yes, we did," Tanya answered. "Where's Curtis?"

"Pastor had a regional Baptist minister's meeting that he forgot about until this afternoon, and he asked me if I would meet you for him. He wanted me to tell both of you how sorry he was, and that he will see you as soon as the meeting is over with."

"Oh, okay," Tanya said, biting her tongue. Then they all started walking. She wanted to lash out at Deacon Roberson for agreeing to take on Curtis's responsibilities. He was always picking up the pieces whenever Curtis left them lying around, and Tanya could barely stand it. She knew none of this was the deacon's fault, and that he was only doing what he had been asked, but some of the deacons acted more like unpaid flunkies than they did officers of the church. They did everything for him, and it was enough to make Tanya sick. Not to mention the fact that she had heard enough of Curtis's lies and excuses to last her and the rest of the world a lifetime.

"So, did you find your parents doing well?" the deacon asked with sincere concern.

"Yes. They're doing very well," Tanya answered, trying to be gracious toward him. She was still fuming inside, but she knew it wasn't right to take her problems and frustrations out on someone who had been caring enough to pick them up from the airport. Especially since Deacon Roberson and his family lived north of Chicago, and would have to drive all the way to the south suburbs to take them home. "So, how is Sister Roberson and the rest of the family?" she continued.

"They're all doing fine. She's hosting some houseware party for one of the women she works with."

"Well, no wonder you offered to come pick us up," Tanya said jokingly.

Deacon Roberson laughed. "No, it wasn't anything like that. But I do admit, I wasn't looking forward to hanging around for the party, either."

Tanya chuckled with the deacon, and then looked down at Alicia, who was strutting along in silence. Tanya knew she was totally disappointed that her father hadn't met them at the airport like he'd promised, but Tanya didn't know what to say to her. She'd been making excuses for Curtis's whereabouts to Alicia day in and day out, but now she was running out of ways to explain things to her.

"Are you tired of carrying that book bag?" Tanya asked, trying to make conversation with her.

"No," she said, still looking straight ahead.

"I can take that for you," Deacon Roberson offered.

"No, thanks. I can carry it," she said, still not looking at her mother or the deacon.

Tanya could tell that she was sad, and that enraged Tanya even more. And it was at times like these when she was sure it would be better for Alicia if she left Curtis.

That way she would never expect him to come home on time or do any of the things he promised her. That way she could get on with her life without a full-time father. She'd miss him at first, but she'd get over it and would adjust to her new lifestyle with time.

No sooner had they driven out of the air-port parking ramp and were on their way home than Alicia fell asleep in the back-seat, and Tanya rode most of the way in silence. She conversed with Deacon Roberson on a few different occasions, but for the most part, she'd been preoccupied with her marital situation. She recalled every lie Curtis had ever told, every night she'd shed a river of tears because of him, and, worst of all, every night she'd watched her daughter glaring out of the living-room window, wondering when her father was going to come home.

But things were getting ready to change. She didn't know what was going to happen exactly, but from this point on, she knew her life with Curtis was going to be different. And that most of all, Curtis wasn't going to like it the least little bit.

Chapter 11

Tanya finished writing her to-do list, and then stacked a few client files on top of her in-basket, so she could finalize some paperwork first thing tomorrow morning. She wished she could complete some of it now, but it was almost six o'clock, and time for her to go set up the conference room for her abused women's support group meeting. Usually they convened on Monday nights, but with Tanya not flying in until late yesterday evening, she'd asked the women if they minded getting together on Tuesday instead. And with the exception of one member who had a previous engagement, they'd all been fine with it.

She walked into the room and started the coffeepot. The women liked having refreshments, so she'd gone out and purchased some cheese, crackers, and cold cuts during her lunch hour to accommodate them. They all had some very serious problems that they were dealing with, but they were some of the nicest women she'd come in contact with in a long time. And it was almost like the women had become her extended family. The women sometimes had their differences, but for the most part they enjoyed being around one another. And Tanya was sure it had something to do with the fact that they all had something in common: an idiot who spent most of his time trying to control them. Not to mention the fact that each of their significant others had seriously beat the living daylights out of them at one time or another.

Tanya sat down in one of the eight folding chairs she'd placed in a circle and crossed her legs. She felt a slight headache coming on, and debated taking a couple of Tylenol. But then she decided to wait and see if it would go away on its own. She didn't like taking medication unless it was absolutely necessary, but she knew she'd have no other choice if her pain became worse during the course of the meeting.

"Hey, Tanya," Barb, a tall, beautiful, classy-looking white woman said, walking in and smiling as usual.

"How's it going, Barb?" Tanya said,

smiling back at her. Barb had been to hell and back with her estranged husband, but she was one of the most pleasant women in the group. She had a whole lot of common sense, and she did well when it came to helping some of the other members come to terms with their abusive relationships. Sometimes she was outspoken when she truly believed in what she was thinking, but she was never rude about it, which was the difference between her and Paula, the attractive, petite black woman who had just strolled into the conference room.

"Hi, Paula," Tanya said.

"Hey, Paula," Barb said, smiling.

"Hey, ladies," Paula said, responding to both women.

"I bought some of that salami you like so well," Tanya said to Paula, who had eaten hers and everyone else's share of it a couple of weeks ago. Of course, if someone else had gone too far with anything at all, Paula Freeman would have told them about themselves outright, without mincing any words. That's just the way Paula was, and it had gotten to the point where the other members either accepted her or ignored everything she complained about. Tanya had more sympathy for her, though, than most of the women, because Paula had been married to a complete drunk for over fifteen years, delivered a stillborn baby only hours after he kicked her in her stomach while she was in her final trimester, and now that he was dead, thanks to a drunk driver, she was struggling to raise two children on her own. So, Tanya couldn't help but feel for her, especially since her husband hadn't left her even one life insurance policy.

"So, how did your trip to Atlanta go?" Paula asked Tanya.

"Oh, it went fine. I really enjoyed being at home and seeing my parents again."

"Well, that's good," Paula said, fixing her salami and Ritz cracker plate. Then she poured a cup of coffee and took a seat next to Tanya.

After about fifteen minutes or so, the other five women came in and fixed themselves a cup of coffee and a food plate. When they were all settled, Tanya distributed next month's calendar, discussed a few therapy techniques, and turned the meeting over to the group members. Their meeting wasn't like one of the more structured Anonymous meetings, but they did take turns sharing their feelings.

"So, who wants to share with us first?" Tanya asked, gazing from one woman to the next. It was strange how no one ever liked going first, but usually after the first thirty minutes passed by, no one could get a word in edgewise.

"Oh, what the hell. I will," Paula offered, and then covered her mouth. "Excuse me, Tanya. You know I always forget you're a pastor's wife," Paula said playfully.

"No problem," Tanya said, and was glad that Paula and the rest of the women didn't know about some of the words she'd been using herself whenever she argued with Curtis. They'd be completely appalled if they did, and Tanya felt ashamed just thinking about it. But she had promised herself this past weekend that she was going to work a lot harder on her serenity and spirituality.

Paula breathed deeply. "Well, my two little boys are still having a hard time dealing with the death of their father, and sometimes I feel bad because, well . . . I'm glad that he's finally out of my life. I know it's not right to be happy about someone being killed in a car accident, but I'm sorry, because I'm happier now than I have been in over fifteen years. To be honest, I'm happier than I've been since the day I laid eyes on Larry," she said, referring to her late husband.

"Well, as far as I'm concerned," Barb added, "you have every right to be happy. That bastard did everything he could to try and ruin your life and now you're finally free. And unlike the rest of us, you don't ever have to worry about seeing that jerk ever again," Barb said, looking at Tanya. "I don't mean to cuss in front of you, Tanya, but you know how I get when I really feel strongly about something."

"Yeah, I do, Barb. We all do," Tanya said, and everyone laughed.

"Now, take me for example," Barb continued. "I'm fighting like hell to get divorced from my children's father and at the same time that son of a bitch is still trying to stalk me. He still calls me on the phone making threats and he keeps saying that if the court gives me the house and full custody of the children that he's going to kill me. So, trust me, Paula, when I say that you are lucky Larry is finally dead and out of your way for good. Eventually, your boys will get over their sad feelings, and all three of you will be just fine." As usual, Barb spoke exactly what she was thinking.

"I sure hope so, because I don't want them growing up feeling lost, or, you know, like their father abandoned them," Paula commented.

Barb frowned at Paula. "Abandoned? Which do you think was better for them? To be abandoned by their father or for them to watch their father beating their mother half to death whenever he felt like it?"

"Look, Barb," Paula said, staring at the only white woman in the room. "Don't keep trying to make me sound stupid, because I'm not. I'm trying to share with everyone what I'm feeling, but I'm not about to let you keep talking down to me. It's not like you really know what the rest of us are going through anyway."

Tanya had known it wasn't going to be long before Barb and Paula's discussion turned into an argument. They always did this at least once or twice a month, and Tanya hated it when Paula told Barb that she didn't understand the rest of the group. Yes, Barb was the only white woman in the group, and on top of that the only one who had a ton of money, but Tanya didn't want Paula or any of the other women saying anything to make her feel out of place. The rest of the women weren't living on government cheese, but they weren't successful businesswomen like Barb was, either. And they definitely weren't married to or living with successful attorneys like her husband. However, being physically and mentally abused didn't require any certain level of poverty or financial wealth, and Barb had just as much right to be at the meeting as Paula and all of the rest of the women did.

"What do you mean I don't know what the rest of you are going through?" Barb asked with her arms folded. "What kind of statement is that?"

"I mean exactly what I said," Paula said matter-of-factly. "You don't know what the rest of us are going through. You may have been in an abusive relationship, but you'll never have to worry about where your next dollar is coming from for as long as you live. But, see, the rest of us have to struggle every day just to make ends meet and then figure out how we're going to keep food on the table for our children and clothes on their backs. So, believe me, you don't have even the slightest idea of what we're going through. Money isn't everything, but from where I'm sitting, it comes pretty doggone close."

"You know, Paula," Barb said calmly, "I really resent the way you view me. Hell, what am I supposed to do? Apologize for getting an education, and for marrying a successful man? Well, I'm not going to do that, because I'm proud of the fact that I went to college and that I worked my behind off to create a successful business. And you know what else? I don't think it's just the fact that I make decent money that bothers you. I think it's the fact that I'm white, and that I'm the only white woman who's a member of this group."

Paula rolled her eyes in the air like she was bored with Barb's entire conversation.

"Okay," Tanya intervened. "That's enough. What we need to do is get back to doing what we came here for. And that's sharing our feelings with each other in a constructive and caring manner. But before we do, let me just say this. Money, ethnic background, looks, success, and any other aspect we can think of doesn't mean a thing when it comes to having a man put his hands on you. Each of you may be as different as can be from each other, but you're all here for the same reason. Which is to help each other. And nobody is any better or worse than the next person," Tanya said, and couldn't help but think about her friend Nicole who was having the same problem with her husband concerning his jealousy over her successful business. Which just went to show that jealousy could come from all possible directions. From both men and women.

"Fine," Paula said, clearly upset. "Then let someone else talk."

"Only if you've shared everything you intended to," Tanya responded.

"I did. But not without someone trying to make it seem like my feelings were stupid," she said, looking straight at Tanya.

Tanya didn't say anything. But Barb did.

"Look, Paula. I didn't mean to make it sound like your feelings were stupid. All I was trying to do was get you to see that you don't have to feel guilty about your husband being dead, and that your children will eventually come to terms with their father's loss. Maybe I didn't say it in the right manner, and if I offended you, I'm sorry."

"Whatever," Paula commented, obviously now accepting her apology.

No one spoke for thirty seconds. And then Arnita began speaking.

Tanya listened as they each discussed their situations, and although she certainly understood the battered-wife syndrome, she couldn't help but wonder why some of the women had stayed in their relationships for so long, and more importantly, why some of them eventually went back to such an unbearable situation. But then, who was she to wonder about anyone's marriage? She'd been taking Curtis's crap for what seemed like an eternity, and still she hadn't mustered up the nerve to leave him. She knew it was what she needed to do, but for some reason she just couldn't seem to do it. And as much as she hated admitting it, a small part of her still wanted to believe that there was some possible chance that things were going to work out for them. For one thing, she could still remember all the happy times. Especially the day she'd told Curtis that she was pregnant with Alicia. She'd left work early, gone home and prepared him a romantic, candlelight dinner, and then waited for him to walk through the front door. When they were living in Atlanta, he would always inform her of his daily agenda, and then he'd always arrive home when he said he would. And if for some reason he couldn't, he'd phone her to let her know what was going on.

She could still remember the look on his face when she'd broken the news to him. He had grabbed her immediately and hugged her like she'd given him the best news he'd heard in his entire life. He'd even shed a flood of tears from his happiness. Which is what he'd also done the day he'd found out he'd been chosen as senior pastor of Faith Missionary Baptist Church. Their lives were going to be better than ever, so he'd promised, but in reality, their lives had turned out to be nothing more than an upside-down fairytale.

She envisioned all the expensive jewelry he wore, the lavish clothing he paid too much money for, and the top-of-the-line automobiles he purchased and replaced faster than the blink of an eyelid. It was all so disgusting, but not nearly as disgusting as his out-of-town trips and the amount of time he spent away from home with his women.

"Tanya," Barb called. "Are you okay?"

Tanya glanced over at Barb, caught totally off guard, and then looked around at the rest of the women. "Pardon," she answered with not the first idea about what she'd been asked.

"Are you okay?" Barb continued. "It seems like you weren't with us for the last few minutes."

"Oh, I'm sorry. I was just thinking about something, but I'm fine," Tanya said, forcing a smile on her face and looking from one group member to the other.

Everyone gazed at her, and it was apparent that they didn't believe what she'd just told them. But they continued their discussion, which went on for another hour or so, and Tanya was glad when their two-hour time slot was over. She felt completely exhausted, a result of lingering jet-lag, she guessed, and she wanted to get home.

Shortly after the women hugged and said their good-byes, Tanya tidied up the conference room, went into her office, grabbed her briefcase from her office, headed out of the building down to the parking facility, and it wasn't long before she drove away from the women's center.

She didn't feel like cooking anything, and it was way too late anyhow, so she decided to pick up Chinese instead. Curtis had probably already gotten something for him and Alicia, but she figured she'd better call him just to make sure. She dialed the number on her cellular phone and waited for someone to answer.

"Hello, Black residence," a soft-spoken woman answered in a polite manner.

Tanya shook her head. Not because she didn't want to talk with Sheila, Alicia's babysitter, but because she knew if Sheila was answering, it could only mean that Curtis still wasn't home. Tanya could already feel the steam forcing its way through her head.

"Hi, Sheila. I didn't expect for you to still be there."

"Pastor Black called and asked me if I could stay here until you left work, and he wanted me to tell you that he's going to stay at the church a little later tonight to prepare for the revival he's doing next week in Indianapolis."

Tanya was fuming. "Well, has Alicia had dinner yet?"

"Yes, we went and picked up some White Castle. You know how she loves that," Sheila said, laughing.

"Yes, I do," Tanya commented, laughing with her. "Well, if you don't mind, Sheila, I'd like you to stay with Alicia for another couple of hours or so, because I think I'm going to go to one of the restaurants down here to have dinner and just sort of relax."

"That's fine, Mrs. Black."

"Thanks, Sheila. I really appreciate it. Now, can you put Alicia on the phone?"

"Sure, she's right here."

"Hi, Mom, what are you doing?" Alicia asked contentedly. Which was how she always sounded whenever Sheila baby-sat for them. Sheila was eighteen, but she seemed to be able to relate to Alicia as if they were the same age. Alicia loved her, and she loved Alicia, which had always placed Tanya's mind at ease. Not to mention the fact that Sheila was so responsible. She was so much more mature than most girls her age, and her education was the most important thing to her. And it was because of her maturity that Tanya and Curtis had no problem with allowing Sheila to pick Alicia up from after-care on the days they couldn't.

"I'm driving over to one of the restaurants not too far from where I work. What are you doing?"

"Sheila and I had some White Castle," she answered happily.

"Is that right?"

"Yep. Mom, when are you coming home?"

Tanya felt guilty as soon as she heard those words leaving her daughter's lips. It was bad enough that her father had abandoned her for the evening, and now her mother was doing the same thing. She wasn't sure what to say, but she knew she had to answer with something. "I'll be there in a couple of hours or so. After I have dinner."

"Oh, because I want Sheila to watch one of my videos with me. And if you come

174

home right now, she'll have to leave before it's over."

Tanya laughed at her daughter. "So, that's why you wanted to know when I was coming home? What about, Mom when are you coming home, because I really want to see you?"

"Well, I do want to see you, but I'll see you after you finish eating dinner."

"That's fine, sweetheart. And don't you give Sheila any trouble, either. You do what she tells you to do, including going to bed when she tells you it's time. And since it's eight o'clock, you're really only supposed to be up another half hour. But I guess we can stretch it to nine-thirty tonight."

"Thanks, Mom. Talk to you later, okay?"

" 'Bye, honey, and put Sheila back on the phone for me."

"This is me again," Sheila said.

"It sounds like you're about to watch one of those Disney videos," Tanya teased. "But as soon as the credits start rolling, I want little Miss Video Queen to go straight to bed, regardless of what excuse she has."

Sheila laughed. "Don't worry, Mrs. Black, I'll make sure she gets there. And you have a nice time at dinner, okay."

"I'll try. Oh, and Sheila? Did she finish her homework?"

"She sure did, and believe it or not, I didn't even have to tell her to."

"That's because she knows she can't watch TV if she doesn't get her homework done."

Sheila laughed. "Yep, that's probably it."

"Okay, then, I'll see you both when I get there."

Tanya and Sheila said good-bye and hung up.

Yeah, right, Tanya thought. Curtis had his lying behind at the church about as much as she'd won a million dollars from some sweepstake. He was such a liar, and it only made things easier for him whenever he could pass messages through the babysitter, or anyone else for that matter. He'd even done that with Alicia a few times, and then hung up before Tanya could get to the phone. And if he'd really wanted to tell her himself, he would have called her at work. She'd been in the meeting with her women's group, but he could have left a voice mail message with no problem.

Tanya drove around for a while, becoming more and more upset as time went on, until finally she decided to do something no decent pastor's wife would even think about doing, let alone follow through with: drive into a parking lot barely footsteps away from one of the most frequented jazz clubs in downtown Chicago. She knew this wasn't one of the best places for her to be, but she didn't know which way to turn anymore. What she needed was peace of mind, and decided that maybe the answer was to mingle with some *normal* people for a change. People who weren't pretending to be one thing on Sunday and something totally different each of the other six days in the week. People like Curtis, and a few other devout *Christians* she could think of.

What she longed for most was to have a really good time, the type of good time that every woman should be allowed to have every now and then.

Chapter 12

Tanya pulled the door open and stepped inside the club. Then she walked over to the host and waited to be seated.

"Seating for one?" the handsome, forty-something maitre d' asked her.

"Yes, please."

"Follow me," he said, smiling, and walked toward the middle of the club. But when he didn't see a suitable table for one person, he continued over to a more isolated corner. Tanya was glad. So far, she hadn't seen anyone she recognized, and was happy about that.

When they arrived at the only empty booth on that side of the room, Tanya took a seat, and the maitre d' set a menu on the table and told her that her waitress would be with her shortly and to enjoy her evening. She thanked him, and hoped that she really would be able to relax and enjoy her dinner.

Tanya glanced through the menu and decided that she wanted the grilled chicken Caesar salad. Then she sat patiently waiting for the waitress. The place wasn't packed, but there was a pretty nice crowd. And the music was wonderful. Jazz always mellowed her out. Made her feel relaxed. But she hadn't had the opportunity to sit down and listen to it for a very long time. It wasn't the kind of music she and Curtis were accustomed to. They'd enjoyed it during their college years, and shortly thereafter, but the minute he'd been called to preach, each and everything he considered to be worldly had ceased. But she didn't see anything wrong with listening to instrumental music. Although she was sure most religious faiths would be in total disagreement with her way of thinking.

"Hi, my name is Carmen, and I'll be your waitress for the evening," a tall, slender, bronze-complexion woman said, smiling. "Could I start you with something to drink?"

Tanya hadn't even considered the idea of having anything except water, and she debated whether she should order cranberry juice or a *real* drink. She hadn't consumed anything with even the smallest percentage of alcohol in years, but she really did need something to help her unwind. Something to calm her nerves and something to prepare her before she went home to sleep in the same bed with Curtis.

"I'll have a glass of white wine, an order of mozzarella cheese sticks for my appetizer, and a chicken Caesar salad." Tanya knew most waitresses liked delivering the drinks before taking the actual food order, but since she'd already decided on her selection, she didn't see any reason to wait.

"Would you like something for dessert?"

"Maybe, but I think I'll wait until after I finish dinner, if that's okay."

"That's fine. I'll bring your wine right out," the waitress said, and then walked away.

Tanya gazed around the club again, and noticed a lot of couples having dinner, and she couldn't help but wish she had someone to dine with as well. And not just some girlfriend, either. Her own husband was who she was thinking of. But the days when they'd gone out for romantic dinners or anywhere fun together were over with, and she'd long since come to the realization that it wasn't worth crying over spilled milk. Especially the kind of milk that had been spilled for so long, that it was now completely spoiled.

The waitress set the long-stemmed glass of wine down on the table. "Your appetizer should be ready shortly."

"Thanks," Tanya said, and watched as the woman walked away from the table. Then she gazed down at the drink in front of her. She'd wanted it when she ordered it, and she still wanted it now, but she couldn't shake the guilty feeling that had come over her. She tried to justify the idea of drinking an alcoholic beverage, but she couldn't see any justification in it. And maybe it wouldn't have been so bad if she wasn't a preacher's wife. It wasn't right for anyone, but she was supposed to be someone who other people in the church could look up to and learn from. She didn't want to become the same hypocrite that her husband had evolved into, but with the exception of her daughter, she was completely fed up with every other aspect of her personal life and needed some sort of outlet.

She debated back and forth for another minute or so, and then took her first sip. And then another. She couldn't believe how good it tasted, and she was already feeling better than she had in a long time.

She took another sip, and then glanced over toward the bar area. She scanned it from one end to the next, but when she looked back toward the center, she saw a gorgeous-looking, seemingly sophisticated man gazing back at her with a comforting smile. She'd been caught completely off-guard, so she had no choice except to smile back at him, but then she immediately looked in another direction. He made her feel nervous, but at the same time, it was all she could do not to check to see if he was still looking her way. She lifted her glass and took yet another sip of wine. But when she glanced in his direction again, she saw the man heading toward her table.

"Are you waiting for someone?" he asked with the same comforting smile on his face, the sort of smile that would make any woman forget what her first name was. And the way he wore his black linen blazer and triple-pleated, cuffed dress pants wasn't making things any easier.

"No, I'm not," she said, not knowing what he wanted or what exactly she should say to this man who looked to be at least six feet three inches.

"Do you mind if I sit down and keep you company?" he asked without pausing.

She couldn't believe how straightforward

he was. But then, maybe this was the way it was done when a man was interested in talking to a woman. And maybe it had always been done this way, and she was only shocked by it, because it had been almost a decade since someone had approached her in that manner. She'd had guys make passes at her in the past, but she'd never had a man ask her if he could sit down to dinner with her. And she couldn't even remember the last time she'd had dinner alone with any other man besides Curtis. But then, she'd never made a habit of going out to jazz clubs all by her lonesome, either.

She didn't even know this guy, but without even thinking much about it, she answered his question. "Sure. Have a seat."

"My name is James Howard," he said, setting his beer down with one hand and reaching his other hand out toward her.

"I'm Tanya," she said, shaking his hand, purposely not revealing her last name. Curtis and Faith Missionary Baptist Church were just a little too well known for her to be disclosing her full identity.

"I hope you don't think I'm too straightforward by asking if I could join you."

Hmmph. That's exactly what she'd been thinking. But, at the same time, she didn't really mind too much at all. She knew there was a chance he was some serial killer, rapist or both, but there was something about him that kept her from pushing him away. Maybe it had something to do with the fact that she felt so alone and unwanted. All women needed to feel like they were attractive, and the fact that he'd spied her from the other side of the room and walked right over to where she was sitting told her that maybe he liked what he saw.

"I guess you could call it straightforward, but then, I'm not much better, because I'm the one who told you to have a seat," she said, and they both laughed.

"So, do you come in here very often," he asked, and Tanya caught him taking a glimpse at her wedding rings.

"No, not very often. As a matter of fact, this is my first time. I'd heard some of my co-workers talking about it from time to time, so I finally decided to drop in to have dinner. What about you?"

"I come here occasionally when I leave work and every now and then on the weekend. It's something to do when you don't have anything else going on. The food is good, and the music is great."

"Yeah, the music sounds really nice. I've

always loved jazz."

"It relaxes you, that's for sure, which is what I always need after work."

"What do you do?" Tanya asked curiously, since he'd said something about coming here after work twice already. But then maybe he wanted to make sure she knew he wasn't some lazy bum out to take financial advantage of women. Which reminded her of the T-shirt one of the young ladies at the church had worn when the church had gone on one of their shopping trips. It said "Every Woman Should Have a BMW," which led any person to believe that the T-shirt was making reference to a car, but under the phrase, in small print, it said: Black Man Working.

"I'm an independent computer consultant for a company called Pierce."

"Oh, okay."

"What do you do?" he asked, raising his beer mug.

"I'm a counselor at a women's center, and I moderate a support group for abused women."

"That sounds like interesting work, but I'll bet it can be depressing sometimes, too."

"Yes, it can. It's hard to imagine some of the things some women have to go through. It's really sad."

"I have no respect for a man who puts his hand on a woman, and it makes me angry whenever I witness anything like that. My father used to slap my mother around whenever he felt like it, and it used to kill me inside. Sometimes it still does when I think about it."

Tanya felt for any child who had to witness their mother being abused by any man, especially the father, but James's last comment bothered her a little bit because a lot of men who watched their mother being abused while they were growing up sometimes resorted to doing the same thing to women. Not every man, and maybe not even James himself, but there were a whole lot of other men who could clearly back up that theory. But there were also men who would rather die than hit a woman, because of what they'd seen their mother go through, and maybe James fit into that particular category instead.

"I really feel for children who have to go through that. It has such a lasting effect, and it stays with you even after you've become an adult," she said.

"I know. My parents have been divorced for over fifteen years, but I still have moments when I despise my father. I'm a lot better about it than I used to be, but I can't understand why he treated her the way he did."

Tanya looked up when she saw the waitress standing at the table preparing to set her appetizer down in front of her.

"Could I get you something?" the waitress asked James.

"As a matter of fact, you can. I'll have your lasagna special."

"What type of dressing would you like on your salad?"

"Ranch is fine," he said, and then looked over at Tanya. "Did you want something else?"

"No, I'm fine," Tanya answered.

"Will this be on the same check," the waitress asked him.

"Yes, it will be," he said, and the waitress walked away.

Tanya couldn't believe he'd just told the waitress to place their orders on one bill. Did he think they were on some sort of date? Because that's not what this was at all. At least that's not what she'd planned for it to be. She didn't know whether to ignore his decision to place everything on one check or to say something about it, but before she could decide, he spoke.

"You don't mind me buying dinner, do you?" he asked.

"Well, you know you don't have to do that."

"I know I don't, but it's the least I can do. You kept me from eating alone, and I'm enjoying your company."

She was enjoying his company, too, but she still didn't feel completely comfortable with any of this. Whether she wanted to accept it or not, she was still a married woman. The wife of a pastor who presided over a well-known church. She must have been crazy to even think about giving him permission to sit down with her.

She smiled at him, but didn't say anything.

"So," he said, sighing deeply, looking straight at her. "I see you have on wedding rings."

She wasn't sure if she wanted to have this discussion with him or not, and he was making her feel uncomfortable. Making her feel like the sinner that she was. It wasn't like she had kissed or gone to bed with him, but somehow she knew hanging out at a jazz bar and keeping company with another man who obviously wanted to be more than just friends wasn't quite right. And, dear Lord, as much as she hated to admit it, she could already tell that she was undeniably attracted to him.

The chemistry had been obvious from the moment she laid eyes on him over at the bar. She hadn't wanted to own up to her feelings, but now as she sat there gazing straight into his dark-brown eyes, there was no more denying it. No more pretending that she wasn't happy he'd made the first move and come over to introduce himself. There was just something about him that she liked, something that she hadn't seen or gotten from Curtis since she could remember.

She finally responded to his question. "Yes, I'm married and have been for a little over eight years."

He looked at her for a few seconds, as if he didn't know what to say to her. But then he spoke. "I hope I'm not out of line, but are you happily married?"

This was the question she'd been hoping she wouldn't have to answer, because she didn't know any other way except to answer him honestly. And that's what she did. "No, as a matter of fact, I can't say that I am. I mean, we've been married for a good while, and we have a beautiful daughter, but that's pretty much where it ends," she said.

James glanced over at the waitress who was headed their way with his salad. She set it down on the table before him, and as soon as she walked away, he looked back over at Tanya. "So, do you think things are going to get better or are you at a point of wanting to file for a divorce?"

"I don't even know why I'm telling you this, but I have to say that I am seriously thinking about doing just that. I don't want to, because when I took my marriage vows, I planned on staying married to the same person until death. And the last thing I want to do is raise my daughter in a broken home."

"I can understand that. Children make the decision to get divorced a lot harder than if you don't have any. I know it made it a lot easier for my ex-wife and me."

She'd been wondering if he'd been married, or still married for that matter. She hadn't seen a ring on his finger, but these days, that really didn't seem to make a whole lot of difference, since some men made it a point of not wearing their wedding bands whenever they went out to a bar or club.

"So, how long have you been divorced?" she asked, sipping the rest of her wine, which was a lot warmer than when she'd first started drinking it.

"Almost two years. We were only together a year and a half before we separated, but it was pretty much a mutual decision. We just weren't as compatible as we were when we first started seeing each other."

"That's sort of what happened with my husband and me. We were so happy when we first met, and for the first few years after we were married, but right after we moved here from Atlanta, things changed. He started staying out all the time, making excuses for not being at home, and everything else with our relationship has sort of gone downhill from there. I kept telling myself that things would get better, but, if anything, they're getting worse," she said, breathing deeply. "And I know with everything in my heart that he's seeing other women."

"Other women? Why do you think it's more than one?" he asked, raising his eyebrows in curiosity.

"Because I just do."

James opened his mouth to speak, but the waitress interrupted them, hopefully for the last time. She set a basket of rolls and garlic bread down toward the center of the table, a plate of lasagna in front of him, and the Caesar salad in front of Tanya.

"Can I get either of you anything else?"

"No, I don't think so," James said, waiting for Tanya to acknowledge his answer.

"No, I'm fine as well," Tanya added.

"Okay. Just let me know if you need anything," the waitress said and walked away.

"Well, that's really too bad. I mean, someone with your personality and beauty? And he's out looking for someone else? Something must be wrong with him is all I can think," James said, taking a bite of his entrée.

"There's nothing wrong with him," Tanya said, slicing her salad into bite-size pieces. "He's just not interested in what he has at home anymore."

"So, what is it that you're planning to do?"

"To be honest with you, I don't know," Tanya said, and wanted to tell him the rest of the story and how complicated it all was. She wanted to tell him that her philandering husband was pastor of a huge Baptist church right here in the city, and that not only would their daughter be devastated, but so would the entire congregation.

"Well, I guess you have to think it through. The last thing you want to do is make a decision to get divorced and then regret it."

"Did you regret divorcing your wife?" Tanya just had to know.

"No, I didn't, but it's like I said, our separation and divorce were mutual. But I have a good friend who thought he'd found the woman of his dreams, and eventually divorced his wife because of it. But now he and the woman aren't together anymore, and he's finally realized that he shouldn't have left his wife and that he wants her back. But of course now his ex-wife won't even consider getting back together with him. And unfortunately, I don't know if he'll ever get over it. So, all I'm saying is that you have to be sure when you do something like this."

"My girlfriend has been giving me the same advice, so I'm going to think long and hard about it before I do anything. One minute I'm sure, but that's usually when he does something to really upset me, and then there's other times when I wish we could work things out with each other. I don't know what I'm afraid of, but I think it's the idea of raising my daughter without a father and then being all alone. I love the whole idea of being married, but I know it's not supposed to be like this. It's supposed to be a lot better than what my husband and I have between each other."

"Marriage can be the best thing in the world, but you have to marry the right person."

"That's for sure, but not everyone gets that lucky, I guess, because look how high the divorce rate is."

"Maybe, but I still say there's someone for every man or woman. It just sometimes takes longer for some to find that person than others."

They sat for another half hour and finished talking and eating their meal, and Tanya couldn't believe how comfortable she'd become with him. She knew it wasn't right, but she wanted to see him again. She felt guilty, but she couldn't help the way she was feeling. James was so caring and understanding, and it was almost like they'd known each other for years and years. She'd heard a lot of people make that statement in the past, but in all honesty, she'd sort of thought people tended to say that because it sounded good. But now she knew exactly what they meant. She could have sat and talked with him all night long, but she knew it was time for her to go. Not because she had a husband waiting at home for her, but because she had a daughter who needed her.

"Well," Tanya said, patting her lips with

the linen napkin. "As much as I've enjoyed talking with you, I really do have to get going."

"So soon?" he asked, smiling his usual way.

"I'm afraid so. But, I really want to thank you for coming over to introduce yourself. You were good company, and I'm glad we met."

"Do you think I can see you again?" James asked in a polite and calm manner.

"James . . ." she said, almost pleading with him not to ask that question again.

"All right, then, can I at least call you?"

At first she hesitated, but then she pulled out her business card and handed it to him. James noticed her hesitation, and pulled out his business card as well. But before he passed it to her, he wrote his home phone number on the back of it.

"You can call me at either place. I won't pressure you, but if you want to talk, just give me a ring."

"Thanks again for dinner," she said, standing up.

James stood up with her. "No problem. You take care of yourself, all right?"

"I will," she said, smiling, and then walked toward the front entrance.

She looked back just before walking

through the doorway, and as she suspected, he was sitting relaxed in the booth, staring at her. Then he waved good-bye one final time. She waved back and wondered what she had just gotten herself into.

Chapter 13

It was such a beautiful Friday afternoon, Tanya left work a few hours early so she could pick Alicia up from school. They hadn't had a girls' day out for some time now, and it was high time for a trip to the mall and of course dinner at White Castle. Alicia had grown out of most of her summer clothing, and Tanya had been planning to take her shopping for more than three weeks. And since they'd only purchased a couple of items during their visit to Atlanta, Alicia still needed a few more things. It was almost the end of May, but for some reason, it already felt so much more warmer than usual.

Tanya drove the utility vehicle in front of Alicia's school and realized that she'd barely made it in time, because her daughter was already walking toward her. Alicia pulled open the passenger door, hopped in, and pulled the door shut.

"Hi, Mom," she said, smiling.

"Hi, sweetheart," Tanya said, smiling back and leaning over to kiss her daughter. "How was your day?"

"It was good. Our teacher didn't make us do very much, because we had an assembly this afternoon," Alicia said, buckling her seat belt.

"I'll bet you guys liked that," Tanya said, looking in both her rearview and side mirrors to make sure it was safe before pulling away from the curb.

"Yep. We didn't do hardly anything at all, except play games on the computer, and some other fun stuff."

"We did hardly anything at all," Tanya said, correcting Alicia.

"I mean, we did hardly anything at all," Alicia repeated after her mother. Tanya had taught her to do that so she wouldn't forget so easily the next time she needed to use those same words.

"Your father said he's going to be home by the time we leave the mall, and then we're all going to dinner. So, how about you and I get some White Castle right now?"

"Yay!" Alicia cheered with excitement.

Tanya drove until she found the first White Castle sign. They entered the restaurant, placed their orders, and then sat down to eat their food. It didn't take them more than thirty minutes to finish eating, and as soon as they had, they left and continued on to the mall.

"Mom, how come Daddy is never at home with us anymore?" Alicia asked out of the clear blue.

Tanya wasn't sure where this was coming from, and she wasn't exactly sure how she should respond to the question. "He's home when he can be, but you know he's real busy with the church," she said, trying to cover Curtis's constant absences. She didn't care to do that, but if it would place her daughter's mind at ease, it was worth it.

"I know, but he used to go to the church and spend time with us, too. Doesn't he want to be with us anymore?" she asked, and Tanya could see through the corner of her eyes that Alicia was looking straight at her.

"Of course he does, honey," Tanya said, still lying. "What makes you think he doesn't want to be with you?"

"He's never at home. And I hear you and him argue every time he comes back from somewhere," Alicia said, and paused for a second. "And you don't like it when he's gone all the time, either, do you, Mom?"

Tanya wished she could vanish into thin air, the same as she always did whenever Alicia asked these awkward questions, because she really didn't want to have this particular conversation with her daughter. And she couldn't figure out at all why Alicia was suddenly in the mood for asking all these questions about her father. Tanya had the same concerns herself, and had for a long time now, but she didn't want her baby worrying about any of this. She was way too young to even think about such things, but Tanya had long ago realized that she wasn't as naïve as most children her age. Alicia knew something was wrong, and there wasn't a thing Tanya could say to fool her.

"Look, honey. Mommy and Daddy are having some problems the same way all adults do from time to time. But remember when I told you that some things that go on between us are not to be discussed by little girls."

"I know, Mom, but when I see you sad, I get sad. And sometimes you're sad all the time."

Tanya could feel the tears welling in her eyes as soon as her daughter finished speaking the last word of her sentence.

Alicia was right. She *was* sad a lot more lately, and when she wasn't sad, she was usually so angry that she felt like taking Curtis's life. Which wasn't healthy for anyone in the household, and it was as morally wrong as anything else she could think of. He'd been trying to do better, or at least better by his definition, and Tanya had pretty much decided that she wasn't going to have heated arguments with him as often as she had been, and that she was simply going to grin and bear the whole situation regardless of how bad it was. But instead of being angry, the only thing holding everything in was doing was making her sad. It had been two weeks since she'd met James at the jazz club, but she'd made up in her mind that she wasn't going to call him, and that she wasn't going to become the adulterer that her husband already was. And then last night, for the first time in weeks, Curtis had finally found his way home right before nine o'clock. They'd even held a halfway decent conversation before dropping off to sleep, and it was during that same conversation that he mentioned the idea of all three of them going to dinner together. She hadn't really believed him, and that was the main reason she hadn't mentioned it to Alicia this morning before she left for school. But when Curtis had phoned her earlier in the day at work to remind her about their rare family affair, she'd finally had no choice but to believe him. She was sort of looking forward to it for Alicia's sake, but she wasn't getting her hopes up about their marriage. She'd gone that route far too many times and ended up with nothing more than total disappointment, and she wasn't going to let that happen again.

"Mom. Did you hear me?" Alicia asked when her mother took too long answering her question.

Tanya hadn't realized that she'd been in deep thought for as long as she had. "Yes, honey, I heard you. Look. Mom's okay, and even if I get sad, it doesn't have anything to do with the way I feel about you. Your daddy and I both love you more than anything in this world, and no matter what we have problems with, it's never anything that you need to worry yourself about. Okay?"

"Okay," Alicia said. Tanya couldn't tell if she was satisfied with the response or not, but she didn't mention anything else relating to their home situation during the rest of the ride to the mall. Then when they'd arrived at the mall, she'd been too excited about the purchase of her new summer clothing to really care about anything else. And when they'd finally started on their way home, she'd been too excited about her father going to dinner with them to think about anything else then, either. And Tanya had been glad that she'd sort of forgotten about the subject. At least for the time being.

After about another twenty miles, they finally arrived at their subdivision. But when Tanya drove into the driveway and pressed the garage door opener, she saw that Curtis still wasn't home. She didn't want to jump to conclusions, but she had a feeling he'd stood them up as usual.

"Mom, where's Daddy?" Alicia asked, sounding confused.

"Maybe he's running a little late," Tanya said, trying to pacify her daughter. It amazed Tanya that regardless of how many times Curtis went back on his word, Alicia still believed that he was going to stand by his word the next time he promised something. But then, she'd only recently stopped doing the same thing herself. As a matter of fact, she'd pretty much believed him this time as well, when he said he was taking them to dinner this evening. Especially since he called her at work to reconfirm it. So, maybe he really was running a little late, like she'd just told Alicia. But just the same, she wasn't going to depend on that theory until she saw him walk through the doorway.

They gathered together all of their shopping bags, and walked through the garage door that led into the kitchen. Then they headed upstairs to set Alicia's new clothing inside her bedroom.

"I'm going to my room for a minute, but I'll be back so we can hang your things in your closet," Tanya said, already heading down the hallway to her own bedroom. When she entered it, she strutted straight over to the phone and picked it up to see if the dial tone was signaling that there had been voice mail messages left. And of course there were.

She dialed Ameritech's voice mail number, entered the four-digit access code, and waited for the messages to play. The first one was from Nicole, checking to see what she was up to, the second call was from the church secretary, checking to see if Curtis could do a revival in Houston three months from now, and the third was from Curtis himself.

"Hi, Tanya. I know you're going to be upset, but there's no way I'm going to make it home in time to go to dinner with you and Alicia. The Davis family has asked me to come and pray with them at the hospital, because the doctor has given their mother twenty-four to forty-eight hours to live, at the most. But I promise I'll make it up to both of you tomorrow. We'll go out to dinner, and then we'll take Alicia to a movie or something. I love both of you, and tell my baby girl how sorry I am for not making it home in time. I should be there around nine or ten. Talk to you then."

Tanya didn't even bother listening to any more of the messages. She didn't have the energy or the interest in whomever else was calling. She hung up the phone, and sat down on the side of her bed. She hated when he did this, and as much as she'd promised herself that she wouldn't get upset over his lies any longer, she couldn't help but contemplate what she was going to do to him as soon as he found his pathetic way home. Maybe if she hurt him physically, he'd see that she wasn't playing games with him, and that she meant business once and for all. But it would've been so much simpler if he'd have a car accident on the way home and then died on arrival at the hospital.

But what in the world was she thinking? It was as if she didn't even know herself anymore. She'd always been a decent person, and she knew it was wrong to even consider the thoughts she'd just played through her mind. She couldn't believe how far Curtis had pushed her over the edge. And the sad part of it all was that he really didn't care how she felt about the situation anyhow, one way or another. She didn't want to wish such cruel things on him or anyone else, because she knew when a person dug a ditch for someone, he or she usually fell in it themselves. But she clearly understood why Paula was happy that her husband had been killed in a car crash. Now there was no more waiting for him to come home, no more pain, no more anything that had to do with him. Curtis wasn't physically abusive the way Paula's husband had been, but he was mentally abusive, and mental abuse was sometimes worse, because the effects from it usually lasted for all eternity.

Now she wished she'd checked the messages before they'd gotten home, because then she could have taken Alicia to dinner on her own. Not to mention the fact that it probably would have been easier if they'd just gone to the restaurant without coming home, because now Alicia had had time to sit in her room, wondering where her father was.

"Mom, when do you think Daddy's going to get here, because I'm ready to go eat," Alicia said, walking into her mother's room, almost as if she was reading her mind.

"He's not going to make it, sweetheart. Mother Davis is very, very sick, and he has to go pray with her family. He said he was really sorry and to tell you that he loved you," Tanya said, intentionally leaving out the part about him making it up to them tomorrow.

Alicia looked at her mother with tears rolling down her face.

"Honey, come here," Tanya said, reaching her arms out to her daughter.

Alicia ran over to her mother, laid her head on her chest, and wept silently.

"It's going to be okay. You and I can go get something to eat, and then we'll rent some videos. And maybe Lisa can come for a sleepover if her parents don't mind," Tanya said, referring to Alicia's little friend next door.

Alicia didn't respond at first, but then spoke. "Can I go sleep over at her house instead?"

"Well . . . if you want, and if it's all right with her parents," Tanya said, wondering what the difference was, and why she preferred to stay with Lisa instead.

Alicia raised her head away from her mother. "Can we call her now?"

"Okay. I'll call Lisa's mom," she said, pulling her black leather phone book from her purse. Then she dialed her neighbor's number.

Lisa's mom said they didn't have any plans, that they had just ordered a pizza, and that Alicia could come right over. Tanya really didn't want to be left alone, and was sort of hoping she and Alicia could do something together, but at the same time she was glad that her daughter was excited about her outing. At least that way, she'd have something to do that would keep her mind off her father. Maybe not completely, but at least to the extent that she could have a good time doing something else.

Tanya helped Alicia pack her Pocahontas overnight bag and then walked her next door to make sure she got in okay. Lisa's mom said that they were planning to go to a matinee around one the next day, and wanted to know if Alicia could go along with them. At first Tanya had thought twice about saying yes, but when she realized that Curtis wasn't going to keep his word about taking Alicia to the movies himself, she said it was okay, and that she would bring some money over tomorrow morning.

When Tanya walked back into her home, she debated what she was going to have for dinner. She opened the refrigerator and looked around, and then searched the freezer until she found a package of Polish sausages. She really wasn't in the mood for going out, so she pulled out the package of meat, opened it, and threw two of them into a pot filled with water. Then she placed them over the fire on the stove, and covered them with a top. It wasn't what she really wanted to eat, but it was going to have to do.

After she'd eaten her street-corner meal, which included potato chips and a Coke, she threw her dishes, along with the ones left from this morning, into the dishwasher and headed back upstairs. Then she pulled off the blazer, jeans, and shirt she'd worn for casual day at work, and then threw on a Jazzercise T-shirt and a pair of black leggings. She hadn't gone to Jazzercise class in over six months, and she was starting to feel like she needed to get back into it. Not because she was gaining weight, but because it always made her feel so much better. Both physically and mentally. It helped relax her, and whenever she experienced a tension headache, exercising always helped relieve the pain.

She picked up the remote, turned on the television, and laid her head back on two king-size plush pillows. She searched through the basic cable channels and didn't see anything, but when she turned to one of the pay channels, she saw that *Soul Food* was just about to begin. She and Nicole had gone to see it at the movie theater, but since that had been at least two or three years ago and she'd really enjoyed it, she decided to watch it again.

When the movie was finished, the credits rolled, and Tanya cried as she listened to "Mama" being performed by Boys to Men. Partly she cried, because she'd been thinking about how it would feel if her own mother passed away, and partly because she was so unhappy with the way her life was going. She listened to the end of the song, and then flipped the channel to CNN.

She glanced over at the clock and saw that it was ten o'clock, but, of course, there was no earthly sign of Curtis. Her blood was starting to boil again, and she was having the same criminal thoughts as she'd had earlier in the evening. But the more she thought about it, the more her fuming ceased, because Curtis wasn't worth going to jail for or losing her soul over.

She sat for a while longer, and after she'd listened to the top news stories, she picked up her purse and pulled out her phone book again, until she remembered that James had written his home phone number on the back of his business card. So, she opened her wallet, recited the phone number out loud, and then dialed his number before she had second thoughts.

"Hello?" a voice said on the other end.

"James?" she said, making sure it was him.

"I've been wondering if you were ever going to get around to calling me. As a matter of fact, I was thinking about calling you at work."

She couldn't believe he recognized her voice, since they'd only spoken that one night, but she was flattered just the same.

"So, you recognize my voice, huh?"

"Of course. How could I forget it."

Tanya laughed the way schoolgirls do when they're talking with their teenage boyfriend for the first time on the telephone. "I don't know. I'm sure you meet people all the time, so it could have been anybody," she said, hoping deep down that it couldn't have.

"I don't make it a habit of giving out my home phone number to a lot of women, if that's what you mean. I only gave it to you, because there was something special about you, and because I really wanted to talk to you again."

"Well, I wanted to talk to you, too, but . . . you know how it is."

"No, I don't. So why don't you tell me," he said.

Didn't he know she was feeling awkward and was simply trying to make conversation? He was sounding so serious, and she really didn't know how to respond to him. "Well, you know my situation, so it wasn't that easy for me to do something like this."

"Hey, believe me, I understand what you're going through. I was just joking with you. So, how have you been doing anyway?"

"Pretty much the same. My marriage hasn't gotten any better, and, as usual, I'm sitting here on a Friday night all alone. Usually my daughter is here, and we keep each other company, but she went next door to sleep over with her little friend."

"That's really too bad. A beautiful woman like yourself at home on a warm Friday evening."

They both chuckled.

"So, what about you? Why are you at home?" Tanya asked, assuming that he was probably on his way out.

"There's not a lot to do, and I just didn't feel like the club scene tonight. Plus, I have an early baseball game in the morning."

"Who do you play for?"

"The company that I work for."

"Oh, okay. So, what about the rest of the weekend? Do you have something planned for that?"

"I could have. If you want me to."

Tanya felt a lump in her chest area, right near her heart. She wanted more than anything to be with this man. She wanted to be with him right now, and she wished she could tell him how she really felt. She needed someone to hold her. Someone to show her the love and affection she deserved. The love and affection she wasn't getting from her own husband.

"What is that supposed to mean?" she finally asked, pretending she didn't know what he meant.

"That we could make some plans to get together and do whatever you want."

She sighed deeply. "I really wish I could, James, but you know I can't. I'm married. Remember? And it's bad enough that I called you in the first place."

"Well, the fact that you called me tells me that you have at least some interest in seeing me again. So, I guess I'll just settle for that for now."

"I really felt like I needed to talk to someone, and, I'll admit, for some reason I thought of you."

"What can I say? I have irresistible qualities," he said charmingly.

"As a matter of fact, you do. But it's just that we met at the wrong time."

"Well, I don't know about that, because I'm a true believer that everything happens for a reason, whether a situation is good or bad. So, things will work out the way they're supposed to."

"Yeah, I guess. But I do want you to know something. I've never as much as looked at another man except my husband since the day I started dating him. So, you're the first man I've ever sat and had dinner with and talked on the phone to."

"Well, I'm honored that you thought enough of me to say I could sit with you at the club. Especially since you didn't know anything about me. There's a lot of lunatics out there, so I'm glad you gave me a chance."

She'd been thinking the same thing the night she'd met him, but for some reason, she felt she could trust him. She couldn't guarantee it, because nothing was a sure thing anymore. But there was something about him that told her he was okay. She felt comfortable with him.

"I'm glad, too. But I still feel guilty about talking to you. I mean, I know my husband doesn't give me the time of day, but that doesn't matter, because in God's eyes, I know what I'm doing is wrong."

"Look, sweetheart, all we've done is talk. It's not like we've made love to each other or anything like that."

Sweetheart? She knew a lot of men made it a habit of calling any woman by that name, because it was sort of like a figure of speech, but she could tell he meant it more intimately. He was sounding like a husband speaking to his wife. And she could feel the lump near her heart all over again.

"I hear what you're saying, but it's still not right," she said. Especially since she wanted more than conversation. And she knew he wanted more than conversation from her as well.

"I don't want to make you feel uncomfortable, and it's like I told you that night we met, I won't pressure you into doing something you don't want to do. So, when you need someone to talk to or when you feel like you're ready to spend some time with me, all you have to do is say the word. And I'll be here for you."

He was making everything so hard. And she was feeling more confused now than she had before she called him. She was confused because she didn't know how she could have feelings for a man she hardly knew, a man she'd only seen once in her whole life, and who she didn't know a single thing about. What would her mother think if she knew what her daughter was doing? What would her father think? But then, he couldn't stand Curtis, and since he wanted her to be rid of him as soon as possible, he'd probably love James to death. Just to spite Curtis. But even with disregarding everyone else's opinion, what was God going to think of her?

Surely, he couldn't be happy about the way she was consorting with another man. She hadn't been with him sexually, but truth was, she wanted to. She really, seriously wanted to. And there had to be at least some price to pay for that. She was lusting this man in her mind, and she didn't see where that was any different than actually having sex with him. She'd have loved to believe that there was nothing wrong with talking with him, because certainly it would place her conscience at ease, but she knew better. She'd been raised to know better than that, and there was no sense pretending that what she was doing was acceptable. Because it clearly wasn't.

"I appreciate you being there for me if I need you, but for now, I'm going to have to see what happens here at home. I'm really sorry, but I don't want to add more fuel to the fire."

"Hey, you don't have to apologize for anything, and I understand exactly where you're coming from."

They continued chatting about relationships in general, family, work, and before they knew it, three hours had passed by. Tanya finally felt relaxed and like she'd really found a true friend in James, but a part of her was wondering why Curtis still wasn't home yet. She knew he was probably out sleeping with one of his women, but she still couldn't dismiss the possibility that something bad had happened to him. She'd been wishing for something like that before, but now that there was a chance it might have come to pass, she felt nervous.

"Gosh, where has the time gone," she said, leaning toward ending the conversation.

"You know the old saying about time flying when you're having fun."

"Well, I'd better go, but I really enjoyed talking to you. You really kept me company."

"I know it's not my business, but it's hard for me to believe that your husband still isn't home yet."

"Now you know what I keep having to deal with. He left a message saying that he had to go pray with one of the families at the church, because their mother is very ill, but I'm sure he left the hospital a long time ago."

"What is he, a deacon or something?"

Until now, Tanya hadn't even thought about the fact that she still hadn't told him about her husband being a pastor and, even more importantly, that she was a preacher's wife. She hadn't known how he was going to react, and somehow she'd thought it would be better if maybe he didn't know what Curtis did for a living. And it definitely didn't look too good for a preacher's wife to be carrying on the way that she was. But, she didn't see any reason to continue disguising her secret, because he was probably going to find out one way or the other anyway.

"No, he's not a deacon . . . he's pastor of a church."

"Pastor of a church? And he's staying out to the wee hours of the morning?"

"Believe it or not, yes. And that's what he does all the time."

"That's really somethin' else," James commented, obviously shocked to hear that her husband was a minister.

"So, you can see why my situation is just a little more difficult than the average woman wanting to file for a divorce."

"Yeah, I can see your problem to a certain extent, but as far as I'm concerned, no woman should have to put up with that kind of treatment, whether she's married to a minister or not."

"I know," she said, sighing. "But I've got the congregation to be concerned about, and my daughter."

"I can understand your concern about your daughter, but what other people think shouldn't be reason enough for you to stay in a miserable relationship. And I would think the church would much rather know what's going on, because if your husband is doing the things you say he's doing, they're being totally deceived."

She agreed with him, and she'd been saying the same thing herself, but there was just something about divorcing a minister that made her feel somewhat uneasy. There was something about getting divorced period.

"You're right. But until I feel like it's the right thing for me to do, I can't go through with separating from him."

"And you shouldn't," he said understandingly.

"Well, I hate to go, but I'd better," she said reluctantly. "It's getting late, and I have a million things to do tomorrow morning. But you take care of yourself, okay?"

"I will. So, when will I talk to you again?"

"I have to be honest. I don't know if I can call you again," she said, knowing full-well that she wanted to talk to him every chance she got.

"Well, you know how I feel, and I'll just leave that decision up to you. But, like I said before, I'm here whenever you need me."

She paused for a few seconds. "I'll give you a call next week, all right?"

"Are you sure?"

"I promise, I'll call you."

"Sounds good to me, sweetheart. I'll talk to you then," he said, and they both hung up.

Tanya held the cordless phone close to her chest before placing it back onto the base with her eyes closed. First she'd unintentionally had dinner with him, then she'd called him and held a three-hour phone conversation, and now she'd actually promised that she'd call him next week. She didn't even want to think about what might be next on the agenda.

"Did the family have you praying until two o'clock in the morning, Curtis?" Tanya complained as he stepped into the master bedroom.

Curtis blew out a sigh of disgust. "Tanya, please. Not tonight, okay?" he said, throwing his suit jacket across the chaise.

Tanya reached over toward her nightstand and turned on the light. "So, tell me, Curtis, where have you been all this time?" she asked so calmly that Curtis didn't know how to take her.

"I went to the hospital like I told you."

"You were there all this time?"

"Yes," he said, completely fed up with her inquiries.

221

"So, what you're saying is that if I call any of Mother Davis's family members, they'll tell me that you were at the hospital all night with them."

"That's exactly what I'm telling you," he said, and Tanya knew he was only calling her bluff because he knew for a fact that she would never bother any of those people for something as silly as Curtis's alibi.

Curtis continued to undress in silence, and Tanya sat in the bed with her arms folded, looking at him. Then she said what she'd wanted to say for months now.

"Curtis, I've thought long and hard about all of this, and I've had all I can take of you and your mess. So, I've decided that I'm not waiting until Alicia graduates, I'm filing for a divorce from you as soon as possible."

Curtis pulled up his lounging shorts and stared at Tanya like she was crazy. He couldn't believe what he'd just heard, and it was obvious that he needed some clarification. "What did you just say?" he asked, still staring at her.

"I said I'm filing for a divorce. I've had enough of you and your women, and I'm not about to keep . . ."

Curtis lunged across the bed and grabbed her by her throat. He held on to it with his left hand and pointed his right finger not even one centimeter from her nose. "If you even think about leaving me, I'll make your life a living hell. I'm not about to lose my church and everything else I've worked so hard for because of you. Do you hear me?" he said, still squeezing her neck.

Tanya tried to pry his fingers away, but she couldn't budge them. She tried to speak, beg him to let her go, but Curtis was applying too much pressure against her voice box to do so.

She continued trying to force his fingers open, and finally he pressed down on her neck as hard as he could and let go. Then he backed away from the bed. "Just try to divorce me, Tanya. I'm tellin' you. Just try it and see what happens!" he screamed, and walked out of the bedroom like everything was normal.

Tanya rolled over on her stomach and cried uncontrollably, trying to figure out exactly what just happened.

Chapter 14

Tanya and Curtis rode to church in complete silence. It was obvious that Alicia had sensed that something was wrong, because she'd barely said more than two words since they'd left home. No matter how many times Tanya replayed a mental tape of what Curtis had done to her Friday night or, in actuality, yesterday morning, she still couldn't believe what had happened. She'd tried to justify the whole situation, but she hadn't found one reason why Curtis should have gone as far as putting his hands on her. It had all been so uncalled for, and she didn't know if she was ever going to get over it. She hated him for hurting her the way he had, and she hated herself even more for riding in the car to church with him, just so that he could pretend the Black family was still as happy as ever before. She wouldn't have gone along with it except she hadn't wanted to upset her daughter. And she thanked God that Alicia had wanted to spend the night with the next-door neighbor. Curtis hadn't even known that Alicia was gone, and that meant he hadn't cared one bit whether his daughter might hear or see what he was doing. All he cared about was himself and not much else seemed to matter to him anymore.

They drove into the church parking lot, parked in the space that had been reserved for the pastor of the church, and then stepped out of the car. As soon as they walked into the church, they went their separate ways, Tanya and Alicia into the sanctuary and Curtis up to his study.

It was all Tanya could do not to break out in tears, and she did her best to interact with the church members the same as she always did. They were always so kind to her, and that was one thing she looked forward to whenever she entered the church every Sunday morning.

Tanya and Alicia walked closer to their usual pew, but on their way past the organ, Tanya saw Adrienne Jackson heading toward them.

"Good morning, Sister Black," Adrienne said. "And how are you, Little Miss Alicia?"

"Fine, and you," Tanya said as cordial as

her anger and pain would afford her to.

"I'm fine," Alicia responded.

"That suit is really sharp," Adrienne said, complimenting Tanya.

Tanya couldn't believe she had the nerve to be giving her a compliment when she knew good and well that she was sleeping with her husband every chance she got. But Tanya wasn't going to make anything of it. She had far more respect for the church and the people who belonged to it. Besides, Adrienne Jackson was going to get what was coming to her sooner or later anyhow. Tanya was willing to bet her life on it.

"Oh, thank you, Adrienne," Tanya offered in a far too friendly tone and then strutted right past her without waiting to hear any more of her false words of praise.

A few more members came over and spoke to Tanya and Alicia, and shortly thereafter, one of the deacons started devotion. They sang a hymn, read a scripture, prayed, read the responsive reading, and then they sang another hymn before they were finally able to take their seats. Then the male chorus stood to sing the first song of their A and B selections. Usually Tanya couldn't wait to hear the choir sing, but today her mind was somewhere else. It was in a place where she didn't want it to be, but she couldn't help what she was thinking, either. She wanted revenge. Revenge against Curtis because of how miserable he'd made her life and for physically abusing her like she was some stranger who didn't matter to him. And she wanted revenge against Adrienne for sleeping with her husband and then smiling in her face like she was some innocent little angel. Tanya owed both of them a lot, and as sure as she was sitting inside the church right now, payday was going to come for both of them. She was going to make sure it did.

After Curtis stood and did his weekly pastoral observations and used his normal scare tactics to get more money, the congregation stood and waited to walk around to give their tithes and offerings. Tanya gazed at some of the women parading around and slightly shook her head when she noticed that they were dressed like models strutting down the runway at a fashion show. And it made her sick to her stomach as she watched some of the deacons and trustees in the front row, eyeballing every dress tail that passed by them. Not to mention her own husband's wandering eyes.

When everyone had taken their seats, one of the deacons prayed over the money that had been collected, the choir sang another song, and, after that, Curtis prepared to preach his sermon.

"You know, I thought long and hard about what today's sermon should be about," he began. "And after praying over it and then praying over it again, God finally laid it on my heart to preach on the subject, Hypocritical Christians."

Tanya couldn't believe his audacity. She couldn't believe he had the gall to preach about the very thing he was guilty of being himself. She listened as he cruised further into his topic, and she heard him discuss everything from adultery to abortion to greed, and Tanya wondered how he could fix his lips to criticize anyone when he was committing every one of the sins he was condemning. Maybe not abortion, but clearly, adultery and greed.

He continued preaching his sermon, but the more he elaborated, the more appalled Tanya became. And it wasn't long before she tuned him completely out with fantasies that centered around James. She couldn't get over how wonderful his personality was and how well they connected with each other just in conversation. She longed for the caring and sharing that he was offering her, and she was starting to wonder just how long she could continue denying herself at least some level of happiness, the sort of happiness James was willing and able to give to her in a heartbeat. She could feel his touch right now, and she wanted her fantasy to become the reality it should be. Tanya continued to daydream about what her life could be if she were to leave Curtis, but then she started to feel guilty. She couldn't believe how unfaithful she'd become in such a short length of time, to both her marriage and her religious values.

When Curtis said the final words of his sermon, a young married couple walked to the front of the sanctuary, stated that they wanted to become members, and then Curtis executed the benediction.

Usually Tanya enjoyed everything she heard during the service, that is, everything except what Curtis had to say, but today she couldn't wait to get out of there. She needed to get as far away as she could from anything reminding her of him and Adrienne.

"Daddy, do we have to go back to church this afternoon?" Alicia asked her father at the dinner table. They were all eating the meal that Tanya had prepared the day before.

"Yes, baby girl. We have to go back for a Men's Day Service."

Tanya just looked at him, because whether he knew it or not, she wasn't going anywhere. And neither was Alicia for that matter.

"Mom, am I going to put my same dress back on after we eat?" Alicia asked her mother, who had made her change into her play clothing as soon as they'd arrived back at home.

"No, sweetheart. You and I are going by to see Miss Nicole and then to a movie."

"But Daddy said . . ." Alicia started before her mother interrupted.

"I know what your daddy told you, but we're not going back," Tanya said, ignoring Curtis and pretending as if he didn't even exist. "I'm exhausted, and I don't feel like getting dressed up all over again."

Curtis looked at Tanya angrily, but he didn't say anything. Alicia noticed it, but kept quiet about the whole situation.

When they'd finished their meals, Alicia ran upstairs to her bedroom, and Tanya began clearing her and Alicia's dishes away from the table.

"What do you mean, you're not going back to church?" Curtis finally asked when he couldn't take Tanya's silent treatment any longer.

"Exactly what I said. I'm not going back to church, and neither is Alicia. And to tell you the truth, I don't want to hear anything else about it," she said, scraping the dishes.

"What's the matter with you?" Curtis asked like they were as happy as Mike and Carol on *The Brady Bunch.*

"There's nothing the matter with me, unless you're talking about the fact that you tried to strangle me half to death or the fact that you didn't find your way home until after two in the morning. Or the fact that that little witch Adrienne, had the nerve to speak to me and then compliment my outfit, when she knows good and well she probably just slept with you less than twenty-four hours ago. But if you're not talking about any of that, then like I said, there's nothing wrong with me."

"You're never going to get off of this Adrienne trip, are you? I keep telling you over and over again that there's nothing between us, but you still refuse to believe me."

"Save it, Curtis, for someone who really

gives a damn. Because I really couldn't care less about you or Adrienne anymore. I'm through with you, and as far as I'm concerned, you can do whatever you damn well please with her and any other whore that will have your sorry ass," Tanya said, and didn't feel bad about the words she'd chosen, or the way she'd just spoken to him.

"You sure don't have very much respect for God or any dedication to the church at all, do you?" Curtis asked as though he was shocked over the way Tanya was acting.

She ignored him.

"The problem with you is that you're allowing the devil take control of your mind again," he continued.

"Well, if he is, then I feel sorry for you and anyone else who crosses my path today. And I suggest you leave me alone before something bad happens to you. Something you won't ever forget for as long as you live."

"Tanya, your threats don't mean a thing to me, so if I were you, I wouldn't even waste my breath."

Tanya looked at him and smiled, and she kept looking at him as if he was crazy. And then suddenly she cracked up laughing.

And she continued laughing all the way out of the kitchen and all the way up to her bedroom on the second floor. She laughed as hard as she could, and she didn't stop laughing until she was good and ready to. Curtis was just that funny to her.

Chapter 15

Curtis flipped through his daily planner, taking mental note of what his schedule looked like for the current week. As always, his Monday and Tuesday agenda included visiting members who were sick and shut in at hospitals, nursing facilities, or at their own places of residence, and on Wednesday and Thursday he had to begin preparation of his weekly sermon, not to mention the regional Baptist ministers' meeting, a marriage consultation for a young couple in the church, and a meeting with a young woman who wanted to discuss the final arrangements for her wedding which he'd be officiating about four weeks from now. There were times when Curtis couldn't believe the amount of work his pastoral position entailed. It seemed like it was always something. If it wasn't one thing it was another. He'd known all along that taking on a prominent church such as Faith Missionary was going to be a huge responsibility, but he hadn't known that it would be quite to this extent. He never seemed to have one quiet moment, and it bothered him to know that everyone depended on him. It seemed all the members cared about were themselves and the problems they were going through. Just once, he wished he could tell them how hard it was being pastor of a church, how hard it was to deal with all the pressure and frustrations, and how hard it was to ignore all the women in the church who'd been flaunting and flirting with him from the very beginning. Everyone expected him to be perfect, but he wasn't. He was just as human as the next person, and he wished he could tell them that, too. But he knew they would never understand where he was coming from, because it hadn't taken him much time at all to realize that most of the members worshipped both him and the ground he walked on. When he had first come to the church, he'd been amazed at how easy it had been to gain the love, trust, and respect of his congregation. He could still remember how mesmerized they all had been the Sunday he'd preached his trial sermon. And while he was last of five final candidates, it hadn't taken the deacons' board even a week to call him with the good news — that they were hiring him, and that they wanted him to move to Chicago as soon as possible.

He'd been so happy, and now that he thought about it, he and Tanya had been happier than ever with each other. They had been the model family, and they'd found the American dream, or so he had thought. He wished things could be the way they used to be, and they could, if only Tanya would see things in the same manner he did. If only she could find the same ambition that he had. And if only she could see that running a church was no different than running a business, and that a man had to do whatever was necessary to make a decent living. As far as he was concerned, he was no different than some of the top CEOs in the country who worked aggressively to bring huge profits into their companies. Tanya thought his motivations were based on greed, but she was wrong. He was simply doing his job the way it had to be done if he wanted to be successful. And he couldn't believe she wanted to ruin everything for him. That she wanted to turn his whole world upside down with all this talk about leaving him. But he wasn't going to stand for it. He wasn't sure what he was going to do about this crazy notion of hers, but there was no way he was going to lose his position in the church. He just couldn't have that, and he was going to have to find a way to calm her down a bit. But that was another story. The day was slipping away, and he didn't have any more time to dwell on such subjects. At least not at the moment anyway.

Curtis leaned back in the exquisite black leather high-back chair, pressed the speaker button on his phone, and dialed his secretary's extension.

"Yes," Monique answered.

"Can you come in here for a minute."

"Sure, I'll be in there in a second," she said, and disconnected the call.

Monique picked up her calendar, a notebook, some recently printed documents, and a pen, and then strutted toward Curtis's door. Then she opened it and walked into his elegant study, which was filled with beautiful, plush carpet, a cherrywood desk, and large matching bookcases on each side of the room. She walked past one of two leather loveseats, and sat down in one of the chairs directly in front of him.

"So, how's the monthly calendar coming along?" Curtis asked. She always penciled in the speaking engagements he had approved, but two months ago, he'd decided that he wanted a computer-generated calendar, outlining the next two months, every Monday.

"Fine. I just printed it out, and after I go over it one more time, I'll give you a final copy. But here's the first draft right here," she said, passing the document across his desk.

Curtis reached for it, placed both of his elbows on the desktop, and then scanned through it. When he came to the first week of July, he sighed. "Why people want to get married on a holiday weekend is way beyond me. Most of their guests are either out of town or they have family visiting. It just doesn't make sense to me."

"Well that's the reason this particular bride is having it close to the Fourth of July, because she said that a lot of their family members were planning to be in town anyway."

"Maybe, but I know a lot of the church members who will be gone, and some of them would have definitely attended the wedding if they were going to be here."

Monique continued looking at her copy of the calendar, but didn't comment.

"But who am I to complain?" Curtis continued. "To each his own, I guess," he said, leaning back in his chair again.

"So, how's everything coming along with the church picnic at the end of July? Have we gotten the meat ordered, and figured out the budget for the rest of the food?"

"The last time I spoke to the chairman of the picnic committee was a few weeks ago, so I'll have to check with her again to see what's what. But I'm sure everything is being taken care of."

"That's fine, but I want to be sure it is. The last thing we want is to run out of food. Some of the members bring family members who belong to other churches, and I'm not about to be embarrassed. If there's one thing I can't stand, it's for someone to invite a lot of people to an event and then not have enough food to feed even a small group of children."

"I'll call her up this afternoon to see how far along they are with the plans."

"Have there been any other requests for me to do a revival?"

"No. You have the one three months from now, one in September, and one in October. But that's pretty much it," she said, skipping through her yearly calendar. "I already recorded those in your book, though."

"Well, if there are any more calls that

come through, make sure you let me know, because I want to do as many five-day weekly revivals as I can this year. Not so many that I'll be too exhausted to preach here on Sunday mornings, but enough so that I can get more national exposure."

"Okay," she said, leaning back in the chair with her legs crossed, gazing at him with an inappropriate look on her face.

Curtis had seen this look more times than he cared to, and he didn't know how to react to it. Sometimes she acted as though she was going to seduce him, but he wasn't interested. Her administrative skills were exceptional, but she wasn't the most attractive thirty-something woman he had ever laid eyes on. To be quite honest, she wasn't the least bit attractive to him in any way, shape, or form. She had a beautiful body, but that's where all the beauty seemed to end. He didn't know why she kept looking at him and making comments the way she did. She'd only been working for him for six months now, but he could already tell that her actions were becoming more and more bold as time went on.

"Well, I guess that's about it," he said, hoping she would take the hint and leave without him having to tell her to.

But she didn't.

"You know," she said, smiling slyly, "your wife is so lucky to have such a handsome, intelligent husband. I would give anything to find a man like you."

"Thanks for the compliment, Monique," he said, and waited for her to stand up to leave.

"And you dress so sharply. I don't think I've met anyone who looks as good as you do in a suit. But then, you looked even better that day you dropped by the church with a pair of shorts and a T-shirt on."

At first Curtis wondered what she was talking about, but then he remembered the basketball game he and some of the men at the church had played and how he had dropped by the church right afterward and Monique had been working late.

"Well, I need to make a couple of important phone calls, so if you don't mind, I'll see you after you've reviewed the calendar again and printed it out," he said, ignoring her crazy advances.

Monique finally stood and then smiled at him as she walked toward the entrance of his study.

"Could you please close the door behind you?" he asked politely.

"Sure. Anything you want, Pastor," she said in a beguiling manner.

Curtis sighed deeply and wondered how on earth he was going to get rid of her. And he prayed that it wasn't going to be nearly as hard as it was for him to fire his last assistant — an assistant who couldn't keep her nose out of other people's business. She'd wanted to know why *this* person was calling him so often, why *that* person needed to speak to him again, and why he'd sent *roses* to Adrienne Jackson twice in the last two months. And Curtis wasn't about to have some young girl monitoring his personal activities, which was the reason he'd fired her on the spot once he'd become completely fed up with their working relationship.

Curtis picked up the receiver and dialed Adrienne's work number. She answered right after the third ring.

"What took you so long to answer the phone?" he asked, teasing her.

"I was standing a few feet away from my office when it first started ringing," she explained.

"So, did you get up on time this morning?"

"Yes. But barely. It's sort of hard to get up at six o'clock in the morning when you've just gotten to bed at one," she said, laughing.

"Well, it's not my fault. You could have gone home hours before that if you wanted to," he said, smiling and motioning his chair from side to side.

"Yeah, right," she said in a happy tone of voice.

"So," she continued. "Have you been working hard or hardly working?"

"Shoot. I always work hard. Seven days a week if you really want to know the truth."

"Do you work as hard as you did last night?" she asked.

"Of course. I work hard at everything I do, so I can be the best."

"You're something else," she said, laughing at him.

"What's so funny? I satisfied *you* last night, didn't I?"

"As a matter of fact you did. And that's why I couldn't wait to leave the Men's Day Service. I know it's wrong, but it was all I could do not to lose my mind every time you looked over at me."

"What can I say?" he said confidently.

"So, are we still on for tonight?" she asked, wanting confirmation.

"I'll be there. Probably not until around eight-thirty or so."

"Oh, that's right, Tanya has to moderate that support group on Monday evenings, doesn't she?" Adrienne asked, remembering what day it was.

"Yeah, and I have to stay with Alicia until she gets home. I could have the babysitter stay with her, but Tanya has been on edge lately, and I don't want to make her any more angry than she already is," he said, referring to the choking incident on Saturday, as well as the way she had laughed at him on Sunday. But he wasn't about to tell Adrienne any of what had gone on. It had been a terrible weekend for the Black family, and no matter how many times he tried to push the memory from his mind, he still couldn't get over the fact that he'd put his hands on Tanya. He'd never done it before, and he wasn't sure why he'd done it then. He didn't know what was happening to him, but it was almost as if he could no longer distinguish between right and wrong. Which didn't make a lot of sense to him, because he was supposed to be a man of God. A man who was supposed to lead others onto the path of righteousness for His name's sake.

He wanted to apologize to Tanya, but so far he hadn't found the words or the courage to do so, which was why he'd decided that it was better to wait until she cooled off. If she ever did.

"Well, I hate to run," she said. "But I have a manager's meeting to go to in a couple of minutes." Adrienne was one of the top marketing managers at KTM Corporation, a well-known pharmaceutical company.

"I'll see you tonight," he said.

"I love you, Curtis," she said, waiting for his response.

"I love you, too," he said as convincingly as he could, and then they both hung up.

He hated lying to her, but then again, maybe he did love her but just didn't know it. She catered to his every need, she was extremely attractive, their lovemaking was remarkable, and she was smart. Not so much in the common sense department, but she had loads of book knowledge. She'd gone to college and pretty much cruised through the master's in marketing program at Northwestern.

But even with all her credentials and looks, there was still something missing. He couldn't put his finger on it, but there just was. And he didn't know if he loved Tanya anymore, either. There had been so many arguments that he honestly dreaded going home. But whenever he even thought about staying overnight with

Adrienne, the only thought that stopped him was his sweet little Alicia. Regardless of how bad things had gotten between him and Tanya, his little girl meant everything in this world to him. He didn't mean to neglect her, and he wanted to spend way more time with her than he had been, but that was sort of hard to do without including her mother. Alicia wanted them to be the happy family they used to be, and she didn't like going too many places without Tanya. She didn't mind spending time with Curtis when it was just the two of them, but for the most part, she wanted all three of them to do things together.

Curtis didn't know what he was going to do if Tanya was serious about filing for a divorce. But then, the more he thought about it, the more he doubted that she would actually go through with it. Tanya didn't care too much about appearances, but taking vows before God had been important to her, and it was going to take more than some petty threat to make him believe that she was going to end their marriage.

That's what he told himself anyway. But in the back of his mind, he knew he really could have something to worry about.

Chapter 16

Tanya still couldn't believe Curtis had had the audacity to put his hands on her over the weekend, and then went even further by trying to pretend they were as happy as could be when they stepped inside the church yesterday morning. She was hurt, angry, confused, and shocked. You name it, she had felt it. And now here she was having to put on a front with her abused women's support group. Who was she to tell them anything, when she was obviously in the same situation? Curtis hadn't actually beat her down to the ground, but he had made inappropriate physical contact in a forceful manner. And she knew that when a man so much as slapped a woman, it was only a matter of time before it happened again, and more than likely on a much worse scale.

She still had about thirty minutes before the women would be arriving, and she decided to call Nicole. She hadn't spoken with her since Saturday morning, and since Alicia was sitting in the kitchen when Tanya answered the phone, she hadn't been able to tell her what Curtis had done. And then when she'd seen her at church, she hadn't been able to fill her in there, either. But she needed to tell someone what was going on, and Nicole was the only person she felt comfortable confiding in.

She dialed Nicole's home office number, because, knowing Nicole, she was still working like it was ten in the morning. The girl was sort of a workaholic, and that was the main reason she'd been able to build such a successful career for herself.

"Hello?" Nicole answered.

"Hey. How's it going?" Tanya asked, and then waved at one of her colleagues who was leaving for the day.

"Still working, but I'm about to wind it down in about a half hour or so."

"You're always working," Tanya said, teasing her.

"It's the only way to keep up with the competition," Nicole joked back.

"So, what did you do after church yesterday?"

"Eric and I went to dinner after I got home, and then over to the mall for a couple of hours. What about you guys?"

"I took Alicia to the movies, and Curtis went back to the Men's Day Service at the church."

"Since when have you ever missed any of the annual services?" Nicole asked, cracking up.

"I haven't. At least not until yesterday anyway. I'm fed up, Nicole, and a lot happened over the weekend. Things you wouldn't even be able to imagine."

"Like what?" Nicole asked with concern.

"Girl, you wouldn't believe it if I told you," Tanya said, sounding sad and serious.

"It can't be that bad, can it?"

"Well, it is, and I really need to talk to you this evening if I can. If I don't talk to someone, I'm really going to lose it."

"Well, Eric is out with some of his co-workers, so you can come by here if you want to," Nicole offered.

"I'll tell you what. Since Eric is out, why don't you meet me downtown at the jazz club I told you about a few weeks ago. That way, we can have dinner and talk at the same time," Tanya suggested.

"Sounds good to me. What time do you want me to come down?"

"I'll be finished here around eight, so

249

what about eight-thirty?"

"That'll give me more than enough time to finish up here and then get dressed, so I guess I'll see you then," Nicole confirmed.

"See ya soon," Tanya said, and told her friend good-bye. Then she took a deep breath, and tried to pull herself together before everyone arrived. They would never suspect what was going on with her, but she didn't know how she was going to look them in their eyes. Especially when she had always tried to figure out why they stayed with their abusive husbands after the abuse had taken place. And if they did leave, they always seemed to go back over and over again, like things were actually going to be better the next time around. And now, she'd allowed Curtis to shove her and practically strangle her to death, and she hadn't made even the smallest attempt to walk out on him. As a matter of fact, she'd been putting up the same front he was when she interacted with all of the church members. And she was about to put up one more front with the women in the support group. But she was glad that she'd finally be able to pour her heart out to Nicole within the next three hours. She couldn't wait. She would have loved to tell her mother, but she just couldn't bring herself to bother her with any of what was going on. Her mother wouldn't even be able to sleep at night if she thought her daughter was in some sort of danger. And Tanya didn't even want to think about what her father would do if he found out that that "shifty-eyed Negro" had put his hands on his "baby girl." He was liable to hop a plane to Chicago and kill the son-in-law he couldn't stand and wished he didn't have.

No, it was better not to tell them anything. It was better just to deal with the situation on her own until she came to some sort of a decision in terms of what she was going to do about her marriage.

Tanya said good-bye to Barb, who was the last one leaving the facility and then headed into her office to gather up her briefcase and purse. She was glad that the meeting was finally over, because she just hadn't wanted to be there tonight, and she'd spent most of her time daydreaming about James. She knew it was wrong to ignore what the women were discussing, but she just couldn't seem to help it. She didn't know what her problem was. Maybe she was using James as some sort of escape method. She'd found herself fantasizing about him in ways she didn't care to admit to, and she felt guilty. And in all honesty, she didn't know if it really was fantasy or not, because she was starting to have feelings and thoughts in a way that she never had before. She hadn't even had these sort of feelings and thoughts for Curtis. It was almost as if she was lusting after James, and starting to feel she needed to be with him on a regular basis. As a matter of fact, she longed to be with him more so now than before. She still loved Curtis to a certain extent, and couldn't deny it, but she couldn't shake the feelings she had for James, either. Ever since they'd had that marathon phone conversation, she thought about him all the time, and she had a full understanding of how people really did fall in love while chatting on the Internet. Words were powerful tools of communication, and the way James had spoken to her was living proof of it.

She glanced over at her phone to see if she had any voice mail messages, but there was no light flashing. Then she picked up the receiver to call Curtis. She didn't want to, but she figured the least she could do was let him know that she was going to be late, and she wanted to talk to Alicia as well.

She dialed her home phone number and waited for Curtis to answer.

"Hello?" he said.

"Curtis, I just wanted to let you know that Nicole and I are going out to dinner, so I probably won't be home until after ten or so."

"How come you didn't call and tell me that earlier so I could have kept the babysitter here?" he yelled. "She left as soon as I got here."

"I didn't even know that Nicole and I were going until right before my group meeting," she said, ignoring his anger and frustration. "And anyway, what did you need the babysitter to stay there for anyhow?"

"Because I have somewhere that I have to be. You're going to have to come home, and that's all there is to it."

"I'm not coming home until I finish eating dinner, so I suggest you call Adrienne and tell her that you can't make it," she said angrily.

"I'm not even going to respond to that crazy comment," he said in denial.

"Let me speak to Alicia," Tanya said, moving on to the next order of business.

"Alicia!" Curtis yelled to his daughter, who was in her room sitting at her desk doing her homework. "Your mother wants to speak to you."

Alicia ran into her parents' room and took the phone from her father. "Hi, Mom. Guess what? Daddy burned up some hamburgers on the grill," she said, laughing.

Curtis just looked at her. And although he was furious with Tanya, he couldn't help but laugh at what his daughter was saying.

"How did he do that?" Tanya asked Alicia.

"He was on the phone, and he said he forgot about them."

Served him right, Tanya thought, because she could only guess who he had been conversing with so comfortably that he forgot about the food he was cooking. "Well, have you had anything to eat?"

"Yes. We ordered some Chinese food, and we went to pick it up. It was good, too."

"Well, I'm going to dinner with Miss Nicole, so I won't see you before you go to bed, okay?"

"But, Mom, I want to show you something. I made this picture for you at school today, and I need you to sign my permission slip for the field trip we're taking on the last day of school," Alicia whined.

"Honey, I'll sign your permission slip in the morning, and you can show me your picture, too," Tanya said with tears in her eyes and a ton of guilty feelings.

Alicia was silent.

"Honey, I promise we'll spend the whole evening together tomorrow when I get home from work, okay?" Tanya asked, practically begging for Alicia's forgiveness. The last thing she wanted was to have her daughter lose confidence in her the same way she had in her father, who never kept any promises that he so faithfully made to her.

"Okay," Alicia responded unwillingly, but realized she didn't really have much of a choice. "Daddy wants to speak back to you," she said, and passed Curtis the phone.

"Where are you going to dinner?" he asked after Alicia walked back to her room.

"A restaurant downtown," she lied knowing full well she was going to a jazz club. The same jazz club she had had the pleasure of meeting James at.

"You know I have things that I have to do, so why did you make these plans without telling me?" he said, sounding like some dictator.

"I have things that I have to do, too, Curtis, and on top of that, you never tell me where you're going until the last minute, and sometimes you don't even bother to do that until after the fact. So, don't even try it. I won't be home until later, so deal with it!" Tanya said, and was proud of herself.

Curtis slammed the phone down as hard as he could.

Tanya placed the phone on the base and glanced over at Alicia's latest school picture. She picked it up, and tears began streaming down her face. She hated being away from her daughter, but she needed some time for herself. She needed to discuss her problems with another human being, because if she didn't, she was probably going to explode. And it wasn't like she left Alicia all the time. She was a good mother, she loved her daughter, and she had strong family values. But it killed her as she thought about the way Alicia had sounded when she begged her to come home. Why was it that Curtis could go and come as he pleased, thinking nothing of it, but she was feeling guilty for going out for dinner with her girlfriend? She didn't make a habit of it, and these two jazz club outings had been the only two evening outings she'd really had away from Curtis or Alicia this year. But, somehow, she still felt bad about it. But mothers needed time to themselves the same as anybody else, and she hoped Alicia would forgive her for her absence in the morning.

Tanya walked into the women's restroom, wiped her face, freshened up her makeup, and then headed out to her car. It was a beautiful night. The stars were shining, and it felt like the temperature was still somewhere in the late seventies, which was probably the reason why there were still people walking around as if it were summertime. It was usually a bit cooler downtown because of Lake Michigan, but it was still very pleasant.

She drove her car into the same parking lot as she had the first time she'd come to the jazz club, turned the ignition off, stepped out of the car, placed her briefcase on the floor behind the seat, and headed toward the club entrance. When she walked in, she saw Nicole sitting on a padded bench waiting for her.

"Hey," Tanya said.

Nicole stood up. "Girl, this is a really nice club. I've heard people talking about it, but you know Eric and I never go out anymore."

"Well, I never go out, either, but some of my co-workers had raved about it a while back, so I thought I'd give it a try a few weeks ago. And the food is good, too," Tanya said, wondering when they were going to be seated, until she saw the maitre d' heading their way.

"Just the two of you?" he asked.

"Yes," Tanya answered.

"Follow me," he said cheerfully.

After they'd taken their seats, Nicole didn't waste any time asking Tanya what was going on. "So, what is it that you wanted to talk to me about?"

"Hmmph. Where do I begin?" she asked, sighing. "But to make a long story short, I told Curtis that I was going to divorce him, and he shoved me around and tried to strangle me."

"He what?" Nicole said, frowning in disbelief.

"He actually put his hands on me," Tanya said, almost in tears again.

"Girl, what is wrong with him? Why is he acting so violently toward you?"

"Because he's worried that he'll lose the church. You know if he isn't married, he can't be senior pastor any longer."

"But that doesn't give him the right to put his hands on you," Nicole said in disgust.

"Well, he did. And do you know he

hasn't even apologized to me? It's almost like he doesn't care one way or the other."

"I still can't believe it, Tanya. I mean we're talking about someone who is supposed to be setting an example for hundreds and hundreds of members at church. He has to know that he was wrong for doing what he did."

"Maybe he does, and maybe he doesn't. Curtis lives in an unrealistic world sometimes. He's caught up with the idea of status and having as many material things as he can get his hands on. So, I wouldn't be surprised if he's forgotten about the whole incident by now."

"Well, why were you threatening to divorce him in the first place? I thought things were getting better," Nicole said, looking up at the waitress who was a few feet away from their table.

"Hello, my name is Cynthia, and I'll be taking care of you ladies this evening. Would you like to start out with something to drink?" the petite waitress asked, holding a pad of paper in one hand and a pen in the other.

"I'll have a glass of white wine," Tanya said without hesitation.

Nicole raised her eyebrows and smiled at Tanya. "Well, excuse me." Then she turned her attention to the waitress. "Well, I guess I'll have the same thing."

"Coming right up," the waitress said, smiling, and walked toward the bar area.

"So, since when did we start drinking wine?" Nicole asked.

"The last time I was here. I hadn't had wine in so many years, till I'd forgotten what it tasted like. And it was rather good, too," Tanya added.

"Wouldn't the good reverend love to know about this. He would just die if he knew you were hanging out at a jazz club. And drinking wine on top of that," Nicole said humorously.

"Well, that's just too bad, isn't it, because I'm fed up with him and his sleeping around. I mean, don't get me wrong, I'm not proud of what I'm doing, but I'm to the point where I really don't know which way to turn. That's not a good enough excuse for me to be out drinking, but I just needed to do something different for a change. And that's why I came here a few weeks ago, and why I suggested we have dinner here tonight."

"Actually, I don't see anything wrong at all with going to a jazz club and listening to some good instrumental music. And as far as the wine goes, even Jesus and his disciples had wine at The Last Supper. Everybody has their interpretation of what's right and what's wrong, but as far as I'm concerned, it's only a sin if you drink so much that you become intoxicated."

"I agree. But as a pastor's wife, it still doesn't look right for me to be drinking alcoholic beverages at a jazz club. And you know some of the church members would have a natural fit if they found out about it."

"But what about what a person has in their heart?" Nicole asked, folding her arms. "Or what about someone's personal relationship with God? Doesn't any of that matter? I've met plenty of people who claim to be so self-righteous — you know, not drinking alcohol, not going out to bars, not cursing, not doing this and not doing that, but then they talk about other people like dogs, betray them, steal, lie, commit adultery, fornicate, don't honor their parents, and I don't even want to get into the rest of the commandments a lot of so-called Christians make a habit of violating. I mean, what about all of that?" Nicole asked, wanting Tanya to give her an explanation.

"No, I know exactly what you're saying, and I agree with you one hundred percent, but people these days are so caught up with appearances. My grandmother used to say the worst kind of person you could ever meet was a lukewarm Christian. She would always say that it wasn't good to straddle the fence, and that you needed to get on one side or the other, because if you didn't, you were only playing with God. I really didn't quite understand what she meant when I was younger, but now I know exactly what she was saying. It makes a lot of sense, because how many people do we know who come to church every time the doors of the church are open, sing, shout, praise God to the highest, and then commit every sin imaginable on their way home. And they keep right on sinning until the next Sunday morning rolls around when it's time for them to put up a front all over again."

"It's really sad," Nicole said, realizing just how deep religion and Christianity really were.

They both looked up as the waitress approached them with their drinks.

"So, what would you ladies like to order for dinner?"

"Oops," Nicole said. "We've been talking so much that we haven't even looked at the menus."

"Well, I had the chicken Caesar salad the last time I was here, and it was delicious, so I think I'll have that again," Tanya commented.

"I'll have it, too," Nicole added, and passed her menu to the waitress. Tanya did the same.

"Would you like an appetizer?"

"Do you have onion rings?" Nicole asked.

"We sure do. Would you like an order?"

"Please."

"What about you?" the waitress asked, looking at Tanya.

"Is the onion ring order pretty large?"

"It's huge," the waitress said.

"Well, you can just share my order," Nicole interrupted.

"That's fine," Tanya said, and took a sip of her drink.

"Sounds good," the waitress said. "And I'll bring two plates out when they're ready."

"Thanks," Nicole said, and took a sip of her drink as well. "This is good wine."

"It sure is. So, now tell me. How are things with you and Eric? Has he gotten better about your career and the amount of money you make?"

"No. Things just aren't the same between us, and it seems like we're growing further and further apart. And it really hurts. But at the same time, I'm not going to give up my business just to please his ego. It doesn't make sense, and I didn't spend all that time going to college just to be a housewife."

"It's still hard to believe he's acting like that. He just doesn't seem like the type," Tanya said, trying to figure Eric out.

"Well, he is. And I don't know how long I'm going to be able to put up with his attitude. I need someone to give me emotional support, and he's not doing it. Shoot, maybe I'm the one who should be thinking about divorce."

"I doubt that. I mean, at least he's not out with other women to the wee hours of the morning like Curtis."

"No, but we hardly say more than two words to each other when he is at home, and I'm surprised he even wanted to go to dinner. Of course, he gives me all kinds of attention when he wants to make love, but that's pretty much where it ends. We talk about household stuff, like bills, but we never just sit down and have a regular conversation the way we used to. Oh, and I didn't tell you what he had the nerve to say two weeks ago."

"No, what did he say?" Tanya asked, waiting for the newsflash.

"One morning after I'd gotten up, I took a shower, threw on some shorts, a raggedy T-shirt, and started working. I had a lot to do that day, and before I knew it, he was walking through the door from work. But when he walked into my office, he took one look at me, shook his head like he was disgusted, and had the nerve to tell me that I needed to comb my hair more often and put on some makeup. And then he wanted to know when I was going to start fixing him dinner."

"No way!" Tanya said, and couldn't help laughing. "I'm sorry, but it's sort of funny."

"No, it's real funny," Nicole said, laughing with her.

"What did you say to him?"

"I told him that if he wanted a black Barbie doll, then he should have married one. And that the day I start fixing daily dinners for him would be the same day McDonald's stopped selling Big Macs."

Tanya cracked up. "You've got to be kidding."

"Shoot, I'm sick of him and his crazy attitude. He needs to get over whatever problem he has, because I'm not giving up my business. Not for him or anybody else."

"Well, have you tried to talk to him about it?"

"Yes. But when I ask him what's wrong and why he's walking around pouting all the time, all he says is that nothing's wrong with him. Which is a lie, of course, but the reason he can't tell me what he's upset about is because he knows his reasons don't make a lot of sense. He's just insecure, and that's all there is to it. And I don't know what I can do to change that."

"I really don't know, either. Did you offer to take him on some of your road trips?"

"Yeah, but he made up some excuse as to why he couldn't go. As a matter of fact, I asked him about two different events, and he said no to both of them."

Tanya lifted her wineglass, and the waitress set down two plates and an order of onion rings on the table. She told them to enjoy and then walked away.

"Girl, Eric does have some issues," Tanya said. "That's for sure. And so does Curtis for that matter. And what is a wife to do?"

"I don't know about you, but I don't see where there is anything that I really *can* do.

The only thing that will make Eric happy is if I get rid of my business, and I'm not about to do that. So, my hands are tied."

"And I'm not about to keep staying home 365 days a year all alone, while Curtis hangs out with his women any time he gets ready to. It's almost as if Alicia only has one parent anyway, so I figure it won't make much difference if we get divorced, because Curtis is never home."

"I hear what you're saying. At first I thought you should try to work things out with him, but him putting his hands on you sort of changes things from where I'm sitting. I'm not telling you that you should leave him, but I am saying that you should be careful."

"Those are my thoughts exactly. I was thinking earlier how I've spent most of my career counseling abused women, and now I'm going through the same thing myself. And it's almost like it's different when the ball is in your court. It's easy to tell other people what they should or shouldn't do in a tough situation, but it's not that easy to follow that same advice when it's happening to you. I would love for Alicia and me to pack our things and leave, but where would we go? My parents live in Atlanta, and my job is here."

"Yeah, but if push came to shove, you could always stay with Eric and me until you got situated," Nicole said sincerely.

"I know, and I appreciate that. But it's still not that easy. I know it should be, after all Curtis has put me through, but it's not."

"Plus, it would be hard to give up your house and everything."

"You know, a long time ago that would have been at the top of my list, but I'd give up that house and everything in it if it meant I had a chance of being happy. Material things mean absolutely nothing if you're miserable practically seven days a week."

"I guess you're right," Nicole said, gazing around the club.

Tanya did the same, and her heart did a somersault when she saw James staring straight at her. She couldn't believe he was there, and she hoped he wasn't going to take it upon himself to just walk right over to their table, because she hadn't told Nicole anything about him. It wasn't that she didn't trust her, but she didn't want Nicole thinking that she was some adulterous person who had no moral values.

Tanya turned her head and looked on the other side of the room, and while she tried to keep her composure, Nicole suspected that something was wrong.

"What's the matter with you?" Nicole said. "That wine must be taking major effect," she said, laughing.

"No, it's not the wine," Tanya assured her, and then decided that she'd better tell her the whole story.

And after she did, Nicole looked over at him. "Well, I'll say this. Baby looks good. He looks real good."

"Nicole, shut up. And you sound like some seventeen-year-old hip-hopper," Tanya said, smiling. Actually, she was grinning from ear to ear the same as she had that night she spoke with him on the phone.

Nicole laughed under her breath, and picked up a couple of onion rings. "You might as well invite him over here, because it's pretty obvious that he can't keep his eyes off you."

"No. You and I came here to have dinner, and that's exactly what we're going to do," Tanya said. "Here's our food now anyway."

After the waitress set their salads down, she walked away.

Nicole took the first bite of her meal. "You were right, this is good."

"I told you. They have good food here. I

haven't tried any other entrées, but I've heard other people talking about their steaks and their seafood."

They continued chatting while they ate, and Tanya glanced over at James every chance she got. And of course he never stopped staring the whole time. He was chomping at the bit to get over there, and Tanya didn't know how she was going to keep him away. And she didn't want to.

"Well," Nicole said, wiping her mouth and pushing her plate just a tad toward the center of the table. "I guess I should be getting home before Eric complains about my going out, too. Next thing you know, he'll be trying to place me on some sort of lock-down," she said, and laughed.

Tanya laughed with her. "You're crazy. Well, since you're in such a hurry to leave, I guess I'll invite James to come over and sit for a while."

"Ha. Are you kidding? That man's going to fly over here as soon as he sees me darken that front doorway. So, there won't be any time for invitations."

Tanya glanced at him again.

Nicole continued. "Hey, I'm glad we had a chance to do this, and I hope things get better for you at home," she said, grabbing Tanya's hand. They'd been joking around most of the evening, but now Nicole was serious. "I know we've never actually said that we were best friends, but that's exactly what I consider us to be. And I love you and Alicia dearly. So, please, if you ever need anything, please call me, because I'm here for you."

Tanya squeezed Nicole's hand. "Thanks, girl. And you're right when you say that we're best friends. You've always been the closest friend I've had since we came to Chicago, and that's how I've always referred to you, but truth is, I don't have a closer friend than you anywhere. Not even back in Atlanta. And I guess I've sort of been hesitant about labeling you as a best friend, because the last best friend I had betrayed me in so many ways until I finally stopped counting them. But I'm glad I have you, and I really do believe that I can depend on you. And I want you to know that I'm here for you as well. Always."

Nicole grabbed her purse, hugged Tanya as tight as she could, and told her good-bye. Tanya watched her as she walked away from the table, and she smiled when she saw Nicole say a few words to James, shake his hand, and then leave the club. Then James made his way over to Tanya's table.

"So, what's up, beautiful?" he asked, sitting down in front of her.

"Not much. How are you?" she asked, feeling like she was on a cloud.

"I'm fine now that I can finally talk to you."

"Oh, really," she said playfully.

"Yes, really," he said sincerely.

They gazed at each other, and Tanya could feel her heart beating more rapidly by the minute. She had such strong feelings for him, and she didn't know how much longer she would be able to control them. She was caught between a rock and a hard place, and the temptation was all but killing her.

"Your friend seems really nice," he continued. "I take it you told her about me."

"As a matter of fact, I did. She's the closest friend I have, or I should say the best friend I have in this world."

"There's nothing wrong with that. I think everyone should have one best friend if they can find a true one."

"She's wonderful, and she really cares about what happens to me. We sort of took to each other right when I first moved here."

"So, how are things at home?" he asked, sounding like he really wanted to know. Like he was hoping that she'd decided to leave her husband, and as if he hoped she was going to do it real soon.

"Basically, the same. Things haven't gotten any better, and I don't know if they ever will," she said, wishing she could tell him about her weekend dilemma. But she didn't even want to go into it right now, because it would only dampen the mood, which was currently right where she wanted it to be.

"I'm sorry to hear that," he lied.

They sat for a little while longer admiring each other, and then he pulled her out on the floor to slow dance. She laid her head against his chest, and pretended like they were in love and already living happily ever after. It felt wonderful to have him hold her the way he was, and she wished this night would never end.

When the song ended, another began, and they never missed a beat. She wanted so desperately to spend the night with him. She hadn't wanted to accept the way she was feeling, but she could no longer deny what she wanted. And the fact that he wanted her made him even harder to resist.

This time when the song ended, they walked back over to the table and sat down. And James didn't waste any time saying what he had to say.

"Look, I don't know about you, but I think we've both got some pretty strong feelings for each other. And what I want more than anything is for you to come home with me. I know you can't spend the night, but all I'm asking is that you come home with me for a couple of hours."

"James . . . I can't. You know I can't do that," she said, and it was all she could do not to tell him yes.

"But, sweetheart, you can't deny the fact that you're starting to care about me the same as I am about you. Right?" he said, grabbing both of her hands across the center of the table, leaning toward her.

"James. Why are you doing this? You know what my situation is." He was making things so difficult, and while she was flattered, she wished he wouldn't.

"I'm not trying to pressure you . . . No, wait a minute. I am trying to pressure you, but I'm not trying to make you do something you don't want to do. Am I?"

She knew he was telling the truth, because what she really wanted to do was make love to him all night long and then again when they woke up the next morning. But she had a daughter to think about. A daughter who would be crushed if she woke up in the middle of the night or the next morning and found that her mother wasn't home yet. And then there was Curtis to contend with. God only knew what he would do to her if he even suspected that she was sleeping with another man. But then, she really didn't care what his reaction would be, because he'd been doing the same thing for some time now, as if there wasn't the slightest thing wrong with it. So, her only reason for not going home with him still reverted back to her baby, Alicia.

"No, you're right. I would love nothing more than to go home with you, but I just can't. And I need you to understand what I'm going through."

"I do understand, but I also understand that I really want to be with you. And yes, I do want to make love to you. Hopefully, the way no man ever has before, but at the same time, I genuinely want to be with you because I enjoy your company. I had feelings for you the first night we met, and they weren't like any feelings I've ever had for another woman. So, believe me when I say that I'm not just trying to get you into bed, if that's what you're thinking."

"I know that's not what your intentions are, and I have very strong feelings for you as well, but this just isn't the right time, and it's not the right thing to do, either," she said, taking a deep breath.

James continued trying to convince her, but he couldn't convince her to change her mind. And when he finally realized that he wasn't going to be able to, he told her that he would walk her to the parking lot.

When they arrived, she unlocked the door to the Navigator, threw her purse inside, and then turned toward James, who was standing so close, anyone walking by would have thought they belonged to each other.

"Well, I guess I'll see you later," she said, feeling awkward.

He stared at her for a moment. Then he gently pushed her against the utility vehicle, wrapped his arms around her and kissed her more passionately than she thought possible. And it was almost like a reflex for her to grab hold of his blazer with both hands and kiss him back in a rugged manner. It never even dawned on her that someone she knew might be watching. But if that *were* the case, right now she didn't care, and they didn't stop kissing until they both were ready to. She wanted more. He wanted more. But she decided that this was as far as she was willing to let it go. At least for the time being anyway.

Tanya couldn't believe what she'd just done. She hadn't actually had sex with James, but oh did it feel so much like it. She couldn't describe what she was feeling right now even if she wanted to, and either she was going to have to stop seeing him completely or go all the way, which meant having a secret affair with him. She was mesmerized by him, and she hoped it wasn't because she was so vulnerable right now.

She drove off the expressway, and continued into their subdivision. When she drove into the driveway and pressed the garage door opener, she cringed. Curtis's car was gone. And when she entered the house and walked into the family room, she saw Sheila, the babysitter, sleeping on the sofa.

Tanya shook her head, and wondered why on earth she hadn't gone home with James.

Tanya tossed and turned in her bed the same as she had for the last couple of hours. Sheila had decided to sleep in the guest bedroom until morning, and after Tanya had checked on Alicia, she'd gone straight to bed herself. She was tired, but she just couldn't seem to drop off to sleep, and she knew it was because of everything she was thinking. Curtis still wasn't home, and she even wondered what Sheila must be thinking in terms of their crazy household situation. She was young, but she'd baby-sat more than enough times to realize that Curtis hardly spent any time at home and very little time with her and Alicia as a family.

She lay there for a few more minutes and struggled with the idea of calling James. She struggled for quite a while, but it wasn't long before she pulled his number from her purse and phoned him.

"Hello?" he said, sounding like he was already asleep.

"James?"

"Hey," he said in a groggy but pleasant tone.

"I'm sorry I woke you," she said, feeling bad about waking him.

"No problem. What's wrong?"

"Nothing. I guess I just wanted to talk to you."

"Are you home?" he asked.

"Yes. With my daughter and the baby-sitter."

James chuckled.

"I know you have to get ready for work in a few hours, but since I couldn't get to sleep, I thought I'd give you a call," she said.

"Hey, don't even worry about it. I'll be fine. And I guess I should be flattered, because if you're calling me, that can only mean one thing."

"What?"

"That you've been thinking about me just as much as I've been thinking about you."

She didn't want to admit that to him or herself, but she knew he was right. "You think so, huh?"

"That's what I'm hoping."

"You shouldn't have done what you did to me in the parking lot."

"You're not upset with me about that, are you?"

"No, it's not that."

"Good, because I don't ever want to offend you."

"You didn't, but that still doesn't change the fact that I'm married."

"But you're not happy, and while it's probably easy for me to say, I think you deserve better than that."

"I know, but if we keep seeing each other, my feelings for you are only going to escalate, and I don't think that's a good thing."

"I think it's a great thing."

"I'm sure you do, but it's only going to make things harder for me."

"I understand what you're saying, but it's going to be hard for me to stop pursuing you unless you tell me that you never want to see me again."

Tanya was speechless. She wanted to tell him just that, but in reality she knew she *did* want to see him again. No matter how sinful the whole idea of it was.

James continued. "So, be honest with me. Is that how you feel?"

"No, but it still doesn't make things any easier."

"I'm sorry that it doesn't, but I can't help the way I feel about you, and I don't think you can help the way you're feeling about me, either. I know we met at an inconvenient time, but that's just how things go sometimes."

"I'm sorry for bringing you into all this craziness."

"You don't owe me an apology for anything. I knew what the situation was from the very beginning, and I'm willing to take my chances with it."

"Regardless of what the outcome might be?"

"Regardless of what the outcome might be," he assured her.

Tanya heard a door shutting down on the first floor of the house. "Well, my other half has finally decided to come home, so I guess I'd better let you go."

"Not before you agree to meet me for lunch tomorrow, or I guess I should say today."

"I can't."

"Why?"

"James, I have to go," Tanya said, hoping Curtis wasn't already on his way up the stairway.

"I'll call you at work so we can decide where," James said.

" 'Bye," she said, and hung up.

Then she smiled, because she couldn't wait to see him again.

Chapter 17

It was partly cloudy and humid, but Tanya was glad it hadn't started to rain yet. James had phoned her at work a couple of hours ago, as he'd said he would, and she'd agreed to meet him at a park over in a suburb not too far from where he lived. She'd sort of thought twice about going, but she hadn't hesitated for very long, because she really did want to see him. She'd tried to deny her feelings for the sake of doing the right thing, but before she'd known it, she'd asked him what time she should be there. And he'd told her somewhere around twelve-thirty.

She drove through the winding pavement, searching for the spot he'd given her directions to, and it wasn't long before she spied his black BMW. Then she saw him sitting a few feet away under a shade tree at a picnic table.

Tanya cracked her windows before leaving her vehicle and strolled over to where James was waiting for her.

"So you made it," he said.

"Yeah, I did."

"It wasn't hard to find, was it?"

"No. Your directions were perfect," she said, sitting down next to him.

He stared at her and didn't say anything.

"What?" she asked, wanting to know what the problem was.

"Your husband must be completely out of his mind," he commented, and looked away from her.

"Why?"

"Because no man in his right mind would treat a woman like you the way he does. I mean, damn, what more could a man ask for when he has a beautiful, caring wife? I know that sounds like some sort of line, but I'm just calling it the way I see it."

"Most people never want what they have, and you know the grass always seems just a little greener somewhere else."

"I guess, but I still don't understand it."

Tanya sat down.

"So," James said. "When do you have to be back to work?"

"In a couple of hours. I have a lot of work to do, but I can stay a little later this evening to take care of it."

"I thought about picking up a couple of sandwiches, but I figured we could walk through the park and pick up something at one of the food carts."

"That's fine."

"You want to go now?" he asked.

"Whenever you're ready."

They walked a good ways to the first cart they saw and James purchased two hot dogs, two bags of chips, and some lemonade. Then they found a much more secluded table, sat down next to each other, and ate.

"So, aren't you glad you came?" James asked her.

"I am. I won't even lie to you."

"I thought about you all morning, and I would have done anything to take you home with me last night."

"I know, but I just couldn't do that."

"What about now?" he asked, smiling.

Tanya laughed at him. "I agreed to meet you for lunch and lunch only, remember?"

"Well, you can't blame me for trying."

"Goodness. You give a person some rope, and then they wanna be a cowboy."

They both laughed.

"This is a nice park, and I never would have noticed it," Tanya said. "But then,

I'm never out this way that often, either."

"It's pretty quiet, and that's why I like it. There're a few people out here now, but after the lunch hour is over, there won't be very many people here at all."

They continued chatting, and then finally James balled up his hot dog wrapper and drank the last of his lemonade. Then he moved his body up to the table and rested his feet on the bench.

"Come here," he said.

Tanya looked up at him. "You just won't give up, will you?"

"Just come here for a minute," he repeated.

She set her beverage down, stood up, and positioned herself directly in front of him. He pulled her body between his legs and kissed her.

Tanya felt a queasy sensation in her stomach, and her desire to make love to him was mounting higher and higher. So high that she wished they had gone to his condo for lunch instead, as he'd suggested. The passion was thick between them, and she didn't know how much longer she'd be able to continue putting him off. How much longer she'd be able to remember that she did in fact have a husband and a daughter. Because now, everything was starting to seem a little fuzzy. She was past the wanting stage, and now she *needed* to be with him, if only for one night. Or even one hour, if necessary.

They kissed for a short while, until James could no longer tolerate the situation. "Come home with me."

With all of the desire burning fiercely within her soul, she wanted more than anything to tell him yes. But it was this crazy conscience of hers that just wouldn't allow her to do so. And she felt bad about it, because she didn't want James to feel as though she was leading him on or playing games with him.

"I can't," she finally said.

James released her and covered his face with both hands. He sighed intensely and then looked at her. "How can you kiss me like that, and not want to be with me?"

"It's not that I don't want to. But I just can't let things go that far between us. I know you don't understand it, but that's how I feel. And I'm sorry."

They were silent for a few moments, and Tanya wondered if he was angry with her, because she knew he had every right to be. She shouldn't have ever agreed to meet with him, and now she knew that she couldn't see him again, especially since there was a chance that she was starting to have other feelings for him — the sort of feelings that had absolutely nothing to do with sex. She couldn't be sure if she was falling in love with him or not, but either way, it was best to leave well enough alone while she was ahead.

"Are you upset?" she found the courage to ask him.

"No. Disappointed, I guess, but not upset."

"James, I'm so confused."

"You can't deny what's happening between us, no matter how hard you try."

"I know, and that's why we can't do this anymore. Not until I take care of my marital situation."

"Have you decided what you want to do?"

Tanya thought about his question for a minute.

"I'll be honest with you. For my daughter's sake, I want nothing more than to keep our family together. But at the same time, I want to divorce Curtis and move on with my life. And that's why I feel so caught up and so confused."

"And I'm not helping with all of this pressure I'm putting on you, am I?"

"It's not all your fault, because I wanted

to be with you just as badly. But I do think we need to slow this down a bit."

"I understand. But can I still call you from time to time?"

"That's fine."

"Well, I guess that's that then, huh?" he said.

"I guess so."

"Can I kiss you good-bye?"

"James, you know that's only going to make things worse."

"Well, at least a hug then," he said, standing up.

They held each other firmly, until Tanya made the mistake of looking up at him. And when their eyes finally met, they kissed more intimately than they had before.

Then Tanya grabbed her purse and walked away from him in tears.

Chapter 18

It had been over three weeks since Tanya had spoken with James — that is, with the exceptions of his leaving a few voice mail messages that she'd forced herself not to return and the day she just so happened to be sitting in her office when he'd called her again. He'd wanted to know why she hadn't returned any of his phone calls, and he'd stressed over and over again, that he really wanted to see her, *needed* to see her as soon as he could. But she'd told him in no uncertain terms that she couldn't, and that she had no choice but to stick to her decision of not seeing him again. Maybe if she'd met him before she married Curtis, things could have been different. But the truth of the matter was, she *was* married to Curtis, and until she moved forward with filing for a divorce, she just couldn't live with the idea of committing adultery. She'd been asking God on a daily basis to forgive her for the two evenings and one afternoon that she'd already spent with James as it was, but still, her feelings of guilt hadn't been lifted. She knew there were some women, and men, too, who would have thought she was crazy, with Curtis frolicking around town the way he was. But she really didn't care about any of that, because she knew she had her own soul to be concerned with. She had always tried to do the right thing in the past, and for the most part, it had always worked for her, and she was going to try to do the right thing now as well. She didn't know what the future had in store for her, but she was going to keep her faith in God. It had become much harder lately, with her marriage being turned upside down, but she'd always been taught that a person needed to keep their faith strong, even when things had gone bad.

Tanya had worked through lunch, and hadn't taken one break today, and now she was completely worn out. And since she'd consistently put off washing their clothing for more days than she cared to think about, she walked into the laundry room, turned the washer on, and threw in a load of whites. She waited for the tub to fill with warm water, and then poured in the suggested amounts of bleach and detergent. Then she closed the top of the washer, and walked back out into the family room, which was just a few feet away. If there was one thing she loved, it was having a first-floor laundry. They'd always had that in Atlanta, because most homes in Atlanta didn't have basement dwellings, but when they'd first moved to Chicago and into the church parsonage, they'd had a lower level. And, of course, that's where the washer and dryer were. But after only living there for one full year, Curtis had decided that the parsonage wasn't good enough, big enough, or contemporary enough for them to live in any longer. He complained about it being on an average side of town, and as soon as he'd realized his position as pastor was pretty secure, he'd started looking for a brand-new home. He'd wanted to build one to his own specifications, but when one of the top Chicago developers began building homes in a new subdivision, in the same suburb, he'd quickly jumped on it. Then he hadn't cared so much about building as much anymore, so long as he could buy a home that no one else had lived in. And when he found what he considered to be the perfect home — one with two stories, four thousand square feet of

living space, a three-car garage, five bedrooms, three and a half bathrooms, a formal dining room, formal living room,
sunken family room, an island in the
kitchen, and two beautiful staircases, he
hadn't hesitated to make an offer. And
they'd signed the contract before Tanya
had really known what was going on.
She'd known what she was doing when
she'd signed on the dotted line, but it had
all happened so quickly. And it wasn't that
she didn't love her home, because she did,
but at the same time, she would have been
just as happy living in something half the
size. She liked nice things the same as
anyone else, but Curtis was the status-
minded one, and just couldn't see living in
a home that was valued the same as the
ones his church members might live in.
And now here he was upstairs getting
dressed to go to a monthly business meeting with the deacons, and she could only
imagine what he was going to complain
about this time around.

She'd hardly spoken more than a few
words to him ever since the night she'd had
dinner with Nicole and then found him
gone when she arrived home. But he, on
the other hand, had been trying to make
conversation with her ever since. They

hadn't argued about his being gone, and she could tell that deep down, Curtis was surprised by her whole nonchalant attitude.

She heard Curtis coming down the stairway and pretended to be reading the latest issue of *Essence* magazine. The same magazine that she'd already read cover to cover one week ago.

"I should be back from the business meeting in a couple of hours or so. Do you need anything back?" he asked, standing over her.

"Nope," Tanya said cordially, and kept right on turning pages like he wasn't even there. She could tell he didn't know how to take her, and it served him right as far as she was concerned.

"Well, I'll see you later, then," he said, moving toward the doorway, partly waiting for her to say good-bye, okay, or something. But she didn't. And finally he walked out of the doorway.

She looked toward the kitchen door after he shut it, dropped the magazine down on the table, and started flipping through the TV channels as if Curtis had never spoken to her. And, after a few minutes, she went upstairs to wash and condition Alicia's hair.

"From where I'm sitting, the church isn't bringing in nearly the amount of money I know it could be on a weekly basis. The congregation is capable of giving a whole lot more, and we need to find a way to encourage them to do so," Curtis said with his arms resting on the long, oval conference-room table.

Most of the deacons just stared at him in silence, because they'd heard him bring this money topic up more times than they felt like discussing it. But some of the deacons had become so tired of it, they stressed their opinions pretty openly. Especially Deacon Jackson, Adrienne's husband.

"We're already taking in anywhere between twenty to thirty thousand dollars a week, depending on if we have an evening service or not. And that's more than sufficient to run the church without any problems whatsoever," Deacon Jackson said, staring straight at Curtis.

If Curtis hadn't known better, he would have sworn the deacon knew about him and Adrienne, because he never supported Curtis on anything he brought up, and he always seemed to go out of his way to disagree with his ideas. But then, the deacon loved his beloved wife more than life itself, and would never in a million years believe that his sweet little Adrienne was messing around with another man, and especially not her own pastor. And if there was some chance that he did know about them being together, he probably would have already shot and killed both of them by now. So, Curtis knew it wasn't that he knew any-thing, and that Deacon Jackson simply just didn't like him. Unless he really did know and was just in denial about it.

"I realize we can run the church with no problem, but I have a much larger vision for the church," Curtis continued. "What I want us to do is build a new and more con-temporary educational center, and we need to offer better college scholarships for members who are graduating high school seniors as well. Families are supposed to be able to depend on their church in a time of need, and we have a responsibility to make sure they can."

"Well, it's not like we can force people to give a set amount of money," Deacon Pearson, the oldest gentleman in the room, added. "You can already see how irritated some of the members are as it is, every time you get up on Sunday morning talking about tithes and offerings," he said, and Curtis could tell he was against him as well. But he was older and set in his ways, and Curtis didn't expect him to side with him anyhow.

"Well, paying your tithes is in the Bible, and it's what God has instructed each of us to do. And as pastor of this church, it's up to me to make them see how important it is for them to obey His word." Curtis looked toward the opposite end of the table at his friend, Deacon Roberson, the man he'd sent to pick up Tanya and Alicia from the airport. "Brother Roberson, what do you think?" Curtis asked, knowing he could count on him, even if he couldn't count on anyone else on the board.

"Well, I do think the educational center is needed, and it would be nice to give some larger scholarship amounts, because it would really help out some of the parents in the church," Deacon Roberson commented, but didn't touch on the subject of where the extra money was going to come from. It was obvious to Curtis that he wanted to back him up, but he didn't want to get caught up in an argument with the other deacons, either. And Curtis understood that.

"We really don't have a problem with you encouraging the members to pay their tithes, because it's like you said, that's in the Bible," the chairman, Deacon Murray, said, speaking for the first time since he'd called the meeting to order. "But that's as far as we can allow you to go. We don't want it to sound like you're threatening them in any way. Last Sunday, you sort of made it sound like they were going to hell if they didn't pay their tithes and give an extra offering, and we've gotten a few phone calls about it."

"A few phone calls about what?" Curtis, getting upset, asked the Hank Aaron-looking chairman.

"About the way you keep bringing this money thing up to the congregation, and how you make them feel like they're going to be condemned if they don't give what you want them to," the chairman answered.

"If they don't do what God has told them to do, then they *will* be condemned. My job is to save souls, and how can I do that if I don't teach them what it is God expects them to do," he said, gesturing his hands in anger.

"Some things have to be said in a certain way, or people will be offended, and it's not like you have to bring the subject of money up every single Sunday either,"

Deacon Jackson interrupted.

Curtis wished he could knock Deacon Jackson right out of that chair he was so comfortably reared back in. He was making Curtis sick, and he couldn't wait to tell Adrienne that she had better put her husband in check. That she had better talk to him about his attitude before he ended up getting his feelings hurt. Why couldn't he just go along with the flow and stop adding fuel to the fire every time Curtis spoke? Curtis wanted to tell him a few things or two right now, but then, he'd already gotten his revenge on him. He'd gotten his revenge every single time he'd slept with Adrienne.

"I didn't come here to try and win some popularity contest, and if some of the members don't like what I have to say, then maybe they need to move on to another church."

"Well, we've said what we have to say on that matter, and I think it would be best if we moved on to your next item," the chairman said, and as Curtis glanced around the room, he could tell that the other deacons agreed with Deacon Murray, even the ones who hadn't said one word since the meeting began. But Curtis knew they would all have something to say when he brought up his next request.

"Fine," Curtis said, gazing down at the outline he had prepared late last week. "I've been here for two years, and I think it's only fair that I ask for a raise. I've only been getting three thousand a week for the last twelve months, and I think it's time to discuss an increase."

"A raise?" Deacon Jackson commented, and laughed at Curtis.

"If you don't mind, I'd like to finish what I was saying," Curtis said, not appreciating Deacon Jackson's rude interruption. "I've come up with some figures which include a cost of living increase and some inflation percentages, and I'm requesting five hundred more dollars a week. That's just under seventeen percent, but I think it's fair based on all the responsibilities I have here at the church and away from it."

"As long as I can remember, we've never paid a pastor thirty-five hundred dollars a week when they've only been here for two years," the chairman explained. "And until you came along, we hadn't even paid anyone three thousand a week."

"I just don't see how we can get the church to agree to anything like this," Deacon Jackson said, not looking at Curtis.

"Look!" Curtis said, raising his voice and pushing his chair slightly away from the table. "I have bills to pay. And the cost of living goes up for me the same as it does for everyone else. This church wasn't nearly as organized before I came here, and I've started more programs and taken the congregation more places than they've ever gone before. From what I can see, Faith Missionary didn't even have a *real* leader before I came along anyway. And now you're going to tell me I don't deserve a raise?" He was furious.

"You haven't done any more than what you're being paid to do," Deacon Jackson stated. "You are the pastor of this church and it's your responsibility to plan, organize, or do whatever it takes to run this church. And with all of the rumors floating around about your personal life, the congregation would have a fit if they thought we were planning to pay you any more than what you're already getting. This just doesn't make any sense."

"What do rumors have to do with anything?" Curtis asked him. "People talk all the time, but there's never any truth to what they're saying."

"Well, it's mighty strange that the rumors about you sleeping around with some of these women in the church never seem to go away. We keep hearing them over and over again, and I don't know how much longer we're going to be able to just sit back and ignore them. So, you'd better hope you're telling the truth when you say you're being faithful to your wife," Deacon Jackson said matter-of-factly.

"Hey, I think that's enough," the chairman intercepted. "This has gone way too far out in left field, and we need to get back to the matter at hand." Then he turned his attention directly toward Curtis. "So, Pastor, are you willing to accept anything less than a five-hundred-dollar-per-week raise? I'm not saying whether or not we'll be able to give you a raise at all, but if we do, I need to know where you stand."

"I think five hundred more a week is fair, because most of my colleagues who have similar churches are earning thirty-five hundred a week and more. I've done a lot for this church, and I'm still working as hard as I can to make this one of the most well-known churches in the city. Sometimes we have more interaction with the community than some of the larger churches in the area, and we only have around three thousand members."

"Well, it's not like three thousand members is a small congregation," Deacon Pearson said, remembering where he'd come from. "Some churches out in some of the suburbs are happy when they have four to five hundred in their congregation. And thirty years ago, when I lived in the South, you were considered a huge church if you had one to two hundred members."

"But, Brother Pearson," Curtis said, wondering if the fact that Deacon Pearson was almost sixty-five years old was the reason he couldn't see that things had actually changed over the years, that this wasn't the South, and that the nineties certainly weren't in any way similar to the sixties. "This is the great city of Chicago, and there are churches here who have up to ten thousand members or more, with multiple services throughout the day, every Sunday. And I'm not saying that Faith Missionary is small, but what I am trying to point out is that we do a lot considering the amount of members we have."

"Well, I don't see what the size of the congregation has to do with anything anyway," Deacon Jackson said, still disagreeing with every card Curtis dropped on the table. "We are who we are, and as far as most of the people in the church are concerned, you already get paid too much as it is. And it's like I said before, they would have a fit if they thought we were even thinking about giving you a raise. And I'll tell you another thing. If you think that the size of the congregation should be a deciding factor in terms of how much money you make, why don't you look at it this way. You're already getting a dollar a head. Three thousand dollars for three thousand members."

"Look, man!" Curtis yelled. "What is it about me that bothers you so much? Have I done something to you? Because if I have, I wish you would tell me, so we can straighten whatever it is out," Curtis said, standing up like he wanted to strike the deacon.

"Negro, if you know what's good for you, you'll sit your little arrogant behind back down," Deacon Jackson said, standing up as well. "Haven't you noticed that most of the deacons in here aren't saying hardly anything?"

As a matter of fact, Curtis *had* noticed that nine of the deacons hadn't said more than hello since the moment they'd all sat down for the meeting, but that happened lots of times, and he hadn't really thought too much of it. But now he didn't know what to think.

Deacon Jackson continued. "And do you want to know why? Because they're just as fed up with the rumors they keep hearing as I am. And the only difference between me and them is that I don't have a problem with telling you about yourself. Somebody's got to speak up, because, if they don't, a person like you will try to walk all over this board and the congregation we represent. And as long as I'm a deacon at this church, I'm not going to stand for it."

Curtis opened his mouth to respond, but the chairman intervened again.

"Have the two of you forgotten where you are? This is the Lord's house, and Pastor, you of all people, should have more respect for it. And Deacon Jackson, I know you know better, too."

"Well, we can just end this meeting then, because we're not getting anywhere anyway," Curtis said in a huff. "But before we do, I want to know what you all plan on doing about my raise?"

"We'll take a vote as to whether we agree with you about needing a raise and whether we think we should take it before the congregation, but I have to tell you, based on what I'm feeling from everyone here, I don't see where it's going to happen any time soon."

"Deacon Roberson, what are your feelings about the raise?" Curtis asked, knowing for sure that his only true friend on the board would give him the support he needed. He'd always thought he could persuade most of the deacons to do just about anything he asked, because he always had in the past, but today, they were showing him a totally different reaction. And he couldn't believe they were starting to believe these nasty rumors over what he kept telling them.

Deacon Roberson paused for a moment, and then he spoke the surprise of Curtis's life. "I'm sorry, Pastor, but right is right. You already earn over $150,000 a year, and I think it would be wrong to ask the congregation to consider giving you a raise. I'm sorry, but we have to be concerned about the people who support this church, and they depend on us to make sound decisions when it comes to the finances."

Curtis couldn't believe what he was hearing. Deacon Roberson had always backed him up, and he had always been able to depend on him no matter what. He'd always done anything that Curtis asked him to, and he was so kind and mild-mannered. But worse than that, most of the deacons were acting as if they were conspiring in some way to get rid of him.

He wanted to ask Deacon Roberson why he had betrayed him and why he had humiliated him in front of the entire board. But he didn't see where it was going to make much difference at this point, so he sat back down in his chair instead.

"Well, if there's no more discussion to be had on this subject, now is the time for someone to motion for the vote," the chairman said, looking around the room. But not one single solitary person made even the slightest movement. The chairman felt bad for Curtis, and decided to make the motion himself. "I motion to increase Pastor Curtis Black's salary to thirty-five hundred dollars a week. Can I get someone to second it?" he asked, looking around the room again. And again, no one said a word. "This motion is closed," the chairman said. "And this meeting is adjourned."

Each of the deacons walked out of the room single file, and began talking to each other as soon as they were out of Curtis's sight. Curtis couldn't hear a whole lot of what they were saying, but he heard one of the silent deacons say that Curtis had a lot of gall to come in there asking for more money, and another closed-mouthed deacon say that the church would swear that he only needed more money so he could spend it on his women.

The chairman patted Curtis on the shoulder. "Pastor, I'm really sorry about the way things went tonight, but everyone will eventually cool off, and things will be fine come Sunday."

Curtis was speechless, but he felt obligated to at least acknowledge the deacon, because at least he had kept Deacon Jackson under control and placed a motion for the raise. Curtis knew he had only done it out of pity, but he was thankful to him just the same. "Thank you, Deacon Murray. Thanks for everything."

Deacon Murray left the room, and Curtis continued sitting in the conference room for almost an hour trying to figure out what it was he was going to do to get them to see things his way. He needed more money, and this was the only way he knew how to get it pretty quickly. He'd gone over his financial situation a few days ago, and he didn't know how much longer it was going to be before everything blew completely up in his face. Tanya was already screaming divorce, and if she found out about . . . Or even worse, what if the

307

deacons and the congregation found out that . . . But he wasn't even going to think that way, and he decided that if the deacons really wanted him to remain pastor of Faith Missionary Baptist Church, things were going to have to be his way or no way at all.

Chapter 19

Curtis was totally frustrated and completely beside himself as he drove away from the church parking lot. He couldn't believe what had just happened, and he couldn't stop thinking about the way Deacon Jackson had spoken to him. He'd always made comments here and there, but never quite to this extent. And while Curtis didn't want to think about the possibility of him knowing about his secret affair with Adrienne, he knew he couldn't rule it out. The deacon had become more and more angry as the meeting went on, and if it hadn't been for Deacon Murray, Curtis wasn't sure what would have happened. And while he had no problem with physically putting Deacon Jackson in his place, he hated that he had shown out the way he had in front of the other deacons. They all seemed so surprised at the way he and Deacon Jackson had gotten into it, and they were definitely going to look at him differently from now on. But Deacon Jackson had gone too far with all of his petty criticisms and needless commenting, and Curtis wasn't about to let any man humiliate him in that way and get away with it, regardless of who they were or where it was they were doing it. He was sorry that he'd had to argue with him inside the church, but at the time, he just couldn't seem to help it. What he'd been forced to do was let the good deacon know that he wasn't ever going to back down to him, and that he would knock him back to his senses if it ever became necessary.

Curtis didn't know what he was going to do, and if he'd been a drinking man, right now he'd be heading straight to the nearest liquor store. But since he wasn't, he had to find another way to wind himself down. Another way to relieve this unwanted tension he was experiencing. And he knew there was only one sure way he could do that.

He reached down to his cellular phone and dialed a total of ten digits, since he was dialing into the 773 area code. The phone rang out loud through the speaker, and Curtis waited for someone to answer.

"Hello?" a young female voice answered.

"Hey," Curtis said in a laid-back tone, and was glad to hear Charlotte's voice on the other end.

"How come I haven't heard from you in a couple of days?" she asked immediately, sounding disappointed.

"Baby, you know how my schedule is, and you know I can't call you every single day of the week," he explained.

"Well, sweetheart, I miss you."

"Not more than I miss you," he said convincingly.

"Well, then when am I going to see you again?" she asked, sounding like it had better be sometime this evening. Which was fine, because that's why he was calling her in the first place. But he had to make it seem as if he was making a sacrifice to be with her.

"I don't know. Tanya is expecting me to come home, and I don't think it would be good for me to be away tonight. I just left a business meeting at the church, and I told her I would be back when it was over with," he said truthfully.

And now that he thought about it, he didn't know if calling Charlotte had been such a good idea, because he certainly didn't want Tanya clowning him the way she always did whenever he came home later than he was supposed to. But then, if he did go home, all Tanya was going to do was give him the cold shoulder, and what he needed was to be with someone who was going to take care of him. Someone who was going to push Faith Missionary and the deacons' board completely out of his mind.

"Sweetheart, I really need to see you tonight, so can't we just get together for a couple of hours or so," she begged. "You know I'll make it worth your while," she said, speaking like the immature eighteen-year-old girl that she was. But then, what did maturity have to do with sexual pleasure? Not one thing from where he was sitting.

"You're going to get me into a lot of trouble. You know that?" he said, slightly laughing.

"I'll see you at the motel, okay?" she said, totally overjoyed.

"Okay. You win. I'll see you in about thirty minutes."

"And . . . Curtis?"

"Yes?"

"I love you," she said in a serious tone.

"I love you, too, and I'll see you soon," he said, and pressed the end button on the phone.

He couldn't believe how naïve Charlotte was. She actually believed that he loved her, that he was going to eventually leave Tanya, and that she was most definitely going to be the next Mrs. Curtis Black. He could tell her whatever he wanted, she wholeheartedly believed him, and she never asked too many questions about anything.

But none of that mattered too much to him, because the girl always gave him the pleasure of a lifetime. It didn't matter when or where they got together, she was always able to turn flips around both Tanya, Adrienne, and any other woman he had been with. She was almost like crack to a crack addict. He simply just could not get enough of her. And she was always there when he needed her to be. Adrienne was fine, he enjoyed being with her at the condo, and the sex was good, too, but their relationship wasn't nearly as exciting as the one he had with Charlotte. They always met at this Mom and Pop motel out in the west suburbs, and Curtis loved it. It wasn't the cleanest place, but that made it that much more interesting. Plus, he didn't have to worry about anyone he knew seeing him.

Yes, Charlotte was absolutely the best

when it came to fulfilling his sexual needs, and she gave the best oral sex he had ever dreamed of. She was young, but so experienced when it came to giving a man what he wanted. What he needed from his wife and wasn't getting. And the fact that she was young and almost half his age made another amazing difference. She was so vibrant, and she didn't have one sign of cellulite or any stomach rolls for him to wrestle with. Adrienne had been blessed with a great body, but he'd already come to the realization that it wasn't going to be long before she lost it. He could see the signs already, and whenever he thought about it too long, it turned him off completely. Which was why he didn't think about it too often, and why he was still able to enjoy sex with her at the condo. And he didn't even want to visualize Tanya's love handles. She wasn't totally out of shape or overweight, but he didn't see where she'd be able to get away with wearing a bikini anytime soon, either.

And for the most part, he had the best of three worlds. Adrienne was his woman when he wanted an evening in style, Charlotte was his woman when he needed to be wild, and Tanya was a good mother to their daughter. He clearly understood why some countries allowed men to have more than one wife, because it just wasn't humanly possible to be satisfied with one woman. He'd tried to be happy with Tanya for as long as he could, but it just hadn't worked out for him. But there was a chance that he could be happy with her now, if only she'd come to her senses and understand where he was coming from. There was enough of him to go around, and he didn't know why she was being so difficult. Especially since she had the money, the house, the clothes, and an almost brand-new sports utility vehicle. But some women just didn't know how good they had it, he guessed.

He continued driving until he pulled into the motel parking lot. It was a weeknight, and that meant Charlotte wouldn't have any trouble getting their usual room. Room number 3. He saw her Red Neon parked at the opposite end of the motel, and he parked his car behind the building the same as he always did.

He stepped out of his car, set the alarm, and walked around to the room. He knocked one time, and Charlotte immediately opened the door to let him in. He shut the door behind him and unzipped her dress. She stepped out of it, and they never even said one word.

They kissed wildly, with him caressing her completely naked body. He didn't know where her bra and panties were and didn't care. And after sixty seconds or so, Charlotte pulled his suit jacket off, unbuckled his belt, unzipped his pants, kneeled down to the floor in front of him, and waited for him to kick off his shoes and step out of his slacks and underwear. Then, without hesitation, she did what she did best.

Curtis moaned and groaned with total passion, and wished that this remarkable feeling would never end. Finally, when it had gotten to be too much for him, he begged her to stop, but she didn't pay him any attention. He moaned even louder, and he begged her to stop once again. And this time she did, because she knew he was ready to let himself go inside her. They kissed while moving toward the bed, and as soon as they lay down on it, he entered her, and they made love like Curtis was sure he had never before, until their much awaited climax arrived and felt like some heated explosion.

Curtis sighed, and wiped dripping sweat from his face. Then he moved his body to the side of hers. He'd known that Charlotte would satisfy him the way that he wanted, but he hadn't expected it to feel this good. He hadn't thought she could get any better than she was, but she had. It was almost like she had some special technique, and was the only person in this world who knew how to use it.

He turned his head toward her and gently stroked her hair. "You're the best," he finally said. "You know that?"

"Of course I do. And don't you forget it," she said, smiling.

"Oh, I won't forget it. How could any man, for that matter?"

"Just think," she continued. "When you get your divorce and we get married, I'll be able to satisfy you every single night. I can't wait till the day comes when we don't have to go to motels," she said, envisioning what her life was going to be like when they became one.

Curtis didn't know what to say, and he hated when she ruined the mood with all this nonsense. Why couldn't she just be happy with the current arrangement? He gave her money to buy nice clothing and whatever else she needed. He helped her with her car payment from time to time, and he always reimbursed her for the motel room. Which meant he was basically reimbursing money he'd probably already given her in the first place. So he didn't see why she was trying to make things more difficult for him. But he knew if he said anything, it would probably come out the wrong way, so he chose to keep quiet.

"Sweetheart. Don't you wish we were married now?" she asked, raising her head from the pillow and resting it in her hand with the support of her elbow.

He hated answering her question, but he would just have to lie, the same as he always did. That was all there was to it. "Yes, I do. More than you could possibly know. I've never cared for anyone the way I care about you, and I really want us to be together. But I have to get things situated at home first. We want to do this the right way, because if we don't, your parents will never accept our relationship, let alone our marriage," he said, trying to calm her down about them entering holy matrimony. Her parents were members at the church, and would be livid if they knew about him and their daughter, but he'd always figured that what they didn't know wasn't going to hurt them. But he was afraid that if Charlotte really believed he was going to marry her, she was going to do what most naïve girls would do: start

318

bragging about him to the wrong people. He had told her what the consequences would be if she let that happen, but he wasn't so sure he had really gotten his point across to her. All she knew was that she wanted to be with him, and she really didn't care what her parents, Tanya, or anyone else would have to say about it. But he had to make her see the situation more clearly.

"Baby, something like this takes time. I have a wife and a daughter, and I just can't up and walk away from them just like that. I want to do everything the right way so that you and I can live happily ever after without any repercussions. And I want your parents to be happy about us getting together. I know it seems like it's taking forever, but it won't. And then there's the church. If I don't leave my marriage on good terms, the church will remove me from the pulpit, and if that happens, what are we going to do for money? So, please try to understand why we have to be extremely careful."

"Well, what is this stuff I keep hearing about Adrienne Jackson?"

Why was everyone always accusing him of having an affair with Adrienne? It was true, but where were they getting their information from? He hadn't told a living soul, and he knew Adrienne would take their secret to her death bed if she had to. He didn't know how to answer the question, but he did the best he could.

"Adrienne Jackson?" he said, laughing as hard as his acting skills allowed him to. "What about Adrienne Jackson?"

"Are you messing around with her? I heard some women talking about it at church last week, and that's not the first time I've heard it, either," she said in a concerned yet sad tone and laid her head back down on the pillow, turning away from him.

"Baby," he said, turning her back toward him, "do you actually think that I would betray you like that? After all we've been through together, and how much we love each other? Do you really believe that?" he said, and was happy that he'd almost convinced himself of what he'd just told her.

"Are you sure? I mean, because if you're messing around with someone else, then I can't be with you. I won't be with you from now on," she said, and Curtis couldn't believe she was actually sounding serious. As though she really meant what she was saying.

"I'm very sure. Baby, you know you're

the only one I want, don't you?"

"I don't know," she said, pouting.

"Well, I'm telling you. No, better yet, let me show you," he said, climbing on top of her, and then kissing her.

They made love again, and Curtis didn't know how he was going to find the energy to shower, get dressed, and drive home. After a few minutes, Charlotte went and took her shower, and when she finished, she stepped back out into the room. Curtis watched as she dried off her lean, picture-perfect body, and decided that he was going to have to find a way to make his case with the deacons. Make them understand where he was coming from. Because there was no way he was going to give up his northwest suburban condo or all of the other luxuries he and his women had all become so accustomed to. There was no way on earth he could do that.

Tanya jumped when she heard the phone ringing. It was barely after eleven o'clock, but she still wondered who could be calling at this time of night.

"Hello?" She finally answered after the third ring.

"Sister Black, I'm sorry to wake you, but this is Lena Morris."

Tanya sat up in the bed. "Oh, that's quite all right, Sister Morris. Is something wrong?"

"Our youngest son has had a high fever since early this morning, and the doctors can't seem to keep it down. Once in a while it drops a few points, but then it goes right back up again. And my husband thought it might be best if we call Pastor to see if he could come pray for him."

This really disturbed Tanya, because as far as she knew, Curtis still wasn't home. She didn't want to tell Sister Morris that, but she didn't see how it was going to help things if she lied to her, either.

"I don't think he's back home yet, but I'll page him for you."

"I really, really appreciate it, Sister Black, and, again, I apologize for waking you."

"Please don't worry about that, and I'll be praying for your son myself. And please don't hesitate to call here whenever you need to, no matter what time it is."

"Thank you so much," the woman said sadly.

"Oh, and Sister Morris, what hospital are you calling from?"

"South Suburban over here in Hazel Crest."

"Oh, we've been there before. On South Kedzie, right?" Tanya confirmed.

"Uh-huh."

"Okay, well, you stay strong, and just trust that God will bring all of you through this, and He will."

"I believe that."

"Take care now," Tanya said, and hung up.

Where was Curtis now? He'd claimed that he was coming right home as soon as the business meeting was over with, but, as usual, he hadn't shown. And now the Morris family needed him to pray for their son. Receiving calls in the middle of the night was part of his pastoral responsibilities, but Tanya always seemed to be the one who ended up taking them. Some of the members sounded shocked whenever they called at a late hour and he wasn't home, and while she used to make numerous excuses for him, now she didn't bother with telling them anything. She simply told them that he wasn't there, and that she'd get in touch with him as soon as possible. The same as she'd just told Sister Morris a few minutes ago.

Tanya picked up the phone again, and decided to dial Curtis's cell phone instead of his pager.

"Hello?" he said.

"Where are you?"

"On my way home. I went . . ."

"Curtis, save it, okay. And the only reason I'm calling you is because Sister Morris and her husband need you to come pray for their son."

"What's wrong with him?"

"He has a high fever, and he's at South Suburban in Hazel Crest."

"I'm not too far from there, so I guess I'll see you after I leave there."

"Whatever," Tanya said, and dropped the phone on its base.

She was tired of going through this. And sometimes she could kick herself for ending whatever it was she and James had going on with each other. Even if it was just an affair and not a true loving relationship, at least she'd been happy all three times she was with him. And anyway, who was to say that the relationship wasn't real and that they couldn't eventually fall madly in love with each other?

This was all so completely insane, and now she wanted desperately to call this man who made her feel more loved than her own husband did. The same man she'd been telling over and over that she wasn't going to see again. But she decided against

324

it, because she knew that she was only going to regret it in the end.

And she just couldn't allow that to happen. No matter how terribly she really wanted to hear his voice.

Chapter 20

Curtis was still shocked over the way things had turned out at the business meeting yesterday evening. He was extremely disappointed with the position the deacons had taken when he requested a salary increase. And for the first time in a long time, he was hurt. Hurt because he couldn't get over the way Deacon Roberson had turned on him. He had always been sort of his right-hand man, and Curtis didn't know if things were ever going to be the same between them. He'd wanted to phone him this afternoon, but decided against it, and now that it was after five o'clock, and he was on his way home from the church, he thought about calling him right then. But he didn't know what he would or should say to him. Curtis didn't have a whole lot of close friends and didn't want them, but he really had considered Deacon Roberson to be the best friend he had, the person he trusted with just about anything.

But maybe he was taking things the wrong way, and maybe Deacon Roberson hadn't meant what he said to be personal. Maybe it was strictly a church business decision. Which was what Curtis was hoping for.

Curtis drove down the street and dialed Deacon Roberson's phone number at the same time.

"Hello?" a young female voice answered, and Curtis could tell it was the deacon's fifteen-year-old daughter.

"Hi, Renee," Curtis said. "How are you today?"

"Hey, Pastor. I'm fine. How are you?"

"I'm good. So, are you glad school is finally out?"

"I sure am. But I'm glad I'll be a sophomore this fall. It was hard being a freshman."

Curtis laughed. "So, the older students still give freshmen a hard time, huh?"

"Yep."

"Well, is your dad around?" Curtis asked, hoping that he was, so he could get this over with.

"Uh-huh. I'll get him," she said, and yelled as loud as she could for her father to pick up the phone.

"I have it," Deacon Roberson answered.

" 'Bye, Pastor," Renee said.

"You take care now," Curtis responded.

"Hello," the deacon said as if he didn't know what else to say.

"Deac," Curtis said, using the nickname he always used when they were away from the church.

"How's it going, Pastor?"

"Well, as a matter of fact, not too good."

Deac didn't say anything.

"Okay. There's no sense in me putting this off any longer, so I'll just ask you. Is there something I did to make you turn against me the way you did yesterday?"

"Pastor," Deac said in a most sincere tone. "I would never turn against you, and I hope you can understand where I'm coming from. You've been a good friend to me from the very beginning, but when it comes to the church and congregation, I have to separate friendship from business."

"But why don't you think I deserve a raise?" Curtis asked, really wanting to know.

"I wouldn't say that you don't deserve a raise, but at the same time, you do earn a very good salary, and as much as I know you don't want to hear it, Deacon Jackson was right when he said that the congregation would have a fit if they thought we were giving you over twenty more thousand dollars a year."

"But it's no different than when someone works for a company, and they get an annual or semiannual raise. I haven't gotten one in over a year, and I don't think it's fair for the board not to even consider what I'm saying."

"I think the problem is the fact that when you first came here, we offered you far more than we had planned to. But we really wanted you, and you made it clear that you weren't going to accept anything less. So, even though it may look like we're not being fair, we really are, because we were more than fair when we first hired you for the job."

Curtis didn't like what he was hearing, but he did have to admit that he understood Deac's position. But just because he understood the board's side of the situation didn't mean he agreed with it or that he was going to just roll over and play dead. He'd always fought for what he believed in, and he didn't see a reason to change his philosophy now.

"I hear what you're saying," Curtis said. "But I can't say that I agree with it."

"I understand what you're saying, too," Deac offered. "And I really hope that this doesn't affect our friendship. I know you were pretty upset about what I said at the meeting, but it has nothing to do with you personally. I would have said the same thing, regardless of who our pastor was. I had always hoped that I would never have to draw the line, because it's hard when two people are friends and sort of work together, but I guess it was bound to happen eventually."

"It was. There was probably no way to get around it," Curtis said, still disappointed to a certain extent but glad that Deac still considered him to be his friend. And he really couldn't blame him for standing up for what he believed in, because that's what he and the other deacons had been appointed to do. This whole relationship between the pastor, deacons' board, and congregation worked almost the same as the one between the President of the United States, Congress, and the American people, but on a much smaller and not as formal scale.

"Well, that's what I wanted to talk to you about, and I guess I'll let you go," Curtis said, feeling a little better than he had earlier.

"Are you still at the church?"

"No, I just left there. I had to add the final touches to my sermon, and now I'm on my way home."

"Okay, then, tell Tanya and the little one I said hello."

"I will, and I'll see you Sunday," Curtis said.

He continued down the street, and suddenly it came to him. Tanya was the one who could probably help him persuade the deacons into giving him a raise. The board had always had the utmost respect for her, and maybe if he could get her to speak with them, they'd give his request more favorable consideration.

But then, there was this issue of him and Tanya not being on the best of terms lately. She'd asked him how the Morris's son was doing when he'd arrived home from the hospital last evening but she still wasn't really speaking to him, and he had to find a way to make things up to her. He had to start spending way more time with her and Alicia the way she'd been asking him to. And it wasn't going to hurt if he bought her something special, either.

He drove a few miles until he saw a floral shop that was still open, dashed in and purchased two dozen long-stemmed red roses, and continued on his journey home. And when he finally arrived, he saw her standing at the stove preparing dinner. He knew she'd heard him come in, but she never even turned around to look at him. She had no idea that he was holding such a beautiful surprise in his hand, and he couldn't wait to see the look on her face. She'd always thought that flowers were romantic, and he was sure they would get her attention.

As soon as she moved a few steps over to the sink, he sneaked up behind her, reached the flowers out in front her, and hugged her from behind after she took them by reflex. He'd been right about them getting her attention, but he didn't know what her ultimate reaction was going to be once her state of shock had worn off.

"What are these for?" she asked without emotion, and moved away from his embrace.

"They're for you. They're for the way I've been acting lately and for not treating you like my wife. And I'm really sorry for it."

This was completely absurd, and totally beyond her belief. And she couldn't help but doubt this so-called sincerity of his. He'd put on shows before whenever he wanted something from her, and she couldn't see where this instance was going to be much different. Curtis always knew what to do when he wanted things to work in his favor, and she wasn't going to pay him any attention.

"These are nice. Thank you," she said, laying them on the breakfast table and then walking right past him and back over to the stove. She was making spaghetti, heating up some garlic bread, and their mixed green salad was sitting on the wooden island.

"Baby. Please," he begged. "Is that all you have to say. I'm trying to call a truce here, and I'm really ready to work on getting our marriage back together. I know you've been suffering because of my behavior, but I promise you, I'm going to make it up to you."

"And then after you make it up to me, how long will it be before you go back to your same old ways?" she asked, looking directly at him.

"I won't go back to that way of doing things. I want us to be a family again, and I want you to be happy like you used to be, before we came here."

Tanya didn't respond, because she saw Alicia walking into the kitchen.

"Hi, Daddy," Alicia said, reaching up to hug her father, happy as could be.

"Hey, pumpkin. How's Daddy's baby girl doing?" he said, greeting her in his usual manner.

"I'm fine."

"How was day camp?" he asked her.

"It was fun, and I like it a whole lot better than school."

"I'll just bet you do, because you don't have to do any work," Curtis said, laughing, and then picking his daughter up. "Hey, baby girl," he said in a more serious tone than before. "You and Mom and I are going to spend the whole day together this coming Saturday, and we're going to do whatever you want to, okay?"

"I wanna go to White Castle, to the park, and then to the movies," she said quickly, without having to think twice about it. She was so excited.

"Then that's what we're going to do then, aren't we, Mom?" he asked Tanya, and placed Alicia back onto the floor.

Tanya despised when he put her on the spot like that, because if he didn't come through on his promise, she didn't want to be a part of it. She had no problem spending the entire Saturday with Alicia, because she did it all the time, and she didn't understand why he needed her approval. Like he was all for it, and the only way they wouldn't do it, was if she didn't want to. Curtis was such a joke sometimes, and she wondered exactly what he was up to.

"That's what we're going to do," she said, looking at Alicia and pretending Curtis wasn't even standing there.

"Yayyy!" Alicia yelled. "I'm going back up to my room until dinner gets ready so that you and Mom can finish talking, okay?" she said, and it was obvious to Tanya that Alicia was delighted to see her parents spending time with each other. If that's what a person could call it.

Tanya finished preparing dinner, and they ate until they were too full. Curtis was still on his best behavior. He was acting like the man she'd married, although she still couldn't help but be suspicious of his sudden act of family devotion. However, she decided not to make any waves about it or start any arguments with him, because Alicia seemed so happy. Happy because she probably couldn't remember the last time they'd all had dinner together on a weekday.

After Alicia had talked her parents into watching "Nickelodeon," Curtis told Alicia a made-up bedtime story and tucked her in for the evening. Then he kissed her and turned out her light.

When he walked into his own bedroom, he saw Tanya slipping on an above-the-knee nightgown with nothing under it. And while he hadn't found himself sexually attracted to her in a long while, he couldn't believe how beautiful she looked, and how smooth and toned her skin was. He'd just been thinking yesterday how her waistline wasn't as small as it used to be, but that's not what he was seeing now. The body he saw right now would have turned on any man in his right mind. Had it been that long since he'd really paid attention to the way his wife looked? Had he been so caught up with Adrienne, Charlotte, the church, and all the other responsibilities he had to deal with? So caught up that he was ignoring a wife that most men would have jumped at the chance to be with? How had everything gone so wrong, and how had their marriage gotten so bad that Tanya was talking about divorcing him? And even worse, how could he have physically hurt her that night she had threatened to leave him for good?

He walked across the room, feeling like the jerk that he knew he was, removed each piece of his clothing, and pulled on a pair of navy-blue pajama shorts. Tanya had already climbed into bed, and was reading a book. He couldn't remember the last time he'd come home before dinner, and now he knew what Tanya enjoyed doing before she went to sleep. She had sort of liked doing that before they left Atlanta, but for the most part, there hadn't been any time for reading, because most of their time was spent making love to each other. And he wondered what she did for pleasure. It was clear that he hadn't been giving it to her, and he knew she wasn't the type to have an affair, but he guessed that maybe sex wasn't so important to her. At least not nearly as important as it was to him and most men in general.

He sat down on the side of the bed, and then lay down. Tanya kept reading and never looked over at him, but he couldn't resist saying something to her.

"Do you always look this good before going to bed?" he asked, smiling at her, hoping she would respond.

"Curtis, please don't start, okay. All I want to do is read a few more pages of my book and then go to sleep," she said, wondering where his thoughts were heading.

"Is that book more important than me?"

he said, lightly brushing his finger under her chin.

She wished he wouldn't do that. She'd been angry at him for months now, and she'd decided that they eventually weren't going to be together, but she couldn't deny that she still had feelings for him. She didn't know why, but she did. She wasn't sure if it was love that she was feeling, but she definitely still had something for him. She wanted to tell him to stop, but she was hoping he'd just turn over and go to sleep and that she wouldn't have to deal with him for too much longer.

"Tanya?"

"What?" she said, sighing loudly.

"Can I make love to you?" he asked, pulling her book out of her hand and leaning across her to set it on the nightstand.

"Curtis, why are you doing this?" she asked him.

But instead of answering, he kissed her on her neck in a few different spots, down on her chest in a couple of places, and kissed his way back up to her neck again. And all Tanya could do was close her eyes and enjoy it. She didn't want to enjoy what he was doing to her, but she couldn't help herself. What she wished she could do was keep resisting him, but she was becoming weaker by the second. Curtis had always had that effect on her, but after all that had happened between them, she'd thought for sure that she'd gotten past those feelings.

Curtis pulled her away from the head-board, lay on top of her, and kissed her with total passion. She kissed him back, and for a moment everything felt the way it used to between them. She wanted to make love to him, and there was no sense in pretending that she didn't. And she wished there was some chance Curtis really had come to his senses and that they were finally on their way to working things out. He hadn't kept his word in the past whenever he promised to make things right with her, but if he did, it would certainly make things so much easier, and they wouldn't have to go through a messy divorce.

Curtis pulled off his pajama bottoms, then pulled Tanya's gown over her head and gazed at her. They both breathed loudly with desire, and Curtis couldn't wait to satisfy his wife. But he wanted to tell her something.

"Baby, I love you so much, and I'm so sorry for everything I've put you through," he said. And Tanya felt like melting.

Then they made love the way they used to, and she slept in his arms until morning.

Chapter 21

It took a few seconds for Tanya to figure out if she'd been dreaming or if she and Curtis really had made love together. It was all so out of the ordinary, but she realized now that it had actually happened, and that she still had this warm feeling inside her.

She lay there for a few more minutes, and then it dawned on her. Curtis was already up and gone. She frowned when she thought about how she'd allowed him to use her, when she'd known all along that he hadn't been sincere, and she could kick herself a thousand times over for sleeping with him. He had seemed like he was serious about making things up to her, and she'd sort of believed him when he said that he loved her. She still had her reservations about the way he was acting, but she was trying to give his efforts a fair chance. She'd been practically begging him to do right by her, and why she felt like this was the least she could do.

She continued lying in bed with tears in her eyes, and it was at times like these that she would give anything to be with James. She thought about him often, and there were days when she couldn't keep her mind off him. But she knew she had to get over him, because it wasn't right to start a relationship of any kind with him until she had this Curtis situation settled for good.

Tanya sat on the side of the bed, stroked her hair back, and rubbed her face with both hands. Then she wrapped a robe around her body, opened her bedroom door and started walking toward Alicia's room. But when she walked halfway down the hallway, she heard Alicia downstairs laughing with her father and the beautiful gospel CD, Trin-i-tee 5:7, playing on the family-room stereo.

She couldn't believe what she was hearing, and she knew it couldn't possibly have been breakfast she was smelling. Curtis was on such a roll that it was almost frightening.

She stepped down the stairway and walked into the kitchen where all of the commotion seemed to be going on.

"Good morning, Mom," Alicia said, sitting at the table in her bright pink pajama set. "Look what Daddy's doing."

Tanya could tell that Alicia was just as surprised as she was. And rightfully so. "I see," Tanya said, leaning down to kiss her daughter. "Did you sleep well, sweetheart?"

"Yes. Did you, Mom?"

Curtis looked at Tanya with a huge smile on his face.

"Yes, sweetheart. I slept well, too," Tanya told her, opening the refrigerator door to pull out the orange juice. And just as she did, Curtis kissed her on the lips and said good morning to her.

This was all too much for her to digest in one twenty-four-hour period, and she didn't know how much more her heart and soul were going to be able to take. He was being the perfect husband, he was cooking eggs, bacon, and grits, and he already had out four pieces of bread, preparing to make toast.

"Aren't we cooking a huge breakfast this morning," Tanya told him.

Curtis winked at her. "What I want you to do is sit down and relax, and let me take care of you for a change."

Alicia grinned at what her father said to

her mother. She was having the time of her life.

But Tanya was flabbergasted. And even though he was doing and saying all the right things, she still wondered when all of this unusually wonderful treatment was going to end. Unless maybe he had finally gotten tired of the wild life, and realized that whomever it was he'd been running after out in the street wasn't worth losing his wife and child over. Maybe the idea of getting a divorce had made him wake up and smell the coffee. But with Curtis, who knew?

Curtis finished cooking breakfast, blessed the food, and then they enjoyed a surprisingly well-prepared meal.

"That was good, Daddy. When are you going to cook for me and Mom again?"

"What about tomorrow morning?"

"Good," Alicia said.

Curtis had talked nonstop the entire time they'd been eating breakfast, and Tanya couldn't understand what had gotten into him. He was acting as if he was having the best time ever. And now he was asking her another strange question.

"What are you doing for lunch?"

"I don't have any plans. Why?" she asked curiously.

"I thought I'd drive downtown and pick you up around noon, if that's okay with you."

"That's fine with me," she said, wondering when the monster from two days ago was going to rear its ugly head again.

"Can I be excused? I have to go to the restroom," Alicia said.

"Yes, you may," Tanya said. "And then you and I have to go upstairs to get dressed."

"Okay," Alicia said, and walked down the hallway to the half-bathroom.

"So, did you enjoy yourself last night?" Curtis asked Tanya.

"What do you think?" she said, standing so she could start clearing the dishes.

"I think you enjoyed it a lot," he said confidently, and pulled her onto his lap.

"Curtis, what are you doing?" she said, trying her hardest not to smile at him.

"What does it look like I'm doing?" he said, and kissed her.

Alicia giggled at her parents, and they both jumped, pretending they hadn't been doing anything.

"What are you giggling at?" Tanya said, smiling at her daughter.

"Nothing," Alicia answered, and was still laughing. "Mom, can I watch television until you're ready to go upstairs?" she said, heading over toward the family room.

"No, I want you to go upstairs and brush your teeth, and I'll be right up."

"Not even for a few minutes?" Alicia whined.

"No, now get going," Tanya instructed.

Alicia skipped over to the back staircase and ran up the stairs.

"Now where were we?" Curtis asked, wanting to start where they'd left off.

"Curtis, I have to clear the table and get dressed," she said, and stood up.

"I'll take care of it," he said gently, pushing her into the countertop.

"What in the world has gotten into you?" she asked, starting to feel a little heated up, because Curtis was acting as though he couldn't get enough of her.

"What's gotten into me is you."

"Well, I wish you would stop it," she lied.

"No, you don't," he said, and then they kissed like two people who couldn't remember ever being in love with anyone except each other.

Chapter 22

Tanya couldn't believe it when the receptionist where she worked called and told her that her husband was in the waiting area and wanted her to come talk to him for a couple of minutes. She hoped he wasn't about to make up some lame excuse and cancel their lunch date. It wouldn't be outside of his character if he did, but he'd been doing so well since he arrived home yesterday evening that she didn't feel like going through any turmoil today or hearing any of his usual lies. She didn't know when all of this VIP treatment was going to end, but she hoped it wasn't going to be right now, when she still had another four hours to go at work.

She glanced at her watch and saw that it was eleven forty-five, and then walked up to where Curtis was sitting.

"Hey," she said, walking closer to him.

"Hey," he spoke back, smiling at her the

same way he had this morning before she left. "I already parked the car, so I figured we'd just walk down to that little Italian cafe you always go to instead of driving around in this lunchtime traffic. Is that okay?"

"That's fine," she said, relieved. "It's almost noon anyway, so let me just grab my purse and run to the restroom."

"I'll be here," he said, sounding so agreeable that if she hadn't known better, she would have sworn that this man who resembled her husband was actually an imposter.

They walked outside, and then strolled down three blocks to the cafe. It was a beautiful sunny day, and Tanya was glad to be finally taking a break. When they arrived and were seated, they ordered two glasses of lemonade, Tanya ordered fettuccine, and Curtis chose his favorite Italian entrée, cannelloni. Now, though, they were eating garden salads, and warm, buttery breadsticks.

"So, how was your morning?" he asked.

"Busy, but productive," she answered.

"That's not the same receptionist who used to work for the center when you first started, is it?"

"No, the one you're thinking of left almost a year ago," she answered, and had to bite her tongue, because his question was reminding her that it had probably been that long since he'd last taken her out to lunch.

"So, are you going by the church today?" she asked, making small talk.

"Baby, I don't even know," he said, sounding disappointed.

Tanya wondered what was going on. "Why not?"

"Well, I didn't tell you this, but when I went to the business meeting two nights ago, things didn't turn out the way I thought they would. Most of the deacons couldn't see where I was coming from, and I don't know what to do about it."

"What were you asking for?" she asked, because she knew for sure it had to have something to do with him not getting something that he wanted. She didn't know what that something was, but she knew it had to do with control or money.

"I told them that I need a raise, and that I hadn't had one in over a year."

Tanya wanted to frown at what he was saying, but she was really trying to keep this lunch engagement cordial. They'd been having a pleasant time thus far, and she didn't want to ruin it, if she could help it. "Why do you feel you need more money?"

"Because, baby, I want to take you on a cruise this year, and I want all three of us to go to Disney World before the summer is over with. And I still want to be able to take care of you and Alicia the same as I always have. I tried to explain to them that I need a raise to match the cost of living, the same as anyone else does, and that some of the other pastors in the area make what I'm asking for and then some. But they didn't want to hear it. And not one person backed me up. Not even Deac. Can you believe that?"

Actually, yes. She could believe it, if the deacons were still in their right minds. Curtis was already earning a ton of money from his weekly salary and made even more money when he did revivals for other churches in other cities. So, Tanya didn't know what his problem was. And she was afraid that his greed was starting to get the best of him. More so than she had thought.

"Curtis, you and I earn more than enough money to take vacations or do whatever we want, and I hope you don't get upset, but I think that the church has been extremely liberal with what they're paying you already."

"But, Tanya, I have bills to pay just like the next person," he said, trying hard to make his point.

She'd been wondering how long it was going to take before he called her by the name she'd been given at birth. He'd been calling her baby this and baby that ever since he'd walked through the door last evening, but now she could tell he was becoming a little frustrated with her. Not to his usual extent, maybe, but she could tell he wasn't the same happy camper he'd been before this salary subject came up.

Curtis continued. "And as pastor of one of the most prominent churches, I don't have a choice when it comes to the way I have to dress. I can't spend two to three hundred dollars on a suit like most men, and if we don't live a certain way, I won't be respected by my colleagues or the congregation."

Tanya wanted to disagree with him openly, but decided against it, because she wanted to enjoy in peace the lunch that the waiter had just brought out to them. So, she didn't comment on what he'd said.

"Do you see what I'm saying?" he asked, slicing his food.

"Yeah, sort of, but I see what they're saying, too," she said, looking at him, and right after that, Curtis cut to the chase.

"Well, I hadn't thought about it at the meeting, but I think I have a solution. And if you don't mind, I'm going to set up another meeting with the deacons so that you and I both can explain to them why we need more money."

Tanya felt like screaming. And what was this "we" business all about anyway? She didn't want more money, and she certainly didn't think *he* needed any more, either. He was already making a killing as it was, and she wasn't about to jump on his conniving bandwagon just so he could get what he wanted from the church. And now she was even more appalled as she realized that this was the real reason why Curtis had been portraying the perfect husband for almost twenty-four hours. The least he could have done was waited a couple of weeks or so until she'd gotten used to the nice way he was treating her. It would have been much smarter on his part anyway. And now that she thought about it, why hadn't he played his game in a much smoother and more convincing manner? He had always been so good with fooling her in the past, but now he was slipping. And she knew that could only mean one thing: he had to be in a very desperate situation. The sort of situation she didn't even want to imagine.

"I don't know," she said, trying to find a way to get out of what he was asking her to do. "If they didn't listen to you, I don't know what difference it will make if I talk to them."

"Baby, they respect you," he said with pleading eyes.

"Maybe so, but that doesn't mean that they will give you an increase. And anyway, how much more were you asking for?"

"Five hundred a week," he said, and she could tell he didn't see the slightest problem with the amount he'd come up with.

Tanya shook her head and looked out the window of the cafe. She had a whole lot of comments she wanted to make, but the last thing she wanted was to have an enormous shouting match in front of all of these people who were having lunch. This wasn't the time or place for it, and she knew she had to respond to her husband carefully. He could only pretend so long, and if he thought that she wasn't even considering what he'd asked her to do, he'd lose it the same as all children do when they don't get their way with something.

"I'm not going to make you any promises," she began, "but I'll think about it," she said, knowing she wasn't about to make such a thoughtless and inappropriate request of the deacons. It wasn't right, and she wasn't going to support his little scheme in the least. Especially since he was already earning more than he deserved in the first place, and as far as she was concerned, enough was enough.

"That's all I'm asking," he said. He wasn't totally jumping over with joy, but he was satisfied that she hadn't flat out told him no. "I know you don't see why I need the increase, but you do know how much our mortgage is, and how much all of our other monthly bills come to, not to mention our normal everyday living expenses."

That was just it. She did know. She saw the bills coming in every month the same as he did, and she didn't know how he could possibly feel any financial strain. He was more than able to pay all of their bills, they both deposited money into their Roth accounts, and she bought groceries and household items from her paycheck. And she'd been saving two hundred dollars a week in her credit union savings account for as long as she could remember. She'd only saved a hundred every week when they lived in Atlanta, but when they'd moved to Chicago, and Curtis had begun earning a lot more money, she'd doubled her weekly savings amount. And with the way he was acting, she was glad she had, because he was almost sounding as if they were broke and barely making ends meet.

"Well, we'd better get going, because I need to get back to work," she said, pushing away from the table.

Curtis laid down enough money on the table for the bill and gratuity, and then walked her back down to the center. He told her that he would pick up Alicia from day camp, they kissed each other good-bye, and Tanya walked into her building. Then Curtis walked three more blocks to the six-dollar, self-parking lot he'd parked his car in. But to his surprise, someone was waiting for him. And that someone was Adrienne.

"Why haven't you called me in the last couple of days?" she asked, angrier than he'd ever seen her.

"What are you doing down here?" he asked, trying to figure out how she knew where to find him, and why she was making this surprise visit.

"I followed you from the church. I've been leaving messages for you on your voice mail and with your answering service, and you haven't called me back one time," she said, starting to sound more hurt than furious. "So, what's going on, Curtis?"

"You followed me from the church?" he asked, becoming upset. "For what?"

"Because I wanted to know what you had to do that was so important that you couldn't return my phone calls."

"Look, I've been busy, and I just haven't been able to call you for the last couple of days. That's all."

"What are you doing down here, then?" she asked.

"I had to meet another minister for lunch," he lied.

"Why are you lying?" she asked, folding her arms. "I saw you walk into that building where Tanya works, and after I parked, I saw you guys walking down the street to some restaurant."

Curtis was starting to lose his patience. "Look, don't you ever question me about what I'm doing with Tanya. Regardless of what you and I have between each other, she's still my wife. And I really don't appreciate you following me, either," he said, unlocking his car door.

"Why did you go to lunch with her?" she asked worriedly. "You never go to lunch with her. You never do anything with her."

"Adrienne, this isn't the place for this, so if you don't mind, I'm getting in my car and I'm leaving."

"Honey, why are you doing this?" she asked, moving closer to him.

"Why am I doing what?" he asked, raising his voice and frowning in disgust.

"Why are you treating me like this?"

"Do you want somebody to see us?" he said. "Now like I said before, I'm going to get in my car, and I'm leaving. And I suggest you do the same," he said, opening his car door. Then he sat down inside it, closed the door, and turned the ignition.

Adrienne stood there with tears flowing down her face and watched as he drove off. He drove away without even looking back at her. As if he didn't even know her.

Chapter 23

Tanya didn't know whether to laugh or become highly upset when she walked back into her office and saw a dozen beautiful long-stemmed roses sitting on her desk. They were the same type of roses as the ones Curtis had brought home the night before, except these were yellow. He must have been positive that he'd have no problem convincing her to talk to the deacons' board on his behalf, and the reason why he had probably ordered the roses before he'd come to pick her up for lunch. She hated that he thought she was so predictable, but then, it was her fault, because she'd yelled and threatened him so much that he'd finally come to the realization that she wasn't going to do any of the things she'd been claiming. She'd said she was going to leave him, and never had. She'd told him that she was filing for divorce, yet she'd hadn't called even one attorney. And now she'd allowed herself to get caught up in his latest little plot. But most of all, she wished she hadn't slept with him. And what if she'd slept with her own husband and contracted some terrible disease? She felt a strong wind of terror as she thought about the possibility of having AIDS, herpes, or some other incurable sexually transmitted disease. She was so much smarter than that, and she always criticized women who didn't take any cautious measures when it came to sleeping with men who slept with more than one woman.

She sighed deeply and prayed that what she was thinking wasn't true. She had a daughter who depended on her, needed her, and she didn't want to leave her here in this crazy world all by her lonesome. She had a father, but if Tanya had AIDS, then that meant he was infected, too, since he'd be the one who had given it to her. How had spending one intimate night with Curtis turned into all of this? But she knew how. She knew it was because she'd wanted more than anything to believe that the old Curtis was really back, and because she'd recklessly given in to him much too quickly. So quickly that she hadn't bothered to think about any of these life-threatening consequences until now.

Tanya closed her door and sat down in the chair behind her desk. She glanced at the flowers again in disgust, and then opened the tiny envelope and pulled out the card that was inside it. When she saw what was written on it, she smiled. It said, "Hope everything is well. Please call me."

She knew it wasn't right, since she'd promised herself that she wouldn't have anything else to do with James, but she was elated to know that he was still thinking of her, and that the flowers were from him and not Curtis. And with the way Curtis had used her, now it was even more difficult to resist the urge to see him. She felt happy and excited, but she hoped that no one in her office had been nosy enough to read the card she was holding in her hand right now. She was feeling a tree-load of emotions, and she really didn't know whether she should call James to thank him, chastise him, or what. But she knew she had to call him one way or another.

She dialed his business number, and he answered on the first ring.

"This is James," he said, and Tanya smiled.

"So, are you the guilty party?"

"Guilty as charged," he answered. "So, did you like them?"

"I loved them, but I don't know if it was a

good idea for you to send them to my job."

"Yeah, I sort of thought about that after it was too late. Nobody read the card, did they?"

"I don't know. They were sitting on my desk when I came back from lunch."

"I asked them to deliver them first thing this morning, so you would be there when they arrived. I'll have to call them to see what happened with that."

"Well, hopefully no one read it, and we'll just have to have faith in that."

"And it's not like I signed my name, so if someone read the card, they still don't have any idea who sent them."

"But they'll know that it couldn't be from my husband, because he would never write 'hope everything is well.'"

"For all they know, he could be checking on you, because you weren't feeling too weli before you left home this morning," James said, laughing.

"Well, aren't we just full of humor today," she said, laughing with him.

"No, but seriously," he continued, "I apologize for sending them, and I should have thought about it more before doing it."

"Don't worry about it, I forgive you."

"I wanted to send you red, but I figured maybe that was going a little too far. And that's why I sent you the yellow ones, to let you know how much your friendship really means to me. It really hurt when you said that you couldn't see me anymore."

Tanya didn't say anything.

"The bottom line is," he continued, "that I really want to be with you. I need to be with you. It's been a long time since I've met a woman who has everything I'm looking for. And it seems like we're so compatible."

Tanya closed her eyes and felt her heart fluttering. She was having the same feelings she always had every time she spoke with James or saw him, and she didn't know what she was supposed to do about it. She knew that it was morally wrong to be with him, but didn't the fact that he wanted to be with her for herself stand for anything? Or the fact that he was so thoughtful and considerate when it came to the way she felt? She knew a lot of men sometimes acted this way when they first started dating a woman, and then the attention sometimes ceased as soon as the relationship grew old. But her intuition told her that James was genuine, and that there was nothing at all fake about him. And why did their paths have to cross right now, when she had a husband she had to deal with? It just didn't seem fair, and she wanted so much to change the way her life had unfolded. If she could, she'd have married James and hopefully lived the best life possible.

"Did I say something wrong?" he asked when she didn't respond to what he'd just said to her.

"No," she said, slightly embarrassed because she'd spent so much time in deep thought. She'd been listening to everything he said, she thought, but now she wasn't so sure if she missed anything or not.

"So, can you honestly say that you don't want to be with me and that you don't care about me?"

"No. I can't say that at all, but that still doesn't mean it's right."

"Are things getting any better at home? I mean, are you and your husband trying to make things work? Is that why you can't see me?"

Hmmph. If he only knew, Tanya thought. Curtis had pretended that he wanted to work things out, but now she knew that he'd had a hidden agenda the entire time. As a matter of fact, she'd be willing to bet that he'd concocted his pathetic plan on his way home from the church. But she didn't feel like going into any of this with James, and she definitely didn't want to tell him that she'd made love with Curtis the night before. Or at least love was what it had felt like, but now she knew that love hadn't had the slightest thing to do with it, and that what they'd really done was have plain old sex. The way two people do when they aren't passionately in love with each other any longer.

"It has nothing to do with any of that," she said, being careful with her answer. She didn't want to hurt his feelings, but she didn't want him to think that she was going to be with him any time soon, either.

"Well, what does it have to do with?" he asked, sounding as if his life depended on knowing.

"Look, James. I'll be honest with you," she said, preparing to lay all of her cards on the table in terms of the way she felt about him. "I do care about you, and I would love nothing more than to be with you every single day if I could. But it's just not possible right now. I know you don't understand, but I can't help the way things are. My situation is real messed up right now, and until I get it taken care of, I just can't get involved in a relationship with you. All it's going to do is cause more confusion, and the last thing I want is for you to get hurt. I'm very vulnerable right now, and I honestly don't know if I'd be being with you because I really wanted to or because I need someone to keep me from feeling so alone. Do you know what I'm saying?"

"Why don't you let me worry about getting hurt. I know you're vulnerable. Any woman who's having very serious marital problems would be vulnerable. But I don't care about that. And it's like I told you before, I'm willing to take my chances, if you are."

She knew he was sincere. She'd been thinking it all along, but now that she'd just heard his last plea, she was sure. It wasn't what he'd said, but the way he'd said it. But she was sorry, because she had no choice but to stick to her decision to not see him.

"I'm sorry, James. But I just can't see you. Maybe sometime in the future things will be different, but right now, I just can't do it."

James was silent for the first time since she'd called him, and she could tell that he wasn't happy about what she'd just told him.

"James, I'm really, really sorry. I never should have allowed you to sit with me that first night at the club, because if I hadn't, we wouldn't have gotten to know each other, and we wouldn't be sitting here having this conversation right now."

"No, no, it's not even like that," he said in a low tone, and she could tell he was disappointed and frustrated. "No matter what, I'll always be glad that we met each other. I guess it wasn't the right time, but I don't regret the couple of times we spent time with each other at the club or that afternoon at the park. I felt better than I had in a long time, and, as far as I'm concerned, it was worth it. I believe that there's a reason for everything, and I'm not giving up on you. I won't try to push the issue, but I know you'll eventually call me. I don't know when, but I know that day is coming."

They both sat quietly for a few seconds, not saying anything.

Then Tanya spoke. "Well, as much as I hate to, I really have to be going. But thanks again for the flowers. I really appreciate you sending them."

"You take care of yourself, okay?" he said.

"You, too," she said, and hung up the phone.

Tanya leaned back in her chair, shook her head in confusion, and took a deep breath. "Please, God. Give me strength," she whispered. Which was what she was going to need if she was going to keep rejecting James.

Chapter 24

As soon as Curtis heard his cellular phone ringing, he pressed the send button and said hello.

"Honey, why did you just leave me standing in that parking lot, like I didn't even exist?"

It was Adrienne, and she was already getting on his nerves. He wanted to hang up, because he didn't feel like listening to all of her whining and begging. He had more important issues he had to deal with, and he wasn't in the mood for explaining anything that really wasn't her business.

"Adrienne. Why are you calling me?" he asked, picking up the receiver and placing it against his right ear.

"Because I don't understand what's going on with you. All of a sudden you're acting like you don't want to be with me, and I want to know what's causing it."

"I've got a lot of things going on right now that need to be taken care of, and I don't have time to get together with you this week. That's all."

"Did I do something? Are you mad because of what happened at the business meeting the other night?"

"Oh, so your husband told you about how they shot down everything I had to say, and how they're cheating me out of getting a raise, huh? Well, did he bother to tell you that he was the main one against it?"

"He told me that all of them were against it, and that no one was hardly saying anything. But, honey, if you're mad at me about that, I don't understand it, because I can't control what the deacons decide. And that includes Thomas."

"I'm not mad at you about any of that," Curtis said nonchalantly. "I'm not mad about anything at all."

"Well, then, why haven't you called me back? I left you a message as soon as Thomas came home and told me what happened. He said that the two of you got into an argument. Is that true?"

"Only because he's always running his mouth, and doesn't know when to shut up. And I'll tell you, I'm really getting sick of him. The man despises me, and it makes you wonder if he knows about us."

"He doesn't know anything, because if he did, he'd be acting different with me, and he's not. I think he may have heard rumors, but he would never believe what people are saying. He's just not like that."

"Well, he believes the rumors about me messing around with women in general, because he said it. And you don't know how close I came to telling him that the reason you spend most of your free time with me is because he's not man enough to take care of you at home," Curtis said angrily.

Adrienne didn't respond. And Curtis knew it was because she was scared to death that he was serious. He knew it was wrong to worry her the way he was, because he had no intention of telling Deacon Jackson anything, so maybe it was the devil who was making him upset her.

"Don't worry, I'm not going to tell him anything," he said, relieving her mind.

"I just don't get it, Curtis. All of a sudden this thing happens with the deacons, and the next thing I know, I don't hear from you the next day, and now today I catch you walking down the street getting ready to have lunch with Tanya."

Curtis had had all he was going to take, and he was finally going to put Adrienne in her place once and for all.

"What do you mean, you caught me? It wasn't like I was sneaking around or anything like that. Or didn't you know that a husband doesn't have to sneak around with his own wife? Tanya and I don't have to do that. Just you and I do. And just in case you've forgotten, I don't have to take Tanya out to some suburban hideaway, hoping that no one will see us, and I definitely don't have to worry about her going home to sleep in the bed with another man, now do I? You've gotten to the point where you completely disregard my family situation, and it has got to stop. Tanya is already threatening me with divorce, and the deacons are acting like they believe every rumor they've ever heard about me, and so I think it's time that you and I lay low for a while."

"Curtis, no," she sobbed loudly. "Please . . . don't . . . do this. Please don't throw what we have away."

Curtis felt bad when he heard her crying, and really didn't know what to say to her. She cried lots of times, about a number of things, but this time he could tell that her feelings were deeply hurt.

"Curtis, are you there?" she asked when he didn't respond. "I'll do anything. I'll divorce Thomas. Anything you say, but please don't leave me. I need you, and you know I can't live without you."

"We have to lay low for a while," he repeated calmly and considerately. "Things are starting to heat up from every angle, and if we keep seeing each other as much as we have been, it's just a matter of time before someone starts having us followed. Just look how easy it was for you to follow me this morning from the church without me knowing it. We've got to be more careful, and there's no way getting around it," he tried to convince her.

"So, when can we see each other again? Can we at least see each other this weekend?" she begged.

He knew the weekend wasn't even an option, because he'd already promised Alicia that they were all going to spend the entire day together, doing whatever she wanted. But he didn't want to tell Adrienne that, because then she'd want to know if Tanya was going, and what it was they were going to do. And he definitely couldn't tell her that for the first time in months, he was looking forward to it. He always enjoyed the time he spent with

Alicia, but he was even looking forward to being with Tanya.

"The weekend is a bad time, because I have a lot of church events to go to."

"Well, what about after you leave one of them on Saturday or Sunday?"

She wasn't going to let up, and Curtis didn't know how he was going to end this difficult phone conversation. "I don't know. I'll have to call you to let you know. But I'm not promising anything."

"Curtis," she said, sniffling, "how am I supposed to just pretend we don't love each other anymore? How am I supposed to do that? Huh?"

"Don't you see that we have to tone things down, or something bad is going to happen? Do you want that?"

"No, but . . ."

"Well, then, we'll both just have to deal with the situation, because if Tanya divorces me, and the deacons find a reason to fire me, I won't have anything. It's like I told you before, they'll make sure I never pastor at another prominent church ever again."

"Okay, fine," she said. "But can you at least call me back when I leave messages for you? It makes me crazy when I don't hear from you, and if we can't be together for a while, the only way we'll be able to communicate is by phone."

"I'll call you," he said.

"I'm serious, Curtis. Don't just leave me hanging like you did these past couple of days."

"I won't," he said, wanting to hang up. "Well, I'm on my way up to my office at the church, so I'm going to have to let you go. But you take care of yourself, all right?"

"I will. And, honey?"

"Yeah."

"I love you. I love you so much that sometimes I don't know which way to turn. You mean everything to me, and all I want to do is make you happy."

"I know."

They spoke a few more words and then hung up.

Curtis didn't know why he was treating her the way he was, and why all of a sudden even her voice was starting to irritate him. He was so confused, and everything he'd spent two years building up seemed to be ripping at the seams. He wanted to be with Adrienne, but he had to admit that he was enjoying the time he was spending with Tanya and Alicia as a family. At first, he had only bought the flowers because he needed Tanya to speak with the deacons, but now he was feeling like he really wanted to make their marriage work. It wasn't that he didn't care about Adrienne, because he did, but the stakes were rising too high, and he could tell that it wasn't going to be long before someone found proof that he and Adrienne were in fact having an affair. And there was no way he could allow that to happen. He'd come too far in his career just to lose it all, and the line had to be drawn somewhere.

He stepped out of the Mercedes and set the alarm. He didn't see any other cars except Monique's and wondered why, until he remembered that the rest of the clerical staff were attending a seminar at a hotel in one of the north suburbs.

He walked into the building, up to his office, and greeted his secretary, who was busy working.

"I forgot that the other girls were going to be gone this afternoon," he said.

"The seminar is for a day and a half, so they'll be gone all day tomorrow as well."

"What was it they went to?"

"The one this afternoon is Time Management, and the one tomorrow is How to Work Together as a Team."

"Oh," he said, and walked into his office

and shut the door behind him.

When he'd rested his blazer on the wooden coatrack, he sat down at his desk. And no sooner than he did, he heard a knock on his door.

"Come in," he said.

Monique opened the door, walked inside his office, and closed the door behind her. "Can I talk to you for a minute?" she asked.

"Sure. Have a seat," he said, loosening his tie and opening the top button of his dress shirt, the way he always did when he was about to work on his sermon.

"I've wanted to say this for some time now, and it's not that easy," she said, sitting down and crossing her legs.

Curtis didn't know if he liked the sound of this. He couldn't tell if what she was about to say had something to do with him or her, and he wished she'd just come out with it.

She continued. "I've worked here for six months, and I've been attracted to you ever since the first day I saw you."

Curtis was speechless, because he had hoped it was never going to come to something like this. He'd known all along that she was attracted to him, but he hadn't thought she would ever have the nerve or courage to come right out and tell him how she felt. "Monique, you know that I'm a married man, right?"

"Yes, but now, let's be honest with each other," she said, smiling. "I know you see Adrienne and that girl Charlotte from time to time. And I'm here to tell you I can give you way more pleasure than the two of them put together. I can make you happy," she said, standing. Then she sashayed around to where he was sitting and rested her behind on the edge of his desk.

"Look, let's get one thing straight right now. I'm not seeing either of those women you just mentioned, and, quite frankly, I'm tired of hearing all these rumors," he said, and wondered how she knew about Charlotte. There were rumors about him and women in general, and even rumors about him and Adrienne, but not once had he or Charlotte heard anything about the two of them. "And where did you hear that anyhow?" he asked, filled with curiosity.

"I hear things," she said seductively.

"Well, regardless of what you've been hearing, I'm not interested in having an affair with you or anyone else," he said, feeling uncomfortable.

She caressed the side of his face, and then leaned forward and kissed him on his neck in three different places. Curtis closed his eyes.

"Monique, why are you doing this?"

She ignored his inquiry and kissed him on his lips. He couldn't believe he'd allowed himself to be seduced by Monique, and he couldn't believe how she was making him feel. He hadn't been attracted to her in the past, but he could tell that she really did know how to make a man feel the way she'd said she could.

They kissed a while longer, but when Curtis opened his eyes, he crashed back to reality. What was he doing? He didn't want Monique in that way. And he didn't care about the body she had and how good it looked to him, because he could never get involved with or make love to a woman who looked like her. Some men didn't care if a woman had homely facial features, so long as the sex was good, but he wasn't like that. He had certain standards when it came to his women.

He pushed Monique away. "If you want to keep your job, this can never happen again," he said. "I'm married, and even if I weren't, I'm not attracted to you in that way. You're a good employee, but that's where my relationship with you ends."

"So, what are you saying? That I'm not

good enough? That Adrienne and Charlotte and all of the rest of them are better than me?"

"I'm not saying any of that, and I wish you would stop accusing me of messing with other women, because everything you've been hearing is a lie."

"No, the only person lying is you, because I know for a fact that you mess around on your wife," she said, smoothing out her dress. She sounded angry, and Curtis couldn't understand why.

"I think it would be best if you leave now," he told her.

"What I hate more than anything is to be blown off. And that's what it sounds like you're doing to me," she said, walking away from him.

"Like I said before, I'm a married man, and if this happens again, I'll have to let you go."

"No, you're not going to let me go anywhere," she said matter-of-factly. "You see, I'm not like the rest of these church members. I know exactly what you've been up to since you came here. Truth be told, I've learned more about you in the last six months than they have in two years. And if you even think about trying to fire me, I guarantee you, you'll be going out the door right along with me. The deacons will make sure of it. So, I'm telling you now, don't mess with me," she said, glaring at him.

Then she continued. "And as a matter of fact, I'm gonna pay you back for what you just did to me this afternoon," she said, and slammed the door.

Why was she doing this? Curtis didn't know whether she had proof about his affairs or not, and wondered about what else she knew. Yes, she had access to most of the church files, and yes, she was intelligent. He hoped she hadn't been putting two and two together, and that she hadn't stuck her nose where it didn't belong, like in his personal filing cabinet. She was sounding as if she had the goods all lined up on him, and it made him nervous. More nervous than the deacons had a few days ago. It seemed like everyone was out to get him, and he couldn't understand why. He was a good pastor, but he was starting to feel like the deacons and Monique were trying to concoct some sort of conspiracy against him.

He tried to work on his sermon, but he just couldn't seem to think straight. And after an hour had passed, he gathered his things together and walked out to the parking lot. He'd glanced over at Monique on his way out, wanting to say something to her, but she hadn't even bothered to look up at him. She'd been so angry when she'd stormed out of his office, and he'd debated whether he should apologize to her. He hadn't done anything wrong, but something told him that she really did have something on him, and that she wouldn't hesitate to use it if it became necessary.

"Daddy, why are you so quiet?" Alicia asked, looking up at her father. Curtis had just picked her up from day camp, and was still preoccupied with the Monique incident which had taken place earlier that afternoon.

"Oh, I don't know, baby girl. I've just got a lot on my mind, I guess."

"Well, Daddy, I want you to talk to me," Alicia said, wanting her father's full attention.

"Okay, okay. What is it that you want to talk about," he asked, smiling at her. Then he looked in his rearview mirror and changed lanes.

"Can we still go anywhere I want to this Saturday?"

"Anywhere at all," he promised.

"Good. And Mom's going to come with us?"

"Yep."

"We're going to have so much fun," she said excitedly.

"We sure are," he said.

"Can we do it every Saturday?"

"Well, maybe not every Saturday, but we'll try to do it more often than we have been."

"I'm glad you and Mom made up."

Curtis looked at her strangely and wondered what she meant. "Why do you think we made up?"

"Because you yell at each other all the time. But last night you didn't, and Mom was really happy this morning, too."

Curtis couldn't believe how much she paid attention to what was going on, and it hurt him to know that their problems were affecting her. He didn't want that, and he had never meant to hurt Alicia. But somehow things had run completely out of control. Maybe it was time for him to stop seeing Adrienne and Charlotte, so he could spend more time with Alicia and Tanya. So he could do right by them the way that they wanted him to.

"I know she was, and things are going to be different from now on. And baby girl,

381

I'm sorry if we've been upsetting you."

"I don't want you and Mom to get divorced. I want us to always be together, Daddy. Okay?"

"Baby girl, we're not getting divorced," Curtis said, feeling even worse. "You and Mom and I are a family, and we always will be," he said, hoping that Tanya would forget about her threats of divorcing him, because things really were going to get better once she spoke to the deacons. She hadn't agreed to do it just yet, but he was sure she wasn't going to let him down. She'd been hesitant, but when he'd explained to her that they really did need more money, she seemed to understand it better. And now that he was giving her the attention that she wanted, he was sure she didn't mind doing whatever she could to help him.

"You promise," she said, gazing at him.

"I promise," he said, stopping for a red light.

"I love you, Daddy," Alicia said, smiling.

Curtis stroked her hair. "Daddy loves you, too."

Chapter 25

Tanya was still in awe over the way Curtis was acting. It had been over two weeks since he'd asked her to speak to the deacons, and while she still hadn't agreed to do it, he was continuously showering her and Alicia with all of his attention. He'd done everything from taking the three of them to expensive restaurants to giving Tanya intimate, nightly body massages — something he'd always done when they were first married. But Tanya still wasn't convinced. She'd been praying that his intentions were sincere, but she just couldn't be sure. And it was only a matter of time before she found out one way or the other, because last night he'd told her that he wanted a yes or no answer by this evening.

She heard footsteps coming down the hallway, and she had a feeling that their new blissful way of living was about to be thrown right out of the window, as soon as she told him the bad news, that she couldn't do what he wanted her to.

"So, have you made your decision?" Curtis asked, walking over to the bed where she was sitting, but he didn't sit down beside her.

"Curtis, I've thought about this situation over and over, and I'm sorry, but I can't lie to the deacons about us needing more money when we don't."

"Baby, why won't you support me on this?" he asked, and sat down next to her. "I mean, why can't you just do this one small thing for me?"

"Because I know we don't need more money, and I just can't lie about something like that. The members of the church give a lot of money as it is, and I don't think it would be right for you and me to insist that three thousand dollars a week is not enough money for us to live on. Especially since that money comes from people who mean well. People who expect that the church will do the right thing with their tithes and offerings."

Curtis blew a deep breath and dropped his head into the palm of his hands. Tanya could tell that he was frustrated, and she didn't know what else to say to him. "Do you understand why I can't do this, Curtis?" she asked, hoping he did.

"Understand what?" he said, standing up. "That you won't stand by your own husband? That you want what *you* want, but don't care in the least about what *my* wants and needs are? No. I don't understand anything," he said angrily. "I've gone out of my way over the last couple of weeks trying to be the best husband I could, but that doesn't seem to matter to you. You said you wanted us to work on our marriage, and that's what I've been trying to do. But, Tanya, marriage means both giving and taking."

"So, what you're saying is that the only reason you've been spending so much time with Alicia and me, is because you thought I was going to lie to the deacons for you?"

"No, you're twisting my words. You were the one who said you would think about it. And I assumed that if you weren't going to do it, you would have said no right then and there the first time I asked you about it. But I guess you thought it was better just to string me along."

"Curtis, I wasn't stringing you anywhere. I told you that I would think about it, because I knew you were going to be

385

upset if I didn't do what you wanted me to."

"Well, what's the difference if I'm upset now or two weeks ago."

"Hmmph," Tanya grunted. "You really want me to tell you why I held off for as long as I did?"

"Enlighten me. Please," he said sarcastically.

"Because I knew as soon as I told you no, you were going to start hanging out all night, and that it wouldn't be long before we started having all those arguments again. And I didn't want to go back to that. Alicia doesn't need it, and I don't need it, either."

"So, you thought it was better to just deceive me? Make me think that you were going to support me on this, even though you knew two weeks ago that you weren't. You are really something else," he said in a huff. "And for your information, I wasn't spending time with you just so that you would talk to the deacons."

"Curtis, do you think I'm crazy? I knew from the moment you brought me those roses that you were up to something. And to be honest, I'm surprised you kept it up for this long."

"Doesn't your boss give you raises every six months or so?" he asked.

"Yes, but I don't get twenty percent."

"I'm not asking for twenty percent," he said. "As a matter of fact, it's just over sixteen percent."

"Yeah, but you're talking about sixteen percent of three thousand dollars."

"I deserve it," he said arrogantly. "You know it, the deacons know it, and the congregation knows it."

"Well, like I said, I'm sorry, because I don't agree with that."

"So, that's your decision?" he said, hoping she'd change her mind.

"Yes. I know you don't like it, but that's what my decision is."

"I really thought that things were going to be different with us. I thought that if I gave you what you wanted that you would stand by me until the end. But I guess I was wrong."

"I will stand by you until the end, but not when it comes to something I don't believe in."

Curtis walked into the closet, pulled out a pair of jeans and a polo shirt.

Tanya felt her stomach turning. "Where are you going?" she asked, praying he had a good answer.

"Out," he said, barely acknowledging her question.

"Out where?"

"It doesn't really matter," he said steadily, dressing himself.

"So, now all of a sudden you're going out when the last couple of weeks you've been all over me. Acting like you couldn't get enough of me. Well, two can play that game, brother."

"Threats, threats, and more threats, Tanya. Give it a rest, okay?"

"You know, Curtis. You have really made my life a living hell."

Curtis looked at her, sat down on the loveseat, and slipped on his black loafers. Usually he dressed up whenever he went out, trying to make Tanya believe that he was going somewhere on church business, but not tonight. Tonight, he was dressed like any other man who was about to go out and have a good time with another woman or just have a good time in general. And now that he wasn't being discreet, Tanya was hurt more than ever. She'd told herself that he wasn't being sincere and that he was only using her to get more money, but like any other woman who really wanted her husband to love her, she'd gotten caught up in some whirlwind fantasy.

"So, you're just going to leave? Just like

that?" she asked him when he didn't respond to her last comment.

"That's exactly what I'm going to do."

He picked up his keys and headed out of the bedroom.

When he arrived downstairs near the family room, Alicia looked up from the television. "Daddy, where are you going?"

"Daddy's going out for a while, baby girl."

"Can I go with you?"

"No, not this time," he said guiltily.

"Please, Daddy," she said with watery eyes.

"Sweetheart, come here," he said, reaching his hands out to her.

Alicia ran into his arms and sobbed like it was going to be the end of the world if she couldn't go with him.

"Daddy has to go out, but we'll do something tomorrow, okay?"

"But, Daddy, I want to go with you now," she said between sniffles.

"I know, sweetheart, but Daddy can't take you this time. Now, I have to go, okay," he said, and kissed her on her forehead. She gazed at him sadly, and he walked out of the door.

Tanya walked into the family room just as she heard Curtis leaving and saw Alicia crying. She'd been standing in the living room, listening to their whole conversation but hadn't wanted to see his face again before he left. If she had, she wasn't sure what she might have said to him. "Honey, don't cry," Tanya said, reaching out to hug her daughter.

But Alicia moved away. "Mom, why do you always have to start stuff with Daddy?" she yelled, still crying. "That's why he always leaves us."

Tanya felt a lump in her throat, and she couldn't believe Alicia was speaking to her this way. "Honey, I didn't start an argument with your father."

"But I know you started it, because you start stuff with him every time."

Tanya knew Alicia was hurt and disappointed, but she'd taken all the sass she was going to. "Look, Alicia, I'm the mother in this household, and I'm not going to have you talking to me like I'm one of your little friends. Do you hear me? Now, enough is enough."

Alicia sat silently for a couple of minutes, and Tanya felt bad about the pain her daughter was feeling. But she still couldn't allow her little girl to get beside herself.

Tanya strutted over to the kitchen, drew some water into a glass from the Sparkling

Spring receptacle, shook two pills out of the Extra Strength Tylenol bottle, and swallowed them. She had a horrendous tension headache, and all she wanted to do was lie down. But she sat on the sofa next to her little one instead.

"I'm sorry I had to yell at you, Alicia, but you know better than to talk to me that way."

"I'm sorry," she said, and laid her head on Tanya's lap. Then she asked her mother something Tanya hoped she'd never have to answer.

"Mom, are you and Daddy going to get a divorce?"

And Tanya couldn't lie to her any longer. She wasn't sure if she and Curtis were in fact getting divorced or not, but it certainly was a strong possibility. "I don't know, honey. But no matter what happens, I want you to remember that our problems with each other are not your fault, and that we will always love you."

Tanya hoped that Alicia believed what she was saying, because the last thing she wanted was for her daughter to blame herself for her parents' crazy mess. It wasn't fair that she would probably have to grow up in a broken home, but Tanya was starting to see that there really wasn't anything else she could do about it. She'd tried to make it work, and she'd prayed daily for Curtis to be the husband and father he knew he was supposed to be. But now Tanya knew that all of her efforts were in vain. And that it was time for her to accept things for the way they were. It was time to think about life without Curtis. She hadn't wanted it that way, but there just wasn't any other alternative.

"Girl, I can't take this anymore," Tanya said, leaning back in her bed on a backrest. It was after ten o'clock, Alicia was sound asleep, and, of course, Curtis still wasn't home, and now she was talking to Nicole on the phone.

"But he was doing so well, and you guys seemed so happy," Nicole said.

"Well, we're far from being happy now. And I'm telling you, Nicole. I've had it. You should have seen how hard Alicia was crying when he left."

"Why do you think he needs so much more money?"

"I don't know, but something tells me that he's hiding something. I don't know if he's in some kind of trouble or what, but he's acting so crazy about all of this," Tanya said, bending her knees up toward the middle of the bed.

"You think?" Nicole asked curiously.

"I wouldn't doubt it, because with the way Curtis has been acting, I think anything is possible."

"Maybe he's on drugs," Nicole said, snickering.

Tanya cracked up laughing. "We're joking about it, but I wouldn't put that past him, either."

"Well, what are you going to do?"

"I really think I'm going to file for a divorce. I never wanted to have to do that, but the love between Curtis and me is gone. And now I know that too much has happened to ever get it back, and that the only reason I didn't want to file for a divorce is because I wanted to be like my grandparents. I wanted to stay married until death, because when you take vows before God and become one, you make a lifetime commitment. You're supposed to work your problems out no matter what. Or at least that's how I wanted my marriage to be."

"I know what you're saying, but sometimes it just doesn't work out like that," Nicole said sadly.

Tanya picked up on it. "So, how are you and Eric?"

"I asked him for a divorce two days ago, and all he had to say was 'have the papers drawn up.' "

"Nicole, no," Tanya said, sympathizing with her best friend.

"I finally realized that things weren't going to get any better, and that our marriage has actually been over for a long time now."

"Nicole, I am so sorry."

"Don't be, because I know it's the right thing for us to do. A part of me will always love Eric, but we're just not meant to be together as a couple. And it really makes things easier when the feeling is mutual. We both want this, so I guess I should just be thankful for that."

"I know, but divorce is never easy for anyone."

"No. It isn't. But we'll get through it," Nicole said, sounding as though she was trying to convince herself.

"Well, I'm here for you," Tanya assured her. "Day or night."

"I know you are, and I'm here for you, too, whenever you need me."

"So, do you want to get together for lunch tomorrow?" Tanya asked.

"Sounds good to me. I'll just meet you at your office around noon then."

"Why don't you make it around one, because I scheduled an appointment with one of my clients during her lunch hour."

"That's fine," Nicole agreed.

"Well, I guess I'll see you tomorrow."

"See you then."

Tanya told Nicole good-bye and hung up. Then she wished for this night to be over with.

Curtis paced back and forth until he was tired. He was a nervous wreck, and he wondered what was taking Adrienne so long to get there. He'd called her from his cellular phone and explained that he really needed to see her, but she still hadn't arrived at the condo.

He'd tried to reason with Tanya and she'd let him down the same as she always did. He'd really tried to do right by her, but she just couldn't see things the way he needed her to see them. She was his wife, and a wife had an obligation to her husband. She was supposed to go along with his program, but all she'd done was betray him in every way she could. He'd even made the decision to break things off with Adrienne, and he'd sworn to himself that he wasn't going to see Charlotte again, either. He was going to concentrate on being the family man that Tanya claimed she wanted him to be, but now she'd ruined everything for all of them.

He paced a while longer, and then he heard Adrienne's key turning the lock inside the door.

"What took you so long?" he asked.

"I had to wait for my girlfriend to get home so I could have her call me. You know Thomas would have gotten suspicious with me leaving the house after ten o'clock for no real reason."

"Well, I hope you were careful," Curtis said, sounding worried for the first time.

"I was. I had her call me, and then I told Thomas that she needed me to take her to the emergency room."

"But how do you know he believed you?"

"Thomas doesn't give me the third degree like that, and you know it."

Curtis sat down on the sofa. Adrienne followed behind him and took a seat close to him.

"I couldn't believe you wanted to get together, and I'm really glad you called. I've been praying that you would call all week, and I was going to find a way to get out of the house one way or the other, no matter what," she said, starting to undo her sleeveless shirt.

"No, Adrienne," he said irritably. "All I want to do is talk, all right?"

"What?" she said, frowning. "What do you mean, talk?"

"Look, I'm sorry for the way I've been acting, and I'm sorry that I haven't been spending any time with you, but I've got a lot on my mind, and I've got some serious stuff going on here."

"Like what?"

"For one thing, Tanya and I are worse off than ever before, and there's this thing with the deacons and them not wanting to give me that raise," he said, and paused. "And I'm telling you, baby, if I don't start making more money, you and I are going to have to give up this condo, I won't be able to buy you nice things like I have been, and we can forget about moving away together."

Adrienne stared at him fearfully. "Well, what are we going to do?"

"Well, I don't see any other alternative except for you to convince your husband that my family and I need more money. He'll listen to you, and if you explain it to him in the right way, he'll understand."

"I don't know, Curtis. He's adamant on not giving you a raise, and it sounds like the rest of the deacons feel the same way."

"But he'll listen to you. Tell him that Tanya and I need to start saving for Alicia's college education, and anything else you can think of, if you think it'll work. And if you have to, tell him that they should give me the raise before I start looking for another church."

"But what if he doesn't care about that?" Adrienne asked.

"Then it's up to you to make sure he sees why it's unnecessary for the church to have to go looking for another pastor when they've already had three pastors within the last six years. From what I've heard, the congregation is a little sick of the deacons getting rid of every minister who becomes pastor, so I'm sure they'll think twice if they believe that I'm going to leave."

"I don't know," Adrienne said, sounding as if she wasn't sure that any of what he was saying would work.

"Baby, what other choice do we have?" he said, trying to convince her.

"Maybe you shouldn't ask for so much all at once."

"Damn it!" he yelled. "Why does everyone think they're the expert when it comes to *my* financial situation?"

Adrienne gazed at him in amazement, and it was obvious that she couldn't believe he'd just dropped a four-letter word from his mouth. And he wished he could take it back. He never used words like that, but his back was pressed against the wall, and he didn't have time for all of these silly questions.

"Look, I'm sorry," he said, and sighed. "But I need what I need, and it can't be anything less than that."

"Okay, fine. I'll talk to him."

"Good, because if you can convince him, I guarantee it won't take much to convince the others."

"I missed you so much," she said, leaning over to kiss him.

"I missed you, too," he said, and pecked her on the lips. Then Adrienne stood up and walked toward the bedroom.

"Where are you going?" he asked.

"Where do you think? To get undressed."

"Baby, not tonight. I've got too much on my mind, and I'm too stressed out to make love to you."

"Sweetheart, don't do this. We haven't made love in over two weeks, and I need you."

"Until I get this financial situation

straight, nothing is going to be right. I'm sorry, but that's just the way it is."

Adrienne stood before him with a look of shock on her face, but he couldn't help her, because he didn't have the desire to have sex with her or anyone else. His time was running out, and if he didn't get the money he needed fairly soon, he didn't know what he was going to do. He'd been paying them like they'd told him to, but now they wanted more. And they'd promised him that if he didn't do what they told him, life was never going to be the same for him again. And he'd been dealing with them long enough now to believe it.

Chapter 26

Tanya sighed with relief when Donna Richardson finally announced that it was time to cool down and prepare for the toning exercises. She hadn't worked out since she didn't know when, and the aerobic portion of the videotape had worn her completely out. And she'd even had to slow down a bit after she'd checked her heart rate and saw that it was heading close to one-seventy. This was the best exercise video she'd purchased in a long time, and now she knew why Donna always looked so good. Tanya wanted to look like that, too, and that was the reason why she'd decided yesterday that it was time to tone her body up.

When the workout was over with, Tanya picked up the VCR remote control in the fitness room and zapped the power off. Then she wiped sweat from her face with the plush bath towel, drank sixteen ounces of water, and headed upstairs to her bedroom.

Curtis was in his home office working, the same as he had been for the last couple of evenings, and Alicia was next door having a sleepover with Lisa. Tanya almost didn't know what to do with herself whenever her baby was gone, and she felt all alone. Curtis was still upset about the decision she'd made a few nights ago concerning his salary situation and really didn't have too much to say to her. But it wasn't like she had anything great to say to him, either. So, this whole silent arrangement was just fine with her.

Tanya slipped out of her black two-piece spandex exercise outfit, strolled into the bathroom, and turned on the sink faucet. She eased her hands under the water, rubbed them across a bar of Cuticura soap, smoothed the lather across her face, and rinsed it off with lukewarm water. Then she patted her face dry with a hand towel. She'd had a long day at the center, was totally exhausted, and she couldn't wait to step into the hot, steamy water. Not to mention sliding into her nice, clean bed to relax. She'd changed the sheets right after she'd arrived home, and she could already imagine how good it was going to feel.

She started her bathwater, poured in way too much bubble bath, which was the way she liked it, eased her body into the whirlpool tub, and turned on the jets. Then she closed her eyes. The force of the water felt so soothing, and she could tell that if she stayed in too long, it would only be a matter of time before she dropped off to sleep.

She sat quietly for a few more minutes, and then smiled with her eyes still closed. She was thinking of James, and how gorgeous he was. She'd tried not to think about him, but ever since that day she'd told Curtis that she wasn't going to lie to the deacons and then he'd walked out on her, she hadn't been able to keep her mind off him. It was wrong, and she knew it, but she just couldn't help it. She fantasized about him often, and it felt good when she pictured herself being with someone who really cared about her. Someone who wanted to spend time with her. And someone who wasn't superficial like Curtis. She'd wanted to call James for the last two days, but she'd decided that talking with him was only going to make things worse. She didn't want to see him under rebounding circumstances, and it was better just to leave things the way they were. She wasn't happy about it, but it was best for his sake nonetheless.

Tanya finished her bath, brushed her hair into wrap position, and covered it with a silk night scarf. The wrap style was the best thing someone had come up with for African American hair, and she was grateful for the convenience. Sometimes it dried her hair out too much, but she loved it just the same.

She walked out into the bedroom and saw Curtis entering from the hallway. They looked at each other but didn't say anything, and Tanya wondered why he was even home. Especially on a Friday evening. She hoped he wasn't going to start with her, because she wasn't in the mood for it. She felt relaxed for a change, and all she wanted to do was find a good movie on one of the satellite channels and then fall right off to sleep while watching it. She was getting to the point where she liked it better when he was gone, and now all of a sudden he was hanging around the house.

She moved her body from side to side in the bed until she was comfortable, and then she searched through the TV channels.

"Tanya, I need to talk to you," Curtis said, sitting down on his side of the bed.

Why wouldn't he just leave her alone? Why? Hadn't he had enough of all their arguing? She certainly had.

"Talk to me about what?" she said as calmly as she could.

"Our financial situation is in a mess."

Tanya turned to look at him, and she hoped he wasn't serious.

"What do you mean, our financial situation is in a mess?"

"We have way too many bills to pay, and if I don't start earning more money, I don't know what we're going to do."

Tanya's stomach felt nervous, because for the first time, she could tell that Curtis wasn't lying to her. She didn't know how they could be having financial problems with all of the money he made, and she was afraid to even ask how things had gone wrong.

"How can we possibly have any money problems?" she asked, bracing herself for the answer.

"Because we have more money going out than we have coming in," he said pitifully.

"I know you're kidding," she said, wanting to kick herself for allowing Curtis to handle all of their finances. He'd flat-out insisted on it when they moved to Chicago, reminding her that God had made man head of the household, and that this was the way things were supposed to be done. But now she could tell she was going to be sorry over it. It wasn't as if she didn't pay attention to the bills that came in, because she reviewed every single one of them, and Curtis always paid them from their household checking account. No bill collectors had been calling, no utilities had been turned off, and no vehicles had been repossessed, so she didn't know what he was talking about.

"No, I'm not kidding," he said, unable to look at her.

"What did you do to cause all of this, Curtis?" she asked, raising her voice. She was worried and angry at the same time.

Curtis squinted at her. "Have you taken one look around this house you're living in?" he said defensively. "And look at all the clothes and shoes you have in that walk-in closet," he said, pointing in that direction.

"Oh, now, you just wait a minute," she said, preparing to set him straight. "I'm not the one running around here buying six- and seven-hundred-dollar suits every other week, and I'm certainly not the one who uses a limo service to drive me to the airport or drive me to cities that are barely three hours away from here."

"Tanya, please. You want me to give up everything, but I'll bet you aren't willing to stop getting those expensive hairdos and manicures. And I'll bet you don't plan on staying away from those malls you go to, either."

"No, I don't, because I go to work every day, and the least I should be able to do is get my hair and nails done. And you know good and well that I don't go to the mall on a regular basis. And most of the time when I do go, I'm buying something for Alicia."

"Yeah, whatever," Curtis said, disregarding what she'd said. "Well, all I know is that something has got to give, and if you don't want to see us lose this house and everything in it, I suggest you talk to the deacons like I've been asking you to," he said, looking away from her.

"I know you're not back on that trip again, because I'm not talking to anybody."

"Well, what do you expect me to do?" he asked abruptly.

"I expect you to take that three thousand a week and do the right thing with it. And I suggest you do the same thing with the extra money you earn from doing out-of-town revivals. I trusted you, and if you've forced us into some financial bind, then you'll be the one suffering the consequences, because Alicia and I are going to be fine no matter what."

"Tanya, I know all about your little credit union savings account, so don't make it sound like you've got all this money, because you don't."

"The last time I checked, saving one hundred dollars every week for six years, and two hundred dollars a week for the last two years equals well over fifty thousand dollars, and while that may not seem like a whole lot to someone like you, I'm very proud of it. And it's like I said before, Alicia and I will be fine."

"You never would have even been able to save that much money every week, if it hadn't been for me paying all the bills," he said, sounding jealous.

"When we were in Atlanta, we lived in the church parsonage free of charge, so it wasn't like you had any major bills to pay, and God knows the church here pays you more than enough to stay out of debt."

"Look," he said, raising both of his hands in disgust. "If you're not going to help me out, then I think it would be better for us to end this conversation."

"I never wanted it to begin in the first

place," she said, standing her ground.

"I can't even talk to you anymore," he said, walking toward the doorway.

Tanya ignored him and pretended to watch what was on television. Curtis stood glaring at her, and finally left the room. She could tell that he was really worried, and that he really did need more money for something. Maybe not for household bills, but definitely for something. And it was high time for her to get to the bottom of what he was up to.

Curtis got up from the family room sofa in a frenzy. Beads of sweat covered his face and neck, and he was panting like a dog in ninety-degree weather. He scanned the room, glanced at the woman singing on the gospel channel, and realized where he was. He'd fallen asleep shortly after arguing with Tanya about their financial situation, and had just awakened from a terrible nightmare. It was awful, and just thinking about how vivid the illusion had been made his skin crawl. He'd lost everything. Tanya, Alicia, the church, his home, and his Mercedes. His whole world had collapsed around him, and there hadn't been any way for him to stop it. The congregation had turned completely against him,

409

the deacons had changed the locks on the church and then called the police when he showed up the next Sunday morning to preach. He knew this was nothing more than some crazy dream, and he could've accepted that if it hadn't felt so real. And what if all of this really was going to happen? What if everyone really was out to get him, and there wasn't a single thing he could do about it? His life would definitely be over with. That was for sure.

Why couldn't Tanya just do what he asked? He'd been working on Adrienne for the last couple of days, but so far she hadn't been able to get the deacon to budge one inch. He was wholeheartedly against authorizing Curtis a raise, and Adrienne didn't see where he was going to change his mind about it. She claimed that she'd done everything she could, but Curtis wasn't sure if she had. He didn't trust anyone at this point, and he couldn't tell who was in his corner. With the exception of Tanya, that is, who proved time and time again that she was dead set against him.

Curtis thought about going back upstairs to reason with her one last time, but he knew it wasn't going to change the way she was thinking. Her mind was made up, and whenever it was, she rarely changed it. She had always been that way, and that was another thing he couldn't stand about her. He couldn't stand a lot of things about her, and he wished there was some way he could get his hands on that credit union money she'd thrown in his face. It would solve all of his problems single-handedly, and he'd be able to get back to the life he was used to. But he knew there wasn't any way he could get his hands on it, because he'd seen the quarterly statements, and, unfortunately, his name wasn't anywhere on the account.

No, what he had to do was make Adrienne see how important this was to him, and how he wasn't ever going to speak to her again if she didn't convince the deacon to authorize that money. She wouldn't be able to stand that, and she'd do whatever necessary to make things happen in his favor. And right now, that's all he had to depend on.

Chapter 27

"Can you drop Alicia off at day camp?" Tanya asked Curtis as he stepped out of the master bathroom and moved into the walk-in closet.

"I suppose. Why? Aren't you going to work?"

"I'm taking the day off," she said, pulling out her dirty-clothes basket.

"Taking the day off for what?"

"Because I don't feel like going," she said, wondering why she was having to explain herself to him. She'd already spoken with her *real* boss almost an hour ago, and she didn't know why Curtis felt like he needed to give her the third degree.

"Are you going to pick her up?" he asked in a tone that told her he might not be able to.

And she didn't expect him to anyway. At least not now that he was back to his same old unreliable self.

"Yeah. I can pick her up. Don't even worry about it."

Curtis dressed in silence, and Tanya checked on Alicia to make sure she was almost ready. Then Tanya fixed eggs, bacon, and toast for all three of them. And with the exception of Alicia chattering like she always did, Tanya and Curtis didn't say more than a few words to each other at the table. The tension between them felt as cold as Lake Michigan in December, and Tanya could hardly stand it. She just couldn't keep living this way. Living in the house with a man who didn't want her, let alone spend time with her. Something had to give. She didn't know what, but she knew that things couldn't continue going the way they were.

"You ready, baby girl?"

"Yes," Alicia said, and drank the last of her orange juice. Then she stood up. " 'Bye, Mom," she said, hugging her mother.

"You have a good day, sweetheart, and I'll see you this afternoon when I pick you up."

"Okay," Alicia said, picking up her nylon backpack.

"I'll see you later," Curtis said, pulling

on his suit jacket without even looking at his wife.

Tanya ignored him and turned her attention to Alicia. "You be careful when you guys go hiking today, all right?"

"I will," she said happily. The camp coordinator sometimes scheduled a hiking trip for the children a few times before the summer break was over, and Alicia loved it. She loved anything resembling the great outdoors, and she was always so excited on the days when they went. But Tanya always worried about her, thinking that she might be injured. So far, no accidents had happened, but like all caring mothers, she still worried about it.

As soon as Curtis and Alicia left the driveway and Tanya watched them drive out of the subdivision, she dashed into Curtis's home study and sat down behind his desk. She hadn't been able to tell him the real reason she was taking a day off from work, but this was it. She needed desperately to search through his things to see what was going on. To see why all of a sudden he was spending so much time closed up in there.

She pulled open the left-hand drawer and thumbed through a batch of file folders, but all she saw were sermon outlines, tax information, and a few other legitimate business documents. She continued searching toward the back until she noticed a metal lock-box. She pulled it out, and tried to open it, but it wouldn't budge. She searched throughout the rest of the desk looking for the key but couldn't find it. She knew Curtis was hiding something, and she had to see what it was no matter how she went about doing it.

She sat for a few more seconds, and decided that Curtis would never leave the key lying around out in the open, and that he more than likely kept it on his key ring. Which was why she was going to have to sneak it away from him as soon as he stepped into the shower this evening.

Tanya placed the lock-box back where she'd found it, closed the drawer shut, and opened the one on the right side. She pulled out a stack of Visa credit card statements, but didn't see any charges out of the ordinary. There were way too many of them, but purchasing overly expensive items was the norm for Curtis, so she stacked those on top of the desk, and pulled out a stack of MasterCard statements instead.

"What?" she yelled. She glanced through statement after statement and couldn't believe how many times she saw Bombay Florists listed on each page. A feeling of anxiety latched on to her soul, and her stomach felt like she'd just dipped a few hundred feet on a roller coaster. She didn't know why she was so hurt, but she was. Their marriage was over. She'd decided that herself, but she still didn't want to accept the idea that Curtis had been sending flowers to another woman on a weekly basis when all she'd received from him were the lousy two dozen roses he'd tried to bribe her with not even one month ago. She felt so humiliated, and she couldn't believe he'd actually had the nerve to leave them in his office, practically wide open. And even worse, she couldn't believe she hadn't searched through his desk on a more regular basis. She'd gone through it from time to time, but when she'd come to the realization a few months ago that Curtis probably wasn't stupid enough to leave incriminating material around for her to see, she'd become lax with her detective work. But maybe he'd just placed those statements there this week, and had become too careless to hide things in the proper manner.

She pulled out another folder and cringed again when she flipped through statements from Saks Fifth Avenue and Marshall Field. They'd opened a joint account at both stores, but these statements were boasting an account number that didn't look familiar to her. And she knew full well that she hadn't purchased any lingerie, expensive fragrances, or much of anything at all from Saks in almost a year.

She couldn't believe Curtis would go this far. He'd been spending *their* money, placing charges on *their* account for one of *his* mistresses. She was starting to feel those violent tendencies again as thought after thought gyrated through her mind. She wanted revenge, and she didn't know if she'd be able to sleep at night without paying him back for what he'd done to her. He deserved whatever he got, and she wasn't going to feel sorry for him in the least little bit when he received it.

She dropped the statements on the desk the same as she had the others and leaned back in the chair. She tried to calm herself down because if she didn't, she was going to explode and do something that she would regret for the rest of her life. She kept telling herself that Curtis wasn't worth it, that no man was for that matter, but she was having the hardest time convincing herself of this theory.

She closed her eyes, took a deep breath, and clasped her hands together with her elbows resting on each arm of the chair. She meditated for a while, and opened her eyes. Then she placed each of the statements back into their original filing quarters, shut the drawer and left the office.

She was calm now, and she was going to stay that way until she was able to snatch Curtis's lock-box key from his key ring.

Tanya had wondered if Curtis was ever going to take his shower. He hadn't come home until after ten o'clock, but now it was after midnight, and he was just closing the bathroom door. Finally.

She waited a few minutes, but when she heard the water running and the glass door shutting, she hightailed it over to the chair where he'd laid his clothing and found his keys in his pants pocket. She tossed the keys from side to side. "Shoot," she whispered to herself. There were two small keys on the ring, and she wasn't sure which was which. She didn't know if she should take both of them or not, because the last thing she wanted was for him to miss them and then become suspicious about what she was up to. But on the other hand, if she only took one and it wasn't the one she needed, she'd have to go through this same sneaky process all over again, something she didn't want to do if she didn't have to. Which was why she'd just have to take her chances removing both of them.

She placed them inside her purse and went to check on Alicia one last time, and saw that she was sound asleep. Then she lay back down in the same position she had been in before Curtis walked into the bedroom. She'd pretended to be asleep, and she was planning to do the same thing for the rest of the evening. She didn't want him saying anything to her, and she certainly didn't want to say anything to him, either, because she wasn't sure what might come of their conversation. She'd learned a lot this morning after he and Alicia had left, and she wasn't sure she'd be able to keep it to herself if an argument developed.

No, it was better to play possum for now. At least until she uncovered the remaining pieces to Curtis's hidden puzzle.

Curtis slipped into bed as soon as he finished showering. He tossed from side to side for more than a few minutes, and he was starting to get on Tanya's nerves. She didn't know what his problem was, but whatever it was, she wished he'd get over it. She needed to go to sleep so that they could all get up tomorrow morning as usual and she could drop Alicia off at day camp and then pretend that she was on her way to work.

Curtis sighed deeply, and then sat up. Then he kneeled down on the side of the bed to say his prayers, she guessed. She'd sort of wondered why he hadn't prayed before getting into bed, because praying in bed was completely out of the question for him. He'd always said that a person needed to humble themselves before God, and kneeling was one of the best ways to make that happen.

He stayed on his knees longer than usual, but Tanya still didn't move the slightest inch when he climbed back into bed. He moved his body from side to side again trying to get comfortable, and then called her name. "Tanya?"

But she didn't say anything.

"Tanya?"

She wanted to say something, but didn't.

"After all the moving around in this bed that I've been doing, I know good and well you're not sleeping. So, why are you ignoring me like I'm some child?"

Tanya lay there with her back to him,

staring into the darkness.

"You know, if I weren't a man of God, I would make you sorry that you ever even knew me."

She felt like bursting wide open. She was so angry that she wanted to roll over and shove him off the bed.

But she still didn't say anything to him.

Curtis laughed sarcastically when he saw that she wasn't going to acknowledge his comments, and it wasn't long before Tanya heard him breathing deeply. She tried to envision what was in the mysterious lockbox, and while she couldn't wait to make her discovery, she was fearful at the same time. Fearful that Curtis really was up to something outrageous. Something that neither one of them would ever be able to fix.

Chapter 28

Tanya couldn't wait to get back home, which is why she surpassed the speed limit all the way home from work. Last night she'd planned on skipping another day from work, but when she'd awakened this morning, she decided that she really did need to go in, but that all she actually needed was a few hours in the afternoon, anyway, in order to carry out her investigation.

As soon as she arrived home, she dropped her keys, purse, and briefcase on the kitchen table, kicked her shoes off while walking through the family room, and continued into Curtis's study. She'd already taken the two potential lock-box keys from her purse as soon as she pulled into the garage.

She slid open the right drawer, pulled out the lock-box, inserted the first key into the lock, and opened it. She couldn't believe she'd been successful with opening it on the first try, but she knew it wouldn't have turned out that way had she left one of the keys on her husband's key ring.

She lifted the top of the box and withdrew the first few items lying on top. She opened the white envelope, pulled out a fairly thick document, and covered her mouth. It was a rental/lease agreement for a condo over in Barrington, a prominent northwest suburb of Chicago. The one-year lease appeared to be eight months old, but when she opened the next envelope with the same company name on it, she saw that there had been another lease agreement signed twelve months before the current one. She couldn't believe he'd been secretly renting some condo for almost two years without her knowing one thing about it. Had she been that naïve? She had asked herself that same question more than enough times in the past, and she wondered how she could have been so blind to everything Curtis was doing. She'd accused him of almost everything she could think of, but now that she had proof of his infidelity, and no telling what else, she felt numb. And at the same time, she felt like laughing, because this was all way too much for her to fathom. Her husband, the man who claimed that he'd been called by God, was behind all of this, and she couldn't help but wonder where his conscience was.

She pulled out a stack of envelopes, which were rubber-banded together, and opened them one by one. They each were signed with the inscription "Missing you" or "I love you," but it was obvious that the sender had been extremely careful not to sign her name — with the exception of the last one in the pile that Tanya pulled from a lavender envelope, which was signed, "Yours forever, Adrienne."

Tanya leaned back in total astonishment. The evidence was finally concrete, and there was no more denying the fact or even hoping that Curtis really wasn't sleeping with Adrienne. She'd heard rumor after rumor and now she had to face up to the reality of the entire situation. Curtis had made a fool of her, and that was all there was to it. She'd always told the women in her support group that when a man slept around with other women or physically abused them, it wasn't their fault. But now she wanted to ask herself what she'd done wrong or what she hadn't done for that matter to make things better between them. But she knew there was no sense in trying to figure out any of this, because, in actuality, there wasn't any real logic to it.

She pushed the cards and lease agreements to the side, and pulled out the next document. It was folded in half, so Tanya opened it. And it was all she could do to keep her composure. She scanned down the page and slowly moved her head from left to right in total confusion. How many more surprises were there going to be? She was stunned beyond her wildest imagination, and this had to be the worst thing he'd done thus far. He'd actually paid for Adrienne to have an abortion. She gazed through the document again, and wondered once more why Curtis had been careless enough to keep this pathetic information in their household. Right under her nose. Was it that he didn't care whether she found out, or simply that he truly believed she would never go probing through his things? Either way, it didn't make much sense to her. And how stupid was Adrienne for even thinking that they could continue to get away with any of this? And if Tanya had been a gambler, she'd be willing to bet everything she owned that Adrienne had somehow allowed herself to believe that she and Curtis really would eventually marry and then ride off into the beautiful sunset. She was almost as naïve as Tanya, but from a different perspective. Adrienne believed that the impossible was going to happen, and Tanya believed that the obvious wasn't really going on. Or at least she'd wanted to believe that nothing was going on, because deep down she'd always known that Curtis wasn't sneaking around town for nothing. But the killing part of it all was that he walked around every day like nothing unusual was happening, and that he was doing nothing more than what God told him to do. It was all so insane, and Tanya was starting to think that maybe Curtis needed help. That maybe his apples weren't lined up on the table the way they needed to be.

But Tanya knew that there wasn't the tiniest thing wrong with Curtis's mind, and that the only problem he had was money, women, and power. All three of the above had slung him completely over the edge, and the reason he thought he could do whatever he pleased whenever he felt like it. But now, though, the truth was out. It always came out in every other situation, and Curtis's predicament wasn't any different.

Tanya searched through a few more documents, but didn't find anything else as eye-opening as the previous one. She still couldn't get over it, and now she had to figure out a way to bring Curtis down. She despised having a vengeful nature, but she didn't care about morals or values anymore. She'd placed all of her faith in God, and gone out of her way to do the right thing, but where had it gotten her?

She was angry, and she had a mind to leave the lock-box sitting right on top of Curtis's desk, just to let him know that his skeletons were hanging completely out of the closet. But she decided that it was better to place it back in the drawer where she'd taken it from.

But just as sure as the rain in April, Curtis was going to be sorry.

Because Tanya had come up with the plan of the century.

After picking up around the house, and warming up day-old chicken, Tanya sat down to watch *Judge Judy* like everything was fine. She'd decided what she was going to do with her newfound information, but after that, she needed to see James. She needed to see him tonight, and she was going to give him a call just as soon as she made sure that Alicia's babysitter was available. She hadn't wanted to resort to being with him, at least not under these circumstances, but now she didn't care about that. And she didn't know what she was going to do if she wasn't able to contact him. She didn't want to use him because of what she'd found out about Curtis, but she needed to talk to him. She needed someone to listen to her problems. Someone to hold her if it became necessary.

She finished eating her leftovers and then picked up the telephone. She'd decided that she was only going to tell one other person what she knew, but after thinking about it, she realized that there was no way she could keep all of this information from Nicole. She had to tell her as well, and there wasn't going to be any better time than right now. She dialed her best friend's phone number and waited for her to answer.

"Hello?"

Tanya started right in. "Girl, if you're not sitting down, you'd better find a chair quick before I say what I have to say."

"I am sitting down, so what's up?" Nicole asked curiously.

"I worked this morning, but I decided to take the afternoon off so I could come home and do a little investigating."

"Investigating?" Nicole laughed. "What kind of investigating?"

"I found this lock-box in Curtis's desk here at the house, and when I opened it, I found a lease agreement for a condo, and a bunch of cards from Adrienne telling Curtis that she *missed him* and that she *loved him*," Tanya mocked Adrienne in a girlish tone of voice. "And I won't even discuss all the credit card statements I found with charges for flowers, lingerie, and a lot of other women-related purchases that I know I didn't make."

"Tanya! Girl, you have got to be kidding."

"No, I'm not. And you wouldn't believe what else I found. You won't believe it in a million years."

"What?"

"Some paperwork showing that Adrienne had an abortion up in Michigan."

Nicole was flabbergasted.

"Get out! Are you sure? I mean, maybe you read it wrong or made a mistake."

"Oh, it wasn't a mistake. It said what it said, and it was very clear. And that bastard is going to pay for everything he's ever done to me. I guarantee you that."

"Look, Tanya," Nicole said, sounding concerned. "Don't you do anything you'll regret later, because Curtis and nobody else is worth going to prison over."

Tanya didn't respond.

"Tanya? Do you hear what I'm saying?"

"I hear you, but Curtis has to get what's coming to him. Every dog does eventually, and that's just the way it is."

"What are you planning to do?"

"I don't know yet," Tanya lied.

"I hope it's not anything that will get you into trouble, because you have a daughter who needs you. So, if you don't think about anything else, please think about her well-being."

"Don't worry, everything will be fine when it's all said and done. Just watch."

"I don't like the sound of what you're saying," Nicole said worriedly. "Gosh, I hate that any of this is happening, because I don't want anything bad to happen to you, Tanya."

"Girl, stop worrying. I told you everything is going to be fine. But I will tell you one thing. I'm calling James as soon as I hang up with you. And if he still wants to see me, I'm going to be with him."

"Do you think you should? I mean, given the situation?"

"Why shouldn't I?"

"I don't know, but I hate to see you do

something just to get back at Curtis."

"Yeah, I thought about that, too, but I really do like James. I like him a lot. And it's not like I have a marriage any longer, because I'm telling you, it's over between Curtis and me. I'm through with him for good. Or at least I will be after he gets what's coming to him. I'm going to give him ten times the dose of his own medicine, and I'm going to teach him a lesson he won't ever forget for as long as he lives."

"I don't know, girl," Nicole said cautiously. "I hope you think about what you're doing before you do it. You've got me worried sick, and I won't rest until I know that you've let this whole Curtis thing go."

"Nicole," Tanya said, cracking up. "I'm not some crazed maniac. It's not like I'm going to slit his throat open or anything like that."

"I sure hope not, because what sense would it make for you to hurt him? And it's like I said, Alicia needs you."

"I'm not going to do anything that will hurt my baby. And I'm not going to do anything that will take me away from her, either. I promise."

"Well, that makes me feel somewhat

better, but not a whole lot."

"Why not?"

"I don't know. I guess because you sound so calm about all of this. You know they say that people who stay calm in the wake of tragedy or pain are the most dangerous people you can mess with."

Tanya laughed again. "Nicole, the only reason I'm so calm is because I finally have proof of what Curtis has been doing behind my back. At first it really hurt me, but now I feel more relieved than anything. There's no more wondering, and now I won't have to shed any more tears. And the best thing of all is that I won't have to listen to any more of his lies."

"Well, when are you planning to confront him?"

"I'm not. At least not until the time is right."

"I don't know how you're going to be able to look him in the face and, even worse, sleep in the same bed with him knowing that he's sleeping with Adrienne."

"I've already been doing it for months now, so what's the difference?"

"The difference is that you didn't know for sure if he was messing around or not."

"Trust me, I can do it. As a matter of fact, I'll be killing him with so much kindness that he'll swear I've lost my mind."

"I guess. But like I said . . ."

Tanya interrupted. "I know, I know, I know. Don't do anything I'll regret."

"I mean that," Nicole said sincerely. "Because if you do, you'll just be stooping to Curtis's level."

Tanya didn't say anything, because the payback she was planning for Curtis was going to make *his* sins seem like child's play. She was making all the rules for this game she was about to play, and there was no way Curtis and Adrienne would recover from it. And if they did, it wouldn't be until a long time from now.

"I told you, there's nothing to worry about. I've got everything under control. Now let me get off this phone, so I can call the babysitter and then call James. But I promise I'll call you tomorrow and fill you in."

"You take care of yourself, okay?"

"I will, and I'll talk to you later."

Tanya pressed the flash button on the phone and called the babysitter's mother, who said she'd have Sheila come right over as soon as she arrived home from the community college where she was taking summer courses. Then Tanya flipped through Curtis's Rolodex that listed all of the deacons' daytime phone numbers, and called Deacon Jackson. And, of course, he'd agreed to meet with her as soon as she told him how urgently she needed to speak to him.

Tanya glanced at her watch and saw that she only had two hours to drop by Kinko's, meet with the deacon, and then pick up Alicia. But she had to call James before she left the house.

"This is James."

"How are you?" she said somewhat nervously.

"I'm fine. How are you?" he asked. She could tell he was happy to hear from her.

"I'm fine. Hey, I don't have a lot of time, but I was wondering if we could get together this evening."

"Where? At the club?"

"No. If it's okay with you, I'd rather meet you somewhere that will give us a little more privacy."

"Whoa," he said shockingly. "Where is all this coming from?"

"I'll explain it to you when I see you. If that's okay?"

"No problem," he said. "Do you want to meet me at my condo?"

"That's fine."

James told her his home address, she

told him she'd be there no later than seven, and they ended their phone conversation.

Tanya wondered if revenge was as sweet as everyone made it seem. But whether it was or not, she was only minutes away from paying back both Curtis and Adrienne for every single heartache, every single tear, and every single worry that they each had caused her over these last two dreadful years.

She hadn't wanted things to end up like this, but now she knew that this was the only way to secure at least some satisfaction for what she'd been putting up with. And she hoped Deacon Jackson wasn't going to be too hurt over what she had to show him. He'd always seemed like a decent man, and the last thing she wanted was to cause him a load of unnecessary pain. But he was going to find out sooner or later anyhow, and it was better for him to receive the information in private than for him to hear it later, when he was totally and completely caught off guard. And besides, telling the deacon all but guaranteed that Tanya would finally be able to pay Adrienne back in the worst way possible.

Tanya parked in the area where Deacon

Jackson had instructed her to. He worked for an insurance company out in Skokie, one of the north suburbs, and now Tanya was waiting patiently for him to walk outside of the building.

She waited for almost ten minutes, and then finally she saw him heading in her direction. He looked just as neat as ever in his navy-blue business suit, and Tanya could tell from the look on his face that he didn't have even the slightest clue about what she was about to disclose to him.

He opened the passenger door to her SUV and hopped in.

"So, how's it going, Sister Black?" he asked, smiling.

"Unfortunately, Deacon, not so well. I found out some things today that were pretty shocking, and I really thought you deserved to know what's going on."

He wrinkled his forehead with curiosity. "Like what?"

"Like your wife has been sleeping with my husband almost the entire time we've been living in Chicago."

"What?" he said, and Tanya could tell he didn't want to believe what she was saying.

"Yes. They've been renting a condo over in Barrington."

"Barrington? How do you know?"

Tanya removed from an envelope the set of copies she'd made for him and passed it to him. He searched through each one, and leaned his head back against the headrest. He was hurt, and that was the one thing Tanya had been afraid of.

"Where did you find all of this?"

"Curtis had it locked up in his desk at home."

"I can't believe this," he said, looking out of the window. "I can't believe that ungrateful *bitch* would do something like this."

Tanya saw him staring at the statement from the abortion clinic, and didn't know what to say.

"They actually had nerve enough to get rid of a baby," he declared. "Here, I can't even have a child, and they think they have the right to just kill one?"

"I'm really sorry, Deacon, but I had no choice but to call you." Tanya felt bad for him, because she'd had no idea that he was sterile. And she could only imagine how painful all of this must be for him, wanting a child and then finding out that his wife had been pregnant by someone else.

"I've never loved a woman the way that I love Adrienne, and I've gone out of my way to try and give her everything she could possibly want."

"Well, I know I've tried to be the best wife to Curtis, but as you can see, none of that made any difference to him, and it certainly didn't stop him from being unfaithful to me. I've been hearing rumors about Adrienne for the longest time, but it wasn't until today that I actually had proof of it."

"How long have you been hearing them?" he asked, looking at Tanya directly for the first time.

"Almost the whole time we've been living here."

"I've never heard anything like that," he said sincerely. "I heard that he was messing around with a bunch of different women in the church, but not once did anyone tell me that Adrienne was supposed to be one of them."

That was hard for Tanya to believe. But then, maybe no one in the church had found the courage to tell him what they knew. But even if he hadn't suspected her and Curtis, it still didn't seem logical that he hadn't suspected at least something. Especially since Adrienne had to be spending an awful lot of time away from home.

But then who was she to judge anyone, because she hadn't been the brightest student in the class over the last couple of years herself. And it was always a whole lot easier to slip into denial than it was to admit that the person you loved wanted someone else.

"So, does he know that you found all of this?" he asked.

"No, and I don't want him to until I've figured out how I'm going to handle it."

"You know, people get killed for less than this every day."

Tanya didn't like the sound of that. "But they're not worth it. I'm not planning to let Curtis just get away with this, but I'm not going to prison for him, either."

"You know, I've asked Adrienne a hundred times to tell me if she's not happy, and she always says that everything is fine. And it really pisses me off that she's been lying to me all along. And I don't even want to tell you how I feel about your husband, because he's supposed to be the leader of our church."

Tanya blamed both Curtis and Adrienne equally, but she could see Deacon Jackson's point, with Curtis being a pastor and all.

"I know what you're saying, but I think that you and I ought to benefit from all of this, one way or another," Tanya suggested.

"We didn't go through all of this for nothing."

"How in God's name could she do this to me?" Deacon Jackson said, not paying the slightest bit of attention to Tanya's comments. And he was acting as though he was in his own little world.

"Deacon Jackson!" Tanya called.

He looked at her, and Tanya felt sad when she saw tears rolling down his face. She tried to console him, but she could tell that the pain was almost too striking for him to bear.

They sat there for almost another hour, and Tanya finally convinced him that they had to do something. Not violently, but in a very intelligent manner.

Then Tanya left to pick up Alicia, stopped at a pizza place for an all-cheese pizza, the way Alicia sometimes liked it, and headed home. When Sheila arrived, Tanya kissed Alicia good-bye and told Sheila that she would be gone for at least the next three to four hours.

Chapter 29

She'd been so eager to see James, but the more Tanya drove, the more nervous she was starting to become. His condo was barely minutes away now, and she wasn't sure if she'd made the right decision by calling him. She'd been so upset this afternoon, and maybe she had reacted too quickly and hadn't allowed herself enough time to think everything through. Maybe Nicole had been right when she'd told her to think before doing something she just might regret.

But it was too late now.

She'd already pulled in front of James's condo and parked. And there was clearly no turning back. She sat there for a few minutes gathering her thoughts and trying to calm her nerves, then she stepped out of her Navigator and walked up the driveway. She glanced around and prayed that there wasn't anyone watching her. At least not anyone who might know her from the church. She'd been nervous about that same thing the three times she'd been with him, and she hoped that no one she knew lived in this vicinity.

She stepped up to the door and rang the bell. James opened it and smiled at her.

"Hey," he said. "Come on in."

Tanya walked through the doorway. "So, how are you?"

"I'm fine now that you're here," he said, hugging her.

Tanya smiled back at him and sort of waited for his next move. But in the meantime, she gazed around his living room. "You really have a nice place," she said, complimenting his black leather furniture, glass coffee tables, and beautiful artwork.

"For a man, you mean. Right?" he said, laughing.

"No. For anyone. I really like the way you have it decorated," she said, wondering if his ex-wife or some other female friend had helped him put everything together. But who knew? Maybe he had great contemporary taste and knew how to mix great color schemes together on his own. A lot of men didn't, but there were quite a few who did.

"Thanks." James walked toward the

kitchen. "Why don't you have a seat, and I'll be back in a minute."

"What's that I smell?" she asked, sitting down on the sofa.

"I thought I'd throw a little something together. I hope you have an appetite."

"As a matter of fact, I do. I ate one piece of my daughter's pizza, but that was about it."

"Good. The casserole is just about ready, and I'm taking the dinner rolls out now."

She was impressed. A man who looked good, was intelligent, and thought enough of her to cook dinner. Not to mention the wonderful jazz that had been playing since the moment she walked in. The atmosphere was filled with romance, and it all seemed too good to be true. Her nerves had settled, and she felt content. Even if it might only be for one night.

"Would you like something to drink?" he asked, walking toward her with two glasses in one hand and a bottle of wine in the other.

"Sure, why not?" she answered without thinking twice about it.

James poured wine into both glasses, set the bottle on the coffee table, and took a seat next to her. "It's still hard to believe that you actually called me and wanted to get together."

"I know."

"So, what happened?" he asked, taking a sip of his drink.

"Where do I begin?" she said, lifting her knee up on the sofa and turning her body toward him. Then she took a sip of her wine as well.

"That bad, huh?" He set his glass down on the table, turned his body toward her and leaned his elbow comfortably on the back of the sofa.

"I found out some things today that sort of surprised me. Well, I don't know that they surprised me as much as they shocked me. But either way, I wasn't prepared for any of it."

"I'm sorry to hear that."

"First of all, I found out that Curtis has been renting a condo over in Barrington for almost two years, and the killing part of it all is that we've only been living in Chicago for just a little over two years in the first place. He moved here a couple of months before Alicia and I to get everything situated, but it looks to me he started seeing Adrienne as soon as he relocated."

"How do you know her name?"

"She's a member of our church, and

she's one of the deacons' wives."

James chuckled. "I know this isn't funny, but I can't believe that all of this is going on right in the church."

"I know. It's really sad, but unfortunately, it happens all the time. Look at all the trouble Henry Lyons was involved in, and he was head of the National Baptist Convention USA."

"Yeah, and now he's sitting in prison somewhere," James said.

"I know, and if he hadn't been convicted, he probably would have been able to keep his position, because a lot of the other members of his organization had nerve enough to defend him right on national TV."

"I saw that. And it makes you wonder what they've been up to as well, because there's no way anybody in their right mind could justify defending a pastor who has stolen money and one who sleeps around with other women. His wife didn't burn down that house for nothing. You can believe that."

"You're right. But the sad part of this all is that there really are some wonderful, committed pastors in this country, and not every minister is out to deceive people. But it's the few like Curtis who give all of the rest of them a bad name."

"What I think," James said, standing up, "is that people have to really pay attention to who their church leaders are, and they need to make sure that they are placing their faith in God more so than in the man who stands up in the pulpit on Sunday morning." He walked back into the kitchen.

"Those are my thoughts exactly. It's almost like some people worship their pastor, and that's not how it's supposed to be. And some women seem to lose their minds over ministers. Especially ministers who have money, power, or both. Women are attracted to that."

"This is true," James said, and Tanya could hear him removing something from the oven.

"Can I help you with anything?" she asked.

"You can help me bring everything to the table if you want."

Tanya drank the last of her white wine, and walked around to the dining area and into the kitchen. She hadn't been able to tell for sure when she'd been sitting in the living room, but she'd thought she saw a reflection of burning candles. Which was exactly what it had been. James hadn't forgotten anything, and she couldn't remember the last time she'd had a candlelight dinner. His condo was huge, almost the size of a small house. And he had to be paying a pretty penny for it, too.

Tanya moved the bowl of salad and a bottle of vinaigrette dressing to the dining-room table and then the basket of rolls. James sat an iron trivet on the table and set the tuna casserole dish down on top of it.

"Do you want anything to drink? Like a soft drink or juice or something?" he asked.

"No, but I will have some water."

He fetched two bottles of Perrier from the fridge, and Tanya watched him. He looked gorgeous in his black linen shorts and white polo shirt. And it was almost as if he was reading her mind, because when he sat down at the table, he complimented the way she looked.

"Did I mention how beautiful you look this evening?" he asked her with a sexy smile on his face.

"No. You didn't."

"Well, you do. That dress was made for you," he said, and she was glad she'd chosen to wear her sleeveless, navy-blue dress that dropped all the way down to her ankles.

When Tanya finished her salad, she took a decent helping of casserole.

"You're a good cook. Probably better than I am."

"I doubt that, but I do okay," he said, tearing a dinner roll in two.

"So, tell me," James continued, "how do you know for sure that your husband has been seeing this Adrienne person?"

"She's been giving him cards that say 'I love you' or 'I miss you,' and she made the mistake of signing one of them. And there're a few other things that I don't even want to go into," she said, not wanting to tell him about the abortion paperwork she'd discovered. She still couldn't get over it. Especially since Curtis preached about it all the time and how wrong it was for people to commit such a vile sin. But it was all going to come out in the open in just a short period of time. She was going to make sure of it.

"So, have you confronted him about any of it?"

"No, and I'm not going to for a while. I've got to think things through, but I'm definitely filing for a divorce, and I know for sure that our marriage is over with for good."

"Well, all I can say is that I've been

there. And if you need to talk, all you have to do is let me know."

"I know that. And I appreciate it," she said, smiling at him.

They finished their dinner and walked back into the living room. Tanya prepared to sit down, but James pulled her into his arms before she could. Then he looked down at her.

"So, are you enjoying yourself?" he asked, placing her arms around his neck.

"Yes. And thanks for dinner. I wasn't expecting anything like that, so it was a nice surprise."

"So, what do we do now?" he asked, still gazing into her eyes.

"I don't know. You tell me."

He looked at her for another split second and then he kissed her much more passionately than he had that afternoon in the park. She kissed him back, and she wished that her time with him would never end.

They kissed for a long time, and Tanya was sure that it wouldn't be long before they placed this passion of theirs on much higher ground, but James gently pulled his lips away from hers.

"I think we'd better sit down before we do something you'll regret," he said, pulling her by her hand to the sofa.

"So, what are you saying? That you won't regret it, too?"

"You know *I* won't regret it, because I've wanted to make love to you ever since the first time we met. But I don't want to push you into doing something you won't be able to live with tomorrow morning when you wake up."

Tanya wanted him so badly, but she knew he was right when he said that she might regret it when it was all said and done. "I don't want to hurt you, James."

"Well, tell me this, are you only here because you want to get revenge on your husband, or are you here because you really wanted to spend time with me?"

She paused for a minute and thought about his question. "I have to admit, getting revenge was part of my reason when I called you this afternoon. I didn't want it to be, but it was. But I know now that I'm here because I genuinely want to be with you. I'm attracted to you like I've never been attracted to anyone, and the feelings that I have for you are just as real."

"Well, you know I feel the same way," he said, caressing the side of her face.

She closed her eyes and enjoyed it.

He eased her body down on the sofa and lay on top of her. They kissed again, but in a much more erotic manner. Things were heating up between them, and they both knew that their making love to each other had become inevitable. There was no way getting around it, and neither of them wanted to.

James lifted his body and stood up. Then he pulled her up and led the way to his master bedroom upstairs. They stood in the center of the floor kissing and removing their clothing. The music was still playing just as clearly as it had been on the first floor, and Tanya was thankful that he had a speaker positioned in his bedroom. The sound of it had set the mood, and it had allowed their feelings for each other to escalate to a whole new level.

James turned the comforter and top sheet back and waited for her to lie down. And when she did, he lay to the side of her. "All I want is to satisfy you."

"You already have," she said, and this time she initiated the kiss between them.

He rubbed her body down with coconut oil and caressed her breasts with both hands. She moaned with great desire for more, and he took each one in turn into his mouth.

She moaned even louder. The foreplay had gone on for way too long, and what she wanted now was the icing on the cake.

But he ignored her moans and groans for a while longer, teasing her.

"Please," she begged him in a breathless tone of voice. "James, please."

He stroked his hand slowly and smoothly between her legs, and she wailed loudly with pleasure.

Then he eased inside her and gave her what she'd been pleading for. They made beautiful love with each other, and when they climaxed, tears streamed down each side of Tanya's face.

They lay there for a few minutes catching their breaths until James felt her stomach shaking beneath him. He raised up and looked at her and saw that she was crying silently.

"Sweetheart, what's the matter?" he asked.

Her body shook a few times before she spoke. "I've never felt this way with anyone before. I can't even explain how wonderful you make me feel."

"I know what you mean. There's something special between us, and I knew it from the very beginning. I've had chemistry with other women, but not like there is between us," he said, moving over on his back and pulling her toward him.

She snuggled next to him and laid her head on his chest. "I feel so close to you, and I just don't know how that could be."

"Why? Because we haven't known each other very long or because of your other situation?"

"Both. I just didn't know I could feel this way about another man. And to tell you the truth, I've never felt quite this way about any man. Not even my own husband."

"Sometimes two people can be compatible in every way except when it comes to their passion for each other. And eventually, if the passion isn't right, the relationship is guaranteed to go downhill. It's just human nature to look somewhere else for what you're not getting at home. It's not right, but that's usually how things happen. That's the reason my ex-wife and I separated. She wasn't content with me sexually, and I wasn't one hundred percent content with her, either, and I knew it was only going to be a matter of time before one of us started looking elsewhere. And I can't be sure that she didn't, because toward the end, she spent a lot of time away from home. But I don't blame her, because now I know that there has to be this certain attraction before it can be right for two people and stay that way for years to come."

"But wouldn't you know it. We have the attraction and the passion, but I'm married," she said, sighing deeply.

"Things never turn out perfectly, do they?"

"Not for me anyway."

James didn't comment.

Tanya continued. "I've got to get out of this situation as soon as I can, though, because I can't live this lie between Curtis and me any longer. It'll kill my daughter, but I don't see how an unloving marriage is helping her, either."

Tanya raised up and saw that it was getting late. "I need to get ready to go."

"Why don't you stay the night?"

"I can't. I don't want my daughter waking up in the morning and I'm not there."

"At least stay a little while longer."

"I really want to. You know I do. But I can't."

"I understand," he said disappointedly.

"Sorry," she said, raising her head from his chest to look up at him.

He pulled her body on top of him, and they kissed even more intimately than they had earlier, something Tanya hadn't thought was possible. But this particular kiss felt different, and it wasn't just about their sexual passion for each other either. It was more about their true feelings for each other. She felt her heart beating, and she couldn't tell whose was beating more rapidly, his or hers.

James stopped kissing her, but hugged her tightly. Then he sighed in frustration. "Damn," he said. "I'm in love with somebody else's wife."

She didn't know how to respond to what he'd just said. Was he serious? Maybe he was just playing head games with her, but that didn't seem like his way of doing things. She wanted to tell him that she was having those same feelings for him, but she didn't know if she should, given her problems at home.

"Do you really mean that?" she asked.

"Yes. I do. I've been in love with you since the day I met you. I know people always say that, but now I know what they mean by it. I mean, I wasn't madly in love with you that first night, but it was love nonetheless. Then when I saw you again at the club that night you were with your girlfriend, my feelings for you grew just a little more, and I haven't been able to think straight ever since you called and told me that we couldn't see each other anymore. And I was prepared to live with that if I had to, but now, after making love to you, I know for sure that I don't just love you, but that I'm *in* love with you."

"Are you sure? Maybe it's just infatuation," she said, sort of making a joke.

But it was obvious that he didn't see the humor in it. "Sweetheart, believe me. I'm much too old to be infatuated when it comes to being in love with someone. So, trust me. The love I'm feeling for you is real."

"Too old?" Tanya said, and realized they'd never discussed their ages. James looked to be in his middle thirties or so, but she hadn't really thought too much about it.

"I'm thirty-nine. And if I don't know what's real and what isn't by now, I never will."

She hadn't thought he was almost forty, because he didn't look it. But it really didn't matter to her how old he was, and his age was probably the reason why he knew what he wanted in a relationship and the reason why he knew how to treat a woman in the manner that she needed to be treated.

"And I'm telling you," he continued, "I

would marry you right now if I could. People get married every day, but a person only gets one chance to marry the person who is really meant for them."

She stared at him, and she could no longer hold back what she was thinking. "James, I love you, too."

They kissed each other, caressed each other, and made love until almost midnight.

Chapter 30

Tanya drove most of the way home by instinct, because her thoughts were completely consumed with James and what had evolved between them. It had been hard to leave him, and now that it was almost one o'clock in the morning, she hoped for the first time that Curtis wasn't home yet. She'd told Sheila before she left that if for some reason she ended up staying out a little later than eleven, Sheila could spend the night in the guest room. Sheila had said that was fine, and that was one reason why Tanya hadn't exactly rushed when it came time to leave James's condo. She'd wanted to spend the night with him like he wanted her to, but she knew it just wasn't possible. Curtis would have been livid, and she didn't want to explain her whereabouts to Alicia, either.

She wanted to call Nicole, so she could tell her about her intimate evening with

James, but it was much too late to be calling anyone at this hour. Well, too late to be calling and waking up Nicole's husband Eric, anyway, who wasn't going to be moving out for at least another couple of weeks. But Nicole, on the other hand, wouldn't have cared what time it was in the least, once Tanya filled her in on the details. But it was better to wait until tomorrow morning instead.

Tanya drove into the subdivision and noticed that the light was dimmed in the family room. She figured maybe Sheila had left it on by mistake before going to bed, but when she pressed the garage-door opener, she saw Curtis's Mercedes parked on the right-hand side and then realized that Sheila's car was no longer in the driveway. Tanya swallowed hard, because she didn't know how Curtis was going to take her being out to the wee hours of the morning for the first time since he'd married her. The tables were finally turned, and she hoped she wasn't going to have to argue with him, because she wasn't in the mood for it.

She couldn't believe that of all nights, he'd decided to come home early. She'd been so sure that Sheila was still going to be there when she arrived, and now she didn't know what was about to happen between her and Curtis now that she was gone.

She parked her vehicle and walked into the house. The security system was already set, and she knew Curtis had done that on purpose, because they almost never set it until everyone was in the house for good.

She typed in the code to disarm the system and kicked off her sandals. She heard the television playing. It was turned down fairly low, but, still, she could hear it. She saw the back of Curtis's head, and she decided that it was better just to keep walking until she arrived in her bedroom upstairs.

But Curtis wasn't having it.

"Where in the hell have you been all evening?" he yelled.

"Curtis. Don't start with me, okay?" Tanya said, preparing to head down the hall to the stairway.

"Oh, you're just going to ignore me like I'm not even here, I guess?" he said, standing up. "Well, you can either answer me down here, or we can take it upstairs where Alicia is, and I know you don't want that."

Tanya blew out a deep sigh. She didn't want to deal with him, but she had a feeling that if she didn't discuss this situation with him right now, he really would follow her upstairs. And he was right, she didn't want to disturb her daughter.

"Curtis, for months and months you've been leaving this house, going wherever you feel like going, and you have the nerve to ask me where I've been? You're the last person who should be worried about that, as far as I'm concerned."

"I'm your husband, and I want to know where you've been till one o'clock in the morning. And I want an answer right now," he said in a hostile tone.

She folded her arms and stared at him in silence.

"So, you're not going to answer me, I guess? Well, I already know anyway, because any wife who stays out this late on a weeknight can't be doing anything else except sleeping with another man."

"Whatever, Curtis," she said, knowing he was right.

"So, who is it? Who have you been screwing around with, Tanya?" he asked, moving closer to her.

She hoped he wasn't going to put his hands on her, because she didn't want to go through any more physical ordeals with him. He'd put his hands on her that one

461

time, and that was all she was willing to take. But the desperation in his eyes frightened her. He was yelling like a madman, and she didn't like the idea of him inching closer and closer to her. So she moved away from him.

"Look, Curtis, what I do is my business, and what you do is yours. And as far as I'm concerned, the only woman you need to worry about is Adrienne."

"Don't even try it," he said, pointing at her. "This is about you and your whoring around. Not about me."

"I'm not whoring around, and if I were you, I would get my life in order, because your days of deception are becoming more and more numbered by the minute. Now I'm going to bed," she said, and turned to walk away.

"Is that a threat?" he asked, grabbing her by her throat just as he had that night in their bedroom.

"Curtis, stop it!" she yelled, trying to pry his hands away from her neck.

"You think I'm playing games with you, don't you? Well, I'll show you how much of a game I'm playing," he said, shoving her onto the couch, then dragging her off it by her legs and kicking her in her side.

She rolled away from him as quickly as

she could, but he lunged on top of her. They tussled back and forth on the floor, both of them gasping for breath . . .

Until Tanya reached her arm back toward the fireplace and picked up the poker. She forced it into his stomach as hard as she could, and he rolled off her, yelling.

She stood up and struck him across his legs with it.

He jumped up. "You crazy bitch!" he screamed.

She swung at him again, but he moved out of her way. She rushed over to the kitchen sink, jerked a butcher knife from the drawer, and dropped the poker down to the floor.

Then she chased him through the hallway and into the living room, with the knife raised over her head. She wanted to kill him.

But when she swung at him, he jumped out of her way again, grabbed her arm and then twisted it behind her back, forcing the knife to fall onto the carpet.

"Mommm!" Alicia yelled at the top of the stairway. "Daddy, stop it! Why are you hurting Mom like that? Stop it!" Alicia screamed.

Curtis released Tanya from his hold and

ran up the stairs to comfort his daughter. "Baby girl," he said, reaching out to her.

"Nooo!" she screamed at the top of her lungs, moving away from him. "Mom, make him leave me alone."

"Come here, sweetheart," Tanya said, crying. "It's okay."

Alicia took three steps down, and before they all had a chance to realize it, she slipped and tumbled down the rest of the way.

And there was no movement from her body after she landed.

"Oh, God, no," Tanya wept. "Please, not my baby. Pleeease."

Curtis ran down the stairs, and checked for Alicia's pulse.

"Call 911," Tanya ordered him, and he did.

"Alicia. Baby. Wake up. Come on, honey. Please wake up," Tanya pleaded with her unconscious little girl.

"They'll be here as soon as they can, and they said not to move her," Curtis said, walking toward her with the cordless phone.

Tanya had already thought of that. She'd wanted to grab her into her arms, but she was afraid that something might be broken, since she'd toppled down at least ten steps of the staircase. So, instead, she sat next to her caressing her face and gently rubbing her arms.

The ambulance arrived within minutes, Tanya rode to the hospital with her daughter, and Curtis followed behind in his car.

They'd been sitting in the emergency room for almost two hours now, and the long wait was starting to drive Tanya completely insane. She couldn't believe this was happening, and she was never going to forgive herself for staying out as late as she had, because if she hadn't, this fight between her and Curtis never would have erupted. And she didn't even want to think about what she'd been doing with James. This had to be God's way of punishing her for the awful sin she'd committed, and she was so sorry for it. All she wanted was for her daughter to be okay. She prayed that she didn't have any serious head injuries, and no broken bones. She couldn't understand why something like this had to happen to Alicia and not her. She and Curtis were the ones who were committing adultery, so why did Alicia's well-being have to be sacrificed for their selfish mistakes? It didn't make any sense, but then, she knew God worked in mysterious ways, and that He had a way of getting a person's attention whenever He needed to. She'd been planning revenge on Curtis ever since she found those credit card statements two days ago, and her attitude had only gotten worse after she'd discovered all that other horrid information as well. But now she knew that she'd been wrong, and that instead of planning revenge on Curtis and sleeping with James, she should have separated from him and then simply filed for a divorce. But that had seemed too mild and merciful, and it had felt almost as though she'd be allowing him to get away with everything he'd been doing to her.

But now she wished she'd taken a much different route. She really did love James, and she really did want to be with him, but things needed to be handled from this end of her life first. And she hated that she'd made those two sets of copies at Kinko's yesterday afternoon and then given one of them to Deacon Jackson. The plan had been all worked out and finalized by the end of their scheduled meeting, but now Tanya wished she could get them back. She wished she had kept her mouth shut and allowed God to take care of Curtis and his wrongdoings. It hadn't been up to her to play God, and now she had a feeling that something terrible was going to result from it. Maybe if she called the deacon later today, she'd be able to convince him to forget about the whole thing. He had always been pretty reasonable in the past, and maybe he'd listen to her if she explained it to him in the right way, if she explained that revenge wasn't the right way for the two of them to handle this outrageous situation.

Tanya continued in deep thought, until she heard a man's voice speaking to her and Curtis.

"Are you Reverend and Mrs. Black?" the young resident asked.

"Yes," they both answered in unison.

"Your daughter is going to be fine. She has a slight concussion, and a few bruises, and it looks like her left arm is broken."

"Oh, no," Tanya said with tears building in her eyes again.

"My Lord," Curtis added.

"Did the social worker already speak with you?" the resident asked.

"Yes, she did," Curtis answered. "She wanted to know how it happened, and we explained it to her. We would never abuse our daughter," he said defensively.

"We understand your frustration, but you have no idea how many children come in here with bruises and broken bones and concussions the same as your daughter, except the reason they've been injured is because their mother, father, or some other adult has been physically abusing them. It's our job to protect any child who comes here, and the social worker is required to ask your daughter a few questions. Which she'll be doing in a few minutes or so."

"She's awake?" Tanya asked.

"Yes, she is," the doctor answered. "She's been asking for you, but I think it would be better if she spoke with the social worker first."

"Are you people crazy?" Curtis raised his voice. "Our little girl is probably in there frightened to death, and you're going to make us wait till some social worker has a chance to interrogate her?"

"Can I at least look in on her and tell her that we're here and that she's going to be okay?" Tanya asked, standing.

"I'm sorry, but hospital regulations won't allow us to do that," the resident insisted. "The social worker shouldn't be too long, though, and we'll come and get you as soon as she's finished. Your daughter

468

will need you when we set her arm in place to cast it."

"This is ridiculous," Curtis said irritably. "I'm a minister, and you people are acting like my wife and I are common criminals."

"We're sorry for the inconvenience," the resident said, and then walked away.

"Can you believe this?" Curtis asked Tanya.

Tanya ignored him. She'd wanted to forgive and forget, but she couldn't bring herself to do it. She knew it wasn't right, but she didn't know how she was ever going to forgive him for jumping on her the way he had, for dragging her off the sofa like she was some animal, and then kicking her like she was his most hated enemy.

Curtis said a few more things to her, but when he saw that she wasn't going to respond, he leaned his head back against the wall, closed his eyes and waited for the doctor to call them in to see Alicia.

Which didn't take more than fifteen minutes.

Alicia had told the social worker and the residents how she'd slipped and fallen on her way down the stairs, and that the reason she was up so late was because her parents had been arguing. The hospital staff members had bought the story, but still wanted to keep Alicia for a few hours for observation. Both of her parents took chairs on each side of her bed once she'd been admitted, and Alicia finally fell asleep as soon as the pain medication entered her bloodstream.

Tanya slept on and off, twenty minutes here and twenty minutes there, but Curtis slept soundly, like he didn't have a problem in the world, and Tanya didn't know how he could do it. How he could sleep knowing that their whole lives had been turned upside down and were going to be changed forever. But he always did that. Never seemed to worry about anything for more than a New York minute.

But one thing was for sure. If she couldn't stop Deacon Jackson from carrying out that plan they'd come up with, Curtis was going to have many sleepless nights and more than enough to worry about for the rest of his life.

And she was afraid that there wasn't going to be anything she or anyone else could do to help him.

Chapter 31

It was one of the most glorious and sunniest Sunday afternoons of the year, and the Black family appeared to be the happiest family in the state of Illinois. It had been almost four weeks, since the knock-down, drag-out fight between Tanya and Curtis, and Alicia still had two more weeks before her cast would be removed. The little white concoction had been irritating to her in the very beginning, but she'd been thrilled to death when people started asking if they could autograph her arm in all sorts of colors.

She had been extremely careful with it the first week, but now she was getting around like her arm wasn't broken and like the cast wasn't bothering her in the least little bit — with the exception of the severe itching she sometimes experienced.

But today, they were on their way back to church for the second time to attend the

Annual Pastor and Wife Appreciation Day. And of course Curtis was totally ecstatic, because this was the one day each year that members always gave huge monetary gifts which usually amounted to somewhere between forty-five and fifty thousand dollars, with some members each giving fifty dollars or more. It was almost like a bonus that CEOs and other officers at major corporations were given.

Tanya didn't really see a reason for it, but that's the way it had always been. Here at Faith Missionary and at each of the other churches she'd belonged to down in Atlanta.

She still hadn't filed for a divorce, but she was planning to meet with her attorney within the next couple of weeks. She'd wanted to separate from Curtis right away, but after Alicia's terrible accident, she hadn't wanted to cause her daughter any more pain than she was already having to deal with. She decided that she had to put her own plans and feelings on the back burner so that she could concentrate more on Alicia and the emotions she'd had to tolerate after seeing her father physically abusing her mother. Tanya had been worried that Alicia had seen her chasing her father with a knife, but fortunately she hadn't. The only part of the fight she'd actually seen was Curtis grabbing Tanya's arm and then twisting it as hard as he could behind her back.

And Tanya thanked God that things turned out the way they had. She wasn't happy that Alicia had been hurt, but she was glad that Curtis had stopped her from stabbing him to death, and that her anger had plummeted to a slow simmer as soon as she'd seen her daughter lying on the floor in an unconscious state.

Tanya had been talking with James on a daily basis, but she hadn't seen him more than a couple of times since the night they first confessed their love for each other. She'd told him that they needed to slow down their visits with each other until she or Curtis had moved out of the house, and James, of course, had understood. He'd told her that she was more than worth waiting for, and that his love for her wasn't going to change.

She and Curtis had pretty much been going their separate ways without disagreement, and he was spending his nights in the guest bedroom. Tanya had purposely gone out of her way to remain cordial with him for Alicia's sake, and because she was hoping that they could somehow end their marriage on a mutual basis. She knew there was little chance that Curtis would even consider ending their marriage on a nice, quiet note, but she was so tired of arguing and fighting with him, and she just wanted this all to be over with.

Regardless of how immensely she wanted to end their relationship on decent speaking terms, she still despised him for what he'd done to her, and she'd been praying daily that she would somehow, someday, be able to forgive him. Not because she wanted to, but because she genuinely wanted to live her life in a more Christian-like manner. She'd asked God to forgive her for her sins, and she'd recited the Lord's Prayer enough times to know that she was obligated to forgive those who trespassed against her.

But it was just that every time she thought about Adrienne, the condo, and everything else that had to do with Curtis, the idea of forgiveness seemed to fly right out of the window. And most of all, she still couldn't shake the fact that he'd dragged her off their sofa and kicked her in her side. She'd felt the pain for more than two weeks, and there had been times when she seriously wanted to hurt him. She wanted to make him feel the same pain that he'd forced her to endure.

Domestic violence wasn't something

she'd ever thought she would have to deal with in her lifetime, but it had happened to her. It had happened twice, and she wasn't waiting for three strikes. Lately, she'd been glancing back on her entire life with Curtis, and she couldn't believe she'd been in denial for as long as she had been. She couldn't believe she'd taken so much mess from him, simply because he was a minister and, even more so, because they had a child together. She'd probably caused more harm than good by doing that, but now she was finally thinking more clearly. Clearly enough to escape a horrid situation and move on with her life, one way or another.

Curtis drove into the parking lot, pulled in front of the sign that said Senior Pastor, The Reverend Curtis Black, and they all began their usual Sunday family ritual. They pretended that everything was A-okay on the home front, and that the three of them couldn't be happier if someone paid them. They hadn't said more than a few words all the way there, and Alicia still wasn't on the best of terms with her father. She'd been talking with him more frequently, but Tanya could still tell that things weren't the same between them. They hadn't been since that terrible incident.

They all entered the church, and Curtis pretended to be a gentleman by allowing his wife and daughter to proceed into the church in front of him. Then they walked down to the lower level of the church, up to the vestibule and waited in a small lounge. Two women from the Appreciation Day committee pinned corsages on Tanya and Alicia, and a boutonniere on their pastor. They exchanged smiles and small talk, and told the first family that someone would be in to escort them into the sanctuary at the beginning of the service, which would be starting a half hour from now, at four o'clock. Then the women left.

They sat quietly for a few minutes until Alicia spoke.

"Mom, I have to go to the restroom."

"Sweetheart, I thought I asked you to go before you left."

"I did, but I have to go again."

"Okay, but you'll have to hurry before the program starts," Tanya said, because she knew if Alicia ran into some of the other little girls who belonged to the church, she'd be downstairs with them forever.

"I will," Alicia acknowledged, and then headed back down to the lower level.

Tanya crossed her legs and folded her arms, but didn't look at her husband, because she knew it was just a matter of time before he tried to strike up a conversation with her.

"I really messed up, didn't I?" he said, closing the door.

"Yeah. You did," she answered blandly.

"I'm so sorry for causing you and Alicia all this pain, and I don't know what came over me a few weeks ago."

"You had no business putting your hands on me, Curtis. I told you that the first time you did it, and you ignored me."

"Tanya, everyone makes mistakes. I've made a lot of them, but that whole incident between you and me. And then . . ." he said, sighing, "Alicia hurting herself the way she did has made me realize that there isn't anything else in this world I care about more than the two of you. And that's the truth. You don't know how many sleepless nights I've spent in that guest bedroom thinking and waking up from nightmares of Alicia falling down those stairs."

Tanya didn't know what to say to him, and she had no desire to listen to any more of his explanations, apologies, or promises. It was too late for all of that, and all she wanted was to get through the next couple of weeks as quickly and as peacefully as she possibly could.

"I'm under so much pressure, and when you stayed out that night, I lost it. And I've regretted it ever since. I've wanted to apologize to you every day since it happened, but I didn't even know how to look you in your face."

"A lot has happened, but what we need to do is get through this afternoon, and then talk about this later at home," she suggested.

"You're not thinking about leaving, are you?" he asked, grasping her hand.

She didn't want to lie to him, and she didn't want to give him false hope. He looked pitiful, but she didn't feel a whole lot of sympathy for him, because she was used to his begging and pleading every time he did something disgraceful.

"I don't think we should discuss this right now."

"Look," he said, trying to convince her that things were going to be different. "Everything is finally starting to look up. I didn't tell you this, but the deacons finally agreed to give me a raise. It's only two hundred dollars more a week, but at least they realized that I deserved more money.

And with the gifts that we'll get today, I'll be able to take care of all of our financial problems."

Money, money, money. Is that what he thought? That this whole situation between them was about money? It had taken all the willpower she could muster not to mention anything about that lock-box and what she'd found in it. She hadn't said a mumbling word about anything pertaining to Adrienne, or the money he'd been spending on her, and God only knew who else. She'd wanted to confront him on more than one occasion, but she'd decided she wasn't going to reveal her new knowledge until she filed for a divorce. It was the ammunition she needed to prove to the court that their differences were in fact irreconcilable. And while she wasn't afraid of Curtis, she hadn't wanted to provoke him, or cause him to get physical with her again, because if he did, she wasn't sure what might end up happening to him.

"It's not just the money," she finally said. "It's everything."

"I know, but at least the money situation is one less thing we'll have to work on. And I agree with you now about us needing to see a marriage counselor. I didn't see it before, but I know now that we need help."

Hmmph. The only help she needed was help with getting rid of him.

He grabbed both her hands. "I know you probably despise me for what I did to you, but Tanya, please. Don't divorce me. I'm begging you. I'll do anything."

They both switched their eyes toward the door when they heard a knock.

"Come in," Tanya said.

"Look at the two lovebirds," Sister Coleman, the committee chairman, said, laughing when she gazed down and saw Curtis and Tanya holding hands.

If she only knew, Tanya thought. If they all only knew for that matter.

"Are you all ready?" Sister Coleman continued.

"We sure are, but we have to get Alicia," Tanya said.

"Oh, she's standing right out here," the sister informed them. "I brought her back up with me, because I knew we were just about ready to start."

Tanya and Curtis strolled behind the attractive fifty-something woman, stood by Alicia and waited to be escorted into the sanctuary.

Three members, a husband and wife and a young boy, ushered the Black family to their designated seats, which were three beautiful high-back chairs in the pulpit. The church was completely full, and Curtis was smiling from ear to ear. Tanya hadn't seen him this happy in a long while, and she knew it was only because of the financial gifts he was just about to receive. Which was really a shame, because it was all he seemed to care about.

"First giving honor to God," the mistress of ceremony began. "To the first family, other pulpit ministers, members of Faith Missionary Baptist Church, visitors, and friends. I'd like to take this time to thank all of you for coming out this afternoon as we celebrate our Second Annual Pastor and Wife Appreciation Day."

She paused for a second and continued. "We have a wonderful program in store for everyone, but first we're going to have our devotion. Then we'll have a selection from our choir, and continue on from there," she finished, and sat down.

Three of the deacons carried out the devotion, with a hymn, scripture, and a prayer. Then the choir sang just as the mistress of ceremony said they would. They sang beautifully, and Tanya cried tears of joy as she sat holding Alicia's hand. She was so thankful that God had blessed her with a daughter, and she praised God for keeping her safe from serious injury when she'd slipped and fallen down the stairway.

When the choir was seated, the mistress of ceremony stood at the podium again, and Tanya saw Nicole smiling at her.

"Praise the Lord," the MC said. "Thank you, choir, for that wonderful selection. Next, we'll have a few words from our chairman of the deacon board, Deacon Murray," she said, and took her seat again.

Deacon Murray reached for the cordless microphone and stood before the congregation. "Well, I guess I've been given the job of welcoming all of you here this afternoon, so I don't know any other way to say it except, welcome." He smiled, and the congregation laughed. "But mainly I'm supposed to give you an overview of what the church has accomplished since Pastor Black came to us two years ago. We've increased the amount of days our soup kitchen is open from two to three. We have our clothing shop open for the needy five days a week, when it used to be only four, and we give larger college scholarships to high school seniors than we ever have in the past. And I'll just tell all of you right now that Pastor has already suggested that he wants to give even bigger scholarships to help the families of the church, and he wants to build a new, more contemporary educational center. And while our membership had sort of slacked off before Pastor Black came here from Georgia, it's up twenty-five percent since he's been here. So, Pastor," he said turning toward the pulpit, "we want to thank you for your dedication and commitment to the church and for everything you've done to help make Faith Missionary Baptist Church the best place of worship it could be. And I don't know if any pastor has gone to see the sick and shut-in members as faithfully as you have, and we appreciate that."

Curtis nodded his head in acknowledgment.

"And we appreciate you, Sister Black, for being the loving, patient person that you are, because we know that sometimes Pastor receives calls at all times of the night, when people are ill or have had death in their family. And so, we just want you to know that we love you for that."

Many members of the congregation shouted Amen to what the deacon was saying, and Tanya smiled.

"And we love you, too, Little Miss Alicia," the deacon continued, smiling at her. "You're one of the sweetest young ladies in the church, and I want to thank you for asking me if I would be kind enough to autograph your little cast for you," he said, and the congregation laughed again. Alicia smiled with great pride.

"And finally, I just want to say to all three of you that we're glad to have you, and we look forward to having you as part of our church family for years and years to come. We love you, and God bless each of you."

Tanya and Curtis smiled as the congregation applauded.

When Deacon Murray stepped over to his seat on the front pew, Deacon Jackson stood up before the mistress of ceremony could make her way over to the microphone. He stepped in front of the podium and asked if he could have a few words to say, and she shook her head yes in agreement.

Tanya wondered what he was about to say, and she felt a bit uneasy.

"I won't take too much of your time, but there're a few things I'd like to share with all of you. Things that I feel you really need to know about," he said, pulling out a stack of paper from a large manila envelope.

Tanya didn't move, and she didn't think she could even if she wanted to.

Deacon Jackson shook his head in confusion, as though he couldn't believe what he was about to say himself, and Tanya knew he'd gone back on his word to her.

"This great pastor of yours is renting a condo over in one of the northwest suburbs, and my wife has been meeting him there for almost two years now. And I know it's true, because I have a copy of the lease agreement right here," he said, holding it up. "And on top of that, sweetheart," he said, looking out into the congregation at his wife, Adrienne, "I followed you there three weeks ago on five different nights just to make sure of it."

"Lord have mercy," a woman spoke out.

"Mmm. Mmm. Mmm," another grunted. And there were other gasps and deep sighs throughout the sanctuary. The congregation couldn't believe what they were hearing.

"And then," he continued, "this same great pastor of ours also had nerve enough to get my wife pregnant and then pay for her to have an abortion at a clinic in Michigan. And if you're wondering how I know it wasn't my child they got rid of, well I'll tell you how. I can't have children, and I've never been able to."

"My Lord!" an older man shouted.

"Mmmmmm," another woman sang.

"Lord, please help us today," one of the elder mothers of the church offered.

Curtis turned to look at Tanya, but she ignored him. Alicia looked as if she'd just seen a ghost.

Deacon Murray stood up and walked over to the podium. "Deacon Jackson, I think that's enough. This isn't the time for this, and I think we've heard all we need to hear."

"Oh, hell, no," Deacon Jackson said angrily. "I haven't even gotten to all the lingerie and flowers he's been buying *my* wife."

Adrienne stared at her husband in horror, and she looked as if she'd seen Alicia's ghost and a few more to go along with it.

Curtis didn't know what to do or which way to turn, but he knew Tanya was the culprit. He knew that she was the one who had given Deacon Jackson all this incriminating information.

"Hey, I said we've heard enough," Deacon Murray repeated. "Now, Deacon, please."

Deacon Jackson politely placed the documents back into the envelope and set it down on the podium. Then he turned toward the pulpit where his worst enemy was sitting. "I oughta drag your no-good ass down from there right now," he said, and stormed up into the pulpit.

The deacon yanked Curtis from his seat, and threw him to the floor. Then he grabbed him by his collar and struck him with his fist.

Women and children were screaming and crying in every area of the church. The rest of the deacon board tried to pull Deacon Jackson away from their pastor, but he kept throwing one blow after another, beating Curtis unmercifully.

But finally they succeeded in separating the two men.

"This isn't the end of this," Deacon Jackson yelled while he was being contained by two other deacons. "I promise you that," he warned, and the deacons forced him out of the sanctuary.

"How could you do this to me?" Charlotte, Curtis's eighteen-year-old mistress, sobbed with tears drenching her entire face, walking toward the pulpit. "How could you? I'm three months pregnant with your baby!" she shouted. "And you promised me that we were going to be together. You've been meeting me at motels all these months, and now I find out you've been messing with Adrienne? I knew you were, and you denied it every time I asked you," she wailed. "Why, Curtis? Why did you do it?" she asked like the innocent teenager she wanted to be.

Curtis wanted to zip to another galaxy. He didn't want to believe that any of this was really happening. But unfortunately for him, it was.

"*Negro,* don't you know I will kill you," Charlotte's father said, rushing toward Curtis, shoving past some people standing in the aisle, but the rest of the deacons barricaded his pathway before he could swing at him.

"You said you loved me," Charlotte continued. "Why'd you lie?" she asked as her mother, who was weeping just as uncontrollably as her daughter, pulled her away.

Alicia lay in Tanya's arms doing the same thing, with her face covered.

"Honey, I am so sorry," Tanya said, stroking Alicia's hair.

Tanya hadn't expected for any of this to happen. She'd been so angry when she'd found out what Curtis was up to and hadn't thought twice about calling Deacon Jackson. But then, when Alicia had fallen, and she'd had more time to think about what she and the deacon were planning to do, she tried to stop him. And he had agreed to it. He hadn't wanted to let Curtis and Adrienne get away with what they'd done, but she'd convinced him that in the long run it would be better for everyone involved if they waited a while and then used the evidence for each of their respective divorce proceedings. And he'd given her his word that he would keep quiet about it.

And she certainly hadn't meant for Alicia to hear all of these deplorable things about her father, regardless of how true they all were. But she only had herself to blame for all that was happening, because how could she possibly have expected a married man to simply pretend that he didn't know anything when he knew for sure that his wife was having sex with his pastor on a regular basis? No man that she could think of would have gone for that, and she was surprised that he had kept the information to himself for as long as he had. But it had probably been worth it for him to wait, because he'd had time to come up with a much more revengeful plan. A plan that she didn't know anything about. Because what *they* had agreed to do was confront Curtis and Adrienne together in private so they could force Curtis into resigning from his position at the church and could pressure both of them into signing divorce papers that would grant Tanya and Deacon Jackson all material and monetary possessions, leaving Curtis and Adrienne with absolutely nothing. But this whole idea of broadcasting Curtis's life story in front of the whole congregation, children and all, wasn't something she would have ever agreed to being a part of. Deacon Jackson had really shown out in the worst way, and this day was going to be one that no one would ever forget. And one that Curtis would never live down for as long as he lived in the Chicago area.

Deacon Murray stood before the microphone and apologized to the congregation. He told them that it would be best if everyone prepared to go home.

Hundreds and hundreds of members entered the aisles and began moving outside of the church, and Nicole pushed through the crowd toward Tanya.

"You can ride home with me if you need to," Nicole offered in tears.

"I appreciate that," Tanya responded, and held Alicia close by her side as they began walking toward her best friend.

"Tanya? Alicia?" Curtis called.

But all they did was pause, look back at

him, and then walk through the doorway. There wasn't a single word they could think of to say to him.

"Mom, can I go up to my room?" Alicia asked as soon as she, Tanya, and Nicole stepped inside the house.

"Are you going to be okay?" Tanya asked, hugging her.

"Why did Daddy do all that stuff?" Alicia wanted to know the same as she had in the car a few minutes ago.

"I don't know, sweetheart, but what I want is for you to try not to worry about any of this, okay? I know you don't under-stand what's going on, but the important thing is that we love you."

"Daddy doesn't love me, and he doesn't love you, either," Alicia said, crying again.

"Your daddy does love you, and no matter what happens between us, that won't ever change."

Tanya placed her hand on her daughter's shoulder and led her upstairs. "Nicole, go ahead and have a seat, and I'll be back down as soon as I help Alicia out of her dress."

"Go right ahead, I'll be fine," Nicole said.

When they arrived upstairs, Tanya unzipped Alicia's dress, and helped her slip into her pajamas. Then wet her washcloth so she could wash her face. Alicia was pretty capable of handling all of this on her own, but Tanya didn't want her to get her cast wet, and it was still a bit difficult for her to unzip her dress, so she thought it was best to help her out with it. And she wanted to comfort her as best she could as well.

Alicia climbed into bed, and Tanya sat down on the side of it.

"Mom, we're getting divorced, aren't we?" she asked as if she was part of the marriage, and Tanya realized that she was.

And Tanya couldn't lie to her about it. Her days of sugar-coating the situation were over with. "Yes, we are. But it won't change the way we feel about you. I know things will seem different at first, but no matter how bad everything seems, I want you to always remember that your daddy loves you, and I love you, too. And that you're the most important person in the world to us."

"Will I get to see him?" she asked.

"Sure you will," Tanya answered, and hoped for the best, because if Curtis ended up moving to another city or state, she wasn't going to see him very often.

"Mom, why was Deacon Jackson saying that Daddy paid for Mrs. Jackson to have an abortion?"

"He said a lot of things he shouldn't have." And that was the best Tanya could come up with.

"My friend Tisha, at school, said that abortions kill babies."

"It's a little more detailed than that, but I don't want you worrying about that, either. But what I do want you to do is try to take a nap. Okay?"

Alicia nodded yes. But then she asked another question. "Mom, if that other lady is having a baby by Daddy, does that mean I'm going to have a new baby brother or baby sister?"

Tanya had been hoping that Alicia wasn't going to bring this Charlotte topic up, but she should've known better than that, because Alicia always paid attention to everything she heard. But Tanya didn't want to have this discussion. It was hard enough as it was, accepting the truth about Curtis's sleeping with some teenager, let alone the fact that she was going to have a baby with him. But she knew it wasn't going to help by lying to Alicia, and that it was best to prepare her for the worst.

"Honey, I don't know if Charlotte's baby

is your daddy's baby or not, but if it is, then yes, you'll have a new baby brother or a new baby sister."

"Will he love the baby more than me?"

"Of course not. It's like I told you before, he's going to love you the same no matter what. Always. All right?"

Alicia nodded her head in agreement again.

Tanya kissed her on her forehead. "I'll be right downstairs if you need me."

Alicia watched her mother walk out of the room and then closed her eyes. Tanya strolled back down to the family room where Nicole was sitting.

"Girl, you didn't tell me you gave copies to Deacon Jackson," Nicole commented.

"I know," Tanya said, dropping down on the opposite end of the sofa. "And I'm so embarrassed about what I did. But I never thought he would do anything like that. And I can't believe he did it in front of all those children. And in the church on top of that."

"I don't think anybody could believe it. I knew you were upset that day you called me, and that's why I kept telling you not to do something you'd regret."

"And I should have listened to you, but all I could think about was how I was going to pay Curtis back for everything he'd been doing to me."

"Believe me, I can understand that, because I know you were hurt by what you found out, but I just didn't want you to cause yourself any more heartache."

"I don't know if I will ever forget the look on Alicia's face when Deacon Jackson started rattling off that information. And on top of that, she just asked me why her daddy paid for Adrienne to have an abortion. I hate all of this."

"What did you tell her?" Nicole asked, slipping off her shoes.

"I really didn't tell her much of anything, but she told *me* that someone at school said that abortions kill babies. And I hope she doesn't start dwelling on that," Tanya said, stroking her hair toward the back.

"You're going to have to find a way to explain it to her, or there's no telling what she might be thinking. And you don't want her asking anyone else, either."

"Definitely not. And then she wanted to know about Charlotte's baby and if that means she's going to have a new baby sister or brother."

"Girl, you've got your hands full."

"Don't I, though."

"What are you going to do?"

"First I've got to find the courage to call my parents and tell them about what's going on. It will kill my mother, and my father will be angrier than he already is. Although he'll be glad to hear that I'm divorcing Curtis, because that's all he's been telling me to do ever since I went to visit them."

"Are you going to ask him to leave?"

"We're all going to have to leave, because there's no way we'll be able to pay for this house if Curtis loses his position at the church. And you know that that's exactly what's going to happen."

"You're probably right about that."

"This is all such a mess," Tanya said in frustration.

"But you'll get through it. You just have to stay strong for yourself and for Alicia."

"I know, and right now, she's my main concern."

"Have you spoken with James lately?" Nicole asked.

"Yesterday."

"Well, this might not sound like the right thing for me to say, but at least you have him."

"That I do. He's so patient, and it's hard

for me to believe that he's as wonderful as he seems."

"Some things are meant to be, and if he's willing to wait for you through all of this, then you'll know that he really does love you as much as he says he does."

"I know, but I still have a long way to go before this will all be over with."

Tanya jerked her head toward the kitchen door leading to the garage when she heard it opening. It was Curtis.

"Baby, I really need to talk to you," he pleaded, not caring whether Nicole was there listening or not.

"I'd better go," Nicole said, slipping her shoes on. "But I'll be home if you need me."

"Thanks," Tanya said, and Nicole left without saying a word to Curtis.

"What is it that you want to talk about?" Tanya asked him.

"I want to explain all of this to you," he said, sitting down beside her.

"Everything I found was self-explanatory, so I don't know what else you can tell me about any of it."

"Why didn't you just come to me, instead of going to Deacon Jackson?" he asked, wishing on everything he possessed that she had.

"Because I was hurt, angry, and everything else. That's why."

"I know, and I'm sorry. I know I keep saying that, but I really am."

"Curtis, you're always sorry. But that never stops you from doing something worse next time around."

"What is it you want me to do? Just tell me, and I'll do it. Tell me how to make this right," he said with tears rolling down his face.

"I know you don't want to hear this," Tanya began. "But there isn't anything left for us to discuss, and our marriage is over with."

"Please, Tanya. I can't live without you and Alicia, so don't do this."

Tanya gazed at him, and for the first time, she really believed him. She really believed that he meant what he was saying.

But the only problem was, she wasn't in love with him, and, to tell the truth, she actually hadn't been for a very long while.

Chapter 32

"Where's the money, Reverend Black?" the female voice on the other end inquired.

"I told you, you'll get your money," Curtis answered, plopping down on the bed in the guest bedroom.

"And we told *you* that if you didn't have it by today that we were mailing copies of your little freak show to the deacons' board, your wife, and anyone else who might wanna see it."

"Look, I don't even know what's going to happen with my position at the church. Or if I'll even be allowed to go back in there again," he said in hopes that the woman would have at least some sympathy for him.

"We already know about that. And that's why we're calling you. We told you before that this little scrappy allowance you've been paying us every month isn't going to cut it. And if you wanna keep your little secret safe, you'd better come up with the fifty thousand dollars before tonight is over with. You've known for weeks now when the deadline was, and we're not playing with you," the woman said matter-of-factly.

"Didn't you hear me?" Curtis asked, wondering if she had or not. "I don't even know if I have a job anymore. So, how in the world do you think I'm going to come up with fifty thousand dollars?"

"We really don't care *how* you get it, but I do know one thing. If you don't, the FedEx man will be making some very special Next Day deliveries by tomorrow afternoon."

Curtis's hand shook like a leaf on a tree. What was he going to do? He'd been sure that he was going to be able to give them the money or at least part of it right after the Appreciation Day service at church yesterday, but things hadn't turned out the way he had expected them to. And he couldn't believe they were calling him at home. They'd been threatening him weekly, and until now, he'd been able to hold them off. But now that he couldn't deliver on his promise, they were threatening to ruin him for good.

He continued holding the phone, trying to figure out what to say.

"Did you hear me?" the woman yelled.

"Yes, I heard you."

"Well, then answer me when I'm talking to you."

"I don't have fifty thousand dollars, so I guess you'll just have to do what you have to do," he said, trying to stand up to her. Then he thought about it. "But if you give me a few more days, I'll get you the money."

"Tonight or never," the woman said, and hung up.

Curtis felt his heart jerking. He wished he could take back that hot summer night, almost eleven months ago. He'd been driving around town, doing practically nothing until he bumped into a woman at a convenience store near the church. To his surprise, she claimed that she recognized him, because she'd attended Faith Missionary a few weeks before with a friend of hers. They'd exchanged a few words, and one conversation had sort of led to another. And eventually the conversation had led to her asking him if he wanted to get together with her and her girlfriend and have a nice time.

He didn't know why, but when they'd

stripped away all of their clothing at the apartment they'd taken him to, he'd been turned on in a way he couldn't even understand. But he knew that it had something to do with the fact that he'd always fantasized about being in bed with two women at the same time. The same as most men, whether they admitted it or not.

And while he'd been so ashamed of what he'd done, he couldn't deny the fact that he'd had the time of his life. They'd taken care of him in a way that couldn't be put into words, but what he hadn't known was that they'd videotaped the whole affair without his knowing it. And now they were blackmailing him. They had been for months. And he'd been sure that the monthly stipends were going to suffice, until that day they'd come up with this greedy little lump-sum idea.

He wondered how they knew about the incident that had taken place at church yesterday afternoon, and that made him nervous. Nervous because it almost sounded as if they had an inside contact of some sort. Come to think of it, they seemed to know a lot of things about him that they shouldn't have.

But that was the least of his worries, because if the deacons ever caught wind of that tape, there wasn't going to be an in-kling of a chance that he'd be able to beg them to keep him on as pastor. And if Tanya found out, matters were only going to be worse. She'd said she was going to divorce him anyway, but he was still hop-ing that somehow he'd be able to change her mind about it. But once she saw the tape, he knew there wasn't going to be anything else he could say to her.

Curtis stood and wrapped his body with his bathrobe. He walked down the hallway, preparing what he was going to say to his wife, but when he arrived at her bedroom, he saw that she wasn't there. Then he went to Alicia's bedroom and saw that she was gone as well. He yelled for both of them down the stairway, but there wasn't any answer. He hadn't heard either of them stirring around this morning, but it was probably because of the two sleeping pills he'd taken shortly after midnight. He'd heard Tanya on the phone last night telling someone that she wasn't going in to work today, but he hadn't thought she'd be gone by the time he woke up, either. She was acting as if he didn't even exist, and even worse, Alicia had treated him like a stranger when he'd tried to talk to her last evening.

He dragged himself back into his new sleeping quarters, and dialed Deac's office number. When Deacon Roberson answered, Curtis told him that he needed to talk to him, and Deac agreed to meet him for lunch.

"It doesn't look good for you, man," Deacon Roberson said sadly after the waitress sashayed away from their table. Curtis had told her to give them ten minutes or so before coming back to take their order.

"What are they planning to do?" Curtis asked nervously.

"They're calling an emergency, church-wide business meeting for Thursday evening, and they're asking every member to attend."

"That's only three days away, so how do they plan on contacting everybody," Curtis said, hoping that there wasn't enough time for them to notify the entire membership.

"They've asked the clerical staff to do a mass mailing, which will be going out this afternoon."

They hadn't missed a beat, and Curtis was starting to feel sick.

"Man, what were you thinking?" Deac asked as if he still couldn't believe what he'd witnessed the day before at church.

Curtis sighed heavily, and burst into tears

like a newborn baby. Deac looked around the restaurant at the few people who were eating in their vicinity and noticed that they were all staring in their direction.

"Pastor, get a hold of yourself," Deac said, reaching across the table and patting him on his back.

Curtis tightened his face, which was soaking wet, and continued weeping.

Deac waited for him to pull himself together, and after a while Curtis finally spoke.

"I don't know. All I ever wanted was to be pastor of a prominent church. But as soon as I came here, Adrienne and every other woman practically threw themselves on me, and I was weak. I thought I was stronger than that, but I wasn't. I wanted to be faithful to Tanya, but the more time I spent with her, the more it seemed like I wanted to be with other women."

"But why? You had every man's dream. A beautiful wife and a beautiful daughter who loved everything about you."

"I don't know. I've thought about it a hundred times, but I can't explain it. It just seemed like the temptation was too much for me to bear, and I acted on it. But, Deac, man, I've never regretted anything the way I regret all of this."

"Well, I don't know what's going to happen, but I think you'd better prepare for the worst. Because I doubt very seriously if the church is going to vote in your favor come Thursday."

Curtis wanted to tell him about his blackmail situation, but he was much too embarrassed, and he didn't see what good it was going to do anyway.

"What is Tanya saying?" Deac asked.

"She says she's through, and that she's filing for a divorce."

"Do you believe her?"

"I think she's serious, but I'm not giving up on her, because if I lose her and Alicia, that's it for me."

"What do you mean, that's it for you?" Deac asked, frowning.

"My life will be over."

"Man, I know you've got some real issues going on here, but you've got to stop talking like that. God never burdens us with any more than we can bear. You've said that enough times yourself."

"If Tanya leaves me, there won't be anyone left for me to turn to."

"You have God to turn to. And regardless of what has happened, it's up to you to ask Him for forgiveness."

Curtis wiped the wetness from his face

with his hands and sniffled a couple of times. "Deac, I'm sorry I let you down. I know you believed in me, and that has always meant a lot. And to tell you the truth, I don't even know why you're still speaking to me."

"Look. It's not up to me to judge you or anybody else. So, if you ever need someone to talk to, I'll be here the same as I've always been."

"You're a good man, Deac, and I appreciate that."

When they had finally ordered and eaten their meals, Curtis and Deac left the restaurant and walked over to where their cars were parked.

"Deac, I love you, man, and thanks for coming," Curtis said, hugging the only friend he had left in the world.

"No problem. I love you, too, and you take care of yourself," Deac said, patting him on the back again.

Curtis slipped inside his car and sat there for a minute. He wondered about everything imaginable, but he couldn't find any solutions.

He thought about a lot of things before driving away from the restaurant, but what he thought about the most was committing suicide.

Chapter 33

With the exception of Deacon Jackson, who had been suspended, each of the other eleven members on the deacons' board assembled into the main conference room of the church. Deacon Murray had decided to schedule an emergency meeting shortly after receiving a videotape that carried an attached note stating that it shouldn't be viewed until the entire board was present. The sender hadn't signed his or her name, but the deacon had thought it was only fair that he share it with the rest of the board members right away. He'd decided that it would be best if they all viewed it together a couple of hours before the churchwide business meeting.

"I received this in the mail late yesterday afternoon, and that's why I thought I'd better call all of you here to view it," Deacon Murray began.

"What's on it?" one of the younger deacons wanted to know.

"I don't know," Deacon Murray answered. "But I guess we'd better find out."

"I hope it's not something else about *yall's* pastor, because I'm too old to keep hearing about all this corruption in the church," Deacon Pearson commented, disowning Curtis.

"Shoot, I'm only forty-one, and I'm tired of it, too," another deacon said.

"Let's just look at it," Deacon Murray insisted. Then he popped in the tape, and waited for the snow-filled screen to clear up.

They all looked dumbfounded when they saw Curtis lying on his back, butt naked, and a woman riding him up and down, swerving her body round and round. And they were completely shocked when they saw him kissing a second woman all at the same time.

"Unreal," one of the deacons finally said.

Another deacon laughed out loud, before realizing it.

Deacon Murray pressed the stop button on the video player and then ejected the tape.

Deac sat in silence, not wanting to believe that Curtis had gone this far.

"Well, I guess we all know what we have to do," Deacon Murray said.

"Lord, Lord, Lord," Deacon Pearson gasped. "What is the world coming to? The end is near, I'm telling you. The Bible speaks about all of this in Matthew 7:15. 'Beware of false prophets, which come to you in sheep's clothing, but inwardly they are ravening wolves,'" he quoted from memory.

"The minute we started hearing all those rumors, we should have started keeping a close watch on Pastor Black," one of the deacons said.

"But rumors spread around the church all the time. They always have, and you never know what's true and what's not," Deacon Murray added.

"We've got to get rid of him. That's all there is to it," another deacon insisted.

"It's still going to be left up to the members of the church."

"You know they're going to vote him out," one of the youngest deacons said. "Especially after we tell them about this tape we just watched."

"I don't think we should tell them about that, because all it's going to do is give the church a bad name."

"I think they have a right to know about

everything that's going on in the church," the young deacon pointed out, and the rest of the deacons voiced their opinions all at one time.

"Okay," Deacon Murray said, quieting them down. "We'll take a vote. I motion that we not tell the congregation anything about the videotape."

"I second it," Deacon Pearson uttered loud and clear, and all but three men voted to keep the videotape concealed.

"The ayes have it," Deacon Murray confirmed when the vote was complete.

They discussed a few more items and left the conference room fifteen minutes before the much-awaited business meeting.

"Well, I think we need to see more proof before we just go puttin' somebody out of the church," a rather short woman said with an attitude.

"Yeah," another woman agreed. "Every time the pastors at this church make a mistake, we get rid of them, and then we have to go months and months before we find one again. I'm getting sick of this, and I know a whole lot of other members who are sick of this, too," she said, and a variety of members shouted amen in agreement.

"Well, we can't have someone like Pastor

Black leading and representing this church," a tall, thirty-something gentleman said. "It's not right, and there's no way I'm giving my money every Sunday so some pastor can take care of all his women. Somebody's got to make sure these ministers walk the straight and narrow."

"Who are you to judge the pastor or anybody else?" the short lady asked in a loud tone. "You're not God!"

"I'm not God, but I know a hypocrite when I see one," the tall man argued back.

"Well, I still say we need more proof before we do anything," the short woman reiterated.

"How much more *proof* do you need in order to see what type of man Pastor Black is?" the youngest deacon asked.

"All I saw was Deacon Jackson waving around a few pieces of paper, and that doesn't prove anything. I mean, how do we know what was on those documents anyway?" she asked.

"Well, first of all, every member on the deacon board saw all of the paperwork," Deacon Murray interrupted, "and Pastor Black hasn't tried to deny any of what Deacon Jackson told the church last Sunday."

The short woman listened with an unsatisfied look on her face.

"The board voted to relieve Pastor Black of his duties, but we need a vote from all of you," Deacon Murray said.

"Deacon Roberson?" another female member of the congregation said. "You were pretty close to the pastor, weren't you?"

"I was," Deac responded.

"And you mean to tell me that you didn't know about all this mess he was involved in?" she asked, squinting her eyes.

"No, I didn't. It wasn't my responsibility to question Pastor about any of his personal business," he explained.

The woman pursed her lips in disbelief, and Deac looked embarrassed.

Members of the congregation argued back and forth, trying to determine Curtis's fate, and after another half hour had passed, Deacon Murray instructed them to vote. And surprisingly enough, only sixty percent of those in attendance voted to oust Curtis, while the remaining forty percent voted to keep him or couldn't decide one way or the other. Some even threatened to move their membership to another church, and one man suggested that they get together with Pastor Black to start a new church.

Nicole had been sitting quietly, and when the meeting was over with, she eased down the center aisle and into the vestibule. Deac saw her walking out and yelled to get her attention.

She turned around. "How are you, Deacon Roberson?" she asked, giving him a sisterly hug.

"Okay under the circumstances," he said.

"I know what you're saying."

"How's Sister Black?" he asked.

"She's having a hard time with all of this, and Alicia's not taking it too well, either. But they're hanging in there."

"This is all so unbelievable," he said, folding his arms.

"I know," she said, forcing a smile.

"Well, I won't hold you, but please give Sister Black and Alicia my love, and tell them that if they need anything to please call me."

"I will," she said, and exited the church.

"Girl, the meeting was just as upsetting as you said it would be," Nicole said to Tanya after calling her from the car.

"I'm sure I already know, but what did they decide?" Tanya asked.

"They voted him out, but believe it or

not, I'd say if not half, then pretty close to half wanted to keep him."

"Are you serious?" Tanya was shocked.

"Yes, and people were arguing with each other like they were enemies."

"I told you a long time ago, a lot of people believe in Curtis and the last thing they want to see is him leaving."

"One man even had the nerve to say that Curtis should start his own church."

"Amazing."

"Oh, and Deacon Roberson asked about you. And he wanted me to tell you to call him if you need anything."

"That was nice of him, but I'm not surprised, because he's one of the nicest men I've ever met. He's such a family man, and such a good person, and I don't know why he took to Curtis the way he did."

"Strange, I know, but opposites do attract," Nicole said.

"How many people were there?"

"Maybe not quite a thousand, but more than the amount of people who usually attend regular business meetings."

"Did you vote?" Tanya asked, and sort of laughed.

"No. I wasn't about to vote for or against him."

"Why not?"

"I just didn't feel comfortable doing it. I guess because I'm so close to you, but still, you know I don't agree with what he's been doing. And now that we're on the subject, where is the man of the hour anyway?"

"The phone rang a couple of times and he answered it. And then about an hour ago, he told me he was going out to take care of something."

"Are you guys speaking?"

"He's been begging me to stay with him every waking minute, and I'm really getting tired of it. I've told him, I don't know how many times, that things are over between us, but he keeps saying that things are going to be different, and that he's learned his lesson."

"He knows he messed up and that he'll never find another woman like you."

"I don't know about that, but I do know it's too late for us, because even if you put everything else aside, I will never forget how he jumped on me that night Alicia broke her arm. And there's nothing that could make me stay married to him after that," Tanya said, and heard the doorbell ringing.

"Nicole, somebody's at the door, so I'll give you a call a little later, okay?"

"Talk to you then."

Tanya left her bedroom, went down to the front door and opened it.

"Hi, Sister Black." It was Monique, Curtis's secretary from Faith Missionary.

"Is Pastor here?" she asked.

"No, he just stepped out, but I'm sure he'll be back shortly."

"Well, actually I came to see you."

"Oh. Well, come in," Tanya offered, wondering what this was all about.

"No, that's okay. I just wanted to bring you this," she said, pushing a package into Tanya's hand.

"What is it?"

"It's something I really think you ought to see. Your husband isn't right, Sister Black, and I just wanted to let you know what he's really about."

Tanya gazed at her silently with curiosity.

"Well, that's all I wanted, and I'm really sorry," Monique said. "Oh, and could you please tell Pastor something for me?"

"Sure, what is it?"

"Tell him that I meant what I said when I told him I was going to pay him back, and that as far as I'm concerned, we're even. And secondly, tell him that the only reason I applied for this secretarial job with him six months ago was because my two best friends are the same women he's been paying every month to keep quiet," Monique proudly pronounced and then strutted away like she didn't have a care in the world.

Tanya was speechless.

She opened the package while walking back up to her bedroom. When she arrived, she shut the door, picked up the remote control to the VCR, turned it on, and pushed the tape inside it. She waited a few seconds and then stretched her mouth wide open in disgust. She wanted to believe that this was a dream, but she knew it was just as real as all of the other scandalous acts Curtis had masterminded.

It was never ending with this man, and now she knew that something was clearly wrong with him. And that she had to get away from him as soon as logically possible. She had to get her daughter away from him before something worse happened.

"I know you don't understand, but this is the way things have to be," Curtis said, trying to explain things to Adrienne as best he could. He'd phoned her earlier in the day and asked her to meet him at the condo so he could talk to her, and now he'd just informed her that their relationship was over.

"No, Curtis. Don't do this. I'm begging you, please don't leave me," she said.

"Look, I know you don't want to hear this, but I have to make things right with Tanya and my little girl, and that's all there is to it."

"What about me?!" she screamed like a madwoman.

"You need to make things right with your husband."

"How do you expect me to do that when he's told me that I have to be out of the house by next week? He's filing for a divorce, and there's not one thing I can do to stop him."

"Well, I'm sorry, and I don't know what else to tell you," Curtis said, wishing that he'd never rented this place he was standing in.

"What do you mean you don't know what else to tell me? You can start by telling me why you left all of those papers lying around so Tanya could find them."

"I didn't. She broke into my lock-box, and I never expected that she would go into my office looking for anything."

"What was all of that stuff doing in your

house anyway? I thought you had the lease agreement locked up in your desk at the church?"

"I did, but then Monique started acting funny, so I thought it was best to move everything until things cooled down with her."

"Acting funny how?"

"Just acting funny, like she was up to something," he said, not wanting to tell her about how Monique had tried to seduce him.

"You should never have done that, because if you'd left those documents where they were, this never would have happened," she said, shedding her usual tears.

"Look, Adrienne. I know this isn't easy, and I know you will never be able to forgive me, but I can't do this anymore. I can't do this to Tanya ever again. And more than that, it's time that I make things right with God."

"Make things right with God?" she yelled. "You didn't want to make things right with anybody when you were lying up in here screwing me every chance you got."

"Adrienne, please," Curtis said, moving away from her.

"Don't walk away from me," she protested.

Curtis wondered where all of this gall of hers was coming from, because he'd never seen her act like this before.

"What do you want me to do?" he asked, hoping he'd be able to leave there soon.

"I want you to give Tanya the divorce that she wants, and I want you to make good on every promise you ever made to me."

"I told you, I can't. And I don't know how many times I'm going to have to keep repeating myself."

"How can you just dismiss me like this? Curtis, I killed a baby for you. Don't you even care about that?"

"That's a sin that you and I will have to live with for the rest of our lives, but that still doesn't change the fact that what we had is over with."

Adrienne yanked a small African statue from the end table and threw it across the living room, but Curtis ducked before it hit him.

"You bastard!" she screamed, crying simultaneously.

"Adrienne, will you stop all of this!" he said, moving toward her. Then he grabbed her by both arms.

She tried to pull away from him, but he was holding her too tightly.

"Let me go."

"Not until you cool down, because this isn't getting us anywhere."

"I said let me go," she repeated.

"Look, baby, I'm sorry. I never should have let things go this far between us, but you knew I was married from the very beginning."

"I hate you," she said, and spat in his face.

Curtis slapped her across her cheek as hard as he could. "You must not know who you're messing with," he said, wiping her saliva away. "And I'm through standing here playing these crazy games with you. If you want anything out of here, you need to have it moved before the first of next month. You can take it all if you want to, because I don't want any of it."

"Curtis, please," she said, sounding more hurt than angry.

"I'm out of here," he said, and strutted through the door.

But as he drove off, he really felt sorry for Adrienne and for the pain he had caused her. And he couldn't understand where this violent nature of his kept coming from.

Chapter 34

Curtis dropped his keys on the kitchen counter and tried to figure out the best way to approach Tanya, who was pouring salad dressing on a bed of lettuce. He'd driven around for more than an hour after leaving Adrienne, and now it was almost eleven o'clock.

"Hungry?" he asked, making small talk the way children do when they don't know if their parent is angry with them about something.

Tanya continued what she was doing, ignoring him.

"Is Alicia asleep?" he asked, bypassing the island in the center of the room, moving closer to where his wife was standing.

"Yes, and if you're thinking about waking her up, just forget it."

"I don't want to wake her up, I just

wanted to see if this was a good time for you and me to talk."

Tanya turned to look at him. "Hmmph. You just don't get it, do you?"

"Tanya, please let me talk to you for a few minutes, and if you still don't want to make things right with me, I promise you this will be the last time I bother you about it."

"Talk," she instructed with her arms folded.

"I went to see Adrienne a little while ago, and it's over between us."

"Oh, really?" she said sarcastically.

"Yeah. I told her that what we did was wrong, and that we couldn't ever see each other again."

"Well, if that's what you want, then I'm happy for you."

"It is what I want, and the other thing that I want is for you and I to work things out, because Tanya," he paused, "I love you so much, and I'm willing to spend the rest of my life making things up to you if that's what it takes."

"Is that a fact?" she said unemotionally.

"Yeah. It is."

"And what about the church situation? You do know that they voted you out to-night, don't you?"

"No, I didn't, but I figured they would anyway."

"So, what do you plan on doing now?" she asked. She didn't really care one way or another, but she was curious about what might be going on in his head.

"Well, first of all I want to devote all of my time to you and to rebuilding our relationship with each other and as a family. And I know that that has to be my priority, because while I was driving around tonight, I prayed to God for guidance, and when He spoke to me, He told me that my marriage still has a chance if I do the right thing. And then, as far as finding a new church, I think it would be best if I start searching for a position in another state, because we need to make a totally new start."

He couldn't have been serious. And she was glad that she'd had time to calm down after viewing that perverted video. Because if she hadn't, there was no telling what she might have done to him after hearing all of *this* nonsense on top of it. She was so sick of his manipulative behavior, and she was tired of him assuming that she didn't have a brain in her head and that she would love him and remain committed to him no matter what.

"So, that's your plan, huh?" she asked.

"It's not a plan, it's what I'm dedicated to doing, and what God has led me to tell you."

"Well, before you continue, why don't you follow me over here for a minute," she said, walking down into the family room.

Curtis followed behind her.

"Have a seat," she said.

He wondered what this was all about, but he didn't want to ask any questions. He didn't want to do or say anything that might set her off. So, he sat patiently waiting for her to speak again.

Tanya glanced over at Jay Leno, and then pressed the VCR remote control.

"So, did God tell you to have sex with these two women," she said as the tape rolled.

Curtis swallowed hard. "Baby, I don't know what to say."

"Well, that's a first," she said, rolling her eyes at him in disgust.

"My mind has been so messed up these last couple of years, and I'm not going to tell you that I have an explanation for any of this, because I don't. It seems like the devil has been working on me every day of the week, and for some reason, I just couldn't resist the temptation. But now I know that I have to follow God much more closely than I have been. He's been speaking to me all along, but I've been ignoring him. And I'm not going to do that anymore. Tanya, sometimes people have to reach rock bottom before they turn their lives around, and that's what I think had to happen to me."

Tanya looked at him and then over at the television screen. She hadn't played this much of the tape the first time around, and she was becoming more and more nauseated every time she heard another moan and groan from her worthless husband and his two sex mates.

Curtis wished she would turn it off, but he knew better than to tell her to.

"You really had a great time, didn't you?" she said.

"That wasn't me. I don't even know who that person is right there."

Tanya flicked the VCR off, and threw the remote on the sofa next to him.

"You've had your say," she said, still standing. "Now it's time for you to listen to me."

"Why don't you sit down, so we can talk about this face-to-face." He tried to reason with her.

"I think it's best if I sit over here," she

said, taking a seat in the chair.

Then she continued. "When Monique brought me that video, I didn't know what to expect, and regardless of how many vicious things you've done, I never thought that even you would stoop to something as low as this. I really didn't. And while I had no intention of staying with you before I saw the tape, I'm glad I got the chance to see that you're capable of doing just about anything."

"But —" he interrupted.

"But what? What did Monique have to do with it, right? Is that what you were going to ask me? Well, lucky for you, Monique is best friends with those two women you had your little fun with and who you've been paying all of that blackmail money to. See, what you didn't know was that the only reason she took that job at the church was so she could keep an eye on you. And she also wanted me to tell you that this was the payback she promised you, and that as far as she's concerned, the two of you are even. Whatever that means."

Curtis couldn't speak even if he wanted to. But now he finally knew how those women had known so much about him, and why they'd had no problem demanding such an astronomical amount of money.

"Now, as far as you and me moving to another state, I'm not going anywhere. And as far as us staying married, it's not going to happen. And I really do feel sorry for you, Curtis, because you don't have a clue."

"I know you don't believe me, but I'm telling you, Tanya, God really has spoken to me this time. He really has."

"Curtis, it's really not for me to judge one way or the other, but after going through these past eight years of marriage with you, I doubt very seriously that God ever even called you to preach, let alone anything else. Because when God truly calls someone to preach His word, it's hard for me to believe that that person could do all the horrible things you've done. I know you're human, and that no man falls short of sin, but you've been getting up in the pulpit every Sunday morning teaching people to do as you say, but not as you do. It was almost like you thought you were the only one exempt from God's word. And I'll tell you another thing. I don't know where you were getting the money to pay those women, but I sure hope you weren't stealing it from the church, because there's no way you could have been paying all of our bills, spending money on Adrienne like it was going out of style, or blowing money on yourself the way you do, just on your salary. When you said that we were in financial trouble I couldn't figure it out, but now I see exactly why you were so worried."

"Doesn't it matter to you that I love you. That I'll never love anyone the way I love you? What about the vows we took? You've always said that our vows meant everything to you."

"And they did, but there are some things that just aren't meant to be."

"How can you say that after all the years we've been together?"

"How could you sleep with all those women, and how could you even think about putting your hands on me? Because every time I even walk past this family room, I picture you shoving me on that sofa and dragging me off it."

"I told you I'm sorry, and that I'm willing to get help for that."

"I hope you do get help for your sake, but Alicia and I are moving out of here just as soon as I can find us a place to live. And that's all I have to say about any of this."

Curtis blinked back tears, but that didn't

stop Tanya from leaving the room. She picked up her plate of salad from the kitchen, sauntered through the hallway, and didn't even look back. And he knew for sure that she'd run out of all possible sympathy for him. He didn't know what he was going to do without her, and he didn't know how he was going to survive without any real income.

He worried about a lot of things as he sat there for the next few hours, and while ending his life seemed like the most logical and convenient solution, he knew he couldn't go through with it. He wasn't the Creator, and he knew he had no right taking any life. Even if that pathetic, sinful life was his own.

No, what he was going to do was ask God to forgive him and then show him the right way to go. Something he should have been concentrating on from the very beginning.

Chapter 35

Tanya lay in bed with her eyes fixed on the ceiling in deep thought. She'd been thinking about a lot of things the night before, but she was glad that she'd finally had the chance to make Curtis understand that they each had to move on with their lives in a separate manner. A major burden had been lifted, and she was already starting to feel as if there was going to be a much brighter future for her. There were still many problems that needed to be ironed out, but she was sure that things were eventually going to get better.

Alicia was her main concern, and she knew she was going to have to work extra hard to help her through the divorce she'd soon be filing for. It wouldn't be easy, but Tanya had faith that her daughter would adjust with time.

It was still much too early to start getting dressed for work, but she didn't feel like going back to sleep, either. What she wanted to do was call James. She needed to talk to him, update him about her marital situation and about what had gone on at the church business meeting last evening. She didn't want to wake him, but she didn't think he'd mind, because he always seemed pleased whenever she called him regardless of what time it was.

She dialed the number and waited for him to answer.

"Hello," he said, sounding wide awake.

"What are you doing up so early?" she asked, smiling.

"I'm getting ready to do my morning run. So, the question is, why are you up so early?" he asked, chuckling.

"I couldn't go back to sleep. Too much on my mind, I guess."

"So, how are you?"

"As well as can be expected. I had a long talk with Curtis last night, and I think he finally realizes that it's over between us, and I told him that I was going to start looking for somewhere else to live."

"How did he take it?"

"Not well, but it's not like I expected him to be real happy about it anyhow."

"Well, at least he knows where you guys stand."

"The church voted him out last night, so now he's got that to deal with as well."

"Well, he had to know that they weren't going to keep him."

"Yeah, but I don't think it was real to him until it actually happened."

"Is he there now?"

"I suppose. You know he sleeps in the guest bedroom, but I don't know if he ever even came upstairs."

"So, when are you planning to start looking at apartments?"

"Very soon."

"Well, you know you and Alicia are welcome to stay with me if you have to?"

"I know, and I appreciate your offer, but I have to get things right with her first. This split between her father and I is going to take a toll on her, and the last thing I want is to subject her to something else she's not used to. And I'll be honest with you, I wouldn't feel comfortable shacking up with you. It's not right, just like the other situation that happened between us wasn't right, either."

"Are you saying you regret making love to me?"

"No, I'm not saying that at all, because you know how wonderful that night was for me. But, at the same time, neither of us can deny the fact that I was committing adultery. And after all I've been through with Curtis, I realize now that I have to get my life together both spiritually and as a mother or things will never be right for me."

"I hear what you're saying. But you do know that I'm here, and that all you need to do is holler, right?"

"I know, and I love you for that," she said sincerely.

"Is that *all* you love me for?" he said, teasing her.

"By now you ought to know that I love you for just being you."

"I hope you always feel that way, because I love you from the bottom of my soul."

A warm feeling eased through Tanya's heart, and she wanted more than anything to be with him. She wanted to be with him right at this very moment.

"I can't wait to see you again," she said.

"I want to see you, too, but our time will come. And when it does, I'm going to do everything I can to make you and Alicia happier than you've ever been."

"Will you stop it before you make me cry," she said.

He chuckled softly. "Okay, okay. I need to get out of here anyway, so give me a call when you can."

"I will."

"I love you, sweetheart."

"I love you, too," she said, and hung up the phone.

She smiled as she replayed everything he'd just said to her. But what thrilled her the most was the fact that he didn't just want to make *her* happy, but wanted to make Alicia happy, too. A little girl he had never even laid eyes on, with the exception of her latest school picture.

He was almost too good to be true. But even if he was, Tanya was still going to take her chances on him. It just wouldn't make sense not to.

Chapter 36

Faith Missionary Baptist Church was filled with the holy spirit, and Tanya couldn't remember when she'd ever enjoyed the service the way she had this particular morning. She had still been attending church every single Sunday since the week Curtis had been voted out as pastor, but now that two months had passed, she couldn't have felt better.

She'd found a condominium not too far from the suburb they'd always lived in, and the divorce proceedings were finally underway. She hadn't seen Curtis very much at all, but Alicia was adjusting much better than Tanya had expected. And that was the only thing that mattered to her.

Tanya gazed down at her daughter and smiled when the interim pastor announced that the doors of the church were open, and that it was time for the moment of decision. Nicole was sitting on the other side of Alicia, and Tanya smiled at her best friend as well. They all knew that it was time for Tanya to speak to the congregation. She'd phoned the chairman of the deacon board and asked him if it would be okay, and he'd told her that although he had to clear it with the rest of the board members, he was sure that it wasn't going to be a problem.

Tanya strolled to the front of the church, and one of the ushers passed her a microphone.

"This is the day the Lord hath made. Let us rejoice and be glad in it," Tanya began with her favorite scripture.

"Not once did I ever think I would stand before you asking for forgiveness. But after all that has happened, I feel a certain responsibility to all of you. Especially because each of you has gone out of your way to treat me with the utmost respect, and you have always given me the support I needed as the first lady of this church. And I apologize for my husband's actions. I know that we all have to give account for what we do, but I feel obligated to tell you that I am so very, very sorry for all that has happened here over the last two years. And the unfortunate part of all of this is that I was actually losing faith in God and the church, but now I realize that my problems had nothing to do with God, the idea of being Baptist, or with any of the members here at the church and that it had everything to do with my own individual situation. And as I stand here, I'm not only asking for your forgiveness, but I am openly asking God to forgive me for the sins I've committed as well. There were times when my marriage caused me so much pain and caused me to feel so much anger that I was at the point where I didn't care what I said to Curtis or even how it came out. And I won't even go into some of the terrible thoughts I've had over the last few months or some of the regrettable actions I've taken. Things that were totally outside of my spirituality. Things that I never would have thought to do before moving to Chicago. I wasn't raised that way, and I've always tried to do the right thing. I've always tried to teach my daughter high moral standards, but now I know that even with the strongest Christian upbringing, it is so easy for any human being to step onto the wrong path if they place too much faith in man and not enough trust in God. Which is what I did when I married Curtis. And which is what seems to be going on with a lot of Christians in churches throughout this entire country. We need good pastors, but instead of worshipping them, we need to follow them as they follow God."

The congregation acknowledged her with outspoken amens and applause.

Tanya continued when it was quiet again.

"So, I'm standing here today to rededicate my life and to tell you that my personal relationship with God is now my first and foremost priority, my daughter is second, and that I have found such a wonderful sense of salvation and redemption through being a member of Faith Missionary Baptist Church. And if it's okay with all of you, Alicia and I would like to keep this church as our church home.

"Thank you so much, and God bless all of you," Tanya said with silent tears, and every member of the congregation stood to their feet and gave her the warmest ovation she'd ever witnessed. And she felt a sense of peace that wasn't even explainable.

Epilogue

Two years later

The past two years had been an absolute struggle for Curtis, but now he was finally getting his life on track. He'd lost everything — his Mercedes, the house, and everything in it, but after losing Tanya and Alicia the way he had, material possessions didn't mean a single thing to him. It was so strange how he'd started out with all the right intentions and then somehow ended up leading a life of terrible corruption. He'd tried to figure out what happened during the move from Atlanta to Chicago, and now he knew. It had been his acceptance of the position at Faith Missionary Baptist Church. There hadn't been anything wrong with the church or the members of the congregation, but for some reason, he hadn't known how to react to so much money, so much power, and so many beautiful women. The three temptations together were a deadly mixture, and he was sorry he'd indulged in every one of them.

But it was just that he couldn't seem to resist any of it. And he'd been so blinded that he really hadn't seen the ultimate consequences. He'd thought twice about a few things from time to time, and he'd even felt a touch of remorse on two or three occasions, but that was as far as his guilty conscience had risen to. He had preached Sunday after Sunday, practically ordering his congregation to follow God's word, and here he hadn't been doing any of that himself. What he'd done was follow his own rules and regulations, which had been the biggest mistake of his life. And the reason why he'd lost his beautiful wife to some other man. A man who even his daughter seemed to love unconditionally.

Just picturing Tanya with James caused his heart to ache, and when he heard Alicia even mention her future stepfather, he wanted to cry. And he had cried for quite a few months after they moved out of the house, when he realized that Tanya wasn't going to take him back. But he knew he only had himself to blame for all of this. He'd had to pray on a daily basis just to keep his sanity, and things had only gotten worse that day Tanya informed him that she and James were in fact going to be married. He'd tried to tell himself that she wasn't going through with it, but with the wedding barely a few weeks away, he knew now that she was more than dead serious.

And while he wasn't happy about any of this, he did thank God for giving him a second chance with Alicia. She'd sort of resented him for a short while, but he'd made it a point to spend as much time with her as he could. As much time as his new career allowed him to. He'd taken a position as a counselor for delinquent teenagers, and it hadn't taken him very long at all to become director of the organization. He hadn't really wanted the job in the beginning, and the only reason he'd applied for it was because he desperately needed to earn some money. It didn't provide him with the sort of income he'd been accustomed to, but after six months of working with some of the young people, he started to see where he really could make a difference. He even ministered to them from time to time, and took them to church on Sunday mornings. He didn't consider himself to be an ordained minister any longer, but he spoke at a different church each week, telling his life story. He told congregations throughout the city about the mistakes he'd made and how those mistakes had been the source of his devastation. He told them how God had called him to preach and how he'd taken that calling and turned it into what he wanted it to be. He told them about the baby boy he'd had with Charlotte and how her parents had forbidden him to see him. And he even told them about how he'd ruined Adrienne's life, how he'd manipulated people in his church and how he'd lied to his wife on an almost daily basis.

But most of all, he told them that there was no reward in gaining the whole world just to lose their own souls. A lesson he'd learned the hard way.

A lesson he hoped other people would learn, before they lost everything.

L